PRIME

Other books by Poppy Z. Brite

PRIME

a novel

POPPY Z. BRITE

THREE RIVERS PRESS · NEW YORK

Published in the United States by Three Rivers Press, an imprint of the Crown Publishing Group, a division of Random House, Inc., New York.

www.crownpublishing.com

THREE RIVERS PRESS and the tugboat design are registered trademarks of Random House, Inc.

Library of Congress Cataloging-in-Publication Data

Brite, Poppy Z.
Prime : a novel / Poppy Z. Brite.—1st ed.
1. New Orleans (La.)—Fiction. 2. Male friendship—Fiction.
3. Dallas (Tex.)—Fiction. 4. Restaurants—Fiction. 5. Consultants—Fiction. 6. Cookery—Fiction. 7. Cooks—Fiction. 8. Psychological fiction. I. Title.
PS3551.R4967P75 2005
813'.54—dc22   2004026480

ISBN 1-4000-5008-1

Printed in the United States of America

10   9   8   7   6   5   4   3   2   1

First Edition

For Ti Martin and Neil Gaiman,
two of Liquor's patron saints

Acknowledgments

Prime is a different sort of novel from any I've attempted before and required a great deal of research. For help with this, as well as moral support and general care and feeding, I want to thank Adam & Leslie Alexander, Ella Brennan, Doug Brinkley, Connie Brite, Bob & Anita Brite, Ramsey & Jenny Campbell, Dale Carter, Fr. Patrick Collum, Ben Everett, Wayne Favre, J. Grant, Kenneth Holditch, Rosemary James, Melissa Kaplan, Eman Loubier, Louis & Elly Maistros & family, Gerard Maras, Kevin Maroney, David McMillan, Tory McPhail, Wendell Nelson, Greg Peters, J.K. Potter, George Rico, Van Roberts, Tom Robey, Richard Shakespeare, Ira Silverberg, Carrie Thornton, David Uygur, and Peter & Janis Vazquez.

An extra debt of thanks is due to Harry S. Tervalon, Jr., who helped me to understand the inner workings of the District Attorney's office and other New Orleans legal arenas. Any errors in this area are of course my own.

Without my husband and favorite chef, Christopher DeBarr, obviously none of the writings about Liquor would have been possible.

A character in this story uses the pen name "Humphrey

Wildblood," which was reportedly the name of protagonist Ignatius J. Reilly in an early draft of John Kennedy Toole's great New Orleans novel *A Confederacy of Dunces*. It seemed too good a name to waste, and I hope the late (but still very much present) Mr. Toole will forgive me for recycling it.

To cook a pig, apply heat;
to win a lawsuit, apply money.

—Chinese proverb

PRIME

In another month the New Orleans lakefront would stink of fish, filth, and boat fuel, but right now it was a softly gorgeous spring day on Lakeshore Drive. Two young men sat on the seawall, their feet propped on the algae-slimed steps that descended into the murky brown water. Behind them, the levee rose up lush and green; before them was a vista of sailboats, small yachts, an occasional Coast Guard cutter, and far in the distance, the causeway that stretches twenty-four miles across Lake Pontchartrain to Mandeville, Covington, and other pretty little towns collectively known by sardonic city dwellers as "New Orleans North."

One of the young men—his name was Gary Stubbs, but everyone called him G-man—had a cane pole baited with a rubber worm. He sat with his long legs crossed, the pole balanced on the fulcrum of his knee, and stared out at the boats on the sparkling water. His myopic eyes had always been painfully sensitive to light, and his omnipresent dark glasses could not ward off the beginnings of a headache. G-man wasn't the kind of person who got a lot of headaches, though two years of restaurant co-ownership had certainly increased his familiarity with them. Like many native New Orleanians, he had known how to fish for most of his life, but he was not especially dedicated to the practice. Today he would have been unlikely to notice if Leviathan had risen from the depths and clamped onto his line. His attention was wholly absorbed by a creased and partly crumpled piece of newspaper from which his friend was reading aloud.

His friend was John Rickey, generally addressed as Rickey except by the younger and more timid underlings in the restaurant's kitchen, who just called him Chef. He read in a loud, fierce voice, gesticulating to emphasize points that struck him as particularly egregious. Rickey was very much the kind of person who got a lot of headaches.

They had been together for more than a decade, had worked in kitchens all over New Orleans, had sautéed, chopped, guzzled, and scammed their way from fifteen-year-old dishwashers at a Lower Ninth Ward diner to chef-owners of an award-winning and success-ful restaurant. The restaurant had been Rickey's idea from the beginning, and though he had recently insisted on making G-man his co-chef rather than his sous chef, he was still in charge. Rickey always had to be in charge of everything he did; otherwise it didn't strike him as worth doing. He was sharp-featured and intense, handsome despite a slight tendency toward paunchiness. Even the article he was reading commented on his good looks, though that seemed to irk him as much as everything else about it.

"'Like so many youthful ventures, Liquor is a fine example of why no one under thirty-five should be put in charge of anything.'" Liquor was their restaurant, so named because all the dishes fea-tured that ingredient; as Rickey had predicted, it was an idea per-fectly suited to this most alcoholic of cities. " 'The menu shows a certain ambition, verve, and raw talent. So may have the young Michelangelo's daubings, but they do not belong in the Louvre.' What the fuck is the Louvre, G? What does any of that *mean*?"

"I think it's a museum," said G-man, hoping Rickey wouldn't pursue the other question, though he knew he might as well hope for Jesus Christ to come strolling across the lake and put a nice bull redfish on his line. He tilted his face up to the cloudless sky, concentrated on the lapping water, the bass on a passing car's stereo, the gulls screeching and mewing and saying "You! You!" It was relaxing out here, or would be if Rickey would let it. This was one of the places they'd always come for peace: from their families when they were still teenagers living at home, from the stress and exhaustion of the various kitchen jobs they'd held during most of their twenties, from their own restaurant over the past couple of years. He felt as if Rickey wasn't honoring that peace now, and it made him a little sad.

" 'Of course, most young entrepreneurs have to come up with their own cash,' " Rickey read. " 'These two gentlemen haven't even done that, instead relying on Daddy's money. Celebrity restaurateur and Maine native Lenny Duveteaux isn't really either chef's father, but he may as well be for all the work they had to do to obtain his considerable financing. The question of *why* he chose to bankroll them remains—' "

G-man tucked the end of his fishing pole under his arm, reached over, and snatched the article out of Rickey's hand. Before Rickey could grab it back, he had torn it into small pieces and scattered it on the surface of the lake. "There," he said. "Maybe now I'll get a bite. I always heard it helps if you chum the water with something really rank."

Rickey stared at him, speechless. G-man stared back, meeting Rickey's bright blue eyes with his own calm brown ones. There weren't many people who could hold that blazing near-turquoise glare, but they had known each other since elementary school, had fallen in love at sixteen, had pretty much stood together against everything life threw at them since then. Rickey could do a lot of things, but he couldn't intimidate G-man. After a couple of minutes, Rickey shook his head and laughed. There wasn't much humor in that laugh, but G-man supposed it was a start.

"You know I'm just gonna get another copy," Rickey said. "The goddamn paper's free. You can pick it up all over town."

"Yeah, but until you do, I won't have to listen to it anymore."

"I think I got parts of it memorized."

3

"Rickey—"

Whatever G-man had been about to say was cut off by the ringing of Rickey's cell phone. Rickey removed it from the side pocket of his mushroom-patterned chef pants, glanced briefly at the caller ID. "Lenny," he said. "Again."

"You gonna talk to him this time?"

"I don't feel like it."

The phone stopped ringing.

"You ought to do it sometime today. That article fucked him over pretty good too."

"I know. I just can't do it yet. *Daddy's money*," Rickey said bitterly. He'd been making wishful noises about buying out Lenny's share of the restaurant for a while now, and this phrase in particular rankled. He started to return the phone to his pocket, but before he could, it rang again. Without any apparent premeditation, Rickey pulled his arm back, snapped his wrist forward, and sent the phone flying out across Lake Pontchartrain. It skipped a couple of times and was gone forever.

"Dude!"

"I didn't even know I was gonna do that," said Rickey, who looked just as surprised as G-man.

"Dude!"

"What?"

"Was that the phone from the walk-in?"

"Yeah," Rickey admitted guiltily. "Ungrateful bastard, aren't I?"

Lenny Duveteaux sat in his office at Crescent, one of two successful local restaurants he owned. He had come to New Orleans more than a decade ago, fallen in love with the place, and proceeded to make his own indelible mark on its culinary landscape. Now he ran a pair of restaurants, had published a bestselling series of cookbooks, marketed his own spice line, made frequent appearances on Leno and Letterman. A couple of years ago he'd heard about a young cook who had a great idea for a restaurant, but no money

Poppy Z. Brite

to pull it off. In a city where public drunkenness was considered a right and sometimes even an obligation, Lenny knew a menu based on liquor would pull in both tourists and locals. Fortunately, the young cook was talented enough to back up his gimmick with excellent food. Lenny decided to invest in the idea. That was how he'd gotten involved with Rickey and G-man.

Lenny was a stocky man, broad through the shoulders and thick in the neck, slightly seedy-looking. He shaved every day, but usually looked as if he were thinking about starting a beard. His square face was otherwise unremarkable except when he smiled, which made him appear demented. He was not smiling now. He had a closet full of expensive clothes, but right now he wore a pair of houndstooth check pants with frayed cuffs, a white chef jacket, and a New Orleans Saints baseball cap. He didn't look like a multi-millionaire, let alone the "dangerously ruthless businessman" this rag accused him of being.

On his desk was a copy of *Cornet*, a biweekly giveaway paper that covered New Orleans entertainment, food, and politics. This issue's cover story was about a dowser who had been brought to town in hopes of divining the exact location of Buddy Bolden's grave in Holt Cemetery, the local potter's field. A marker shaped like a musical note had already been erected for the jazz pioneer, but no one was sure whether it marked the right spot; he'd been buried in an unmarked grave in 1931, and the city had since lost track of him. Ordinarily Lenny would have been interested in the story—he liked old-time jazz, and the dowser was from Maine, his home state—but today he was only interested in what passed for *Cornet*'s restaurant review.

LIQUOR? I HARDLY KNOW HER!
By Humphrey Wildblood

Much has been made recently of the so-called Broad Street restaurant renaissance. It is true that a certain Mid-City stretch of Broad near the New Orleans courthouse/jail complex—formerly a rather bleak industrial area rife with bail bondsmen, gas stations, muffler shops, and the like—now boasts a number of upscale restaurants of varying quality. The restaurant usually credited with beginning this renaissance is Liquor, located at Toulouse and Broad. Though Chef John Rickey describes the menu as "eclectic French-influenced," local diners know it better as "that place that puts booze in everything." As well they might, for that is the first gimmick that made this restaurant famous, though unfortunately not the last.

Food cognoscenti and haunters of bookstores' true-crime sections may recall the gripping events that took place shortly after Liquor's opening, almost as if choreographed. A grudge-bearing former boss of Rickey's trapped him in the restaurant's walk-in cooler, threatened his life, and actually winged him with a bullet before Rickey was able to use his cell phone to alert coworkers to his plight. Readers who wish to know more can find the full story in *Dark Kitchen*, a sensational little paperback penned by Chase Haricot, the former *Times-Picayune* food critic who gave Liquor a glowing four-out-of-five-bean review. I am here neither to question Haricot's motives nor to examine the questionable wisdom of using red beans to rate fine-dining establishments. I am here only to suggest that a near-tragedy in the kitchen—though it may fascinate *Gourmet, Bon Appétit*, and other denizens of the American food press—does not a great restaurant make.

The aforementioned publications came to Liquor for the story, stayed for the food, and appear to have been impressed. (*Bon Appétit* spoke of "innovative cuisine with an impeccable grounding in local and global culinary tradition," whatever that may mean.) It is worth mentioning that both magazines also ran prominent color photographs of Rickey, a handsome fellow with a winning smile. Chefs are sexy these days, you know. Doubtless it is only a matter of time before the better culinary schools require 8×10 glossies to be submitted with all applications.

Poppy Z. Brite

Rickey runs the kitchen with his co-chef, Gary "G-man" Stubbs, a lanky young man with the slightly dazed expression of a California surfer who's just smoked a lid of dynamite grass. The two have worked together for most of their careers. Both are thirty years old, both lifelong New Orleanians complete with dat scrappy ole how's-ya-mama'n'em Lower Ninth Ward accent, just a couple local boys who done made good. Horatio Alger meets *A Confederacy of Dunces*, perhaps. Of course, most young entrepreneurs have to come up with their own cash. These two gentlemen haven't even done that, instead relying on Daddy's money. Celebrity restaurateur and Maine native Lenny Duveteaux isn't really either chef's father, but he may as well be for all the work they had to do to obtain his considerable financing (Liquor is reportedly turning a handsome profit now, and Duveteaux still owns a share of the business). The question of *why* he chose to bankroll them remains unanswered. Some sources say Duveteaux— chef/owner of Lenny's in the French Quarter and Crescent on Magazine Street—believed he had lost touch with contemporary cuisine and hoped these hip young chefs would restore his credibility. This seems unlikely, since Crescent is already excruciatingly hip and the two young chefs were nobodies when Duveteaux met them. More sinister motives have also been suggested. Lenny Duveteaux is known in certain circles as "the Nixon of the New Orleans restaurant world." He is said to record all his telephone conversations, indexing the tapes in his office by the hundreds, and to have the sort of business connections you don't want to cross if you value your health. A former associate remarked on the condition of anonymity, "Lenny is a dangerously ruthless businessman. He plays by the rules—the problem is that he also makes the rules."

But most local diners could care less who's paying the rent as long as the food is good. Is it? Like so many youthful ventures, Liquor is a fine example of why no one under thirty-five should be put in charge of anything. The menu

7

shows a certain ambition, verve, and raw talent. So may have the young Michelangelo's daubings, but they do not belong in the Louvre. I concede that my meals at Liquor have been well-prepared and reasonably tasty. The problem lies not in the execution but in the conception. A year after it opened, Liquor won a James Beard award for Best Newcomer, something that doesn't impress locals much but continues to bring in culinary tourists by the score. Sadly, the publicity and acclaim seem to have gone to the heads of Chefs Rickey and Stubbs; they want to have it both ways, wooing the out-of-town foodies but still professing to stay true to their roots. The result is a menu that lacks basic coherence—it's almost a stunt. Pecan-crusted Gulf fish with rum beurre blanc nestles uneasily alongside grappa-flamed pork shank with rattlesnake beans. Tequila-scented Creole tomatoes joust for attention with Galliano-marinated fresh sardines (a fish fit only for cat food, in this diner's not-so-humble opinion).

Is Liquor a contemporary Louisiana restaurant? Is it one of those upscale American places that mingle the culinary traditions of France, Italy, and other hazily imagined Old Countries with no regard for accuracy or palatability? You may decide for yourself, since the chefs surely can't—these days, "eclectic" seems to be a code word for "I don't know what the hell I'm doing."

But at least they look good doing it.

Lenny had already read the article three or four times, but he still couldn't quite take it in. Though he'd had his share of bad reviews, he had never seen one like this. He wasn't even certain it *was* a review; it scarcely mentioned the food, seeming rather to take umbrage at Liquor's hype, Rickey's looks, and, of course, Lenny's involvement. That had to be the kicker. He'd had Rickey and G-man investigated before he went into business with them. G-man, who was so easygoing that Lenny occasionally wanted to give him a good shake, had no known enemies. Rickey's only

Poppy Z. Brite

enemy—Mike Mouton, the former boss who'd tried to shoot him—was currently cooling his heels in Angola Prison. Lenny, though, had plenty of enemies. He knew the article was directed at him, though he didn't suppose that would be any comfort to Rickey.

He dialed Rickey's cell number again. This time it didn't even ring, but shunted him off to a recording that told him the number was temporarily out of service. He checked the recording light on the tape machine attached to his phone, then called his attorney, Oscar De La Cerda. He knew De La Cerda had read the article, because he'd faxed it to the lawyer earlier today. "Run down our options for me," he said without preamble when De La Cerda answered. "I know this is actionable, but tell me the best way to approach it."

"The best way to approach it is to stay the hell away from it," said De La Cerda. "It's obvious this guy's a wingnut. Don't give him the satisfaction of acknowledging him, and make sure Rickey doesn't either."

"Bullshit. We don't answer the charges, we look like we're admitting to them."

"That's what I figured you'd say," sighed De La Cerda. "OK. Everything he says about the restaurant is a matter of opinion—that's not actionable. The stuff he says about you is murkier, legally speaking. We can make a good case for libel, but he can probably duck all the charges."

"What do you mean, he can duck all the charges? He stops just short of calling me a crook and a thug."

"Well, that's just it—he stops short of it. You *do* tape your phone calls—you're taping me right now, aren't you?" Lenny was silent. "See, that's not libel. Everything else, he attributes to sources. That's protected. There are ways to get around the protection, but most of them are about as subtle as a lead pipe to the skull. You use them, you're gonna look like a crook and a thug, or at least a guy who's got something to hide."

"No, I don't accept that," said Lenny. He had taken out a book

9

of matches printed with Crescent's logo and was lighting them one by one, letting them burn all the way to his fingertips before dropping them in a crystal ashtray. The ashtray already contained dozens of burnt matches, but no cigarette butts; Lenny was not a smoker. Among other things, it was bad for the palate. "In fact, I hate that attitude, Oscar, and you know it. A righteous man doesn't defend himself because he's got something to hide. He defends himself because his good name is worth something, and he doesn't let the jackals shit on it just because he's afraid of looking like a *meanie*."

"Lenny . . ." He heard De La Cerda light a cigarette. Lenny had warned him about his palate, but the attorney didn't seem to care. "Do you really need reminding that certain of your past actions might not look so good in the harsh light of the courtroom? That you *have* acted, shall we say, outside the law now and again?"

"I've been guilty of *malum prohibitum*—I'll give you that. *Malum in se*, never."

"Christ, Lenny, spare me the Gordon Liddy shit. I've already got a headache. Look, let me do some research on this Humphrey Wildblood. Maybe we can get something nasty on him. I'll call you later this afternoon, all right?"

De La Cerda hung up. Lenny lit another match, let it burn until the flame licked his fingertips, let it burn a little longer, then dropped it in the ashtray. He hated it when his attorney spoke disparagingly of his "Gordon Liddy shit." Liddy's autobiography, *Will*, had been a formative influence on the young Lenny Duveteaux, and if it had never been written, he suspected Oscar De La Cerda would be short one extremely profitable client—and a client who had recently agreed to finance De La Cerda's upcoming run for District Attorney at that. It would be good to have the DA in his pocket; the current one was a real head case.

Lenny had read Liddy's bio just after he opened his first restaurant, and it had changed the way he looked at everything. Liddy made him understand that a righteous man not only had a right to be utterly ruthless; he had an obligation. In particular, the doctrine of the two *malums* had made a deep impression on him. *Malum in se* was evil in and of itself—the example Liddy gave was the sexual assault of a child—and it was morally indefensible. *Malum prohibitum* was wrong only because of laws prohibiting it—Liddy's two examples were the running of a stop sign and the assassination of a newspaper columnist who'd revealed sensitive information about CIA operatives overseas—and it was morally neutral. Lenny had based his entire business career on this doctrine, and it had served him well.

He'd also been intrigued by Liddy's technique of strengthening his will by mastering his reaction to pain, but Lenny's match trick was more of a habit than a way of fortifying himself. After twenty years in the kitchen, his hands were so inured to heat that he barely felt the little flames.

Someone knocked on his office door. He put the matches away and called, "Come in."

It was Polynice, one of his line cooks. "Scuse me, Chef. My cousin wanna know if you can interview him today."

"The porter position? Tell him I'll be there in a minute." Lenny thought of all the nasty jobs a porter had to do: lugging heavy bags of wet garbage, scrubbing out the coolers, hosing down the greasy rubber mats that protected the cooks' feet from the punishing concrete floor. Most restaurants went through porters like a compulsive gambler went through money at the track, but Lenny's tended to stay on because they knew there was the possibility of advancement. Just a few years ago Polynice himself had been a porter.

Polynice left. Lenny ejected the tape from the machine attached to his telephone and marked it in a way only he could understand before going out to interview Polynice's cousin. He decided to hire the kid, but he still couldn't get his mind off the *Cornet* review. He tried to call Rickey again and got the same out-of-service recording. Dinner service started in a couple of hours, but today was Monday, a slow night. "How are you set up?" he asked his sous chef.

"Got everything I need and then some."

"Good," said Lenny. "I'll be back in an hour."

G-man parked Rickey's old black-and-gold Plymouth in front of the little shotgun house they rented on Marengo Street. Rickey had spent most of the drive from the lake mired in silent gloom. "God, am I glad to be home," he said, just as if they had put in a full day's work. The sweet olives in their front yard were in full bloom, and not until they were halfway up the walk did they notice the figure sitting on their porch.

"Catch anything?" said Lenny heavily, eyeing the pole in G-man's hand.

"Nope."

"You know, I respect your days off. I usually try not to bother you. But would it be too much to ask"—Lenny was looking at Rickey now—"if, on the day you get the worst review of your career—a review that seriously impugns me too—maybe you could turn your *goddamn cell phone on*?"

Neither a New Orleans public school education nor twelve years of life in the kitchen had taught G-man what *impugns* meant, but he could tell it was nothing good. "His phone was on," said G-man.

"Then why couldn't he *answer*—"

"Because I didn't want to fucking talk about it yet!" said Rickey. "Why'd you have to call me every ten minutes? I could see it was you. I would've called you back eventually. I was trying to get some perspective."

"I've had bad reviews before. I could have helped you get some perspective."

"Maybe I didn't want your perspective, Lenny, did you ever think of that? Maybe I wanted to decide how I felt about it before you told me how I ought to feel."

"It doesn't matter how you *feel* about it. We need to decide what we're going to *do* about it."

Poppy Z. Brite

"What do you mean, *do*?"

By now Lenny and Rickey were standing nose to nose on the porch steps, waving their arms at each other. "Can we at least go in the house?" said G-man.

They ignored him. "We're not gonna *do* anything," said Rickey. "It's a bad review. Restaurants get them. After the insane amount of hype we've had, I'm not even surprised. I don't like it, but we're not gonna have the guy killed over it."

"I wasn't suggesting we have him *killed*," said Lenny. "I'm just saying we should consider our options. I like to think I have a talent for finding something useful in every misfortune."

"Yeah, well, I like to think you have a talent for being a big asshole."

G-man stifled a laugh; he couldn't help it.

"That was uncalled for," said Lenny. "But I apologize. Sometimes I forget who I'm dealing with. Sometimes I think I'm dealing with a mature person, and it just slips my mind that I'm actually dealing with Chef John Rickey, Boy Wonder."

"Lenny, I swear to God, if you say one more word—"

"Shut up!" said G-man loudly. "Shut the fuck up! Both of you fucking idiots just shut the fuck up!"

G-man hardly ever spoke with such force. Lenny and Rickey both gaped at him, glanced back at each other, looked away half-pissed, half-sheepish.

"Get in the house if you want to scream at each other. Maybe you forgot, but I own part of the restaurant too, and I don't want everybody on Marengo Street hearing my business."

He stepped between them and unlocked the front door of the little house. The door swung open, and G-man ushered them in, giving Rickey a none-too-gentle poke in the shoulder as he went by.

"I can't believe you guys still live here," said Lenny, gazing at the milk-crate coffee table and thrift store sofa. "You could afford something a lot more comfortable."

"Thanks for pointing that out," said Rickey. "Pardon us for not

13

taking the Lenny Duveteaux route. I guess we should've moved out to Lakeview and bought an ugly-ass Spanish Colonial cracker palace full of sectional furniture."

"Never mind where anybody lives," said G-man. Lenny was working his nerves too, but he was most interested in getting the two of them to quit bickering. Lenny and Rickey bickered quite a lot, but they seldom really argued. G-man was afraid this might spill over into a genuine argument if he didn't head it off. "Just shut up a minute and think about this: if that Humphrey Wildblood guy could see us right now, he'd be laughing his ass off."

"What do you mean?" said Rickey sullenly.

"I mean, maybe he thinks Liquor is a shitty restaurant, but at least he thinks *we* all believe in it. He thinks Lenny's got our backs. Imagine how fast he'd change his mind if he saw you two yelling at each other on the damn porch."

"You're right," said Lenny, spreading his hands in a conciliatory way he had. The gesture always looked so sincere that G-man wondered if Lenny practiced it in the mirror. "We shouldn't let this drive a wedge between us."

"Who is this Wildblood clown anyway?" Rickey asked. "He hasn't been writing for the *Cornet* very long."

"No, this is only his fifth review. And the others were puff pieces. I've got Oscar checking him out."

"I'm surprised you don't have new food critics checked out as soon as they get hired."

"I usually do," Lenny confessed. "I've got dossiers on everybody who's even *applied* for the *Times-Picayune* job. But the *Cornet* sort of slipped under my radar. They didn't hire a new food writer when their last one left, and until last month, they hadn't printed any restaurant reviews in a year or so."

"This is just weird," Rickey said darkly.

"I know. That's why I think we ought to look at it a little closer."

"Maybe so. But Lenny . . . the guy panned *my* restaurant. I know he said some ugly shit about you, but it's *my* menu that takes the hit. Don't you think *I* ought to decide how we're gonna react?"

Poppy Z. Brite

In moments of stress, Rickey sometimes forgot that G-man was supposed to be his co-chef. G-man didn't especially care about the title; he was grateful not to endure as much of the media hype and sniping as Rickey did. People who knew them well said that the restaurant wouldn't have opened without Rickey and wouldn't have lasted without G-man.

Lenny was silent for a minute, and G-man wondered whether he was going to blow up again. Lenny was pretty even-tempered most of the time, but the *Cornet* write-up seemed to have shaken him as badly as it had Rickey. Finally Lenny said, "Yeah, you're right. I'll leave it alone, for now anyway. Take some time to think it over."

G-man wasn't sure he believed that—Lenny thought nothing of saying one thing and doing another as long as he believed his actions were in the service of the greater good—but there was nothing he could do about it right now. At least they were talking rather than yelling.

"Keep one thing in mind, though," said Lenny. "You can talk about *your* menu all you like, but he hardly said anything about your menu. He made you and G-man sound like a couple of pretty-boy pawns. It's not inconceivable that somebody could use you guys to spike me."

"I know it," said Rickey. "I'm just not gonna assume it's all about you when my name is on it too."

"Fair enough. Look, I need to get back for dinner service. I'll call you tomorrow, OK? Turn on your cell phone."

"I can't. I—"

"It broke," G-man said hastily. "It just started making this weird noise, then died."

"What'd you tell him that for?" said Rickey when Lenny had gone.

"Because he already thinks you're a hysterical asshole. He doesn't need to know you're completely psychotic."

Rickey swallowed some Excedrin PM and went to lie down. G-man stood at the kitchen sink washing dishes. He didn't want a fancy house in Lakeview, but he supposed there was some truth in what Lenny had said; for one thing, it was ridiculous that they'd never installed an automatic dishwasher. *Why bother?* he thought. *We're never home enough to need much more than clean coffee mugs and a plate here and there.* He supposed it would be fun to have a huge, gorgeous home kitchen like Lenny's, but how often would they ever get to use it?

When Rickey and G-man were eighteen, their parents had tried to separate them by sending Rickey to culinary school in New York. The four-month stretch Rickey had spent there was the most desolate time of G-man's life. He figured he would have ended up dead in a gutter somewhere if Rickey hadn't come home, expelled for beating up the queer-baiting roommate who'd dogged him once too often. The roommate thought he'd met a few queers, but he had never met one from New Orleans' Lower Ninth Ward, the hardscrabble downtown neighborhood where Rickey and G-man had grown up. They'd moved into their first apartment with a few pots and pans, a saggy-springed old double bed one of G-man's sisters had given them, and little else, and had never progressed very far beyond the homemaking level of a couple of clueless eighteen-year-olds. Since then, G-man didn't much care where he lived as long as Rickey was there too. Their little house wasn't going to be featured on the Spring Fiesta Tour of Homes any time soon, but it was clean and comfortable.

He finished the dishes and went into the darkened bedroom. Rickey lay sprawled facedown on top of the covers, his head buried in the crook of his arm. G-man was still a little irritated with Rickey, but he always got over it fast. Things were harder for Rickey, that was all. "How can you *be* like you are?" Rickey had asked him on numerous occasions, not critical but honestly mystified and slightly envious. G-man didn't know. Things annoyed him sometimes—you couldn't be a restaurateur without getting annoyed on a regular basis—but they didn't gnaw at his vitals as they did Rickey's. He supposed that was a blessing; they could never have lasted so long together if they were both high-tension types.

Poppy Z. Brite

He put his hand on the back of Rickey's neck. The muscles were as tight as violin strings, the skin hot and damp. Rickey sighed into the pillow. G-man sighed too, feeling sunburned, wrung out, and a little horny. He began trying to massage the tension out of Rickey, starting at the top and working his way down. It wasn't always possible, but tonight he thought it was worth a try.

Rickey was poaching marrowbones for a sauce to go over the ribeye steak he always kept on the menu. Steak bored him, but some people didn't think they were dining well unless they could gnaw on a big hunk of meat, so Rickey tried to think of different ways to make it interesting.

It was a little past noon, and he and G-man had arrived at the restaurant about an hour ago. G-man was in the cooler writing up a seafood order. Usually this was one of Rickey's favorite times of the day: just the two of them in the kitchen, sometimes talking about the specials they were going to run, sometimes companionably silent, getting the dinner prep started well before anyone else showed up. He liked working with all his cooks, but G-man was the only one he trusted completely; they'd been working together for so long that they were almost like physical extensions of each other.

Today, though, there was no joy in the work. Everything felt strange and unwieldy and wrong. For minutes at a time Rickey would forget why he was so gloomy; then he would remember the terrible review and the sick feeling would settle deeper into the pit of his stomach. He wondered if he might be getting an ulcer, figured he probably was but decided it was the least of his worries. Who the hell was Humphrey Wildblood, and why had he said such terrible things about Liquor? Why would *anyone* say such things? Rickey couldn't understand it. He knew there were nutcases who formed weird psychotic grudges against actors and musicians and such, but those were real celebrities. People talked about "celebrity chefs," but Rickey believed there were very few such creatures. Although chefs occasionally had to go out and swan around the dining room, they spent most of their time sweating behind the scenes. Even with the pictures that had appeared in *Gourmet* and *Bon Appétit,* he suspected not one in a hundred people he'd fed would recognize him on the street. He didn't want them to. His hair had been very short in those pictures, and he'd let it grow since then, so that he almost needed to put it in a ponytail now. He wouldn't, though; ponytails were for hippies and bikers. Instead he shoved it behind his ears and kept it off his face with the same blue bandanna he'd always used, and . . . and what the hell was he thinking about his hair for?

Lenny's a celebrity chef, said an annoying little voice in his head. *A real one, the kind who gets recognized on the street. In your heart, you know that review was aimed at him, not you.*

This suspicion didn't help; if anything, it pissed him off worse, made him feel like Lenny's bitch. This was the kind of thing he'd been afraid of when they accepted Lenny's help. How had he ever thought he could build his own reputation riding on the jacket-tails of a superstar?

He'd said as much to G-man last night. As they were edging toward sleep, Rickey started talking again about how he wanted to buy Lenny out someday, to own a hundred percent of the restaurant. "Sure," G-man had said sensibly, "that'd be great. But we don't have that kinda savings."

"Maybe something will come along."

"Maybe. But you know, Rickey, nobody thinks of Liquor as a

19

Lenny Duveteaux joint. Maybe this Wildblood character thinks he can use us to get to Lenny, but when most people hear "Liquor," they think of you. Don't lose sight of that, huh?"

Rickey wondered. He had always been worried about the effect Lenny's shadow would have on his restaurant, and just now that shadow seemed to be longer than ever. Best to lose himself in work, to get so busy that he couldn't think about anything but the food.

He removed the marrowbones from the pot, chilled them briefly, and ran a paring knife around the hollow of each bone to make the chunks of marrow slide out. He didn't have a great deal of experience with marrow, and the paring knife technique was only working so-so. He was thinking about letting the bones chill a little longer, maybe doing something with a batch of fresh chanterelle mushrooms in the meantime, when the phone rang. "Kitchen," he said into the receiver.

"Is that John Rickey?" asked a genteel-sounding male voice with a slight Southern accent.

"Who wants to know?" he said, deliberately brusque. People constantly called this number trying to sell him shit he didn't want.

"This is Jasper Ducoing."

The name sounded familiar, but Rickey couldn't quite place it. "Uh, yeah, hi," he said, trying to fake it, knowing he was doing a crappy job.

"I'm sorry—I forgot you know me better as Chase Haricot."

Of course: the former *Times-Picayune* food critic who'd given Liquor a stellar review, then left the paper to write a book chronicling the weird events that took place shortly after the restaurant opened. A friend of Lenny's, he had the demeanor of an elegant middle-aged queen but always dined with his wife, upon whom he appeared to dote. *Dark Kitchen* had been quite a hit—one pundit called it "the *Midnight in the Garden of Good and Evil* of the restaurant world"—and Rickey still wasn't comfortable with the knowledge that some people came to eat at his restaurant because of the

Poppy Z. Brite

book rather than the food, but he didn't blame Haricot. You got by however you could in the restaurant business, and Rickey supposed it wasn't much different for writers.

"Sorry, Chase. I should've recognized your voice if not your name, but I'm a little frazzled here."

"Don't give it another thought. I'm certain you are a bit frazzled after that dreadful piece of writing in the *Cornet*. Obviously the gentleman has more ego than taste. Even when I found it necessary to pan a restaurant, I didn't feel the need to *annihilate* it."

Rickey, not previously aware that he'd been annihilated, wanted to get off the subject. "Anything I can do for you? I don't mean to be rude, but I got something on the stove."

"Certainly. I won't keep you much longer. I just thought you might like to know a thing or two about the gentleman in question."

"Humphrey Wildblood?"

"Yes. I use the word *gentleman* only from habit, of course—he's no such thing. For starters, Wildblood is a nom de plume he picked up somewhere. He's actually Humphrey Treat, the younger son of our most beloved local shyster, Placide."

"The DA?"

"None other."

Placide Treat had been the Orleans Parish District Attorney for the past twenty-four years. Occasionally someone would run against him, but he was very popular and defeated all comers without much trouble. In the last two elections he had run unopposed. He was an old-school Louisiana politician who reportedly believed no one was unbuyable; some people were just more expensive than others. In certain circles he was known as "Tricker" Treat because he had so many ways of getting defendants exactly where he wanted them, whether that was scot-free or in front of a grand jury.

In addition to his legal shenanigans, Treat was known for having married into one of the wealthiest families in New Orleans. His wife, the former Yvonne Geigenheimer, was heiress to the Geigenheimer hot sauce fortune. Several decades ago the first notable Geigenheimer, a spice distributor, had patented a method of injecting turkeys, chickens, and hams with ersatz "Cajun" seasonings. Hypodermics full of his products (each printed with the slogan SHOOT YOURSELF A LITTLE CAJUN!) were now sold in supermarkets all over the country. From there he had gone on to invent the pepper sauce that was his biggest moneymaker, as well as a variety of other seasonings, and now the family was very wealthy indeed.

"So the DA's kid hates us, and he's a Geigenheimer too," said Rickey. "Great."

"I don't know if it means anything. I've known Humphrey for years—he's always fancied himself a food critic; used to hang around me when I was writing for the paper—and I never got the idea that he was close to his father. But I *do* know that several years ago, when Lenny had just opened his first restaurant, Placide Treat brought in a big party of lawyers and judges. They sent back bottles of wine, said the portions were too small, disturbed other diners, patted their waitress on the fanny, then expected to have everything comped. Lenny wouldn't do it. He went to their table himself and told them he probably would have done it if they'd behaved decently, but that they were a perfect example of how fine dining *shouldn't* be done and they could damn well pay for their meal."

"And you think Treat still holds it against him?"

"I've heard he is the sort of gentleman who bears a grudge. And of course you know Lenny's attorney, Oscar De La Cerda, wants to throw his hat in the DA ring next year. Lenny, shall we say, would *greatly encourage* his campaign."

"It *is* about Lenny, then," said Rickey. "Goddammit."

"Not necessarily. If I were sure of that, I would have called Lenny. As it is, I simply think you should know what sort of people you're dealing with, so I called you."

"Thanks. I'm glad you did." But as he hung up, Rickey wondered if he really was glad. What good could the knowledge do him? Probably none; it could just make him eat his liver, and he was already doing a pretty good job of that.

Rickey returned to his marrowbones. They had cooled while he was talking to Chase Haricot and now released their unctuous plugs of marrow nicely. He had already made his Bordelaise sauce, a mixture of red wine and veal stock reduced until it took on a deep, almost bloody richness. For service, it would be ladled over the ribeye, with disks of marrow melting fatly on top.

G-man came back from the walk-in carrying a clipboard upon which he had written the seafood order. "How many pieces of redfish you think? Gonna be kinda slow, probably."

"Say twenty."

"We got crabmeat on anything?"

"Yeah, the tomato salad."

"Got it." G-man picked up the phone. "Want me to call Mr. Ernesto too?"

"Already called him. I got a kick-ass shrimp special."

Most of Liquor's seafood came from Old Country, a Croatian-owned wholesaler near the French Quarter. Croatians controlled most of the best seafood in New Orleans. Their shrimp, though, came from Mr. Ernesto, who lived thirty miles away in Delacroix, about as far as you could go in that direction and still be on dry land. The shrimp boats went out from Delacroix every day, and Mr. Ernesto bought up the catch and drove it to New Orleans. Rickey had ordered fifteen pounds of his largest shrimp, the 10/15 count, which meant there were between ten and fifteen in a pound.

Mr. Ernesto was at the back door now, a dark-skinned little man with ropy forearms and a Hook & Line of Chalmette freebie cap pulled down low over his eyes. Rickey glanced at the shrimp, but didn't examine them as closely as he would the order from Old Country. Mr. Ernesto never brought him anything less than translucent, gorgeous, barely dead shrimp.

"You got my bonus?" he asked Rickey. This was a joke of which the shrimp man never seemed to tire: since the restaurant was named Liquor, he thought he should get a free shot of liquor with each delivery. Rickey had tried to send him up to the bar a couple of times, but he just laughed, baring the gold tooth that was one of the few remaining in his head.

When Mr. Ernesto had gone, Rickey told G-man about the phone call, but tried not to make it sound like a big deal. He knew G-man already thought he had overreacted to the *Cornet* review and didn't approve of him and Lenny gathering intelligence on Humphrey Wildblood. Part of G-man's problem was that he had been raised in a traditional Catholic family. He'd left the Church years ago, but his upbringing still seemed to resonate in his character, giving him a weird mixture of free-floating guilt and unearned serenity that sometimes annoyed Rickey almost beyond endurance.

But G-man didn't chide him for listening to Haricot; he was interested. "The DA's son, huh? That Placide Treat is a fucking wingnut."

"Yeah?" said Rickey, who looked at the newspaper over his morning coffee but didn't really follow local politics.

"Yeah. Don't you remember when he was talking about suing the Saints for having a thirty-year losing record?"

"Oh yeah . . . it blew over, though, didn't it?"

"Only because Tom Benson has even more money than Treat." Tom Benson was the owner of the city's luckless football team. "And then there was the case he wanted to bring against anybody who played rap music in their car, and the time he sued the paper for libel because they said he was spending his wife's money on prosecutions, and I think there was something about the King of Carnival . . ."

"Nice."

G-man shrugged. "He's a superfreak. So what are you doing with those shrimp?"

"I'm making vermouth shrimp gratin with artichoke hearts."

"Scuse me." G-man stuck a finger in his ear, swiveled it around and pulled it out again. "I had, like, a time slip there. I thought maybe I was at Galatoire's or Lemoyne's circa 1972. You know, one of those old-school French Creole joints. I thought I heard you say you were making shrimp gratin."

"There's nothing wrong with old-school cuisine," said Rickey. "You talked me out of flaming dishes tableside on gueridons. It was my dream. Don't give me a lotta shit if I want to make something classic once in a while."

"Prehistoric, more like."

"You just wait. This is gonna be good."

"Guess I better take that sea bass I got coming in and do something ultra-modern with it, just to let people know we're in the twenty-first century. You used those chanterelles already?"

"No."

"Give 'em here, then."

The rest of the crew began to trickle in around two o'clock. On slow nights they usually ran the kitchen with five cooks and a dishwasher. Rickey would expedite, calling out orders and finishing plates. G-man would work sauté, the hottest and most fast-paced station in the kitchen. Sometimes they traded off. Tonight they also had Terrance, an old friend Rickey had trained to work the grill after rescuing him from a bad French Quarter hotel restaurant; Tanker, formerly the chef de cuisine at a failed restaurant of Lenny's, who could work any station but usually did desserts; and Marquis, a young cook with little experience but in whom Rickey thought he saw a spark of real talent, doing salads and cold appetizers.

Terrance's shaved head was clammy with sweat, and his huge body seemed to sag in all the wrong places. "Rough weekend?" said G-man.

"Yeah, my sister left her kids with me for the day. I used to think I wanted kids of my own. Now I ain't so sure."

"Funny, I thought you looked sorta hung over."

"Well, after she picked up the little monsters, my cousin come by and took me out. 'Them kids done run you ragged,' he says. 'You gotta cut loose once in awhile, Terrance.' Someday I'll learn not to listen to that ign'ant-ass fool. He just got these new wheel rims, and he gotta drive up and down Lakeshore Drive ninety miles an hour, showing 'em off while I try not to piss my pants."

"Rims?" said Marquis, perking up. "What kinda rims?"

"Aw hell, I don't know. I ain't into all that car stuff."

"How'd they look when he was rollin?"

"How should I know?" said Terrance a little testily. "I was in the car. I couldn't see 'em."

"Sound to me like *you* the ign'ant-ass fool." Marquis was eight inches shorter than Terrance and weighed perhaps half as much, but he spoke with no fear; Terrance never minded being kidded.

"Hey, Rickey," said Tanker from his little dessert nook at the back of the kitchen. "You happen to know if Shake made any Chambord mousse on Sunday?" Shake was their sixth cook, who usually worked the cold apps station but sometimes made desserts on Tanker's day off.

"I couldn't tell you," said Rickey. "Don't you see any?"

"Nuh-uh."

"Better prep it up, then . . . G, what are you doing?"

"Trimming fiddlehead ferns."

"I can see that. Where the hell did you get fiddlehead ferns?"

"Called City Produce. They dropped 'em off along with my tomatillos and crosnes."

"What's a crosne?" said Marquis.

"This is." G-man held up something that looked like a large white grub. "It's a tuber from France. Tastes kinda like a Jerusalem artichoke."

"Christ, it's like pulling teeth." Rickey took a deep breath. "I see you're not gonna volunteer any information, so I'll ask: *What the fuck are you making with fiddlehead ferns, tomatillos, and crosnes, you weird fucker?*"

"My fish special," said G-man imperturbably. "I'm gonna top it with the braised fiddleheads and serve it with a tomatillo-Herbsaint vinaigrette. On the side I'm doing a little salad of chanterelles and crosnes sautéed in butter."

"I take it this is a smartass reaction to my shrimp gratin."

"Hey, we got something ancient and something modern. Everybody's happy."

"Yeah, except me when I see the food costs."

"I got everything cheap. The City Produce guy owes me a bag of weed."

"Tell him I want one too," said Marquis.

"I dunno about that," said Terrance. "Not so sure you could handle it. Produce guy gets the chronic, and you used to that ghetto dirtweed."

Marquis cut his eyes at Terrance but said nothing; he knew this was payback for calling the big man an ign'ant-ass fool.

The first dinner ticket that came out of the machine at Rickey's station included orders for both seafood specials. "Marquis, ordering two tomato salads," Rickey called out. "G, ordering one sea bass, TWO SHRIMP GRATINS, you doubting slob."

"I bet it's somebody with their parents," said G-man. "Or maybe their grandparents. Go look out there, you'll see a young dude with some old maw-maw and paw-paw."

"Yeah, and the maw-maw and paw-paw know how to eat," said Rickey. "They don't think the more weird things you can cram on the plate, the better it's gonna taste."

"Fuck you—my special came out great. I'm gonna set one aside for you and make you eat it after service."

"I don't even like Herbsaint."

"You'll like this."

"Betcha I won't."

From his station, Marquis followed the conversation anxiously. He hadn't been at Liquor very long and wasn't sure whether the chefs were arguing. Everyone else in the kitchen knew how Rickey and G-man liked to bounce off each other; to them it was part of the background noise, just like the clatter of pans, the sizzle of hot fat, and the splash of dishes going into a sinkful of soapy water.

After a short rush, orders began to taper off around nine, and they had the kitchen broken down by eleven. When he first conceived of Liquor, Rickey had imagined it as a late-night restaurant. There weren't many in New Orleans, and the ones that did exist only served burgers, eggs, and the like. When he tried staying open past midnight, Rickey found out why: most people who wanted to eat that late were drunk, obnoxious, and craving grease. The wait staff took a lot of abuse, and soon Rickey gave in to yet another of the city's annoying vagaries: you could only run a viable finedining restaurant between the hours of six P.M. and ten-thirty or so.

The crew congregated at the bar and ordered libations from the bartender, Tanker's girlfriend Mo. Rickey had always considered this one of the hallmarks of a good restaurant crew: they didn't just take off when their shifts were over, but often hung out and drank together. Of course, that could be carried to an extreme. At the Peychaud Grill, the restaurant where he and G-man had earned their chops, the crew partied so hard that they seldom had the time or energy to do anything else. But that was years ago, and they'd learned to pace themselves since then. It was entirely possible to own a restaurant and still be an alcoholic fuckup—the proof was all over town—but Rickey didn't want to.

He sipped his single shot of Wild Turkey on ice and watched his waiters and cooks talking to one another. No one had mentioned the *Cornet* review to him all night; either they hadn't seen it or they were scared to bring it up. Rickey was surprised to realize that in spite of the review and the phone call from Chase Haricot, he felt unusually calm and contented. His shrimp gratin had sold well, and while G-man's bizarre dinner special had moved more slowly, Rickey was secretly pleased by it; as recently as a few years ago G-man would never have thought to make such a dish. He was stretching his boundaries as a cook, and Rickey knew the restaurant would ultimately reap the benefits.

When he remembered the plate G-man had promised to set aside for him, though, he decided not to mention it. Probably it was good—the few customers who'd tried it had raved about it—but he wasn't hungry and he really didn't like Herbsaint.

On their next day off, Rickey and G-man were invited to dinner at G-man's parents' house. Rickey always liked going over there. Mary Rose and Elmer Stubbs had raised their six children in the bosom of the Catholic Church, and Mary Rose had come close to disowning her youngest when he was sixteen, but over the years the Stubbses had grown to accept their son's relationship better than Rickey's unreligious mother had. Rickey's father, a chiropractor who lived in California now, wasn't in the picture at all. He had paid for Rickey's abortive trip to cooking school in New York, and that was the last time he had involved himself in his son's life. Rickey didn't miss him, though he grew resentful if he let himself think too long about it.

So the Stubbs house was a comfort when they could get there. They stopped by the restaurant to get a bottle of wine—they weren't big wine drinkers, but Elmer and Mary Rose liked it—then sped downtown until they came to the St. Claude Avenue railroad tracks. A long freight train blocked the street, tank cars full of deadly chemicals as far as the eye could see. It rolled forward until the end had almost cleared the crossing, hesitated for nearly two minutes, then started rolling backward again. G-man groaned.

"I'm gonna cut over to Robertson and take the bridge," said Rickey, who was driving. He did so, angling through narrow pot-holed streets crammed with wood and tarpaper houses, nail salons, storefront churches, fragrant barbecue shacks, and the occasional overgrown vacant lot. They approached the drawbridge that crossed the Industrial Canal, a toxic but useful body of water that formed one boundary of the Lower Ninth Ward. The bridge was just cranking ponderously open, with not one but two tall boats waiting to pass underneath. "Fuck!" said Rickey.

"Don't worry about it. If we're a little late, they'll figure we caught the bridge or the train, one."

"I know it. I just hate catching 'em *both*."

G-man shrugged. The train and the bridge were hazards of the neighborhood, no more annoying to him than a sudden rainstorm, a heat wave, or any other force of nature.

"Is Rosalie gonna be there?" said Rickey.

"No, but I think Henry and Leonetta are."

"Great," said Rickey, meaning the opposite. Rosalie was the second-youngest Stubbs child, the one who had given them the bed. Henry was a middle kid, younger than Mary Louise, Little Elmer, and Carl, older than Rosalie and G-man. Rickey liked Henry fine—all the Stubbs men were sweet-natured and easy to spend time with—but had never gotten along with his wife. Leonetta Stubbs was the sort of woman Rickey privately thought of as a high-toned bitch. She took advantage of Henry's gentle nature, bullied him mercilessly, and considered him to be at the disposal of any weird scheme she happened to cook up. Though she'd grown up downtown, she cultivated a rich Uptown accent, practically rolling her *r*'s. Rickey saw her type in his dining room all the time, with maybe more money but not a bit more class, pretending to appreciate their fine dining experience but really just liking the fact that they could get soused in a fancy place.

When they finally pulled up in front of the big clapboard house on Delery Street, Elmer was sitting on the stoop taking in the warm, clear evening. Rickey didn't blame him; soon it would be too hot to sit outside until well after dark. Unfolding his lanky body, Elmer stood to hug his son and shake Rickey's hand, just as he did with his daughters and their spouses. It was easy for Rickey to feel close to this man who looked so much like an older version of G-man. The other Stubbs kids were mostly black-haired and stocky like their mother, who'd been a Bonano before she married. G-man was nearly the spitting image of his tall, skinny Irish dad, though his darker eyes and blunt Sicilian nose hinted at his mother's heritage.

"How y'all doing?" Elmer said. "Which one you caught—the bridge or the train?"

"Both," said G-man.

"Aw, no! Well, c'mon in—your momma's just finishing up dinner."

The inside of the house was hot—only the kitchen and a few upstairs rooms were air-conditioned—but rich with the smells of garlic, toasted breadcrumbs, and simmering red gravy. Mary Rose Stubbs turned away from the stove and offered her cheek to G-man, then to Rickey. She was a small woman, far from thin, with a sweet suffering face and jet-black hair that had once been natural but was now obviously assisted. For years her daughters had begged Mary Rose to rethink her towering ebony bouffant—Rosalie's exact, oft-repeated words were "Why don'tcha get rid of that damn old-lady hair?"—but Mary Rose enjoyed the beauty shop almost as much as she did Mass. Between the two places she got to see everyone she knew.

"You need any help?" said G-man.

"Yeah, babe, you can take them artichokes and put 'em out on the table. Lemme just finish the veal and we ready to eat."

"Where's Henry and Leonetta?"

"Henry's upstairs looking for something in the junk room. Leonetta ain't here. She got her a headache and decided she better stay home with the baby."

"Good," said Rickey. Mary Rose let out a shocked little laugh, then swatted him on the butt as if she'd remembered she wasn't supposed to agree.

As they carried dishes to the table, Henry came down the stairs carrying a big cardboard box. He was tall like Elmer and G-man, but much broader through the shoulders, with a plain, honest face. "Hey, Gary!" he said, reaching instinctively for his brother and nearly dropping the box. "How's my baby brother? Hell, I don't even remember the last time I saw you. Hey, Rickey, or do I gotta call you Chef now?"

"Please don't. This is the one day I don't have to be Chef."

"I heard that. Hey, look, y'all, I found some of our old baby toys for Matthew. He's just about old enough to play with 'em, I think. Look, Gary, you remember this thing?" Henry reached into the box and pulled out a plastic wheel decorated with pictures of zoo and barnyard animals. You could point to a particular animal, then pull a string to hear the sound that animal made. At least Rickey guessed that was the theory. When Henry turned the pointer to a picture of a chicken, the sound that came out was a cross between a dog's snarl and a dying man's last wheeze.

"Well, maybe that one doesn't work so great any more. But look at this—remember Guv'nor Long-neck?" Henry held up a stuffed giraffe with a key in its side. Rickey figured it wouldn't do whatever it was supposed to do either, but when Henry turned the key, a music box inside the toy began to play "It's a Small World."

"Jeez, did we have to wind up *all* our toys to make 'em do anything?" said G-man. "No wonder we ended up with these high-strung partners."

Henry looked blank, then started laughing. Rickey did too. Though he didn't appreciate being compared to Leonetta, he had to admit G-man had gotten off a good one.

Henry put away the toys and they all sat down at the long dining table. Mary Rose had prepared pannéed veal with a delicate golden breading, spaghetti with red gravy, green beans smothered with bacon and onions, stuffed artichokes, and eggplant baked with shrimp and mozzarella. No doubt some rich dessert was waiting in the kitchen. Rickey knew Mary Rose had learned to turn out heroic amounts of food growing up in her own big family, then perfected the art while raising six healthy kids, but he didn't know where she had gotten such a light touch. This kind of food (he thought of it as Yat Italian) was often stodgy and leaden, but Mary Rose's never was. He was particularly fond of her artichokes, which overflowed with herbed breadcrumbs, grated Romano cheese, and coarsely chopped fresh garlic, all liberally drizzled with a fruity green olive oil from Sicily. G-man had learned to cook from his mother and sisters—the other Stubbs boys knew their way around a kitchen, but none had shown such an affinity for it—and he took such food for granted. Even after two decades' worth of dinners at the Stubbs house, Rickey did not. "What'd you fry the veal in?" he asked.

"Lard, babe. That's the only thing that crisps it up nice without making it greasy, and if you got your pan hot enough, your breading don't soak up too much fat."

"This is practically health food," said Henry. "Look at all these vegetables."

"Y'all don't use nothing like that at the restaurant, huh?" said Elmer. "I can just hear them Uptown ladies if they found out they was eating lard."

"F— forget them, I'd love to use it. The flavor's great. But it's too smoky. We gotta keep our pans so hot all the time, we use clarified butter. You can just about burn the crap out of it before it starts to smoke."

"Language!" said Mary Rose.

"Sorry."

They started trading work stories—Elmer and Henry both worked at Tante Lou's Confections, a Mid-City candy factory that shipped pralines, pecan rolls, and chocolate eggs all over the country—and eventually Rickey got on the subject of the *Cornet* review, Humphrey Wildblood, Chase Haricot, and the District Attorney. In truth, he wanted to pick Elmer's brain; Elmer Stubbs knew the unlikeliest people all over New Orleans. But it was Henry who began to frown as he listened to the story, then said, "I know him."

"Who? Humphrey Wildblood?"

"No, Placide Treat."

"Henry, don't take this wrong, but you grew up in the hood and you work in a candy factory. How do you know the DA?"

"Well, he came in the store one day a couple years ago." Tante Lou's was not a retail outlet, but Henry and Elmer always referred to it as the store. "Wanted to buy two hundred thirty-seven boxes of Treasure Eggs, and would I give him a good deal."

"I hate those things," said G-man.

"That's cause you and Rosalie ate most of a case one Easter when y'all were little," said Elmer. "They were supposed to be for the whole family."

"I don't remember that."

"Lord, I do," said Mary Rose. "I never seen two children vomit so much. I was washing towels for days."

"*Anyway*," Henry said pointedly, "Old Tricker left his driver parked outside and came in by himself. Said if I gave him a good price on that candy, he'd personally see to it that I never had to pay a traffic ticket again."

"Don't believe you ever mentioned this to me," Elmer said.

"It kinda slipped my mind."

"I hope you turned him down," said Mary Rose without much hope.

"Course I did, Momma. And the river's clean and the Saints are gonna win the Super Bowl next year. You know how much money I saved just in the past six months? I don't get a lot of tickets, but Leonetta's always speeding around town and leaving her car in no-parking zones and all."

"So how come he wanted so many boxes of candy?" Rickey asked.

"You got me. I figured it was none of my business—I just gave him a good price and helped him and his driver load 'em in the car. Big old Rolls-Royce he got, and in perfect condition too.

Gorgeous car. Anyway, he gave me a number to call, and every time she gets a ticket, somebody in his office fixes it right up."

"Nice."

"One time she even parked on the Napoleon Avenue neutral ground when Bacchus was rolling. Three hundred dollars they wanted for that, but Tricker's office fixed it."

"I bet they did," Elmer said. "Placide Treat fixes all kinda stuff."

Rickey looked at Elmer. He'd never known a man less likely to indulge in any sort of corruption, but Elmer had been around the city a long time, and he was a good listener. He knew things, he knew people who knew things, and sometimes he could get things. A few years back, he'd gotten them tickets to the only playoff game the Saints had ever won. "What kinda stuff?" Rickey asked.

"Well . . ." Elmer frowned; he was an inveterate gossip but always liked to pretend reluctance to tell his tales. "He says he just has the one son—your pal Humphrey Wildblood—but lots of people say otherwise. Say back when he was a young lawyer, traveling a lot for one of the oil companies, he had an affair with a lady who . . ." He glanced at Mary Rose. "Who wasn't exactly a lady."

"She was a drag queen?" said Rickey, surprised.

Elmer blushed. "No, no. Just not a real respectable woman. People say she had his baby, and he took care of them both until the kid turned twenty-one. Kid's supposed to be some kinda prominent business type now."

"In New Orleans?"

"I don't think so. That's all I know, really."

Mary Rose sighed. "It's wrong, but worse goes on every day. Anybody want some more eggplant and shrimps?"

"I do," said Rickey, accepting the dish of baked eggplant. "How'd you keep the mozzarella from getting stringy?"

"I put in a little ricotta, just like that lasagna I showed you how to make."

G-man nodded, but Rickey, who had never even mastered the lasagna to his own satisfaction, felt a pang of despair in his heart. As much as he enjoyed Mary Rose's cooking, he was also a little

Poppy Z. Brite

jealous of her talent. He could make probably four hundred different dishes, many of them approaching culinary perfection, but he couldn't cook like this. He reached for his glass and took a swig of Chianti, wincing at the taste. Wine was his palate's worst deficiency; he could tell the good stuff from the cheap crap, but he couldn't make himself swirl it around the glass and taste its nuances and practically come in his pants over it like some people did. He'd learned to drink on liquor, and a liquor drinker he remained.

"You look just like your picture in *Gourmet*," Mary Rose said suddenly.

"Huh?"

"You smiling so pretty and holding that wineglass, you look just like that picture. Well, your hair was a lot shorter then. You should cut it like that again," said Mary Rose, casting a gimlet eye upon Rickey's straggling, slightly tangled hair.

"I keep meaning to, but I never have time. And I wasn't holding any *wineglass* in that picture. I hate chefs who pose in the dining room with a glass of wine, like they think they're some kinda bon vivants. They're not bon vivants, they're working slobs, or they ought to be."

Henry laughed. "Some of 'em don't wanna be called working slobs, huh?"

"Oh my God. Some of them think their job is to make sure nothing gets on their jacket so they'll look extra pretty when they go out to preen in the dining room. I call those the ballerinas."

"Then there's the drill sergeants," said G-man. "We heard about this one chef who lines up his crew before a busy dinner shift and yells at them for ten minutes, just to make sure they got the fear in 'em when service starts."

"And don't forget the frat boys. They let their crew do all the work so they can hang out in the bar doing whiskey shots with the poor bast— poor people waiting for tables. They don't care if their kitchen's in the weeds, as long as everybody gets to see what big fun characters they are."

37

"Larger than life," said G-man, who had been hitting the Chianti fairly hard. "Legends in their own time."

"So is Lenny Duveteaux like that?" said Henry.

Rickey shook his head. "He loves being famous—he knows he's a big cheeseball and embraces it. But he doesn't let other people do his work for him. Lenny's always at his restaurants, except once in awhile when he gets horny and hits the strip clubs."

"Rickey!" cried Mary Rose.

"Well, he does. Never actually *dates* anybody—he says regular women won't put up with his hours."

"I bet some of 'em would put up with his money," Henry said.

"Yeah, you'd think, but Lenny likes his Gold Club girls. I guess they aren't much trouble."

"Not unless one of 'em finds out what *paternity suit* means," said Elmer.

"I don't believe what I'm hearing," said Mary Rose. "Y'all put a lid on this right now. I'm going in the kitchen to check on my cassata, and by the time I get back, I want to hear a nice conversation going on out here."

"I thought you were holding a wineglass in that picture too," said Elmer when she had gone. "Coulda sworn I remembered it that way."

"Great. The photographer tried to *make* me hold a wineglass and I refused. Come to find out everybody thinks they saw one anyway."

"They airbrushed one in," said G-man. "I had it airbrushed back out of our copy before I let you see it."

Rickey stared wildly at him, saw that he was joking, picked up a piece of French bread and threw it at him. G-man lobbed it back. Rickey tried to catch it, but it bounced off his hand and landed in his Chianti. "Stubbs from three-point land!" said G-man.

"Y'all behave now," said Elmer, just as if they were still nine or ten. It was a shame they hadn't learned to obey him in twenty years, Rickey thought, but Elmer never had been the strict type.

Elmer and Henry worked earlier hours than Rickey and G-man,

and Mary Rose liked to attend morning Mass, so the party broke up around ten. "Well, that was relaxing," said Rickey as they drove home.

"It sure was," said G-man, leaning his head against the window.

"Yeah, you're about as relaxed as they come, Mr. Chianti. I don't know how you can drink so much of that shit."

"We just always had it on the table. I don't really like it, but it's there and it gives you a buzz, you know?"

"I can't drink enough to get a buzz. It just gives me a headache. You wanna stop and have a drink somewhere?"

"I don't know. Do you?"

Rickey considered. "I guess not really. Let's just go home."

"I don't even remember the last time we were in a bar. Other than our own, I mean."

"It was in March," said Rickey after a moment's thought. "We went over to the Apostle Bar to see the St. Joseph altar."

"Well, that doesn't count. Anthony B would've gotten his feelings hurt if we didn't go see his altar."

The Apostle Bar was where they had developed much of their menu before opening Liquor, elevating the modest array of bar food to heights that had caught the attention of Chase Haricot and others. Since their departure, the Apostle had gone back to serving burgers, wings, and such, a fact that seemed to relieve the owner, Anthony Bonvillano. Running a real restaurant had made him nervous. He loved his little bar, where he built a St. Joseph's altar every year in accordance with the wishes of his late father, who'd left him the money to open the place.

"It counts," said Rickey. "We had a drink, didn't we?"

"I can't remember."

"Me neither." Rickey turned from Claiborne onto Louisiana Avenue, which would deposit them back in their Uptown neighborhood. "Are we old, G?"

"Well, we've sure calmed down a lot. That's good, though. I don't see how we could run the restaurant if we were still a couple of drunk slackers."

"You don't ever miss it?"

"Sure I miss it. Back then we didn't have any responsibilities except putting out the food and trying to make it good. Now we got nothing but responsibilities. Sure I miss it. Don't you?"

"Yeah, sometimes. But I wouldn't go back."

"Neither would I. I mean, we can still cut loose once in a while. Nothing's stopping us."

"I really wouldn't mind one drink," said Rickey. "How about we stop at the drugstore and pick up a bottle?"

"Sounds good," said G-man, as well he might have, for Rickey was already pulling into the brightly lit parking lot of the twenty-four-hour Rite Aid.

The following week, two envelopes postmarked Dallas, Texas arrived in the same day's mail at Liquor. One was crisp and expensive-looking, the other smudged and creased as if someone had carried it around in his pocket for a day or two before mailing it. Sitting at the little desk in his office, Rickey opened the crisp one first. Its pages gave off a faint smell of cigarette smoke, and he waved it in the air, trying to dissipate the unpleasant odor before he began to read it.

Dear Chef John Rickey:

My name is Frank Firestone and I am the owner of an upscale restaurant in Dallas. The menu at Firestone's is a mixture of traditional and eclectic, blending Continental cuisine with contemporary American.

Last year I hired the award-winning Cooper Stark, former chef/owner of Star K and Capers in New York City. He says he met you many years ago, but doesn't know if you will remember him. I ate at both of Cooper's restaurants many times during the '80s and '90s, and I think he has a whole lot of talent. The fit between him and Firestone's, however, has been shy of perfect. To be blunt, he doesn't seem able to evolve with the changing times or adapt himself to a dining market less sophisticated than what he's used to. Dallas is a cosmopolitan city and will give you a sharp boot in the ass if you say otherwise, but that's part of the problem, if you see what I mean. We're ready to try new things, but we're not necessarily ready to like them.

As <u>Bon Appétit</u> said, you have an impeccable grounding in local and global culinary tradition. That's what I need at Firestone's. I'm not looking to fire Cooper. As I say, he is very talented and I consider myself lucky to have him. He has also been through some personal difficulties in the past few years and I'm not one to kick a man when he is down. What I'm looking for is a consultant. I need a chef who can come to Dallas for a week or so and help Cooper, not only to redesign the menu, but to understand how to cook for a market that isn't New York and is never going to be. The truth is that I am a wealthy man and this restaurant is probably never going to make me much money—I own it because I love restaurants and like the idea of having a fine one. It's kind of a toy for me, like my boat and my racehorses. (If you like the ponies, maybe you've heard of Shape O'Texas, my filly who placed in the Breeders Cup Distaff last year.) I'm prepared to pay you very well for a period of consulting to be scheduled around the needs of your own business. Will you come to Dallas for a minimum of seven days in June or July? I'll pay $10,000 plus all your expenses, and I am a very liberal man when it comes to expenses (I like to send all my guests home with hangovers, gout, sore balls, and a new pair of boots).

Please think over my offer and get back to me at your earliest convenience. I remain very truly yours,

Frank Firestone

Pretty sure he knew what the other letter was going to be, Rickey tore it open and pulled out a single page from a yellow legal pad, the kind many chefs made their daily notes on. The page was covered on both sides with jagged, tightly packed handwriting.

Dear Rickey,

I guess by now you've read Fred Flintstone's letter. If not, you should stop and read it before you go any further with this one.

OK. First of all, I have no idea if you'll remember me. Second, if you do remember me, I don't know if you want to hear from me again. I came to CIA as a guest chef 11–12 years ago when you were a student there. I'd just broken up with my longtime lover. Was doing a lot of coke. It was the beginning of a bad time that still hasn't completely ended.

Anyway, you came up to talk to me after my demo, so fresh-faced, earnest, obviously impressed with me that I asked you out for coffee even though I knew I shouldn't. I ended up taking you into the city, to my office at Star K, one thing led to another, and I'm afraid I wasn't very respectful of your desire to stay true to your boyfriend. You were just 18 and far from home, and I couldn't imagine that the relationship would last. I thought you needed to experience more of the world. Of course I considered myself just the guy to help you get started. When the evening was over, I put you on a train back to Poughkeepsie even though I could see that you were freaked out and due for a bad coke comedown. I'm not proud of that. Actually, I'm not proud of most things I've done since then either, but more about that if you come to Dallas. Won't bore you with it now.

Suffice it to say that I fucked up badly in the subsequent years, lost both my restaurants, lost my apartment, got into serious debt, left New York under a cloud of embarrassment and failure. Picked up kitchen work here and there, finally ending up in Dallas, of all the places to be. What do you think of that?—the guy who once got three stars from the <u>New York Times</u> slinging hash in the Big D? Life's an existential comedy, kiddo. I don't know if you believe that, but I do. If I didn't, I think I'd have blown my brains out by now.

There's a lot of disposable money in this town. Some of it trickles down to people in kitchens. I guess my boss wants to give you a nice chunk of it to come help me stop scaring off his customers. That's not how he puts it, but that's what he means. He wants simple, accessible, fake-ass "French" food, and somehow he got the idea that's what you do. Sure, it's insulting as hell to us both, but you could pick up some easy money and help me keep my job. This is a good gig. In fact it is my last chance. I can't stand to lose another job, have to scramble again. I'm 47 years old. Ancient for a chef. Have bad feet and a bad back and, like a lot of ex-cokeheads, get respiratory infections all the time. But enough about that. If I can keep this job for another couple of years, I think I can get my shit together and save enough money to go do a few things I really want to do. I'd like to tell you about them.

I hope you'll take the job, Rickey. Firestone's an asshole, but he's a <u>rich</u> asshole. Come to Dallas for a week, help me figure out what he wants, let me try to make up for the way I treated you. I've thought of you often in the past ten years. If some big-shit famous guy put the rush on me when I was 18, then dropped me like a hot sizzle platter, I know it would have made me feel like garbage. I hope I didn't do that to you.

You can't imagine how happy I was to pick up <u>Gourmet</u> and see you won that Beard award. Let me know what you

Poppy Z. Brite

decide. I'd like to hear from you even if you don't want the consulting job, tho' I warn you I'll probably try to change your mind.

Your friend,
Coop

Rickey folded the letter and crammed it back in the envelope so hard that he tore one of the seams. His heart was pounding and his face felt flushed. Maybe Cooper Stark really had thought of him often, but he'd scarcely thought of Stark in years, and now he realized he'd liked it that way.

He supposed he had been an easy mark during his four months at cooking school, broke and lonely, separated from everything he'd ever known. The classes had been interesting, but everything else was so foreign: the upstate New York weather, life in a dormitory, life away from G-man. He'd been excited to learn of the demo by Cooper Stark, whose cookbook had provided the first recipe he'd ever used in his first real cooking job, and he had been *very* impressed to learn that Stark was openly gay. He'd known that couldn't be easy in the macho environment of a restaurant kitchen. When Stark said a few kind words to him, Rickey had been stupid enough to believe maybe the older chef actually thought he was an interesting person. Not until the end of the evening, when Stark realized Rickey wasn't going to put out, did the truth become apparent. Stark had given him a hundred-dollar bill for train fare and dropped him off at Grand Central Station, leaving him feeling like a whore who hadn't done his job right. If Stark was sorry now, Rickey didn't give a damn.

G-man came into the office carrying a clipboard, probably meaning to ask Rickey something about the day's menu, but one look at Rickey's thunderous face told him something was up. "What's going on?"

Rickey handed him the letters. G-man read them, occasionally glancing at Rickey but not speaking until he had finished the last page of Stark's letter. "You know what my mom likes to say. A bad penny always turns up."

Rickey wasn't sure he had ever heard Mary Rose Stubbs say that, but he didn't doubt that she might; she was full of favorite expressions. "What do *you* think?" he asked G-man.

"I think there's a lot that's fucked up about getting famous."

Rickey looked quickly at G-man, but G-man's eyes were hidden by the reflection of fluorescent lights in his dark glasses as he laid Stark's letter on the desk and flipped back to Firestone's.

"But there's good stuff too. I mean, damn, Rickey, ten thousand dollars for a week of work!"

"Ten *million* dollars wouldn't be enough to make me want to see Cooper Stark again. What an asshole." Rickey snatched up the letter and scanned it for a particularly offensive line, but he couldn't pick one out; it was the tone of the whole thing that bothered him.

"I don't know. To me he sounds more like somebody who knows he *was* an asshole and wants to make up for it."

"Yeah, but that's just because you expect the best of everybody. Believe me, Cooper Stark hasn't turned into a nice guy. I don't think he even remembers what happened that night." Rickey's eye finally lit upon a bothersome sentence. " 'I ended up taking you into the city, to my office at Star K, one thing led to another, and I'm afraid I wasn't very respectful of your desire to stay true to your boyfriend.' He makes it sound like we had sex. Maybe he even thinks we did—maybe it's, like, inconceivable to him that this stupid kid was able to resist getting his dick sucked by the great Cooper Stark. But we *didn't*. Like I told you a long time ago, I didn't do anything but kiss him a couple times. Then I thought about what I was doing and made him stop. I didn't cheat on you."

"I know you didn't," said G-man. "I wasn't even gonna ask you about that."

Rickey loved him for saying so. If the situation were reversed—if G-man had gotten the letter—it would have been the first thing Rickey mentioned. In their fourteen years together, G-man had never given him a single reason to be jealous, but he was anyway. He didn't even like to see anyone looking speculatively at G-man. A letter like the one he'd just gotten from Cooper Stark would have had him frothing.

"But Rickey . . . are you sure you don't want to think about doing this gig? We're making good money, but we put most of it back into the restaurant. Our overhead's pretty high. Our food costs are through the roof. We always talk about buying Lenny out someday, but how we're gonna do that if we never save anything? We could put this in some kinda money market account, maybe add a couple hundred dollars every month. In a few years we'd really have something."

Rickey folded his arms across his chest and shook his head.

"Hell, I'd do it myself if they wanted me."

"No way!" Rickey sprang up from the desk. "I don't want you within a thousand miles of Cooper Stark!"

"Well, it doesn't matter anyway. This Firestone guy wants you. I doubt he'd be too thrilled to have your co-chef."

"You're just as important to the restaurant as I am."

"Maybe so. But my picture wasn't in *Gourmet*." G-man spoke with no rancor, only a slightly exasperated sort of patience. "Firestone doesn't want to hire our food. He wants to hire a hot, young, glamorous chef he can brag about to his foodie-wannabe customers. Probably that's what he was looking for with Stark too."

"Stark isn't young."

"Yeah, but imagine how cool Firestone would feel if he could say he rediscovered Cooper Stark. Maybe he still thinks he can."

"God, this is just sick on so many levels." Rickey tossed the letters into a desk drawer. "Forget it, G. I'm not interested in consulting. I got too much work to do right here. The minute a chef starts spreading himself too thin, that's when people say his restaurant's going downhill."

"OK. I won't say another word about it."

And he wouldn't, Rickey knew. G-man had always been able to

leave things alone. It was Rickey himself who would keep gnawing at this, not because he was interested in the offer, but just because it was in his nature to gnaw.

That night a scene of decadence erupted at Liquor. No one intended for it to, but these things could happen without warning. Because the moon was full, because summer was coming and a sour smell had begun to rise off the streets, or for no reason at all, people would congregate in the bar after service. Cooks from other restaurants and friends of the crew might stop by. None of this was unusual, but then, instead of having the usual drink or three, everybody would get staggeringly, apocalyptically wasted.

Though he drank as much as anyone, Rickey didn't approve of these excessive evenings and had managed to keep them to a minimum—three or four since the restaurant opened, no more. He knew this one was getting out of control when Shake listed up drunkenly and started to kid him about the *Cornet* review. "What'd you *do* to that guy? Piss in his redfish? What's he got against you anyway?"

"He's got nothing against *Rickey*," said Tanker, who was half-lying in the next booth. "He's got it in for *Lenny*, and you must be some kinda shit-for-brains if you can't see that."

"So what's he got against Lenny?" said Shake, apparently unperturbed at being called a shit-for-brains.

"Damn if I know. If all the bodies Lenny's buried rose out of the muck tomorrow, we'd have fucking *Dawn of the Dead* in New Orleans."

"Fuck the review," said Rickey with bourbon-fueled indifference. "I don't care. I think it was good for us. I read where Jeremiah Tower says getting jacked off by the media is the worst thing that can happen to a young, successful chef. Says it pressures him to keep topping himself. I been feeling like that ever since we opened. A little bad press won't kill me."

"But you never were too good at taking criticism," said Karl, the dining-room manager and maître d'. "How about that time that guy kept sending back his entrée, and you finally went out to see what the matter was, and he said, 'I think you should go back to cooking school,' and you said, 'I think you should bite my crank?' "

"You did *not*!" said Karl's girlfriend Treneice.

Rickey rolled his eyes. "It was right after we got the Beard award and Chase Haricot's damn book came out. We were crazy busy. I was half out of my mind."

"And there was nothing wrong with his entrée," said G-man.

"Course there wasn't—it was a perfectly nice pork shank. But I never should've gone out there. I should've let Mr. Smooth handle it." Rickey nodded at Karl, tall and coffee-colored in a silk suit the shade of yucca leaves. "That's what we pay him for. Sure, he takes reservations and seats tables, but we *really* pay him to deal with the assholes."

"The gentleman in question was from Plano, Texas," said Karl. "He informed me numerous times that no such dish would be served in Plano—an assertion I couldn't argue with."

"Fucking Texans," said Rickey. "They think they got their own goddamn country over there, but they're just a bunch of fucking yahoos."

"As opposed to the urbane sophisticates of New Orleans," said Tanker. "Fat bastards arguing about oysters and dropping cigar ash on their seersucker suits."

"Least they know how to eat."

"You remember that next time one of 'em sends back his tuna tartare because it's raw."

"I admit we're provincial," said Rickey. "But we're not completely ignorant."

"Says the guy who's been out of Louisiana what? Twice?"

"I been to the Mississippi coast lots of times."

"Oh, well." Tanker sat up in the booth, grimacing as he found his cocktail glass full of melted ice. "Shut my mouth. I forgot I was talking to a seasoned world traveler."

"What'd you want us to do?" said G-man, who was even less

traveled than Rickey. "Spend our summer vacations in France? We grew up poor. We been working in kitchens since we were fifteen and living on our own since we were eighteen. There wasn't a whole lot left over for cruises and shit."

"I know it," said Tanker. "Just seems like now you could afford to expand your horizons a little."

"Maybe one of these days," Rickey said sullenly. He hated to travel, hadn't even enjoyed going to New York for the Beard awards.

Tanker looked as if he wanted to say more, but a couple of line cooks from a little French restaurant on Prytania Street appeared at to the table. One of them slid into the booth and slung an arm around Rickey's shoulders. "I think it's *great* you told that guy to bite your crank," he said. "Everybody talks about doing shit like that, but you're the only guy I know who actually *does* it."

"It was stupid," said Rickey. "Every customer you piss off, they go tell ten other people not to eat at your place."

"Aw, man, don't be such a sellout. It was *awesome*."

"Chuckie?"

"Yeah?"

"If you don't keep your goddamn hands to yourself, you're gonna be holding your knife with a hook."

"Sorry, sorry, jeez," said Chuckie.

"And Chuckie?"

"Yeah?"

"If you gotta walk around in a monogrammed jacket even though you left work three hours ago, just so everybody knows you work at Poivre, you could at least find a *clean fucking jacket!*"

Chuckie looked down at the saffron-aioli stains on his white jacket, looked back up at Rickey as though he might cry, then grabbed his beer and backed away from the table.

"Kinda harsh on him, weren't you?" said G-man.

"I can't stand those jerkoffs. Cole Parker's a good chef, but not a one of his crew is worth a damn." Rickey knew he was getting cranky, but he couldn't seem to shut up. "He just hires people who think he's hot shit."

"They think *you're* hot shit too," Tanker observed. "A lot of young cooks make puppydog eyes at you, Rickey. Not us, of course—we know what a wet end you are—but these kids from other restaurants think you're some kinda hero."

"And I hate that too!" Rickey smacked the tabletop, making several glasses jump. "I mean, do they think I'm a good *cook,* or are they just impressed that I won some big-ass award, or that I stuck a peeler in the throat of a guy who was trying to shoot me, or . . ." He paused, looked up at Tanker. "Did you just call me a *wet end*?"

"Yeah, I think I did."

"What the fuck does that mean?"

Tanker thought about it. "I'm not really sure."

"Must be some kinda Yankee expression," said G-man. Tanker had been born in Covington, across the lake from New Orleans, and they liked to rag him about it.

Tanker offered his usual rejoinder: "Suck my ass, yat boy."

From there the evening only got cruder and less coherent. For reasons known only to herself, Mo took off her blouse and tended bar in her brassiere. The young cooks from Poivre thought this was a fine turn of events, and splayed themselves across the bartop oblivious to Tanker's glare. Somebody put on a CD of hits from the seventies. A couple of girls began dancing to "Jackie Blue." The too-smooth, processed-sounding music made Rickey feel slightly nauseated, as if he'd just eaten a stick of margarine on top of all that bourbon. He was on the verge of calling it a night when there was a faint hollow boom in the distance, the music stopped in mid-ripple, and the lights went out. There was a frightened silence. Finally somebody said, "Did you forget to pay the electric bill?" A round of nervous laughter went around the bar. Rickey didn't laugh.

"Everybody stay where you are," he said. "I don't need a bunch of drunks crashing around. Mo, you got a flashlight back there?"

Mo found one and gave it to Karl, who started shooing people out of the bar. "I didn't finish my drink," Rickey heard somebody complain.

"You OK?" said G-man from across the table.

"No, I'm fucking wasted and I gotta get back to the kitchen and check the fuses."

They appropriated the flashlight and made their way to the fuse box at the rear of the kitchen. Everything seemed in order there. When Rickey called the power company to report the outage, a recording informed him that there had been a power spike in the area and service would be restored by noon the following day. He knew from experience that it would probably happen sooner, but he couldn't take a chance on losing the food in the big reach-in cooler and the little lowboys at the various stations. They began transferring it to the walk-in, which was better insulated and would stay cold much longer. No one came to help. They piled load after load into cardboard produce boxes, carried the heavy boxes back to the walk-in, unloaded and returned for more. Rickey began to doze on his feet. He dreamed he was sixteen, hauling bags of sand to fill a pothole in front of his mother's house. "What the hell are you doing?" said G-man as Rickey dumped a hotel pan full of prepped salad greens onto the floor.

"Not gonna work anyway," Rickey mumbled. "First time a truck drives by, this shit'll be all over the street."

"Dude, I think you better sit down for a minute. Look, here's a nice milk crate. I'll finish this."

"Huh?" said Rickey, waking up. "Is the power back on? What's all this arugula doing on the floor?"

"Just sit tight, OK? I'm almost done."

The power returned just as G-man finished carrying the last load to the walk-in. Rickey, still sitting on the milk crate, had nodded off again. G-man slid to the floor beside him, meaning to rest for a few minutes.

They woke up three hours later with cricks in their necks, crusts in their eyes, cotton in their skulls, and what felt like hot razor wire

Poppy Z. Brite

surgically implanted in their spines. Peeking out the back door, Rickey saw that dawn had already come and gone. He went into the dining room. Everybody had left, but there had been a cursory attempt to clean up the bar; the ashtrays had been dumped and the glasses stacked in the sink. He went around checking all the appliances to make sure nothing had been damaged by the power spike. Everything seemed OK until he looked through the tall glass doors of the reach-in and saw that the little interior thermometer read seventy-five degrees.

"We just had a cancellation," said the operator at the refrigeration company. "I can have a technician there in an hour."

Rickey could hardly stand the thought of staying awake for another hour. If they went home right now, they could grab a four-hour nap before they had to be back at the restaurant. If he gave up this chance, though, he might have to wait two or three days for the repairman. "Fine," he said, and went to make a pot of coffee.

"Wiring's shot," said the repairman, showing Rickey a mouthful of eroded gold teeth. The name stitched on the guy's shirt pocket appeared to read PTHALEN, but Rickey thought he might be hallucinating by now. "Power spike musta blown 'er out. How old is this thing anyway?"

"I got it used," said Rickey. The cooler had actually come from a failed restaurant of Lenny's. "So am I fixing it, or am I buying a new one?"

"Hafta rewire the whole thing. Cost you half as much as a new one, but you still got the old compressor and all. I was you, I'd replace 'er."

When the repairman had gone, Rickey and G-man slumped in a booth finishing their second pot of coffee. The wood grain of the table appeared to wriggle and twitch. G-man's eyes were so bloodshot that the veins showed through the dark lenses of his shades. "Good thing we can afford a new cooler," he said.

"Yeah," said Rickey without much enthusiasm.

"You thought about *why* we can afford it?"

Rickey looked up, realized what G-man was getting at, looked back down without answering.

"We got Lenny to fall back on," said G-man. "We've *always* had Lenny to fall back on. If anything happened to him, we'd be fucked next time something like this happened."

"We wouldn't be *fucked*. A reach-in costs a couple thousand dollars. It's a lot of money, but we're doing well enough to afford it."

"Yeah, but you know these things happen in clusters. I bet next week the ice machine goes out, or maybe the grease trap gets clogged."

"You're a real cheerer-upper."

G-man shrugged. "I'm just saying we could stand to have more of our own money, as opposed to always counting on Lenny's."

"Lenny's not going anywhere."

"Hope you're right."

"You really think I should do this thing in Dallas, huh?"

"Don't know," said G-man. "I just think if somebody offers you ten thousand dollars, maybe you shouldn't turn it down because you'd have to work with a guy who pissed you off one time."

"He did more than *piss me off*. God, G, he tried to break us up."

"He didn't know anything about *us*—he just put the make on a cute young kid. Anyway, we're still here and he's in Dallas trying to hang on to his crappy job. Why're you scared of him?"

"I'm not scared of him," said Rickey, but G-man just gave him a level stare. "I'm not *exactly* scared of him," he amended. "He's just a part of my past I'm not real eager to hook up with again."

"Because he made you feel stupid," said G-man. "Go show him you're not stupid. Go show him you're better at what you do than he ever was."

"I'll think about it, OK?" Rickey drained the bitter dregs of his coffee. "I can't decide now. I'll be doing great if I just get through this day without putting myself in the emergency room."

Poppy Z. Brite

"You really feel that bad? We could probably get Tanker to fill in if you need to go home."

"Fuck that." With an effort, Rickey hauled himself out of the booth. "Look—I'm standing up. If you can stand, you can work."

G-man nodded. It was the cook's rule of thumb for calling in sick, and one by which they had always abided.

"Look at this!" said Rickey.

"What's that?" G-man said as he poured hot milk into his first cup of coffee. It was their day off and they were just getting up.

Rickey held up a large, glossy cookbook. G-man squinted at the cover and saw that it was *Stark Raving Flavors* by Cooper Stark. Rickey had owned it since he was seventeen or so, but G-man hadn't seen it in a while.

Rickey had the book open to a full-page color photograph of Cooper Stark in the kitchen. He was dressed not in chef's whites, but in a wide-shouldered pinstriped suit with a purple silk shirt underneath. No tie—that would have spoiled his boyish, tousled image, G-man supposed. His dark hair was sportily gelled, his megawatt smile aimed right at the camera. A row of spotless copper pots gleamed above his head. Behind him, not quite in focus, hapless line cooks bowed their heads over an open fire.

"Look!" said Rickey. "There's his fucking glass of wine!"

Sure enough, there was Stark's wineglass on the granite-topped counter near his elbow. Beside it was a small, square plate of what looked like seared scallops. For a long moment they regarded the photo, silenced by its cheesiness. Then Rickey made as if to close the cookbook, but G-man put his hand on the page, holding it open. "Good-looking bastard," he said.

"Yeah, thirteen years ago when this book came out," said Rickey. "Now, who knows?"

G-man felt a twinge of guilt as he sipped his coffee. What Rickey had just said was uncomfortably close to what he'd been thinking. Did he want Rickey to take the job so Rickey could see Stark as he was today, a broken-down old nobody? Certainly it wasn't all about the money. They could use the money—no doubt about that—but he also thought consulting would do Rickey a lot of good. It was something Rickey had never done, didn't even really know how to do. Rickey thrived on things like that. Most people didn't open their own restaurants without ever having been head chef anywhere except a bar. Rickey had done it through sheer force of will and fearlessness.

No, not quite fearlessness, G-man thought. Rickey was plenty scared sometimes, but he went ahead and did what he wanted anyway. Usually he was good at it. G-man thought he might have gotten a little *too* good at running Liquor: he knew everything about the place, decided how everything should be done, micromanaged it down to the flowers on the table and the brand of toilet paper in the restrooms. He kept it running smoothly, but he had a hard time letting go of things and trusting his crew as much as a chef-owner needed to. A consulting job would not only present Rickey with a new challenge; it would force him to relinquish control of Liquor for a week or so, and assuming the place didn't burn down in his absence, G-man thought everyone would benefit from that.

Rickey closed the book, turned it facedown on the kitchen table, and picked up the newspaper. "Hey, check this out," he said, scanning the food page. "Lance Cowslip is at Saffron now."

"I thought he left town when Fourchette d'Or closed."

"Apparently he's back."

Lance Cowslip had been the city's other trendy young chef during the height of Rickey's publicity blitz. A *New York Times* article on New Orleans dining had almost seemed to pit them against each other, ignoring other worthy restaurants to compare two places doing two very different things. The quote "Where Cowslip would refine a flavor, Rickey exaggerates it" had been a particular thorn in Rickey's side, and they had heard that Cowslip especially disliked "Rickey understands the true and vital pulse of Louisiana in a way Cowslip, a Midwesterner, cannot."

Several months ago, the owners of Fourchette d'Or had locked the doors and disappeared one night. Their phone was disconnected, their apartment was empty, and they owed their staff three weeks' pay. Rumor had it that they were in Vegas blowing the last of their meager profits. Lance Cowslip was livid. "I don't care about the *money*," he'd told the *Times-Picayune* food critic, who was able to reach him on his cell phone as he rode his motorcycle across Colorado in pursuit of the owners. "I can make money anywhere, but these guys took away my *canvas*." How Rickey had sneered at that!

"Let's have dinner there," said Rickey.

"Dude, are you crazy? You know what happens when a place gets mentioned in the paper, especially a hot tip like that. Saffron's gonna be swamped tonight."

"Bet we can get in."

"How?"

Rickey squinted over the rim of his coffee cup. His hair was in wild corkscrews, his face had gone unshaven for two days, and his T-shirt was far from clean. Only his wide, sweet smile saved him from an appearance of complete degeneracy. "I love you, G," he said. "You're a food celebrity and you don't even know it."

"I am not. *You* are, maybe."

"Uh huh. And you got any idea how many people think you're the real brains of the operation?"

"Oh, well." G-man shrugged. "I thought you said I was a food celebrity or something. Now you're just speaking the truth."

•

Poppy Z. Brite

Saffron was located in a downtown building that had once been the master's house on a vast indigo plantation. Hundreds of slaves were poisoned to death picking and processing the toxic plant. Now the site housed a restaurant that seemed to go through chefs as fast as the plantation had gone through pickers. Their first chef had fallen off the deck of a casino boat and drowned in Lake Pontchartrain. The second suffered a spider bite, got gangrene, and lost a leg. The third left the restaurant business to join a gun-hoarding cult in the Texas panhandle. The fourth was Lance Cowslip.

Upon entering Saffron's foyer, the diner was greeted by a series of translucent hanging Plexiglas circles as large as compact cars. These circles bisected the entryway, forcing people to dodge around them in search of the reservations desk. This desk, when located, proved to be a cigar-shaped contrivance made out of glass bricks and brushed copper. The black-clad woman standing behind it, her body about as wide as an uncooked strand of fettucine, would consult a thick leather folder before deciding whether or not to grant the petitioner a table. If the gods smiled, the diner would be led into a dining room softly lit by some concealed source. The thick ecru carpet embraced the ankles as if glad to be walked upon. The ceiling was covered with a tangled web of stainless steel and copper wire. Here and there in the webbing, wine bottles dangled like insects caught by some huge industrial spider.

"Jeez," said Rickey as they were seated at a banquette. "Somebody sure redid this place."

"Mitsy Bing," said the hostess.

"Huh?"

"She did the decorating. The entire restaurant was redone last summer. We're particularly proud of the wire installation on the ceiling."

Rickey reserved comment until the woman had left the table. Then he said, "I know that name. That's the crazy broad Lenny tried to make us use, and I fired her when she wanted to paint a Roman orgy scene on the back wall."

"Now, now," said G-man, perusing the wine card on the table.

"Well, if she'd had her way, our dining room would look like a damn Mardi Gras float."

"But it doesn't. It's very tasteful."

"Especially compared to some places," said Rickey, glancing up at the shiny metal web and shuddering a little.

A waiter appeared beside the table holding two leather-covered menus. "Good evening, chefs. We're so pleased to have you in the house."

"I bet Lance is just thrilled," said Rickey, and noted the waiter's suppressed snicker with no little satisfaction. They studied the menus with the absorption of Biblical scholars coming upon some previously unknown Gnostic text. Rickey was the first to break the silence. "Lance," he said. "Oh, Lance, Lance, Lance. I knew you were a wacky character, but venison with black trumpets and tobacco *jus*? You oughta be arrested."

"See, I knew you were gonna get bitchy before we even tasted a mouthful of food," said G-man.

"Bet the black trumpets are dried too."

The waiter reappeared with two small plates. "Compliments of Chef Lance," he said, setting the plates before them. "This is a potato-chive blintz filled with goat cheese and *Bündnerfleisch*."

"What kind of flesh?" said G-man when the waiter had retreated.

"*Bündnerfleisch*." Rickey ground his teeth. "Air-dried beef from Switzerland. I've never even *heard* of anybody cooking with it in New Orleans." He tasted his *amuse-bouche* and looked pleased. "And if Lance is gonna be the first, he should set a better example. This is way too salty."

"It's all right," said G-man. "It's a little salty."

"It's like the fucking Dead Sea," said Rickey, gulping his water.

G-man looked across the table at Rickey and experienced a small sinking feeling. Rickey had not come here to have a nice dinner. He wanted to pick this meal apart, and the more flaws he could find with it, the happier he would be. It was a hell of a way to spend a date. At least he had brushed his hair and put on the nice dark blue

Poppy Z. Brite

jacket he'd bought for their trip to New York. Even this minimal effort made him stand out from the crowd, and as G-man listened to the constant stream of complaints, he obtained some consolation from knowing he was dining with the best-looking man in the place. He smiled at Rickey and signaled the waiter, eager to order their first round of cocktails.

They had just finished their appetizers when Lance Cowslip appeared at the table. Rickey noted the small sauce and grease stains on his white jacket with grudging respect. He didn't approve of chefs who visited the dining room in disgustingly filthy jackets, but he wasn't impressed by those who took the time to put on fresh, spotless ones either. You didn't have to look like a slob, but there was no shame in admitting that you'd been working back there.

Most of Cowslip's tousled blond hair was hidden beneath the kind of tall paper hat some cooks called a coffee filter. He was a young man with a slightly unfinished look, pink and soft, rather like a large, unusually handsome fetus. His dewy complexion was flushed with kitchen heat. "I'm absolutely slammed," he said after shaking their hands. "Just wanted to make sure you enjoyed your apps."

"We did," said Rickey.

"Real good," said G-man.

"It's just that I noticed the quail stuffed with foie gras and lavender-scented wild rice came back unfinished."

"Oh, that was mine," said Rickey. "It was very filling."

"Really," said Cowslip, cocking an eye at Rickey. "You look like a boy who could eat a few quail if he wanted to."

"Hell, Lance, I hated to say anything. It's so damn easy to overcook those little birds."

"It was overcooked?"

"It was kinda dry."

"A little dry?"

"Bone dry," said Rickey with the air of a doctor telling a patient to get his affairs in order.

"I'll have it taken off your bill."

"Absolutely not. It could happen to anybody. Don't worry about it."

"And the *soupe de poissons*?" Cowslip asked G-man. "How was it?"

"Good. Real good."

"The serrano rouille wasn't too weird?"

"*That* wasn't weird," said Rickey.

Cowslip turned on him. "What *was* weird?"

"Oh, Lance, you know . . ." Rickey made a regretful face. "Nobody loves Louisiana seafood more than me, but I don't know about putting crawfish in *soupe de poissons*. I thought it . . . *interfered*."

"You know how these locals are!" said Cowslip a little too loudly. "They'd no more comprehend a classic *soupe de poissons* than they'd give up beer for Lent!"

The four people at the next table glared at him, then began to whisper irately amongst themselves.

"Anyway, I better get back to the kitchen. I'll try to drop into your place sometime. I saw your menu online—you're doing a duck terrine with kirsch, right?"

"Yeah."

"Good dish," said Cowslip. "I did one just like it at Fourchette d'Or." Before Rickey could reply, he turned and glided off through the crowded dining room, a white beacon that caught everyone's attention but paused for nobody.

"Bastard!" said Rickey.

"Aw, you got in plenty of zingers. Don't begrudge him one good line."

"I wasn't trying to get in *zingers*. I wasn't even gonna mention the quail, but he *asked*."

"Course he asked. You only dismembered it and pushed all the stuffing over to one side of the plate."

Poppy Z. Brite

"That stuffing was nasty."

"You ordered it because you thought it was gonna be nasty. You *hoped* it was gonna be nasty. Just like you're hoping your venison with tobacco *jus* will be."

"Well, maybe I hope it'll be a little nasty, but not too bad. I *am* pretty hungry."

Rickey sniffed suspiciously at the venison when it was set before him, but after a few bites, he pronounced it successful. Though his tone was dolorous, G-man admired his honesty. Rickey might have a penchant for pissing contests, but he wouldn't lie about what his palate told him. G-man's saddle of lamb with artichoke ragout was badly overdone. He found a medium-rare bite for Rickey and didn't say anything about the rest. There was no need to add fuel to the fire.

They passed on dessert, opting instead for a fourth round of cocktails. When the bill folder came to their table, Rickey opened it and found a note:

> **Your drinks are on me. Heard you guys were having a rough time of it lately and figured it was the least I could do. Hang in there—bad write-ups get forgotten in a few years. Hope you enjoyed everything.**
>
> **Lance**

"Bastard!" Rickey snarled. "Smug, swanning, prima-donna, prettyboy bastard!"

G-man hid a small smile as he reached for the bill. He didn't like Lance Cowslip a whole lot better than Rickey did, but he had to admire Cowslip's wiliness in getting the final word.

Pleasantly full and more than a little tipsy, they pulled up in front of their house. The night air was soft on their faces, scented with flowers and a touch of mud from the river. From a passing car came a deep basso throb and a voice that inquired irritably, *"What a nigga gotta do to make a half a million?"* The car turned the corner onto Tchoupitoulas Street and the evening was quiet again. Then, out of the darkness, suddenly someone said, "There they are!"

Two figures came rushing toward them. One, a scruffy young man, held a large camera emblazoned with the letters WNOL-TV. The other, a woman with the kind of makeup job Rickey had previously only seen on the guest of honor at funerals, brandished a microphone. "Chef John Rickey?" she said.

Rickey took a step back and almost fell off the curb. "Yeah. Who wants to know?"

"Kimberly LeBlanc from Channel 5. Do you have any comment on tonight's arrest of Lenny Duveteaux?"

Poppy Z. Brite

Lenny sat in his vast white living room watching the news. Oscar De La Cerda perched beside him on the sectional sofa, staring morosely at the television and occasionally making notes on a yellow legal pad.

"Celebrity restaurateur Lenny Duveteaux was arrested tonight on charges of conspiracy to commit fraud, injuring public records, and failure to pay sales tax to the City of New Orleans," said the lacquered lady reporter standing in front of Lenny's French Quarter restaurant. "He bonded out within hours, but by that time, investigators had reportedly searched his home and office. The investigation was launched by District Attorney Placide Treat."

Treat appeared on the screen. He was a short old man with broad shoulders, wild tangled eyebrows, and a florid face that suggested mumps rather than any sort of normal jowliness. He stared right into the camera as if soliciting its vote. "I shall give no interviews about this until the time is right," he said. "The moving finger writes, and having writ, moves on! He who hath an ear, let him hear! If you know the source of these quotations, you may be able to understand why I have arrested Mr. Duveteaux. If not, don't worry, it will all come clear in time. Due time. And allow me to say that Mr. Duveteaux's time is long overdue. That's it! No comment!"

"I love how Tricker always says 'No comment' after he's finished commenting," said De La Cerda.

"Shhh."

The film cut to Rickey standing in front of his house. G-man was just visible behind him. They both looked rumpled, somewhat drunk, and not particularly reputable. "Plenty of people are jealous of Lenny," Rickey said. "People are jealous of anybody who does any [bleep] thing and manages not to [bleep] it up. This is retarded. Now get the [bleep] out of my yard."

"Chef John Rickey, Duveteaux's business associate," the reporter said primly. "Treat promises new developments within the week. Meanwhile, Chef Duveteaux is still cooking . . . but he may be in hot water. For WNOL-5, I'm Kimberly LeBlanc." The camera panned to a close-up of the hanging sign that read LENNY'S; then the screen showed the two news anchors, who looked outwardly solemn, secretly amused, and even more stiffly lacquered than the reporter. "Hottest summer in fifty years coming up?" said one of them. "Stay tuned for Brent with the weather . . . after this break."

"I SAY I SAY I SAY! WHO SAY I SAY? FRANKIE AND JOHNNY SEZ LET 'EM HAVE IT WITH NOOOO PROBLEM! GET DIS SEVENTEEN-PIECE THREE-ROOM SET FOR ONLY FOUR HUNDRED NINETY DOWN—"

Lenny stabbed viciously at the remote control until the television was struck mute. "I don't know which makes this place look more like a banana republic," he snarled, "the politics or the advertising."

"You mean there's a difference?" said De La Cerda.

Lenny's famous equanimity had been almost completely shattered by the events of the past twenty-four hours. Just before dinner service, Placide Treat, two of his assistant DAs, and a brace of uniformed police officers had shown up at Crescent. Treat read the warrant himself, staring up into Lenny's eyes with an expression of mingled glee and menace. Lenny was completely unprepared for the arrest, but he refused to show distress in front of his crew. "Horace, you got everything under control?" he asked his sous chef. "I have to go take care of this. I should be back in a few hours."

"I got it, Chef," said Horace, staring worriedly at the suits and uniforms that had invaded his kitchen. Most of the crew had disappeared at the first sight of cops.

But Lenny didn't make it back to the restaurant that night. It took hours for De La Cerda to arrange his bail, and for a while Lenny thought he might have to sleep at Central Lockup. That wouldn't have been so bad if he'd had his own cell, but after booking him, they'd put him in with a bunch of wiseass drunk drivers, small-time drug collars, and such. Nobody tried to hurt him, but the ripostes soon grew stultifying.

"Hey, ain't I seen you on that show? Whass that show? Late Night with David Litterbox?"

"Yeah, that him. He some kinda famous chef."

"Yo, Chef, you gonna cook me a rock?"

"Rich-ass motherfucker think he better'n everybody in here, look at his fuckin face—"

That was when Lenny stood up from the wobbly metal bench where he'd been sitting and grabbed a burning cigarette out of the nearest hand. "I don't think you understand who you're dealing with," he said, and jammed the cigarette into the palm of his hand. The pain was instant, huge, and nauseating, but he forced himself not to react. "I don't even feel that. Now if I can do that to myself, just imagine what I'm liable to do to the first person who fucks with me." He surveyed the mass of surprised faces. "Anybody?"

"Be cool," somebody said in a small voice, but Lenny ignored it. He dropped the extinguished cigarette on the floor and displayed his palm, which was now marked with an impressive-looking black-edged hole.

"Fine," he said. "Maybe now we can get a little peace and quiet around here."

The rest of the evening wasn't peaceful or quiet—Lenny had an idea jails never were—but they left him alone after that. In a few hours De La Cerda showed up and took him home, where he showered, helped himself to some of the delicious leftover ham in the refrigerator, fixed himself a triple vodka tonic, and caught a few hours of uneasy sleep.

Today he and the lawyer had taken inventory of his situation. While he was in jail, the investigators had searched his offices at Lenny's and Crescent as well as his home. Many of his files and all his tapes were now in the hands of Placide Treat. Those tapes contained most of Lenny's telephone conversations over the past ten years, as well as certain conversations that had taken place in his restaurant offices, which were bugged. If Treat heard certain exchanges, Lenny would almost certainly be indicted on several of the charges. (The tax charge was completely bogus—Lenny never failed to pay his sales tax—but he supposed it had been something else to put on the warrant.) His hope lay in the fact that it would take several years to listen to all the tapes. The DA's office was notoriously understaffed and underfunded . . . but of course Treat had access to his wife's family fortune.

"Can Tricker fund the investigation himself?" he asked De La Cerda. "Is that legal?"

"No, but I bet he can find ways of funneling money into it. Of course, I don't know if he'd take the risk, because his ass would be on the line if we could prove it. It all depends on how bad he wants you, Lenny. And why."

"Yeah. *Why* does he want me?" Lenny stood up and paced across the room, stared out through the sliding glass doors at his rolling green lawn, paced back. "Not because I made him and his buddies pay for their meal ten years ago."

"You were an asshole to make them pay. You could've had him in your corner for the price of a dozen overdone steaks. Plus you could've told people the DA eats at your restaurant. But no, you had to stand on principle."

"I hadn't been here very long. I didn't really know how things worked yet. And even if it was a mistake, he wouldn't try to nail me on a bunch of bogus charges after all this time. He's not *that* crazy." De La Cerda didn't reply, and Lenny turned to look at him. "Is he?"

"He's pretty fucking crazy," De La Cerda said quietly.

"But nobody would hold a ten-year grudge over a thing like that."

"Lenny, have you ever heard of Clay Shaw?"

"Didn't he have something to do with the JFK assassination?"

"Personally, I think he had nothing to do with it. But Jim Garrison—the DA before Treat—brought him to trial for it and basically destroyed his life. Shaw was acquitted, but he spent a fortune on his defense and died a few years later. Now, some New Orleanians think it all had to do with Shaw being gay, or CIA, or God knows what. But you know what other people say? They tell a story about how Shaw was seated next to the Garrisons at Brennan's one night, and the Garrisons were arguing, and Big Jim threw a glass of wine in his wife's face. And he hated Clay Shaw forever after because Shaw saw that embarrassing scene. When he saw a chance to drag him into the JFK thing and tear his life apart, why, that's exactly what he did."

"My God," Lenny whispered. "He was able to get an indictment and everything?"

"Indictment!" De La Cerda laughed. "Any DA can get any grand jury to indict a ham sandwich. That's no problem. Garrison brought Shaw to *trial*, didn't you hear me? Long, controversial, expensive *trial*."

"All over a scene in a restaurant?"

"Probably not." De La Cerda cracked his knuckles, making Lenny wince. "And I doubt this grudge Placide Treat has against you is the only reason you got arrested tonight. We've got the DA race coming up next year. Tricker knows you're gonna finance my run. Ten years ago I don't think he'd have been worried—I mean, who the fuck am I?—but he's getting old. What do people know him for?

Handing out free candy and saying goofy shit on TV. Meanwhile criminals are getting out of jail, people are getting robbed and murdered. He needs a big, high-profile case."

"But I'm *popular*. I don't mean to sound like a dick, but people in New Orleans *love* me, Oscar. What's Tricker got to gain from putting me in prison?"

"Rich people love you, Lenny. Poor people don't give a shit about you one way or another, because they can't afford to eat at your restaurants. And remember, Tricker's from here and you're not."

"I've lived here for fifteen years!"

De La Cerda shook his head. "Ever look at the obituaries in the *Times-Picayune*? Check 'em out sometime. 'Joe Schmoe resided in New Orleans for 53 years, but he was originally from Asshole Junction, Utah.' That shit matters here."

"Christ."

"And of course it doesn't help that Louisiana's conspiracy law is such a joke. Treat doesn't even have to prove you committed a crime if he can prove you *conspired* to commit it. A guy could be walking around in the bloom of health and the DA could still get somebody indicted for conspiracy to murder him."

"So I can be indicted for thought crimes."

"Basically."

"You don't sound too goddamn optimistic, Oscar. As my attorney, shouldn't you be giving me every assurance that we're going to beat this rap?"

"I told you not to make those fucking tapes. I been telling you for *years* to quit making those fucking tapes. How am I supposed to defend you if you've recorded your own doom on microcassettes?"

"My *doom*? That's pretty melodramatic."

"OK. Let's see. The time you bribed Old Country to send bad shipments of fish to that restaurant that moved in next to your French Quarter place—is that on there?"

"Well, yeah. But they were duplicating my menu. I had to nip it in the bud."

"Right. How about the payoffs to get the Crescent property zoned commercial even though the neighborhood association made a stink about it?"

"Not in so many words." De La Cerda gazed levelly at Lenny. After a minute, Lenny said, "But I guess somebody could put things together."

"Uh-huh. And I guess you taped all your conversations with the Gemelli boys?"

"Of course I taped all my conversations with the Gemelli boys! You think I want those fuckers coming back on me, saying I said shit I didn't say . . . oh, fuck." Lenny buried his head in his hands. "OK, so the tapes are pretty bad. But I still don't like the way you're talking about Treat. If I have to mount a major defense, I need somebody who's not chickenshit-scared of the DA."

"Every lawyer in this state is chickenshit-scared of Placide Treat," said De La Cerda. "The fucking *governor's* chickenshit-scared of Placide Treat. Guy's got something on everybody, and if he doesn't, he'll find something."

"No, Oscar. That's a defeatist attitude and I don't accept it. You keep that attitude, you'll just help Tricker indict me the way he indicted that guy a few years ago—what was his name? You know, the King of Rex?"

"Goddammit, Lenny, you pig. You know perfectly well there is no fucking King of Rex. You only do it to torture me. He's not the King of Rex, he's not King Rex, he's just fucking REX, KING OF CARNIVAL."

Lenny could not, in fact, understand this distinction. He knew that each year a wealthy old Uptown New Orleanian was elected King of Carnival. On Fat Tuesday, the guy was crowned Rex and was actually granted a sort of benign sovereignty for a day. Some locals seemed to see the custom as a form of transubstantiation whereby the (relatively) humble flesh of the old-money Uptowner became the body of a lost king resurrected for a single day in Arthurian glory. Lenny knew all this, had even met several of the past ten or so Rexes, but he still could not quite comprehend the semantics.

A Rex of years past—better known as Spencer Dulac III, president of a local bank—had been indicted for criminal malfeasance in connection with monies that (according to Placide Treat) had ended up in Dulac's Cayman Islands bank account. When the city's Criminal Court judges—many of them good friends of Dulac—sought to oversee the funds Treat was using for his investigation, Treat implied to the press that the judges were involved in racketeering. Said judges promptly tried to hold him in contempt, but were unsuccessful. Several of those judges had subsequently been unseated, and the rest no longer dared to say anything critical of the DA. Though Spencer Dulac himself never went to trial, his reputation had been tarnished and he now spent most Carnival seasons skiing in Vail.

New Orleans was an altogether implausible city, Lenny often thought, so outside the normal frame of reference that there were many parts of his life he could not even begin to explain to his old friends back in Maine. They thought it was Bourbon Street, jazz, and gumbo; they didn't understand the festering miasma of tradition and corruption that underlay all the tourist shit. He no longer tried to enlighten them. But sometimes—now, for instance—he still felt like an outsider himself.

He returned to the sofa and unmuted the television. An elfin-featured weatherman was drawing pinwheels on a large map of the Gulf. "So if these predictions are right," he said cheerily, "this could be the most active hurricane season in twenty years!"

"Glorious," said Lenny.

Rickey opened the Word program on his computer and sat looking at the blank white screen for a few minutes. His so-called education had given him no writing skills to speak of, and he'd had little chance or reason to develop any over the course of his career. He hoped he could write a letter that wouldn't send Frank Firestone running to find a new consultant.

Poppy Z. Brite

Dear Mr. Firestone,

Thanks for thinking of me for your consulting job. I was surprised and flattered to hear from you. Sure I remember Cooper Stark. He's a real good chef, you chose well.

I know what you mean about being ready to try new things, but not necessarily ready to like them. New Orleans is like that too. Seems like some people around here think it's a crime if you don't serve fried seafood, trout meunière, gumbo, etc. That's great food of course but I think it is good to have other options. As many as possible. When I opened Liquor, I wanted to have a restaurant that would appeal to tourists and locals, but as you know the local customer is always the most important. "REPEAT" tourists might come in once every year or 2. "REPEAT" locals might come in 2 or 3 times a month or more.

Rickey scowled at the screen, then pushed back from his desk and went out into the hall that connected his little office to the kitchen. "G!" he hollered. "Can you come here a minute?"

G-man appeared from the direction of the walk-in, his hands dusted with flour. "What's up?" he said. "I thought you were in the bar or something."

"No, I'm trying to write this letter to Firestone and it just sounds stupid. Would you take a look at it?"

G-man sat down at the desk and squinted through his dark glasses at the computer screen. Rickey couldn't stand to watch him read the document, and the office wasn't really big enough to occupy his attention elsewhere, so he went into the hall again. He didn't know why he felt so embarrassed; he and G-man knew everything about each other, but something about the words on the screen just made him cringe.

"It looks fine to me," called G-man.

Rickey went back into the office. "Yeah?"

"Yeah. You probably don't need to put 'repeat' in quotes and capital letters—one or the other would do, I guess. But it's a good start."

"I hate writing. I *know* I'm not stupid, but it makes me *feel* stupid."

"You're not stupid. You just had a shitty education. We all did." G-man remained at the desk, tapping his fingers on the edges of the keyboard. "So you're really gonna do this thing, huh?"

"Yeah, if Firestone still wants me. I told you that last night."

"Well, last night was kinda crazy. I thought you might sleep on it and change your mind. I'm glad you didn't, though. I think you should do it—you know that."

"Yeah." Rickey sighed. "I just wish I was as sure as you. I don't want to go to Dallas, and I sure don't want to spend a week working with Cooper Stark. But we gotta find ways of making our own money. The damn DA's gonna haul Lenny up in front of a grand jury, and I bet he gets indicted. When it goes to trial, who knows what could happen?"

"You really think they can get that much dirt on Lenny?"

"Dude, you know those tapes are Lenny's weak spot. Remember how he told us some chef in Maine betrayed him a long time ago, when he was first starting out in the business? He's convinced nobody can ever spike him again if he just keeps evidence of every single conversation he ever has. Only trouble is, most of those tapes probably make *him* look worse than anybody else. You know the kinda stuff Lenny does. He doesn't start a lot of shit, but if somebody starts shit with him, they're toast."

"Like Mr. Johnson," said G-man. Mr. Johnson was a mean old man who'd lived near the Liquor property and tried to prevent the restaurant from opening. Just before the neighborhood meeting where the matter was to be voted upon, Mr. Johnson was found dead in his home. The death was ruled natural, but G-man had always been convinced that Lenny had a hand in it. Rickey thought that was ridiculous; Johnson was known to have a heart condition, and Lenny could hardly make somebody drop dead of a coronary, could he? At least that was what Rickey had always told himself.

"Never mind Mr. Johnson. Lenny's had lots of enemies more important than that. He takes care of them, and there's gotta be some evidence of it on those tapes."

G-man went back to what he had been doing, and Rickey returned to the desk to finish his letter.

> . . . REPEAT tourists might come in once every year or 2. REPEAT locals might come in 2 or 3 times a month or more. In New Orleans, a restaurant can't survive outside the French Quarter without attracting plenty of local business, and I know how to do that.
>
> Your Dallas market doesn't sound all that different from ours, except that your locals have more money, so maybe your food costs can run a little higher (reflected in your menu prices). If not, I can help Coop figure out how to keep them down. Mine run around 30% at Liquor, but we like to use some specialty items, EXOTIC PRODUCE, PLUGRA BUTTER, ETC. But I don't know if that is a concern of yours. Why don't we talk and you can let me know a little more about your concerns?
>
> The way my schedule looks now, I could come to Dallas the third week in June if that looks good for you. It's a real slow time for us. Give me a call any day between 10 AM and 4:30 PM. Thanks again for thinking of me.
>
> Sincerely Yours,
> Chef John Rickey

He printed the letter, signed it, and slid it into an envelope that bore the restaurant's logo, the word *Liquor* in flowing script with a stylized martini glass in the upsweep of the *R*. He saw the logo every day, but just now it gave him a funny feeling. Two years ago it had been an embryonic concept in his brain. Now it was on stationery, napkins, chef jackets, even in neon on the roof of the goddamn building. He had made it real and it had changed his life. He couldn't stand the idea of failing, of having to work in somebody else's kitchen again, thinking about money all the time, slogging through the month wondering if they would be able to pay the light bill, water bill, rent. He and G-man weren't rich now by any means. After the restaurant started making a profit, Rickey had a picture window installed in his mother's living room, G-man bought his folks a new refrigerator, and they often ate in nice restaurants on their nights off. These things were pretty much the extent of their luxuries, but even so, this was the first time in their lives that they hadn't been flat-out poor. How awful it would be to go back to all that.

When the letter was stamped and ready to go, Rickey sat there a little longer, wondering if he should answer Cooper Stark's letter too. If all went well, he'd be seeing Coop soon. Things might be even weirder between them if Rickey didn't at least write or speak to him beforehand. But he couldn't face that blank screen again, so he turned off the computer and went to get started on his real work. Knives, stockpots, cutting boards, crates of vegetables and Styrofoam boxes of fish: these were tangible things, things that made sense to him. He was happy to leave the written word behind.

7

By day, the French Market is a gaudy, tawdry open-air enclave at the river edge of the French Quarter, a veritable showcase of New Orleans cliché. Tourists swarm through shops that sell overpriced hot sauce, Mardi Gras beads, and mammy-doll saltshaker sets; shady characters hawk preserved alligator heads; pralines are manufactured before your eyes; bad restaurants pump out gallons of Creole-flavored sludge . . . and somewhere in the midst of all this, a small fruit and vegetable market still survives, the original purpose of the buildings relegated to a minor part of a major tourist attraction. Visitors to New Orleans like to imagine local chefs strolling through the market buying fresh produce from the farmers who back their trucks up to the stalls, but most chefs never shop here; the place is too expensive and too crowded.

At night, the market is a different animal. The shops close early, the tourists migrate to Bourbon Street, and the flea market clears out. There are only intermittent pools of light between the black iron colonnades, mostly empty. But the farmer's market is open twenty-four hours, and though most of the vendors leave in the late afternoon and come back in the early morning, it is possible to find a man selling tomatoes, squash, and strawberries at two A.M.

Sal Mariakakis had a truckload of late-season navel oranges he'd gotten from a grower down in Plaquemines Parish two days ago. They weren't moving very well—nobody wanted anything but Creole tomatoes right now—and so he'd decided to stay at his stall all night, catnapping and seeing if he could unload some of the damned fruit to the drunks who occasionally strolled through the market. He was sitting on an upturned milk crate cleaning his nails with his pocketknife when the astonishing car came gliding around the corner of French Market Place and parked illegally on Ursulines.

It was the largest car Sal had ever seen, at least ten feet long and six feet high, with a humped roof and a sparkling silver grille flanked by two enormous headlights. A third, slightly smaller headlight was set at bottom center of the grille, just in case the other two failed to blind any oncoming drivers, Sal guessed. The two-tone paint job—black and cream—had been polished to a high gloss no bird or insect dared sully. The back doors swung open and two men got out. One stayed by the car. The other approached Sal's stall.

If he hadn't seen the car, Sal might have thought this strange little man was a street person; the guy wore a pair of hand-tooled cowboy boots so battered they were almost falling off his feet, a pair of dress pants, and a Hawaiian shirt with a colorful pattern of palm trees, B-52 bombers, and bikini-clad girls. His gray hair fell lankly across his forehead as if unwashed for days. There was a gleam in his eye that reminded Sal of certain French Quarter denizens given to ranting about Jesus, the Pope, black helicopters, microwaves from outer space, the tragedy of desegregation, and such.

"You got some satsumas for sale?" the man asked without preamble. He had one of those New Orleans voices that sound as if they have been dragged through broken glass, then wrapped in sandpaper.

"Satsumas are outta season right now. I got navel oranges."

"Navels be just fine. They nice and sweet?"

Poppy Z. Brite

"Sure."

"Lemme have a taste."

"Sorry. No free samples."

"Boy—what's your name?"

"Sal Mariakakis," said Sal, wondering if the little old guy was going to be trouble. He didn't look like much of a threat, but the other guy, taller and younger with a shock of bright red hair, was still waiting by the car. They'd both gotten out of the back, so there must be a driver in there too.

"Placide Treat," said the man, holding out his hand. Sal looked at it for a moment, then shook it. "Now listen, Sal Mariakakis, I'm a wealthy man."

"I kinda figured from the car."

"Yes indeed. That's a Rolls-Royce Silver Wraith. 1948, and she still runs just as smooth as mayonnaise." He pronounced this last word *mynez*. "Now what I'd like to do, Sal, is buy every one of these navel oranges you got here and take 'em away in that car. But I'm not gonna do it if I can't taste one and see are they nice and sweet."

"Mister, are you kidding? I got four crates left. That's over three hundred oranges."

"Three hundred should be sufficient," said Treat.

Sal wiped his pocketknife on the leg of his jeans, selected an orange, and cut it in two. He offered one half to Treat, who began sucking noisily. The man by the car was watching, and Sal held up the other half. "Try some?" he called, feeling a little stupid but not particularly caring. If these guys weren't just jacking him around, he could get out of here and maybe hit one of the cheap strip joints in the upper Quarter before he went home.

"Thanks," said the redhead, walking over and taking the orange half. He was a nerdy-looking type who wasn't wearing a suit right now, but would obviously feel more comfortable in one, and Sal wondered what he was doing running around with this old freak in the middle of the night.

"They real nice," said Treat. It was funny the way he talked, downtown New Orleans one minute and words like *sufficient* the next. Must be a local boy who'd gotten himself some education. "Your sign says three for a dollar. I give you a hundred dollars, we gonna be square?"

"Sure."

"Woofer, get the driver to help you load 'em up."

"Hey, that's OK," Sal said. "You buy me out, the least I can do is load 'em in your car."

He did, and the old guy gave him five crisp twenties. As Sal put the money away, Treat pointed at the pocketknife Sal had used to cut the orange. Its handle was engraved with a bucolic scene of a lone egret silhouetted against a bayou sunset. "How much you want for that?"

"Aw, I just picked this up by the flea market. You can get you one any day."

"I don't want to get me one any day, I want that one. Twenty dollars?"

"Sure," said Sal, who had paid five.

Treat paid for the knife, shook Sal's hand again, and climbed back into the car. Sal caught a glimpse of buttery leather upholstery and what he felt fairly sure was a portable bar as the door swung shut. The younger man was still standing there finishing his orange; he hadn't chomped into it like Treat, but peeled away the remaining rind and separated the segments in a rather prissy way.

"So, uh, who is that guy anyway?" said Sal.

"Placide Treat? Don't you read the newspaper?"

"Just the funny pages," Sal said truthfully.

"He's the District Attorney of Orleans Parish."

"He don't look much like a District Attorney."

"Well, he dresses a little better when he's in court. He calls those his relaxing clothes."

"What's he gonna do with all them oranges?"

"Give them away to people. Probably claim he's got a grove down in Plaquemines Parish and grew them himself."

"For real? How come?"

"Election coming up," said the man. He didn't quite roll his eyes, but there was the definite suggestion of an eye-roll. "He likes to create good will by giving away snacks. Candy and things. Calls them 'Treats from Treat.' "

"Well, he's got my vote." Sal wasn't even registered, but it seemed like the right thing to say. "So you a lawyer too?"

"Yeah. Woofer Scagliano. I'm his First Assistant DA."

One of the car windows cranked down a couple of inches. "C'mon now, Woofer!" cried the old guy. "Hurry it up!"

"Just a sec, dammit!"

"You like working for him?" Sal asked.

"Well, it's got one thing to recommend it," said Woofer Scagliano, swallowing the last bite of his orange and wiping his fingers on a handkerchief he'd taken from his pocket. "It's never, ever boring."

Placide Treat dismissed his driver and grabbed a few hours' sleep in his suite at the Roosevelt Hotel. The gracious old hotel had actually changed its name to the Fairmont in 1965, but Treat didn't like getting used to new things and saw no reason to change his habit of calling it the Roosevelt. He had kept a suite there since his election in 1979, often finding it more convenient to sleep downtown than to drive all the way out to his Lakeview home. He couldn't get any peace at home anyway; his wife and son always wanted some damn thing or other. It was a hell of a thing, having a son nearly forty years old who still lived at home, whose only ambition in life was to become a restaurant critic. Sometimes he wished his other son was the legitimate one and Humphrey the bastard. Of course, Humphrey did have his uses. That article he'd written for *Cornet* had been the perfect prelude to the investigation that would shut down Lenny Duveteaux for good.

In his twenty-four years as DA, Placide Treat had never felt threatened by another candidate for the job. New Orleans loved him: he was a character, he was tough on crime as long as the criminals were poor people, he understood how things were done here.

But he had a bad feeling about Oscar De La Cerda. The attorney would be nothing to worry about on his own, but with Lenny's public backing and private funding, he could be a strong contender. He was a local boy through and through, and had the makings of a character every bit as colorful as Treat's.

If he could take Lenny down, Treat knew he could nip De La Cerda's campaign right in the bud. There were rumors of things Lenny had done much worse than fraud or tax evasion. He'd heard of an old man who'd died under mysterious circumstances right before Lenny had helped open Liquor. But there were so many of those goddamn tapes. Treat needed some insurance; he needed just one of Lenny's close associates to turn on him, for either personal gain or self-protection.

After his nap, Treat drove to his office on South White Street. The original DA's office had been in the big Criminal District Courthouse at Tulane and Broad, a great, gray, twelve-columned, block-long edifice just up the street from Liquor. The police headquarters, the parish prison, and the morgue were also located in this complex, but several years ago Treat had built himself and his staff a new, modern building behind the old one. It lacked the Art Deco beauty of the older offices, it got hotter in the summers, and it had plumbing problems from time to time, but it was all his; it said so on a large, gaudy metal plaque right outside the front door.

This morning he had given out oranges to the security guards downstairs, to the secretaries, and to everyone who came through the office. Each orange was adorned with a pre-printed sticker that said A TASTE OF SUNSHINE FROM PLACIDE TREAT, YOUR DISTRICT ATTORNEY. He had wanted to add something clever like ORANGE YOU GLAD YOU GOT HIM?, but the stickers weren't very big. In addition to gifting the people around the courthouse, he had sent one of his assistant DAs—not Woofer, who was home sleeping; these young kids couldn't keep up with him—over to the C.J. Peete housing project to distribute oranges to the poor. The ADA hadn't looked too happy about it, but people who worked for Placide Treat knew they had to go the extra mile for the citizens of New Orleans.

Poppy Z. Brite

He glanced at the door of his inner sanctum, making sure it was locked; then he opened the bottom drawer of his desk and took out a hand-held tape recorder. A tape, one of thousands confiscated from Lenny Duveteaux, was already in the machine. All Lenny's tapes were marked with an unintelligible series of letters and numbers that Treat had so far been unable to decode. He had no way of knowing when the various conversations had taken place or even, in most cases, to whom Lenny was speaking. He pressed PLAY, bowed his head, and began listening to Lenny's slightly nasal Maine accent with a depth of concentration approaching prayer.

"I'm not some Midwesterner who doesn't know from fish, OK?" said Lenny's voice. "I grew up on the Maine sea coast, I've been cooking with fresh seafood all my life, and this isn't fresh seafood. Now send me some decent 16/20 count shrimp or I'll take my business elsewhere."

"We'll get 'em right out to you," said whoever was on the other end of the line. "Sorry about that."

Click.

"Lenny? Ralph. Listen, I'm not gonna be able to play tennis tomorrow morning, one of my waiters quit . . ."

All the tapes Treat had listened to—some forty or fifty hours so far—were this kind of stuff, dull conversations with food purveyors, repairmen, golf and tennis buddies. Oscar De La Cerda and John Rickey had turned up a couple of times, but neither had said anything interesting. Treat didn't care. He would find what he needed. The fact that Lenny had been recording the calls for ten years and he'd only made it through a few weeks' worth of tapes did not daunt him.

It drove Woofer crazy that Treat was listening to the tapes himself. "We could hire people to do that," Woofer said.

"Hire people! They wouldn't even know what they were listening for. Everything I need is on these tapes, Woofer, but I won't know it till I hear it."

"We could have every goddamn one of those tapes transcribed

within a couple months. You could read the transcripts and pick out your evidence from them. Your way could take *years,* Placide."

"I can't just look at a bunch of goddamn transcripts. I need to hear his voice. I'm a master at reading voices, you know that, Woofer. I need to hear the guilt in his voice. Lenny Duveteaux will hang himself with his own tongue."

"Ugh, what an image."

Woofer just didn't understand the hard work and finesse needed to destroy a character like Lenny Duveteaux. De La Cerda's run for DA was the crux of the matter, yes, but it wasn't the only reason Treat wanted to see Lenny broken and crawling. He could not precisely account for his loathing of the popular restaurateur, but he knew that part of being an effective prosecutor was trusting one's gut feelings and finding the evidence to support them. If asked flat-out, he would have to admit that Lenny's failure to comp his dinner all those years ago played a part in what he was doing now. There was no percentage in lying to himself. It wasn't a simple matter of wounded dignity, though. Lenny's behavior then had demonstrated his lack of compatibility with the ways of New Orleans, his failure to understand how things were done here. Lenny had made a great success of himself in New Orleans since then, but he still didn't understand how things were done. Only a month ago he had been quoted in *USA Today* saying that many of the city's old-line restaurants were dinosaurs with no relevance to the current dining scene. Even if this were true, you didn't say such things to the national press. The man had to be stopped.

Placide Treat had not read G. Gordon Liddy's autobiography and was unfamiliar with his doctrines of *malum prohibitum* and *malum in se,* but if he had known of them, he would have agreed. With every cell of his old shyster's heart he believed that the corrupt paths and byways of his office had been hacked out as a route by which the Greater Good might travel. The old ways of the city were the right ways, and should be preserved. (This belief included a selective racism common to a great many older white men who could not avoid working with blacks, and had found that many of the blacks were as intelligent, competent, and committed to *comme il faut* as they themselves: such men decided that *their* blacks were all right, but the city would still be a better place if those *other* blacks had remained in their neighborhoods and kept to their stations in life.)

So Treat was not bothered that Lenny Duveteaux was corrupt; he was bothered that Lenny was corrupt in all the wrong ways. The city's embrace of Lenny appalled him, and the fact that Lenny had become one of the city's most beloved ambassadors. People saw him on TV, bought his cookbooks, came to eat at his restaurants, believed him to be a true representative of New Orleans. It was unacceptable.

Treat listened to the tapes for another hour, occasionally rewinding bits and playing them over again. Nothing interesting turned up. All too soon it was time for his lunch date. He needed an indictment from a grand jury on another case, so he was taking them all to lunch at Commander's Palace.

His driver dropped him off in front of the 123-year-old restaurant, a still-vibrant grande dame of the Garden District. The maître d' led him through the main dining room, up the back staircase, and into a sunny buttercup-colored room that had reportedly been a popular rendezvous spot for prostitutes and their customers in the 1920s. The grand jury was already there and well into its second round of martinis. Placide Treat entered to cheers and took his seat at the head of the table.

8

So Rickey was really going. Going to Dallas, going to overhaul somebody else's menu when up until a couple of years ago he'd never even made a menu of his own. Going to spend the night away from G-man for the first time in twelve years. Going to see Cooper Stark again, and somehow that was the weirdest, scariest part of it all, even though no one could say Rickey and Coop had ever really meant anything to each other.

OK, no; if he was to have any chance of getting through this thing, he had to admit the truth to himself. Coop had meant something to him. Coop had been, in fact, his only real glimpse of another possible life. Rickey was a New Orleans boy to the marrow of his bones. The city had birthed him and shaped him, and he could not imagine himself living or cooking anywhere else. Still, he knew there had been the possibility of something with Cooper Stark. He couldn't say whether it would have been a real relationship or just an affair, but either way it would have shaped him differently. For one thing, it would have exposed him to more of the New York culinary world as it had been shaped by the eighties, a milieu he knew little of. When he read about it, he felt like a hick kid poring over lurid accounts of Studio 54's heyday. All that ridiculous excess, the billionaire hotel properties with their gold-rimmed plates, the raspberry vinaigrettes and green peppercorns, the return of serious meat-eating, the sun-dried tomatoes in absolutely everything. Fusion cuisine. Food for the Decade of Greed. Very few of these trends had managed to make it to New Orleans by the decade's conclusion, though some of them came limping down eventually. Some wouldn't have made any sense here at all—for instance, New Orleans had never given up eating meat, except on Fridays during Lent.

Cooper Stark's two restaurants, Star K and Capers, had had a big hand in shaping that eighties scene. If Rickey had gotten involved with Coop, he would almost certainly have gotten involved with the restaurants too. And where would he be today? Living in some Manhattan walk-up, scraping to pay rent, cooking on somebody else's line? Or co-owner of two three-star restaurants in New York, one of the world's great food cities?

It didn't matter. He was co-owner of a four-bean, award-winning restaurant here, and he had no regrets about being with G-man. He had never seriously wished to stray, had never wanted to be with anyone else; sometimes he just looked at G-man and wondered how the hell he had gotten so lucky. He couldn't help wondering what it would have been like, though. Who would he have become in a long-term relationship with a volatile, dominant personality, someone more like himself? Rickey was not a terribly introspective person and hadn't given this a huge amount of thought, but he'd pondered it more than once over the years.

When he wasn't worrying about Coop, he was worrying about Frank Firestone. The guy had sounded nice enough on the phone, but of course he would; he wanted Rickey more than Rickey wanted the job. What if he turned into an asshole once Rickey was in Dallas, trapped? And when he wasn't worrying about Coop or Firestone, he was gnawing out his own liver at the prospect of leaving his restaurant for eight days. Only within the past six months had he begun trusting his crew enough so that he and G-man could take an occasional extra night off, leaving Tanker in charge of the kitchen. Nothing terrible had happened so far, but Rickey was never completely able to relax on those nights. Now he would be hundreds of miles away, committed to another job, unable to be in his kitchen even if catastrophe struck.

It wouldn't strike; objectively he knew that. And if it did, G-man would be there. G-man knew the restaurant as well as Rickey did, and was probably more useful in a real crisis because he could keep a cool head far longer than Rickey could. G-man could handle anything that came up. And yet . . . and yet . . .

He began tossing out hypothetical situations, testing G-man as they drove to and from the restaurant, when they were making groceries at the supermarket, even while they were in the bathroom together. "What'll you do if somebody gets sick?"

"Find somebody to sub."

"What if nobody can sub?"

"Then we work shorthanded."

"You can't do that. Somebody will fuck something up, and word'll get out that the place can't function if I'm not in the kitchen."

"That should make you happy."

"It wouldn't make me happy. A good chef can put together a kick-ass crew, good enough that he doesn't have to be there all the time."

"Well, look, if we're really shorthanded I'll see if somebody can come over from Lenny's or Crescent. But it's not gonna happen, Rickey."

"OK, what if there's a fire?"

"I'll call the fire department. And if there's a murder I'll call the cops, and if Satan appears in the kitchen I'll call a priest."

"That's not funny," said Rickey. He wasn't worried about Satan, but in his present state of mind it seemed entirely possible that there could be a murder at Liquor during his absence.

"No, it isn't," G-man agreed gravely. "But you gotta trust us, Rickey. We know how to run the place. We got a real good menu right now. It's all gonna work out fine. Just get a new cell phone before you go, OK?"

Rickey still hadn't replaced the phone he'd thrown into Lake Pontchartrain the day they got the bad review. He kept meaning to—he hated being unavailable for any length of time in case something happened at the restaurant—but he never seemed to find the few minutes that would be necessary to actually go and do it. He supposed somebody looking for deep psychological motives would say he was asserting his independence from Lenny, who had given him the phone. Lenny had also called him more than anyone else had, and Rickey didn't feel like being at the other end of Lenny's line any more.

It was true that the menu was looking better than ever. Rickey had recently purged a few old dishes that were moving slowly—the Herbsaint-scented rabbit no one ever ordered; the vegetarian lasagna he'd always thought was insipid—and replaced them with some big sellers: a slow-cooked lamb shank with mustard and Armagnac, a softshell crab nestled atop a puree of parsnips spiked with mezcal, a duck confit appetizer with Grand Marnier–stewed apples. The new dishes were getting rave reviews from everybody who ordered them, and G-man, Terrance, Shake, and the rest of the crew were perfectly capable of turning them out. But would they really be able to hold it all together, or would the kitchen just deliquesce into a puddle of confusion as soon as Rickey left?

"What'll you do if you're real busy one night and everybody gets in the weeds?"

G-man gave Rickey a dark look over the tops of his shades. "I *know* how to get out of the damn weeds," he said. "I know how to get my crew out of them too."

"I know you do," said Rickey. "I'm sorry." It heartened him to hear G-man refer to the others as "my crew." Maybe G-man was really a natural leader but had never had to step up because Rickey always got there first.

"Don't worry about it," G-man told him. "I mean that literally. *Do not worry about Liquor.* You spend your whole trip worrying about us, you're not gonna be able to do your own work."

But Rickey was already doing his own work. Firestone had faxed him the most recent menu and Rickey was going over it, trying to figure out its strengths and weaknesses, what could be improved, what needed to be 86'd altogether. It wasn't easy, because he didn't yet know Frank Firestone and had only the barest idea of what he wanted, but a few dishes jumped out at him. For instance, Coop was doing an appetizer of frozen salmon mousse in a tiny tuile—sort of a savory ice cream cone—surrounded by a garnish of pea shoots, very French Laundry. Rickey thought it sounded like a good dish, but he suspected it was just the sort of thing that would make the Dallas dining public turn up their noses, muttering imprecations about rabbit food. More in line with what Texans liked to eat, he figured, was the leg of lamb with a coffee glaze. It was served with a ragout of "wild" mushrooms that were probably about as wild as a stick of butter. Lots of chefs liked to advertise wild mushrooms, but few wanted to pay the price for actual fungi foraged from the woods of Louisiana, Oregon, or other places where such things grew. Most of them were farmed. There was nothing wrong with farm-grown 'shrooms, but Rickey thought it was dishonest to call them wild, and he never did so on his own menu.

He wondered how much this job would cause him to compromise his integrity. Certainly he couldn't show up and read Coop the riot act about calling farm-grown mushrooms wild, or anything similar. He was supposed to help Coop figure out how to make the menu more accessible—to dumb it down, if he wanted to be perfectly honest. Already the idea rankled a little, but he just kept picturing Lenny in front of a grand jury, Lenny on the stand, Lenny in jail. He'd picture Lenny in trouble, and then he'd picture a ten-thousand-dollar check with his own name on it, a signpost on the path to his and G-man's financial independence. There could easily be other plum consulting jobs ahead if word got out that he'd done well on this one.

Poppy Z. Brite

So he studied Coop's menu and pored over his cookbook collection and wrote down ideas in a spiral-bound notebook he'd bought, and he tried to achieve a semblance of calm. Unfortunately, calm had never been a natural state for Rickey, and a week before his departure, something happened at Liquor to throw him way off balance.

It was an average early-summer night on the line, not too busy but not dead. Rickey was expediting, which meant he took the tickets from the printer and called out the orders to the various stations. The plates came to his station at the front of the kitchen for a final once-over, and he either sent them back if there was a problem or set them in the pass for the waiters to pick up. He was finishing a softshell crab plate with a swirl of chili oil and a sprig of chervil when Karl came into the kitchen looking worried. Karl hardly ever looked worried; Rickey had hired him for his unflappability. "What's up?" Rickey asked.

"Well, I didn't know if I should tell you, but Humphrey Wildblood is in the house."

The kitchen suddenly seemed to tilt a little, and Rickey closed his eyes. When he opened them again, he was aware of G-man watching him from the sauté station, waiting for his reaction. "How do you know it's him?" Rickey said.

"Some of us maître d's got a kinda grapevine. We pass around pictures of the food critics, or compare descriptions if we can't get a picture. But I just saw his ugly mug last week."

"Who's with him?"

"He's all by his lonesome."

"Motherfucker," said Rickey. Lines from Wildblood's review began running through his head: *Liquor is a fine example of why no one under thirty-five should be put in charge of anything . . . the result is a menu that lacks basic coherence . . . no regard for accuracy or palatability . . .* "Motherfucker!" he said again, and threw the sprig of chervil across the kitchen.

"You want me to seat him?" said Karl.

"What's he doing now? Cooling his heels in the foyer?"

"He said he wanted to have a drink at the bar, then he'd take a table."

"I'll go talk to him."

"Take over my station for a sec," G-man told Marquis, who was on salads and cold apps.

"But I got five orders—"

"I said get over here and work my station," G-man repeated. Without checking to see if Marquis was going to obey him, he left two pork chops and two redfish fillets sizzling in sauté pans, walked across the kitchen, and grabbed Rickey's arm. "You are *not* going out there to talk to that guy," he said.

"Why not? What you think I'm gonna do? Kick his ass?"

"You might. Maybe you wouldn't mean to, but he could say the wrong thing and you just might. That'd be cute, wouldn't it?—the chef beating up a customer in the bar. Great for our reputation."

"I'm not gonna beat him up!"

"What, then? You just want to yell at him? That'd be almost as good. You're not gonna do *anything,* Rickey. You're gonna stand right there and call out his order when it comes in, and we're gonna make his food. Period. End of story."

"But—"

"Everybody's watching us," G-man said more softly, "and you're putting me in charge of these guys next week. Don't fuck me over now, or you'll make it harder for me when you're gone."

Rickey opened his mouth, closed it again, took a deep breath. He stared at G-man, and G-man, through his dark glasses, looked steadily back.

"It *galls* me!" Rickey said.

"I know. It galls me too, believe it or not. But we gotta make his fucking food anyway, and you know what? We gotta make it *great.*"

As usual, G-man was clearly and infuriatingly right. Rickey gave him one last anguished look, then turned back to his station and began calling out the tickets that had come in while he was otherwise occupied. "Marquis, ordering one green salad, two tomato salads . . . Terrance, ordering one ribeye, medium rare . . . G, ordering two softshells . . ."

Humphrey Wildblood's ticket came in twenty minutes later. A green salad, the soup du jour (a crawfish bisque laced with cognac), and the pecan-crusted redfish. "Adventurous," Rickey muttered to himself. He examined the salad with an eagle eye, stirred the soup to make sure it was hot through and through, gave the redfish a careful once-over even though it had come from G-man's station, the most reliable one in the kitchen. Fifteen minutes after Wildblood's entrée had gone out, Rickey wiped his hands on a side towel and checked the front of his jacket for any particularly egregious stains.

"Rickey," called G-man in a warning voice, for he recognized the signs that Rickey was about to make a tour of the dining room.

"I just gotta pee," said Rickey, heading for the employee bathroom next to the office.

He hadn't lied; he really did need to pee. He relieved himself, washed his hands, splashed his face with cold water, then left the bathroom and exited the restaurant through the back door. He walked around the building and came in through the front. Karl gave him a puzzled look, but was on the phone and couldn't ask any questions. Rickey went into the dining room, a softly lit, forest-green, slightly clubby-looking space that seated eighty. Right now it was about a third full, and Rickey spotted Humphrey Wildblood at once; he was the only solo diner in the place. Karl had seated him up against a wall near the kitchen even though several better tables were available.

When he saw Rickey approaching, Wildblood's eyes took on a panicky sheen. Rickey had always thought the phrase *Like a deer in the headlights* was just a cliché, but that was exactly what Wildblood looked like, except that he was neither as slender nor as graceful as a deer. He was a fat-faced little man with lank black hair and a long, pointed nose. There appeared to be something peculiar about his build; either his sport jacket fit very badly or his arms were far too short, giving him an almost flipperish look. *Like an armadillo in the headlights, maybe,* Rickey thought as he extended his hand.

"I'm John Rickey," he said. "I don't think we've met."

Wildblood shook Rickey's hand as if he expected to get an electric shock. "Actually, we have," he said.

Rickey hadn't expected that. "We have?"

"Yes indeed. I met you and your co-chef at the Harvest for Hunger benefit. You were serving those prosciutto-wrapped figs with the cognac cream that Chase Haricot likes so much. I must admit they were quite good."

Rickey glanced at Wildblood's plate. The redfish was completely gone, and only traces of the accompanying sautéed broccolini remained. Wildblood's silverware appeared to have gone untouched; the full setup of two forks, knife, and coffee spoon still surrounded his empty plate. Balanced on the rim of the plate were a strange-looking fork and spoon.

"I carry my own utensils," Wildblood explained when he saw Rickey looking. "My palate is very sensitive to metal, and I find that silverware spoils the taste of food. These are carved from horn."

Oh boy, thought Rickey. But all he said was, "Well, it looks like you enjoyed your meal."

"Yes, I did . . . though I confess I found the bisque a little spicy."

"Uh huh," Rickey said. "So listen—I don't want to be rude or anything, but after that article you wrote, I can't help wondering . . . uh . . . what the hell you're doing back in my restaurant." *Take it easy,* he cautioned himself. He truly didn't want to make a scene, but he could no more have avoided asking this question than he could have deliberately stuck his knife hand in the blades of his big Robot Coupe food processor.

Wildblood's little eyes took on a darting, frightened look. "I like this restaurant," he said. "I didn't write bad things about the food."

" 'The result is a menu that lacks basic coherence,' " Rickey quoted from memory. " 'It's almost a stunt.' "

"I said my meals were well-prepared and reasonably tasty!"

Poppy Z. Brite

"You said we were a couple of brainless prettyboys who would never have gotten anywhere without Lenny Duveteaux . . . and I guess it's just a coincidence that now your father's trying to burn Lenny at the stake?"

Wildblood buried his face in his hands. "I needed that job at the *Cornet* so badly," he said. "I mean, I didn't need it—my mother's family has all the money in the world—but I *wanted* it. I'm tired of always being 'Placide Treat's son' or 'one of the Geigenheimers.' I want to make a name for myself. I've always wanted to be a food critic. I know it's a stupid dream, but I used to read Craig Claiborne, Mimi Sheraton, Calvin Trillin . . . they're food writers."

"I know who they are!" said Rickey. He was trying to hold on to his temper, but even in his abjectness the guy was so damn condescending.

"Well, my father is good friends with the *Cornet*'s publisher— hell, my father's either good friends or bitter enemies with everybody in town." Wildblood's voice trailed off.

"Are you telling me your dad got you this job so you could write a crappy review of us?"

Wildblood seemed to gather his courage. "Yes. That's exactly what I'm telling you. And I'm also telling you that my father can guarantee you *never* get another bad review in New Orleans if you're prepared to give him information on Lenny Duveteaux."

Rickey shook his head. He obviously hadn't heard right. "What did you just say?"

"You've seen the kind of power he has. Wouldn't you rather have that power used for you than against you?"

"Are you *threatening* us?" Rickey said incredulously.

"Not at all. I'm just extending my father's offer—his service in exchange for yours."

"He can take his service and cram it. I don't know anything about Lenny's business dealings, and if I did, I wouldn't tell a bunch of legal spooks, and furthermore, I don't need his fucking help to get good reviews in New Orleans—"

Rickey never got to complete this elegant tirade, for at that moment a hand clamped down on his shoulder. "You're needed in the kitchen," said G-man.

"What—"

"Go. Hurry. Emergency."

Rickey seriously doubted that a kitchen emergency had cropped up in the past five minutes, but he glanced over and saw the fierce scowl on G-man's face. The expression didn't come naturally to G-man. Rickey went. As he hurried through the dining room, nodding at other diners but not stopping at their tables, he heard G-man say, "Glad you enjoyed your meal, Mr. Wildblood." *Mr. Wildblood!*

Of course there was no emergency in the kitchen, but a few more orders had come in. Rickey began calling them out to the various stations. G-man returned a few minutes later, threw Rickey one withering glance, and took up his sauté station.

For the rest of the night there was a palpable tension in the kitchen, but nothing happened until they were on their way home. G-man hadn't said much except "You ready?" and "Want me to drive?" Finally Rickey said, "Are you ever gonna talk to me again?"

G-man stared straight ahead at the deserted vista of Louisiana Avenue. He was no longer scowling, but there was an unfamiliar set to his chin and a certain whiteness visible around the rims of his glasses. "I'm scared to talk to you," he said. "I'm so mad, I might just start yelling."

Rickey's stomach twisted a little. G-man hardly ever got angry with him. "Why are you mad?" he asked.

"God—Rickey—do you have any respect for me at all? Do you think I'm a total moron?"

"Course not! Of course I have respect for you!"

"I mean *professional* respect."

"Yes! You're one of the best cooks I know. You think I'd leave somebody in charge of my kitchen for a week if I didn't respect him professionally?"

"Then why can't you act like it? I told you not to go talk to that guy. I told you in front of everybody, and next thing I know you sneak out the fucking back door and make a beeline for him. How does that make me look? Do you think it helps my authority over the crew?"

"They didn't know where I went."

"The hell they didn't."

"It's none of their business."

"Rickey . . ." G-man slowed down as they passed a scene of flashing blue lights. A young man was bent facedown over the hood of a police car, two cops going through his pockets. One of the cops glanced at them, and G-man sped up again. "I can do the job, OK? I can run the restaurant. I can run the kitchen. But the whole idea of authority is kinda foreign to me. Those guys are used to answering to *you*. They need to see me as an extension of you. If they see you acting like what I say doesn't matter, they're gonna act that way too."

"Dude, what are you talking about? It's not some bunch of anarchists. It's just Tanker and Terrance and them."

G-man just shook his head. Rickey remembered the first kitchen meeting he'd held, right before the restaurant opened. He knew all the cooks, but he had still felt like the world's biggest poseur, had entertained morbid fantasies of them walking out en masse. It was different when you were suddenly in charge. "I'm sorry," he said. "I know I put you in an awkward position."

"Nice word for it, but what you did was make me look like an asshole."

"I'm sorry," Rickey said again.

"Why'd you do it anyway? I told you it was a bad idea."

"I didn't make a scene or anything."

"You didn't seem all that far from it when I stepped in."

"No! Nuh-uh. I wasn't yelling at him. Well, maybe I was a little, but I yelled *quietly*. And he didn't yell back, he just caved. I think he was really embarrassed. Made me an interesting offer, too."

"Yeah? What?"

As close to verbatim as he could, Rickey repeated his conversation with Humphrey Wildblood. "I wonder if he really thought I

97

was gonna fold," he concluded. "Just say, 'Yeah, sure, set me up a meeting with old Tricker. I'll spill my guts about Lenny.' Like I'd do that even if I didn't consider him a friend. Fuck, man, Lenny'd have me rubbed out if I forced him to. He'd hate to do it, but he'd still do it."

"That's pretty cold."

"You disagree?"

"No." After a moment, G-man said, "He made me the same offer. I told him to go fuck himself too. I just did it a little politer than you."

"Jesus." Rickey shook his head. "Bunch of goddamn cretins. I wonder if they really think we can be bought."

"I just hope buying us is all they try to do."

They reached Marengo Street before either of them spoke again, but this time there was no tension in their silence, just the moderate weariness of a medium-busy night. "I need a drink," said Rickey as they entered the house.

"How come you didn't get one at the restaurant?"

"I didn't feel like hanging out when everybody thought we were mad at each other." Rickey walked into the kitchen. "Last thing we need is a bunch of waiters gossiping about us."

"I'm sure they do anyway."

"Yeah, but the least we can do is try not to give them ammunition. Otherwise they'll have us breaking up, the restaurant closing, God knows what else . . ." Rickey paused, staring into the refrigerator. "Somebody's been in here."

"Say what?"

"Look at the bottles." Rickey indicated a row of Abita beer bottles on the bottom shelf of the fridge. "I always put 'em in with the labels facing out. I don't know why—it's just something I do."

"Yeah, I know."

"Well, look—they're all turned around now. I know you didn't do it, because they weren't that way this morning and we haven't been here all day."

"Why would somebody come in our house and turn all the beer bottles around?"

"I don't know." Rickey slammed the refrigerator door and looked around the kitchen for other things out of place. He couldn't find any, but when he searched the rest of the house, he noticed a few. The towels in the linen closet were slightly ruffled. The top drawer of the dresser, always sticky, wasn't closed quite right. Rickey opened it and rifled through socks and underwear until he found the choupique caviar tin where they kept their small stash of pot. The pot was still there, but the lid of the tin was a little crooked, as if someone had jammed it back on in a hurry.

"Somebody's been in here for sure," he said to G-man, who had followed him into the bedroom.

"A burglar?"

"Well, it wasn't just some crackhead. I left money on the nightstand, and look—it's still there. They didn't steal anything or break anything. They just looked through our shit, and I bet somebody less anal than me would've never noticed."

"Jeez." G-man looked around the bedroom and shivered a little. "Who do you think it was? Something to do with Lenny?"

"You bet your ass it's something to do with Lenny. Hell, that's probably the extra bonus reason why Humphrey Wildblood was at the restaurant tonight. I bet he asked his waiter if we were both in the kitchen, and when he found out we were, he called his dad's people and gave them the go-ahead to break into our house. See if they could blackmail us, just in case they couldn't bribe us with a lifetime of great restaurant reviews."

"Nothing they could find," said G-man. "Nothing worse than the weed, anyway."

"Yeah, but goddamn, it pisses me off. It's bad enough I gotta have health inspectors in my kitchen. At least they're legal. I can't stand the idea of somebody digging through our shit."

"You think we should call the cops?" said G-man. It was a rhetorical question more than anything else. They might be upstanding young businessmen now, but Lower Ninth Ward distrust of New Orleans' finest was deeply ingrained in them.

"Fuck, no. I guess we better just be glad we didn't have any coke or kiddie porn, or a few of Lenny's spare tapes laying around, or whatever the hell they were looking for."

"We gonna tell Lenny?"

"I don't know. You think we should?"

"Nah." G-man turned on the air conditioner and sat on the edge of the bed, pulling off his sweaty T-shirt. "He's got enough to worry about."

"Like we don't?"

"We're not going to *prison*," said G-man.

"Neither is Lenny." Rickey let himself fall back on the bed. "I tell you, dude, Lenny's made of Teflon. I bet he's already figured out a way to beat this rap." His voice sounded confident to his own ears, and he hoped he was right.

"They clean," said the cat burglar. "Nothing in their place but a little weed, not even enough for a felony charge."

"Good," said Lenny, handing the man a fat envelope. "I figured as much, but it never hurts to make sure."

The cat burglar was actually one of Lenny's waiters, but for a while he had moonlighted as a thief, eventually getting too ambitious and ending up in Orleans Parish Prison. Lenny had paid his bail and persuaded the homeowners not to press charges. In exchange, the guy occasionally did small jobs for Lenny, checking up on people and delivering messages, not all of which were verbal. This was the first time Lenny had asked him to break into the home of an actual colleague. He'd hated to do it to Rickey and G-man. He trusted them ninety-nine percent. But any time there was even a tiny percentage of doubt, Lenny made a policy of checking it out.

He'd worked closely with Rickey and G-man when they were starting the restaurant, but since the place took off, they'd pretty much been on their own. He didn't really know what they might have been up to. The pressures on young, successful chefs were tremendous, and Lenny had known such people to develop dangerous habits: coke, pills, even heroin. He had no reason to think they were into anything like that, but on the off-chance that they were, better he should find out before Placide Treat did. Lenny knew Rickey and G-man would be approached about turning on him sooner or later. A serious drug charge could conceivably convince the boys to turn state's evidence, and while they didn't know a whole lot about his business dealings, they knew things he wouldn't want them discussing on the stand.

Fortunately, though, they were squeaky-clean. Well, maybe not squeaky, but he doubted Treat could convince them to turn based on a misdemeanor pot charge. A different operative of Lenny's had checked out the office at Liquor—easy as pie, since Lenny had a key to the restaurant—and gone through the files on Rickey's computer. Nothing to worry about there either. If all went well, he could keep Rickey and G-man out of this matter entirely. Rickey could go off to Dallas and do his consulting gig without being bothered by Placide Treat. They had a good thing going. They didn't deserve to be dragged down by Lenny.

If you looked at it that way, he'd actually done them a big favor by having their home and business burgled this early in the game. He was sure Liddy would have agreed. Lenny escorted the cat burglar out of his office and congratulated himself on another job well done.

There had been a day the summer before when Rickey went downtown to pick up some barbecue, or as he tended to think of it, BBQ. New Orleans is not known for its BBQ, nor does it deserve to be, but there are a few places to get respectable chicken and ribs if you are not afraid of venturing into the hood. Rickey, who had spent the first half of his life in the hood, tended to get antsy if he didn't go back every now and then. His favorite place was a little green-and-yellow shack called Adam's, a couple of miles from where he and G-man had grown up. There you could get ribs or chicken tangily sauced and infused with the alchemy of smoke.

On that day he had called in his order and hit a lull in Claiborne Avenue traffic on his way to pick it up. The city was subject to unexpected lulls during the hottest part of summer days, though it was a little early for that yet. He got to the BBQ place sooner than he had expected and the young man behind the bulletproof Plexiglas window said his order would be a few more minutes. Rickey stood in the doorway to catch a draft, looking at the ramshackle shotgun houses, half-hearing the birdlike clamor of kids choosing flavors at the snowball stand next door. On the other side of Franklin

Avenue, a couple of guys working on their cars. On somebody's radio, an old Peaches & Herb song: *"Sat here starin at the same ole wall . . . Came back to life just when I got your call . . ."* Big oak trees in the neutral ground spreading their shade across the street, not ripped up for passage of an interstate overpass like the ones on Claiborne forty years ago, the heart of the black business district torn out of the city. Nothing like that had happened here. The Ninth Ward hadn't been the heart of anything for a long time, and it had been mostly left alone. Didn't always look all that great, but New Orleanians preferred decrepitude to progress.

"Reunited" segued into "Just My Imagination." The air was filled with a soft urgent heat, not the brutal stew that would arrive in another month or so. Rickey had only spent four months of his life outside New Orleans; he could not savor it in the manner of someone who had spent a long time away. Nor was he a reflective person by nature, or a particularly romantic one. Still, in those idle and ordinary moments waiting for his BBQ, he was struck by the perfection of his city. If he turned his head, he could see trash in the street and a dead cat on the neutral ground; the kids at the snowball stand probably attended decrepit and dangerous schools; somebody would shoot somebody tonight. But none of it mattered in that moment. He had the rare sense of knowing he was exactly where he was meant to be.

He was thinking of that moment as he tried to get comfortable in the death seat of the 9:30 A.M. flight to Dallas. He thought of it as the death seat because it was near the front of the plane and he figured he and his seatmates would be quickly obliterated if the plane took a nosedive. He didn't know enough about the niceties of air travel to register that Frank Firestone had booked him in first class, though he was happy to be offered a drink before the plane even took off. He was normally a bourbon drinker, but he ordered a screwdriver for the vitamins.

The vodka calmed his nerves and he fell asleep soon after the plane took off. The landing woke him. He'd disembarked and gotten halfway down the concourse toward baggage claim when he heard somebody calling his name. He turned, and there was Cooper Stark, who long ago had asked Rickey to call him Coop.

"Hey, you."

"Hey," said Rickey. They stood staring at each other, unsure what to do next. Coop made a little gesture as if he might be thinking about hugging Rickey, but Rickey's face must have shown what he thought of that idea, for the older chef dropped his hands immediately. Rickey had remembered his height and the broadness of his shoulders, but not the way his fair complexion made his dark eyes and hair look almost black. *Dammit, he's still handsome,* Rickey thought, then tried to put it out of his mind.

"Jeez," Coop said at last. "I was afraid you might be a little standoffish at first, but do you really hate me?"

"Huh? No. What do you mean?"

"You've got this fearsome scowl on your face. If I didn't know you were coming to bail me out of a jam, I'd think you wanted to beat me up."

"Sorry," said Rickey. He knew the look he must have had; G-man called it his game face. He forced himself to smile. "Is that better?"

"Sort of."

They stared at each other for a few more seconds before Rickey stuck out his hand. Coop shook it, looking a little amused by the gesture. His palm was rough against Rickey's. At least he'd been working hard.

They collected Rickey's bags and headed for the parking garage. As soon as they stepped outside, heat enfolded them like a dirty sheet of newsprint. Coop's car was a beat-up Saturn coupe, a far cry from the sleek Italian roadster he'd been driving when Rickey met him at the CIA.

"Look, don't get me wrong," said Rickey. "It's actually kinda cool to see you now that we got past the weird part. But from the way Firestone talked, I thought he'd be picking me up in a limo or something. He sounds like a guy who likes to throw his money around."

"Don't you believe it," said Coop. "The fabulously wealthy are all tight-fisted. At least the smart ones are. Firestone drives a Ford Explorer—expensive but not crazy."

"He's not, is he?"

"Not what?"

"Crazy."

Coop half-turned in the seat to look at Rickey. "What makes you ask that?"

Rickey shrugged. "I don't know. It's just something you worry about when you're at somebody's mercy in a strange city. I didn't mean anything special by it."

"Well . . . tell you what. You'll meet him at the restaurant later. You tell me later if you think he's crazy."

"Uh, OK," said Rickey, a little nonplussed. "Where are we going now?"

"To your hotel. I thought you'd want to drop off your stuff, maybe get a shower."

"Fine." Rickey turned away from Coop and looked out the window. At first the area they were driving through didn't look all that alien. They were on a slightly seedy avenue with hole-in-the-wall Mexican places instead of po-boy shops, brown people instead of black people at the bus stops, and hills where New Orleans had none. Gradually, though, the properties turned fancier and the businesses more upscale: bistros, boutiques, salons, and a few whose purpose Rickey could not immediately identify, with names like Successories and The Annuity Center. There were a few prosperous areas in New Orleans—Magazine Street in particular had accumulated more than its share of spas, designer dress shops, and precious little bistros over the past few years—but this was more extensive and far richer-looking than anything Rickey had ever seen. "Is the restaurant around here?" he asked.

"Not too far."

"Where are we now?"

"Just some part of uptown Dallas. I know my way around, but I'm not sure what they call all the different hoods."

Some hood, Rickey thought. He'd never seen so many white

people in one place before, not even Metairie. "Well, where do you live?"

"Firestone's got me installed in one of his apartments across the river. He owns a lot of property in Dallas."

"Installed? You mean he's putting you up?"

"Yeah, he likes it that way. Knows I can't quit because then I'd be instantly homeless. Not that quitting's an option for me right now."

"Jeez," said Rickey.

Coop glanced over at him. "Don't start thinking Frank Firestone's a nice guy, Rickey. I'm sure he kissed your ass on the phone, and he'll probably blow more smoke at you when you meet him tonight, but he's only nice when he wants something. I've seen him with people he thinks have fucked him in business, and he just runs them right over."

"I know the type." *Maybe better than you do,* Rickey thought; he'd been working with Lenny longer than Coop had been at Firestone's.

"Rich fuckers, they're all the same," said Coop. "Some are worse than others, though. Firestone's pretty bad. You want to watch out for him."

"So what kinda specials you running right now?" Rickey asked, just to change the subject.

"Well, I just got some beautiful skate from my fish guy, and I want to do a classic beurre noisette . . ."

They talked about food until Coop pulled up in front of Rickey's hotel. To Rickey the place looked like a royal palace, with fancy iron gates and a uniformed valet waiting to open car doors. "I gotta get to the restaurant," said Coop, handing Rickey a long, heavy envelope. "Whenever you're ready, there's a rental car in the hotel garage for you. A Mustang, I think. Give the claim check ticket to the valet. I wrote out directions to the restaurant."

"But I don't . . . what do I . . ."

"You're all checked in here. Pick up your key at the desk."

Rickey barely had time to grab his suitcase and knife bag out of the backseat before Coop drove off.

Poppy Z. Brite

The hotel seemed to have done its best to hide its registration desk behind banks of lilies, orchids, and the lucky bamboo that seemed to be popping up in pretentious establishments everywhere lately, but Rickey finally found it and collected his key as promised. A bellman tried to grab his suitcase, but Rickey told the guy he'd take care of it himself; he wasn't sure whether a tip would be expected and didn't want to get into an awkward situation. Besides, he hadn't packed much: just his knives, his notebook, a nice outfit in case he went out to eat somewhere, and a bunch of chef clothes. A mirror-lined elevator took him up to his floor. After a few moments spent fumbling with the key card, he entered a room that seemed ridiculously opulent to him.

He'd only ever stayed in three hotels in his entire life. When he came home from the CIA, he didn't want to stay at his mother's house, so he and G-man got a cheap room in Metairie until they could find an apartment. It was near the airport, and the only thing he remembered about it was the bed—after all, they had been eighteen and hadn't seen each other for four months. That was his first hotel room. His second had been the Midtown cubbyhole Lenny recommended when Rickey and G-man went to New York for the Beard Awards banquet, and his third was an old convent turned bed-and-breakfast in Acadiana, where he and G-man had taken a vacation. This was his fourth, and it blew its predecessors all to hell. He poked around the room for several minutes, marveling at the lowboy refrigerator full of liquor and snacks, the gleaming gold-fixtured bathroom with its collection of tiny shampoos and mouthwashes, the folding contraption he couldn't figure out at first but later learned was some kind of ironing board for pants.

He walked out onto the little balcony. Again the heat smacked him in the face. In New Orleans the summer heat felt like a wet, nasty kiss. Here it was more like being inside a dehydrator, the kitchen gadget he sometimes used to make dried tomatoes and such. The gilded railing was hot to his touch and felt faintly grimy. He let go of it and scanned the street six floors below. The asphalt shimmered. The hundreds of cars seemed to waver a little as they zipped by.

The sound of hammering drew his attention upward. Some tiny men atop the much taller building opposite the hotel were erecting a vast and precarious-looking structure at the edge of the roof. After studying it for a minute, Rickey realized it was an enormous letter D made of metal framework and glass tubing, obviously intended to light up when finished. For a moment it reminded him of the martini glass on Liquor's sign, but this was far larger and more conspicuous. He shook his head and retreated into the cool dimness of his room.

"Oh, the Big D on the TransWorld Communication Tower?" said Coop. "That's just the city fathers' latest addition to the skyline. It's going to be the world's largest D."

"But why? Is it advertising something?"

"Dallas is advertising itself. That's what they do here."

"Are the building owners putting it up themselves?"

"No, the city. The building's just leasing them the space. It'll be good publicity for TransWorld."

"How can it be good publicity if it doesn't say their name?"

"Because it'll be a landmark. It'll be right up there with Pegasus, Reunion Tower, the Bank of America building . . . but I forgot you haven't really seen the skyline yet. Just wait until it gets dark."

Skyline? Rickey wondered. They had plenty of tall buildings in New Orleans, and the Superdome was a lot more spectacular than the American Airlines Arena, Dallas's downtown stadium, which looked to him like a huge modern high school or convention center. He had been impressed by the skyscrapers in New York, but that city was so tightly packed and claustrophobic that you seldom got a real sense of vista. What could be such a big deal about the skyline here?

They were in the kitchen at Firestone's, a big, boxy, free-standing, trendily decorated place in just the sort of ritzy neighborhood Rickey had expected. On one side of the restaurant was a Mercedes-Benz dealership, on the other a Jaguar showroom. Rickey had driven here in the brand-new Mustang coupe Frank Firestone rented for him, the nicest car he'd ever driven by twenty thousand dollars or so. Coop's directions had been clear, the streets well marked, easy to navigate, made of smooth pothole-free asphalt. He could get used to driving like that.

This Big D, though, mystified him. Who was paying for it, exactly, and where had the money come from? He couldn't imagine New Orleans doing such a thing. New Orleans' idea of promoting itself was a bumper sticker that said PROUD TO CALL IT HOME, which some local wag had bootlegged into PROUD TO CRAWL HOME. The latter permutation seemed to be more popular. No one in New Orleans would conceive of spending a small fortune to put up . . . Rickey didn't even know what they would put up. A giant neon fleur-de-lis, maybe, but tourists would just wonder what it was.

Dallas obviously had cash falling out its asshole, and Rickey was glad of it, because he was looking forward to working in this kitchen. The kitchen at Liquor was nice enough, but it had been refurbished from an old kitchen already on the premises. Frank Firestone and his people had designed this one from scratch. Coop said the building had been a plastic surgeon's office before, but thanks to the Dallas penchant for lifts, tucks, peels, and augmentations, the doctor made so much money that he decided to take early retirement. All the fixtures were top-of-the-line, the stations set up by somebody who knew what he was doing, the floor carpeted to reduce noise and protect the cooks' tired feet. Rickey had never seen carpet in a kitchen before and couldn't imagine how they kept it clean, but Coop said Firestone just had it replaced once a month.

"He says he wants us to stay in good working condition," said Coop. "He buys us all gym memberships too, but I never use mine. Who wants to go lift weights on their day off?"

"It's like you're his pets or something," Rickey said.

"Tell me about it." Coop grimaced. "More like his racehorses, really."

"Yeah, Coop," said the sous chef. "Watch out he doesn't sell you to the glue factory one of these days." The sous chef was a skinny blonde with a stubborn set to her jaw and too much black liner around her eyes. Why would anybody wear makeup in the kitchen? Rickey wondered. Surely it all got sweated off by the end of the night. She'd introduced herself as Sugar, and Rickey had taken an instant dislike to her. Unlike a lot of male cooks, he had nothing against women in the kitchen, but he thought some of them went around with chips on their shoulders. He couldn't really blame them after seeing some of the crap they had to endure, but it didn't make them very pleasant to work with. This particular one seemed to be angling for Coop's job, and she clearly didn't appreciate Rickey showing up to help him keep it.

Rickey had already made up a list of possible menu changes and additions based on the menus Firestone had sent him, but he and Coop hadn't discussed them yet. Instead Coop had shown him around the kitchen, then given him some prep work to do so he could get a feel for the place. The amount of prep here was minuscule compared to what they did at Liquor—they only had two reservations on the books tonight, and Coop said they might get six or eight more walk-ins—and they found a lot to say to each other as they worked. They couldn't talk openly because Sugar and another cook were there, but Rickey thought that was probably for the best.

"I couldn't believe it when I saw your picture in *Gourmet*. I knew it was you right away—you haven't changed a bit."

"I put on a few pounds, maybe."

"You know what they say—never trust a skinny chef. Hell, nobody ought to trust me."

"That's for sure."

"Those were different days, Rickey. I don't do that kind of stuff any more."

"Hey, it's no concern of mine."

Poppy Z. Brite

"Don't be like that. Know what I'd really like to do? Stick around here a while longer, get the place in a groove, then take off and go to Spain. Some of these young Spanish chefs are making the most exciting food in the world. I'd like to check them out."

"I bet you would," said Rickey, but he was interested. He'd read about the Spanish chefs—Ferran Adrià on the Catalonian coast, Andoni Luis Aduriz in San Sebastián—who were drawing upon centuries of culinary tradition while simultaneously trying to give diners an eating experience unlike any they'd had before. They had started the foam craze, had injected tiny hors d'oeuvres with hot flavored oils that gushed out when you bit into them, had designed their dining environments to the point of perfuming the air to enhance the taste of the food. Rickey found some of this pretty silly, but he admired the fact that they were pushing boundaries and challenging tastes. Though he didn't want to do any such thing himself, he figured somebody needed to from time to time; otherwise fine dining would still be all flour-thickened French sauces and stodgy little chops.

To Dallas diners, Coop's menu probably seemed as surreal as what the young Spaniards were doing. Rickey thought the menu was very good, and while he saw some ways to make it more accessible to the average diner while preserving its basic integrity, he wasn't looking forward to the process. Hell, if some young hot-shot came in and tried to tell him how to change *his* menu, Rickey wouldn't even need both hands to strangle the guy.

Or the girl, since Sugar seemed to have her own ideas about the menu. "Coop, this porcini crust isn't going to work on the chicken, it'll burn." "Coop, these cherry tomatoes take forever to stuff—this dish is a waste of time." "Coop, did you order scallops or do I need to do it myself?" Though Rickey would never have allowed one of his cooks to talk to him that way, Coop didn't seem bothered by it. Maybe he had no pride left at all. Rickey was dying to call her on this, but didn't feel it was his place yet.

"Spain would be cool, I guess," he said. "But wouldn't you need a work permit or something?"

"If I could save up enough money to live for a while, I'd apprentice myself to somebody without pay. Then I could learn while I worked on getting my papers."

Rickey was impressed. He couldn't imagine just picking up and leaving the country without even a paying job at the other end. But then he'd never had any desire to live outside New Orleans. He guessed he just wasn't very adventurous.

"Thanks," said Coop, taking the new potatoes Rickey had tournered for him. Rickey had never used the tourner cut in his day-to-day work before, but he had cut so many potatoes into seven-sided footballs at the CIA that his hands still remembered how to do it. "So listen, Firestone wants you to have dinner with him tonight."

"Here?"

"Yeah. I'm going to let Sugar and Flaco handle all the other covers while I make a special tasting menu for you two."

All what *other covers?* Rickey thought, remembering the two reservations on the books. Even in the dead of summer, Liquor seldom had fewer than twenty reservations going into the dinner shift, and eighty covers was a slow night for them. Coop made it sound like this place would be lucky to do a tenth of that business.

"Cool," he said. "But you don't have to make us anything special. There's lots of stuff I'd like to try on the regular menu."

"Don't worry." Coop looked up from the sauce he was reducing and smiled a little sadly. "I'll let you try everything. I want to show you what I'm capable of before you decide what I get to keep doing."

10

G-man dropped Rickey off at the airport early that morning and felt at loose ends for the rest of the day. He wished Liquor was open so he could do something to occupy himself. He went by G.A. Lotz, the big restaurant supply house near Bayou St. John, with the idea that he might buy a new knife, but found nothing he needed or wanted. He went to his parents' house for dinner, but they got on his nerves and he left before he snapped at them and hurt their feelings. They hadn't done anything wrong; it was just that if he couldn't be with Rickey, he didn't particularly want to be around anyone else.

There was nothing to do at home either. He had a TiVo recorder he'd used to catch all the games during basketball season, but that was over now. Watching basketball had long been a comfort to him, the rhythms of the game simultaneously exciting and soothing. Rickey wasn't as crazy about it, and had been less so since New Orleans got its pro team, the Hornets. They'd gone to a game that was broadcast on ESPN, and when the camera panned the crowd for local celebrities, their image had very briefly been broadcast to millions of viewers around the country. Rickey was embarrassed because he'd been seen eating a foot-long chili dog, and also because he had never quite adjusted to being the latest darling of the celebrity chef cult. He was more of a football fan, with a New Orleans native's hapless, doomed love for the Saints.

G-man got drunk and fell asleep early. Rickey called an hour later. They talked for a few minutes, but G-man couldn't really wake up and the conversation ended too soon. Then he lay in bed unable to get back to sleep. Absurdly, he wished he had slept over at his parents' house. He didn't want to be around other people, but having grown up in a big family, then lived and worked with Rickey, he wasn't good at being alone. The bed felt too big. His mouth tasted of old bourbon. He pounded his pillow into shape. This was ridiculous; couldn't he even get by on his own for one week? He'd have to, but it felt like hours before he could sleep.

In the morning he dragged himself into the restaurant, made his orders, did his prep work, set up his mise en place. Lonesome old soul songs like "Ain't No Sunshine" and "Midnight Train to Georgia" kept running through his head. The kitchen, normally one of the cleanest he'd ever worked in, smelled faintly of rancid fat and garbage. He threw himself into scrubbing all the surfaces and managed to stop thinking for a while.

Just before dinner service began, Marquis said, "G, you mind?" and held up a CD. There was a boom box near the expediting station, but Rickey wasn't fond of music in the kitchen and seldom let anyone use it.

"Sure, go ahead," said G-man. "Maybe it'll wake me up."

It turned out to be bounce, a local variation of hip-hop that relied on calls and responses laid over a heavy, looping beat.

> *Hey wodie, what ward you bang for?*
> *The Third? The Seven? The Lower Nine?*
> *Best be stayin outta mine!*

went one verse, and the next one responded:

> *Fuck alla that ward shit!*
> *Niggas be orderin a hit*

Poppy Z. Brite

Cause you live in the wrong ghetto.
Dawg, I'm all about the 504.

It was repetitive and catchy and got everybody in the kitchen moving a little faster. "What is this anyway?" G-man asked Marquis.

"*It's All Gravy* by N-Word. He just got signed to Gold Frontin' Records last year. Gettin a lotta airplay."

"N-Word, hell," said Terrance, coming in. "That's my cousin NuShawn."

G-man took the CD case down from the boom box shelf and studied the picture on the front: a skinny young man with intricate cornrow braids, many tattoos, and an oversized football jersey that bore the numbers 504, the New Orleans area code. Around his neck was a large medallion stamped with the logo of Gold Frontin' Records: a smiling mouth with two solid gold teeth in front and the rest made of pavé diamonds. "I'll be damn," said G-man. "That *is* NuShawn, isn't it? I didn't know he was a musician."

Rickey and G-man had met NuShawn Jefferson very briefly back when they were still trying to start a restaurant. He had dealt cocaine to Rickey's crazy ex-boss, the one who'd trapped Rickey in the walk-in.

"*Musician,*" said Terrance, rolling his eyes. "Aretha Franklin is a musician. Fats Domino is a musician. A kid yelling 'Work that ass till it bleeds' ain't a musician."

"Aw, you just a old dinosaur," said Marquis.

"Yeah, Terrance," said G-man. "Hell, I'm your age and I like this."

"Got nothing to do with age. Got to do with talent, and NuShawn ain't got none of that. I was glad to see him quit dealing, though. Figure his life expectancy's maybe a little higher now."

"He's doing good, huh?"

"Got him three cars and a big-ass house in English Turn."

"English Turn? That West Bank burb where the millionaires live?"

"Yeah, I told him invest some of that money, it ain't gonna last forever. But he gotta have houses, cars, all kinda shit."

"Gotta keep up appearances," said Marquis.

"Whatever." Terrance started to walk away, then turned back. "Listen, I wasn't gonna go, but he's throwing a party tonight. Gonna have food, drinks, I don't know what all. Y'all like his music so much, I suppose I could take you out there after work."

"Hell, yeah!" said Marquis, suddenly Terrance's best friend.

G-man wasn't even exactly sure where English Turn was, although he had an idea it was far out in the country. He had no real desire to go to a party there, but he knew Terrance was offering because Rickey was gone and his loneliness was probably obvious to everybody. Terrance had a kind heart. Besides, he hadn't been to a real throwdown in years, and he'd never been to an honest-to-God rap star's house. "Sure, what the hell," he said.

The night was slow and they had the kitchen broken down by eleven P.M. "Y'all wanna ride with me or follow me in your own cars?" said Terrance.

"Y'all can both ride with me if you want," said Marquis.

"I rode with you once before. You spend too much time checking out other people's rides and not enough looking at the road."

They ended up taking Terrance's car, a 1984 Oldsmobile with Lou Rawls on the tape deck. "I never knew you were so old-school, Terrance," said G-man.

"Soulasaurus Rex," Marquis commented.

They crossed the bridge—the river shining darkly below them, the city limned in neon at their backs—got off on the West Bank, and headed east. English Turn wasn't as far away as G-man had thought; twenty minutes after leaving the restaurant, they pulled up to the gatehouse that protected NuShawn's neighborhood from the rabble to which he had previously belonged. Terrance gave his name to the uniformed guard, who consulted a clipboard and waved him through.

They drove through a neighborhood of wide streets and tastefully ostentatious mansions to NuShawn's house, a modern-looking place with two big turrets in front and a backyard that rolled gently down to the golf course. The driveway was full, the street lined with cars and SUVs in both directions. G-man was no car freak, but he recognized Impalas, Jaguars, a few Bentleys and Ferraris. All had chrome wheel rims that sparkled like diamonds even at rest; he could only imagine how impressive they looked when the cars were rolling. He saw old Detroit iron here and there too, Cadillacs and Oldsmobiles with patchy paint jobs, like comfortable nags among a herd of sleek and expensive racehorses.

Terrance found a spot far down the street and they walked back toward the house, already able to hear the party throbbing with bass and beats and excited voices and the sound of something smashing. G-man wondered what NuShawn's neighbors thought of all this. He had the idea most people who moved to English Turn did so because there was a private golf course nearby, not because they wanted to mingle with the ghetto-fabulous.

If the cars outside had reminded him of racehorses, the party-goers themselves were like a flock of fantastic tropical birds. The women wore jewel-toned dresses or skimpy tops and pants that appeared to be painted on. The men were resplendent in basketball jerseys, zoot suits, camouflage clothes, sneakers that looked as if they cost more than a meal in a nice restaurant, Stacy Adams alligator shoes. Many of the women had men's names tattooed in flowing script on their chests, just above the cleavage. The men favored initials on the neck and mottoes up and down the arms. The three new arrivals in their kitchen-sweaty T-shirts and check pants looked drab by comparison.

As far as he could tell, G-man was one of only three or four white people at the party, but this didn't make him uncomfortable. He'd grown up in a black neighborhood, gone to a black school, worked in plenty of mostly-black kitchens. In New Orleans, white people either got used to being a minority or moved to the suburbs. G-man had gotten used to it so long ago that he hardly ever thought about it any more. The partygoers glanced at him but didn't stare, which was usually how it was: nobody gave a damn unless you made a big deal of it.

"Mob scene, just like I figured," Terrance said in G-man's ear. "You wanna get a drink?"

They made their way to the bar. Marquis had already peeled off; G-man saw him across the room talking to an unimpressed-looking girl in a strappy red dress. The bartender was setting up flutes of champagne and spiking them with shots of Courvoisier. Terrance grabbed two and handed one to G-man, who sipped it even though he would have preferred a beer. It was surprisingly good, the mellow sweetness of the cognac cutting through the champagne's fizzy bite. G-man figured it for a girly drink, but it had a kick to it; after the first glass he felt relaxed for the first time since he'd dropped Rickey off at the airport. It was only eight days, after all. Two of those days had already passed; he'd see Rickey in less than a week. They shouldn't be so dependent on each other. He could do this.

He got another drink and followed Terrance into the next room, where NuShawn was holding court amidst a thick cumulus formation of pot smoke. The rapper's hair was braided in a complex pattern that resembled row after row of Z's. A medallion around his neck—bigger than the other medallions G-man had seen—and an enormous ring on his left hand both bore the Gold Frontin' logo. He was surrounded by stunning women and dangerous-looking young men, but they parted to let Terrance get to him. The cousins performed a complicated handshake that G-man didn't even try to imitate when Terrance introduced him.

"Seem like I know you from somewhere," said NuShawn.

G-man hadn't planned to mention it, since he didn't know whether NuShawn's coke-dealing past was an embarrassment or a source of pride in his new scene. "Uh, you knew my partner's ex-boss," he said. "Mike Mouton? He's in prison now."

NuShawn's weed-glazed eyes lit up. "Yeah, and your boy helped put him there! I hated that motherfucker. Mean-ass cracker had no respect for nobody. Your partner, he's here tonight?"

"Nuh-uh. He's on a business trip right now."

"Well, you tell him to call me. I got a little sump'm-sump'm for him anytime he wants it. Anybody send Mike Mouton to Angola is a friend of mine, y'heard me?"

A woman who looked like a stripper passed NuShawn one of the biggest joints G-man had ever seen. NuShawn took a prodigious hit off it, then handed it to G-man, who took a smaller hit. He and Rickey could afford better pot these days than the dirtweed they'd grown up with, but they didn't have much time to smoke it, and he was out of practice.

Another stripper, a light-skinned young woman whose complicated upswept hairdo was accented with small rhinestones, kept staring at G-man. "Hey!" she said at last. "I know who you are. Ain't your name Gary?"

"Yeah, it is."

"You went to Frederick Douglass. I'm Terabitha Evans. You don't remember me? Picture me 'bout twenty pounds fatter with real bad hair. I improved myself after I graduated. You still live in the Ninth Ward?"

"No, I moved Uptown. My family's still on Delery Street, though."

"That's nice," said Terabitha, her wide smile revealing a gold tooth with a little star in the center, and she was clearly flirting now. "It's real good to see you, baby. How 'bout a lap dance? I'll give you a freebie for old times' sake."

"Oh, uh, no. Thanks, but no, that's OK."

"Hey man, go ahead," said NuShawn. "I got plenty others. I ain't gonna grudge you one."

G-man looked around for Terrance, but the big cook was talking to somebody else and hadn't heard any of this. He thought about just saying he was gay, but he never did that. He and Rickey weren't closeted by any means, but because they'd grown up in a rough neighborhood and been baptized by fire in the macho kitchen culture, an almost pathological privacy had been deeply ingrained in them. The people who needed to know they were a couple knew it, but they never advertised it to people who didn't need to know. "I'm married," he said at last, not considering it a lie.

"You ain't wearing no ring," Terabitha pouted.

"Damn, girl, leave the man alone," said NuShawn. "Can't you see he ain't interested in your ole stank ass?"

"Most cooks don't like wearing rings," said G-man lamely. "They can get caught on shit or fall down the drain."

The girl just glared at him. He excused himself, got another drink, and wandered around a little, catching bits of conversation. Eventually he ended up on the back patio talking to a sleek young man in a silk tracksuit. At first the man seemed very interested in G-man's check pants, asking all sorts of questions about where you could buy them, why chefs wore them, what the pattern was called. "Houndstooth," he said reflectively, stroking his goateed chin. "I like that. Got an upscale sound to it."

"Hell, checks are about as upscale as my ass," said G-man.

"Your ass *is* upscale now, dawg. You're here, ain'tcha?"

"I guess you got a point," said G-man. Except possibly for Lenny's lakefront place, this was the nicest house he'd ever been in. "Kinda makes me feel like a slice of bologna sitting on the plate with foie gras, though."

The young man laughed loud and long. "Nothing wrong with bologna when that's what you're in the mood for," he said. "Slap it on some white bread with plenty Blue Plate mayonnaise, you got yourself a fine meal."

"Actually, that sounds pretty good right now."

"It does," said the man, "but on the real, I think I'd rather have the foie gras."

"You ever tried the foie gras crème brûlée at the Lemon Tree? Man, I never understood what *decadent* meant until I tasted that."

"Crème brûlée? It's a dessert?"

"Nah, it's savory. He does it with sweet onions and diced Granny Smith apples. Sounds weird, but it's good."

"I'll have to give it a try. Lemon Tree's a great restaurant. Had a cheese plate last time I was there, got this Paul Beeler Gruyère on it . . ."

Poppy Z. Brite

"That real grainy one? From Switzerland?"

"That's the one."

They stood on the patio talking about food until Terrance stuck his head out the sliding glass door. "There you go, G. I been looking all over. You 'bout ready?"

"Sure," said G-man, though he would have liked to stay longer. "Where's Marquis?"

Terrance rolled his eyes. "He said go on without him—thinks he gonna get some high-class pussy. I told him he still gotta work dinner tomorrow."

Not until they were in the car did Terrance ask, "So how'd you start talking to Dirty King?"

"Who?"

"You mean you don't even know who you were talking to out there?" Terrance laughed. "That slick young brother on the patio was Dirty King. Founder and CEO of Gold Frontin' Records. Got him a fleet of Bentleys, his own airplane, all kinda shit. People say he's the richest black man in America."

"Wow," said G-man. "He was cool. Said he liked mackerel. Not too many people around here like mackerel."

"You getting as bad as Rickey. Y'all the only people I know could spend fifteen minutes talking to the top brass of New Orleans rap music and find out nothing but what kinda fish he likes."

"Fish is important."

"Like I said—Rickey's rubbing off on you."

G-man thought about it. Of course Rickey had been the biggest influence in his life for more than a decade, but only in the past couple of years had he developed a curiosity about food that approached Rickey's. He guessed owning a restaurant had forced him along the path Rickey had followed naturally.

"Let's make a mackerel special tomorrow," he said. "I know Old Country usually has it."

"Why? Dirty King coming in for dinner?"

"I didn't even tell him where I worked."

"G, if he has the least little bit of interest in knowing where you work, he'll find out."

"Well, if he comes in, we'll feed him. I don't know why he'd be interested, though."

"I got no idea what you said to him," said Terrance. "But I wouldn't be surprised if he showed up sometime. All I know is when people talk to Rickey, they come away hungry."

11

"**I always did** get along with chefs," said Frank Firestone. "Only one I ever had trouble with was on my yacht. Guy was insubordinate—wouldn't cook what I wanted. I put him off the boat in Rarotonga, but it turned out maritime law forbids you to strand your crew, so I had to charter a plane to bring him back to Texas!"

Firestone laughed heartily. Rickey barely heard the irritating story. He was too engrossed in his fourth course, a crisp, tangy sautéed skate wing in a richly flavored beurre noisette. The flavors were almost too intense, but not quite; the pleasure of tasting them nearly spilled over into discomfort, but stopped just short of it. That was how all the courses had been: beautiful food, exquisitely plated but not stacked into towers, topped with great brittle mounds of sweet potato hay, or tortured into unnatural shapes. The meal had opened with a clear tomato consommé in which floated yellow grape tomato halves and tiny cubes of toasted garlic. Next came a perfect Belon oyster in a grapefruit and black pepper mignonette sauce, then slivers of translucent raw sea scallop draped over a celery gelée and topped with dollops of sevruga caviar. The skate was the first hot course, and Rickey was impressed

123

with the way the lemony flavor referenced the previous, lighter courses. Just as he'd feared, Coop was cooking on a level that was, if anything, higher than Rickey's own. How was he supposed to improve on this?

Frank Firestone ate his food without looking at it and kept talking. He wasn't quite what Rickey had expected. His voice on the phone sounded thickly Texan, and Rickey had pictured him as a short, paunchy, jug-eared cowboy. Instead he was a slender, sallow-skinned man in his mid-forties with a shock of black hair that fell lankly across his forehead and a perpetual beard shadow that reminded Rickey of Coop's nickname for him: Fred Flintstone. His brown eyes were as large and mild as G-man's. A pair of pointy-toed, elaborately stitched boots poked out from beneath the hems of his expensive trousers, but that was the only cowboyish touch. A faint but persistent smell of tobacco smoke hovered around him, irritating Rickey, who shared Lenny's belief that cigarettes destroyed the palate.

"Now, you take Cooper," said Firestone. "He's real easy to get along with. Has his own ideas about things, but he never argues with me. I was a little worried about that when I hired him—owning restaurants in New York and all. I thought he might have trouble taking orders, but he's just as nice as pie."

Yassuh boss, right away boss, thought Rickey, swallowing his last bite of skate with real regret that the portion wasn't larger. The waiter cleared the plates and poured more wine into their glasses. Coop had paired various wines with each course, but the names had gone in one of Rickey's ears and out the other. The wines themselves, though, complemented the food in a way Rickey had never experienced before. Usually when he tried drinking wine with a meal, he wished he had a nice strong cocktail instead, but the idea of Wild Turkey hadn't entered his mind for three courses or so.

Coop really knew what he was doing here. Rickey sighed as the waiter set another plate before him, murmuring discreetly, "This is butter-poached Arctic char with a fennel and green apple slaw."

It was flawless, as were the clam and bacon risotto, roast duck and foie gras terrine, and milk-braised veal cheek with Bleu de Gex cheese grits that followed. Firestone chatted amiably about current events and things to do in Dallas. Rickey began to hate him. What difference did it make whether this restaurant was turning a profit? Firestone didn't need the money. If you had a chef capable of putting out this kind of food, why not just consider the place your own personal dining room and count any customers as gravy?

That was senseless, of course. G-man, with his talent for accounting, would raise his hands in despair to hear Rickey say such a thing. Also, it flew in the face of everything Rickey had come here to do. As he had done so many times over the past few days, he forced himself to picture his bank account being fattened by ten thousand dollars, his restaurant eventually becoming independent of Lenny Duveteaux. It wasn't easy with this veal cheek in front of him, shredding at his fork's touch like a tiny pot roast, caressing his tongue with its deep, gelatinous texture and flavor.

"So whaddaya think?" asked Firestone, finishing his veal cheek in two bites and emptying his wineglass. "Think you can help Cooper get on the right track?"

Rickey measured his words carefully before he spoke. Tact never came easily to him, and now he was about half-buzzed from all the wine. "I think Coop's already on a pretty good track," he said. "I think I can help him figure out how to bring his menu more in line with what your customers might want. But, Mr. Firestone, I gotta tell you this is some of the best food I've ever eaten. Maybe you should let him do a tasting menu in addition to his regular menu or something."

Firestone waved a hand at the waiter, then pointed at his wineglass. "Won't work," he said as the waiter scurried over to pour. "Sure, he can do a tasting menu, but it's gotta have the regular stuff on it. Otherwise you'll get people saying, 'Well, gimme the tasting, but I want the ribeye instead of that veal cheek course, and don't gimme any of those cheese grits, I don't like blue cheese.' I don't mind if he does all this esoteric stuff to impress you, but we cain't have it on the menu every night. Hell, you ask most upscale diners in Dallas what a veal cheek is, they'll probably tell you it's something Mexicans eat."

"Is it?"

"Is it what?"

"Is a veal cheek something Mexicans eat?" Rickey said, feeling faintly stupid.

"Don't know. Never been crazy about Mexican food—I'm a haute cuisine boy from way back."

Christ, Rickey thought, and filed away the phrase *haute cuisine boy* to repeat to G-man later. He wondered whether Firestone's assessment of the Dallas dining scene was entirely fair—the copy of *Where* magazine in his hotel room had listed several upscale-eclectic restaurants that sounded good or at least interesting—but his job wasn't to educate Firestone about whatever else might be going on in culinary Dallas; his job was to make this restaurant work.

The next course, a roulade of venison with artichoke hearts and preserved lemons, was brought to the table by Coop himself. He barely nodded at Firestone, but pinned Rickey with his dark, slightly manic gaze. "How do you like it so far?"

"It's absolutely fucking perfect," said Rickey. "I think I better just get on the next flight home."

"Yeah, well. Listen—don't let this guy hijack you after dinner and drag you to a strip club or something. Stick around till I close the kitchen and we'll go get a drink."

That made Rickey flash back to the night he'd met Coop at the CIA cooking demo. *Stick around for a few minutes,* Coop had said as he signed the other students' cookbooks. *What say we grab a cup of coffee and you can catch me up on New Orleans?* The cup of coffee had led to great quantities of cocaine, a few stolen kisses, and weeks of guilt and humiliation, but Rickey didn't suppose any of that mattered now. The toque was on the other head, as it were. "Sure," he said. "If I can even move after I finish eating all this."

"Is it too filling?" Coop looked worried. "I know there's a bunch of courses, but I thought it was pretty light overall. I wanted to create a sense of satiety without surfeit."

Rickey had the distinct impression that Firestone was rolling his eyes, but he couldn't look away from Coop. The older chef seemed so hungry for praise, but why? Surely he knew he could still cook like the angels. Had it really been so long since anyone had said a kind word about his food? "It's not too filling," Rickey said. "It's just so incredibly good, I'm not gonna want to leave this table."

Obviously pleased by that, Coop returned to the kitchen. The next course was a piece of seared foie gras with roasted pineapple. Rickey admired the idea of serving foie gras after the meat courses, since the lush, fatty liver had an almost dessertlike quality but was usually treated as an appetizer. After that came a selection of three artisanal cheeses, and lastly a scoop of housemade banana ice cream topped with a delicate spindrift of caramelized brown sugar. Recognizing it as a tip of the hat to bananas Foster, Rickey felt absurdly touched.

Firestone recognized the dessert's origins too. "This is kind of a New Orleans dish, isn't it?"

"Yeah," said Rickey. "They invented it at Brennan's in 1951." He reflected that at least Firestone didn't pronounce the name of the city "New Or-LEENZ," or, worse, "N'awlins." Most out-of-towners mispronounced it one way or the other, the ones who butchered it in the latter fashion apparently thinking they sounded local because they saw it written that way on souvenir aprons in the French Quarter. Firestone not only pronounced it correctly, he growled it—"Noo Wahhhlunz"—in a weird Texan approximation of a Lower Ninth Ward accent. Rickey wondered where in the world he'd picked that up.

As the waiter served them coffee with a small plate of chocolate truffles and fleur de sel caramels, all of which Firestone ignored to light a cigarette, Rickey wondered whether he should go out drinking with Coop. Maybe it wasn't a good idea. Something about this meal set off alarms in his head, made him think Coop wasn't just trying to show off his kitchen chops. If Rickey had ever wanted to seduce someone with food, this was the kind of meal he would have cooked. But probably he was just being vain. Coop had everything to prove here. His situation must be incredibly humiliating; the least he could do was show Rickey what he was capable of. It didn't have to be about anything else.

"Oh my God," said Rickey for what must have been the fifth or sixth time that night. This time, though, he wasn't reacting to food. "I see what you mean about the skyline."

They were in a revolving cocktail lounge atop the glittering orb of Reunion Tower, fifty stories above the city. It was cheesy as hell, but Rickey was glad Coop had brought him here, since he had never before seen anything like this view of nighttime Dallas. If a very rich woman with very gaudy taste had upended her jewelry box onto a huge piece of dark blue satin, it might have looked a little like this. There were buildings that seemed to sparkle with gold dust, buildings topped with ruby beacons, a huge building completely outlined in emerald-colored argon tubing, a slightly smaller one whose lights made a pattern like a DNA helix. Far below, traffic moved in glowing chains among it all.

"See Pegasus?" said Coop.

Rickey didn't. Coop moved in close beside him, put a hand on his shoulder, and pointed at the horizon. "That little red neon shape," he said. "It's a flying horse. He doesn't look very big any more, but he used to be a real landmark—the Magnolia Oil sign. The building's a hotel now, but Dallasites love their Pegasus."

"Dallasites, huh?"

"Yeah, that's what we call ourselves."

"I'm kinda surprised to hear you say *we*. I took you for a diehard New Yorker."

"I don't deserve to call myself a New Yorker any more. I was on top of the world in New York and I fucked it all up. This is a new start for me."

Poppy Z. Brite

"So what happened?"

"Nothing very interesting, I'm afraid. Money. Coke. Younger men. Overweening pride. The usual suspects." Coop looked as if he might say more, then shrugged. "I believed my own press. I thought I really was that good, and when they were done jacking me off, they kissed me on the cheek and dropped me off at the train station, just like I did to you. Only this was on a much bigger scale."

"The forehead," said Rickey.

"What?"

"You kissed me on the forehead, not the cheek. And you didn't jack me off. Do you even remember we didn't have sex? I wondered when I read that letter of yours."

"Whoa." Coop raised his hands in a gesture of mock surrender that Rickey remembered well; he'd seen it a few times during that night in New York. At first he'd been impressed by it, as he had been by everything about Coop, but later it had begun to seem like a way of warding off justified criticism. "Yes, I remember we never had sex. I didn't mean to imply anything different in the letter. Did you take this job because you think you can do it, or are you just here to settle some old score with me?"

If Rickey had been just a touch drunker, he might have fired back an inflammatory reply, but something about Coop's question made him stop and think. "I'm not sure," he admitted. "Kinda both, actually. Plus we need the money."

"Isn't your restaurant doing well?"

"Yeah, but there could be problems."

"Aren't there always," said Coop. It wasn't a question, and Rickey was glad not to elaborate. They ordered another round of drinks from the circulating cocktail waitress and sat in silence for a few minutes, gazing out at that astonishing skyline.

"That really pissed you off, what I did all those years ago," said Coop after a while.

"I hadn't thought about it for a long time until I got your letter, but yeah, it pissed me off. That was the first time anybody ever treated me like garbage." Rickey thought about it. "Well, other than my dad."

"Ah, daddy issues. They can make a man hold a grudge longer than just about anything, I think. I don't know what the story is there, Rickey, but you should know I treated everybody like garbage back then. Including myself. It wasn't about you, and I'm sorry you had to get caught up in my bullshit, however briefly."

"So are you some kinda twelve-stepper now?"

Coop indicated the drink in his hand. "Do I look like a twelve-stepper?"

"I don't know how all that shit works. I thought maybe you could give up the thing you were addicted to and still do other stuff. It's just I know people in those programs are supposed to make amends or whatever, and it seems like you're trying to do that with me. All that 'it wasn't about you' crapola."

"Well. Maybe a little. I've been to a few meetings, but I'm not a twelve-stepper. I certainly haven't made amends with most of the people I fucked over." Coop turned away from the skyline and looked Rickey in the eyes. "I don't know if you'll believe me, Rickey, but I really *liked* you when we met back then. You seemed like a cool kid, I admired your curiosity about food, and I couldn't be happier to see you doing well today. Is that so hard to believe?"

"I guess not. But why . . . aw, fuck it."

"No, come on—why what?"

Rickey wished he hadn't brought it up, but it was something he'd always wondered about. "Right after that night, I had a big fight with G-man. My mom didn't want me to come home for Christmas, and instead of backing me up, G seemed like he didn't care if I came home either. I decided, fuck 'em all, I'll stay in New York, call that hot guy I just met, see what happens. I knew I shouldn't, but I did." Rickey drained his drink. "And you never called me back, you shitbag. I ended up spending Christmas in a flophouse in Poughkeepsie."

"Sorry."

"No, when I think about it, I'm glad you didn't call me. I mean,

Poppy Z. Brite

I totally would have fucked you, and then who knows what would have happened with me and G. But damn, it made me feel horrible at the time." Rickey wondered if he was talking too much, but it suddenly seemed like a good idea to hash all this out; it would smooth the way for them to work together.

"I really am sorry. I don't remember why I didn't call you. I'm sure I would have if I'd known you wanted to fuck me."

"I didn't really want to. I mean, I didn't want to cheat on G. Never did, either."

"You two must have done your experimenting at some point. What'd you do? Have threesomes?"

"No!" Rickey was appalled by the thought.

"Did you have some kind of arrangement, then?"

"What are you talking about, *arrangement*? It's called a relationship. We were faithful to each other. *Are* faithful. Always have been."

"Even counting, like, bathroom sex?"

"Bathroom sex?" Rickey was totally mystified now. He and G-man had had sex in the shower a few times, but he didn't see what that had to do with anything.

"You know, public toilets. Parks. The stacks at libraries. Lots of guys call themselves faithful, but don't count that kind of thing." He saw Rickey's face. "No? . . . My God. I can't even conceive of anything like that. I guess you sowed your wild oats early."

"I didn't have any goddamn wild oats!" Rickey wasn't sure if Coop was baiting him, and if so, why he was rising to the bait. "He's the only person I ever slept with, OK? And I'm the only one he ever slept with—at least that's what he says, and he's never lied to me that I know of. I don't guess that makes sense in your world, but that's how it is for us, and we're fucking *fine* with it!"

Again the capitulating hands. "OK! OK! It's none of my business anyway."

"You got that right."

"But Rickey . . . do you have any idea how *unusual* you two are?"

"And what are you? Normal?"

"Well . . ." Coop thought about it, then laughed. "Unfortunately, yes. As gay men go, I'm probably a lot more normal than you are."

"See, I don't even think about all that shit. Gay. Ho-mo-sekshul. I don't give a fuck." Rickey realized there was a fresh drink sitting in front of him. He wasn't sure how it had gotten there, but he picked it up and took a big slug anyway. "I'm just with G. We're not, like, part of some *community*. I hate all that rainbow flag shit."

"God, you're so butch," said Coop.

"Fuck you!" said Rickey before he realized Coop was teasing him. "Well, maybe I am. I didn't grow up in New York. I'm not sophisticated. I'm not politically correct. I don't think about that stuff. I'm just a goddamn cook."

"All of which doubtless makes you extremely attractive to legions of men sick of the usual stereotypes."

Rickey suddenly felt very tired. "Coop, I don't know how to do this kinda talk. It's over my head. Can we either talk about the menu or call it a night?"

"I was sort of avoiding talking about the menu."

"I know, and I don't blame you. It's a real good menu. I wouldn't want to change it if I was you. I don't even understand why you're staying in this job. If Firestone can't appreciate what you're doing, why not go somewhere else?"

"It's not just Firestone. The rest of the city's hardly beating a path to my kitchen door."

"So why stay in Dallas at all? I guess you had your reasons for leaving New York, but, jeez, there's gotta be some middle ground. You could cook in . . . I don't know. Boston, San Francisco, the Napa Valley . . ."

"Expensive places to live. And probably not too many restaurant owners willing to pay me twenty bucks an hour."

"Firestone's paying you twenty an hour?"

"Yup. With OT. Time and a half."

"Jesus." Rickey had never heard of any cook making that kind of money, head chef or not. Most cooks in New Orleans made eight to twelve dollars an hour. Some head chefs and sous chefs pulled good salaries, but they worked so much that if you broke down their pay to an hourly wage, it would be more pitiful than the lowliest line cook's.

"You're probably wondering why I drive that piece-of-shit Saturn," said Coop, though Rickey hadn't been. "I ran up a lot of credit card debt during my last few years in New York. I'm still paying it off, and that's like three thousand a month. Even pulling down twenty an hour, I'd still be fucked without the cheap car and the free apartment."

"Well . . ." Rickey wasn't sure how to respond to this highly personal information dump. It almost seemed as if Coop was trying to make Rickey feel sorry for him. "I hope it all works out," he said lamely.

"Yeah, me too. Say!" Coop sat up straighter, sloshing a little of his cocktail over the back of his hand. "You were going to tell me if you thought Firestone was crazy or not. What's the verdict?"

"Crazy? Nah. Just another rich dickhead."

Coop fell back in his chair laughing. After a moment, Rickey joined in.

The cocktail waitress paused by their table. "Can I get y'all anything else? It's last call in ten minutes."

"Last call?" said Rickey. "What's that?"

Coop snorted. "You're a New Orleans boy, all right. It means they'll be kicking us out of here soon. You feel like taking a ride over to my place?"

Rickey thought about it, then said, "Sure." A few hours ago he would have balked at going to Coop's apartment, but the dinner and the alcohol had eroded his sense of caution, and he was glad of it. If they were going to work together, he needed to be able to relax around the guy.

They exited the Reunion Tower parking lot onto a busy street and zipped along in a heavy stream of traffic. Rickey thought of how pretty the car lights had looked from fifty stories up, like red and gold chains. Now they were too bright and made his head hurt. He wished he hadn't drunk all that wine. Here and there, plastic grocery bags ghosted across barren asphalt. Urban tumbleweeds, G-man called them. From the ground, Rickey decided, Dallas was an ugly city.

"See that triple underpass?" said Coop, gesturing to the right. "On the other side of it is Dealey Plaza."

"Should that mean something to me?"

"Jesus, didn't they teach you any history in school?"

"Not really."

"Dealey Plaza is where President Kennedy was shot. You *have* heard of John F. Kennedy? 1963? Lee Harvey Oswald?"

"Yeah, yeah. Oswald was from New Orleans."

"He didn't have anything to do with it."

"I thought he shot the President."

"See, you must have learned something in school after all."

"What? He didn't do it?"

"Not according to your District Attorney."

"Placide Treat?" Now Rickey was really getting confused.

"No, the one before him. Never mind—it's not important."

Rickey was happy to leave the subject alone. He'd never caught the political bug that infected so many New Orleanians, and he certainly didn't want to think about New Orleans DAs, past or present. He looked out the window and saw that they were crossing a bridge. Far below, he could just make out a tiny stream of water. "What's that canal?" he said.

Coop laughed. "Canal? That's the Trinity River."

Rickey was starting to get mad. "Stop shitting me, would you?"

"I'm not shitting you. That's the Trinity."

"They call that little thing a river?"

"It's not always that small. This has been a dry summer."

Rickey leaned his head against the window and closed his eyes. He suddenly felt very homesick, and just now he couldn't absorb any more of a city that had all the money in the world but didn't

Poppy Z. Brite

want to spend it on Coop's food, that practiced incomprehensible customs like "last call," that was building the world's largest D just for the hell of it, that called a few drops of water a river. It seemed like a delusional place. He wished he were back in New Orleans, where things made sense.

12

Rickey woke up and took immediate inventory of his situation. He was in his own hotel bed. Good. He was alone. Even better. He had a slight headache, but years of practice had left him capable of drinking bouts far more prodigious than last night's. He vaguely remembered calling home, very late. OK. His universe was still in order; he hadn't done anything wrong.

After they left Reunion Tower, they had gone to Coop's apartment. Coop lived in Oak Cliff, a quiet neighborhood across the "river" (Rickey knew it was rude to think of the Trinity in quotes, as if he were one of those assholes who crooked his fingers in the air to signify that something shouldn't be taken seriously, but he couldn't help it; in his world, a river was a fast brown thing nearly a mile wide). Rickey had been completely befuddled when Coop said Oak Cliff was a dry neighborhood. At first Rickey thought he was talking about the climate, and wondered aloud how it could differ from the rest of the city's.

"No," said Coop, "dry as in no alcohol."

"No alcohol? What the fuck do you mean?" Rickey hadn't meant to be rude, but it was as if Coop had suddenly started speaking

Poppy Z. Brite

another language. "Do they stop you at the border and take it away or something?"

Coop laughed. "Nothing like that. You can have it in your home. But the stores don't sell it, and there aren't any bars here."

"What about the restaurants?"

"I never eat over here," Coop admitted. "I think they can serve alcohol, but the customer's supposed to show a drinking permit. I hear the waiters never ask to see it, though."

"A *drinking permit*?" Rickey clutched his head. "How can there be a drinking permit? That's the most retarded thing I ever heard."

"Calm down, Big Easy. I know that's not how they live on Bourbon Street, but you're in the Bible Belt now."

"Fuck Bourbon Street, I don't go to Bourbon Street, that's not how civilized people live *anywhere*."

"I like it," said Coop. "It keeps me from excess. Well, not tonight, maybe, but most of the time."

Rickey had expected Coop's apartment to be rather bleak, but it was a large, high-ceilinged space on the second floor of a big stucco house that seemed older than most of the Dallas buildings Rickey had seen. The wide wooden moldings and 1950s kitchen fixtures reminded him of home. They fixed weak drinks and sat out on a flat section of the roof that had been fixed up like a garden, right outside the tiny kitchenette, talking lazily about food and the weirdness of publicity and the vagaries of life without ever approaching their own shared history again.

It had been comfortable, Rickey thought. He was surprised and pleased that Coop hadn't made a pass at him. They'd gotten through the initial discomfort and found a place in which they could not only work together, but maybe become friends. It was obvious to both of them that there was still a certain amount of attraction, but Rickey thought they would be able to ignore it. At the end of the evening Coop had dropped him back at Firestone's, where his rental car was parked, and he'd found his way back to the hotel. He was probably lucky that some Dallas cop hadn't stopped him for a Breathalyzer test, but other than that he had conducted himself reasonably well.

Rickey was just making his first move toward the bathroom when the phone rang. "Morning!" a loud voice barked into his ear. "Firestone here. Figure you and Cooper put away a few last night, so I thought I better let you sleep in."

Rickey looked at the clock, which read 9:32. "Thanks," he said.

"Thought I'd take you out for a bite and maybe show you around some before you hit the kitchen this afternoon. Say I pick you up in an hour?"

"We're gonna have lunch at ten-thirty?"

"I know a place that does a good brunch."

Rickey had been feeling fine except for the little headache, but now his stomach rolled over. Of all the shifts he had ever worked, Sunday brunch at Reilly's—his first job after coming back from New York—had been the absolute worst. Great steaming hotel pans full of eggy splooge, neon-yellow Hollandaise warming over a Sterno flame, acres of canned artichoke hearts and greasy bacon mired in stiffening cream sauce, bleary-eyed tourists swilling gallons of bad champagne cut with frozen orange juice . . . and the knowledge that he was considered a second-rate cook, since the first-rate ones had all been needed for Saturday night's dinner shift. It was more than a decade past, but the horrors had never completely left him. Rickey decided it was time to assert himself. "Mr. Firestone," he said, "no offense, but I hate brunch. All cooks hate brunch. Why don't you pick me up a little later and we can have a nice, civilized meal like *lunch*?"

Firestone laughed. "OK then. I never could get Cooper to have brunch with me either—now I know why. Nice to meet somebody who doesn't feed me a lot of bullshit."

He feeds you bullshit because he's scared of you, Rickey thought. He wasn't sure where the thought had come from; obviously Coop was sort of at Firestone's mercy, but Rickey didn't know why that meant Coop should be scared of the guy. All he said was, "See you in a couple hours then."

Poppy Z. Brite

He showered, shaved, brewed the little packet of coffee that came with the coffeemaker in his room, took one sip, poured it down the bathroom sink, and ordered coffee from room service. It still didn't taste right since there was no chicory in it, but at least it resembled coffee. He was making notes on last night's dinner when the concierge rang to tell him Frank Firestone was waiting in the lobby. It was 11:17.

Tooling around Dallas in Firestone's Ford Explorer turned out to be fun. Rickey had seen such behemoths on the road for years, usually cursing them because they'd just cut him off or jumped a four-way stop, but he'd never ridden in one. He rather enjoyed being so high above the other traffic, and imagined that it was like riding a luxuriously appointed elephant. They ate at a private club on the thirty-eighth floor of some downtown skyscraper. The food was dull but not actively bad: Cobb salad, poached salmon, filet. Rickey didn't see anyone drinking alcohol, so he didn't order any, though he wouldn't have minded a little hair of the dog. At such a place in New Orleans, people would already be well into their second round of martinis.

Firestone smoked at the table, asked lots of questions about Liquor, and described meals he'd had at other restaurants around the world, many of which Rickey sorely envied. As the plates were cleared away, Firestone asked the waiter, "How's Chef Jerry doing today? Tell him I said hi." A few minutes later the chef came dutifully shuffling out to the table, a decrepit old soul who looked as if he'd started working in kitchens around the time Moses came down from the mountain. He mumbled something to Firestone, who replied, "Because they didn't come any bigger than that." They cackled together. Then came the moment Rickey had been dreading: "Say, Jerry, this is my new consulting chef, John Rickey from New Orleans. He's a real hotshot—won a James Beard award, got his picture in *Gourmet,* even had a book written about his restaurant. Bet you could learn a thing or two from him!"

"Meetcha," said Jerry, radiating animosity at Rickey as they shook hands. Rickey felt sorry for the old guy and didn't take it personally. It must be horrible to work in a place like this, putting out the same food day after day for rich fuckers who mostly had no idea what they were eating, nor cared.

After lunch they visited a suite of offices where Rickey was made to remove his shoes and socks and roll his pants to the knee. A young woman traced his feet on newsprint, measured the rise of his instep and the circumference of his calves. "I never wear stuff like this," Rickey protested, eyeing the photographs of custom-made cowboy boots that covered the walls. He knew they must be very expensive, but to his eye they were gaudy and hideous: every conceivable color of leather and snakeskin inlaid with designs of bucking broncos, yellow roses, lone stars, oil wells, cow skulls, and of course the shape of Texas itself, its flat top jutting proudly into Oklahoma, its pointy bottom tapering off into the Gulf of Mexico. "They'll be wasted on me," he said. "I never wear anything but chef clogs and sneakers."

"You cain't imagine how comfortable our boots are until you put 'em on," said the young woman. "It's like sticking your foot in butter."

Yuck, Rickey thought, continuing to study the needle-toed, whip-stitched monstrosities. But he sensed that while asserting himself about brunch had been appreciated, refusing this gift would be rude. He just hoped Firestone didn't expect to see him wearing whatever they came up with.

"You don't think you'll like 'em, but you will," Firestone said as he merged smoothly back into the downtown traffic. "I've had plenty of people say they weren't ever gonna wear such gaudy hick things, but they all left town with those boots on their feet. They really are comfortable."

"I'll try to keep an open mind."

"Trust me. There's just something that feels good about wearing a seven-hundred-fifty-dollar pair of shoes."

"I wouldn't know. I was pretty much a Payless man until a couple years ago. When I bought my first good kitchen clogs, I thought I was really going all out spending sixty bucks."

Poppy Z. Brite

"Well, I'm fortunate in some ways. Not so fortunate in others."

Rickey realized that, despite having dined twice with the man, he didn't really know anything about Frank Firestone. He had assumed Firestone was an oilman—hadn't every rich Texan made his fortune from oil?—but he wasn't even sure of that. "I guess we all are," he said cautiously.

"Never had to worry about money, that's true enough. Had my share of trouble, though. My mother was an escort—you know what that is?"

"A hooker?"

"She would've slapped your face around to the back of your head if she heard you say that, but yeah, get rid of all the frills and that's what she was. Real good-looking, real high-priced. She didn't need a whole lot of customers, just a few good ones."

"And one of them was your dad?" Rickey guessed.

"Yeah. Lawyer. Not from Dallas, but he met her when he was here on business one time, and kept coming back to see her. Apparently there was a lot of love between them, if you want to call it that. I think she had some idea he might divorce his wife and marry her—when she got pregnant with me, it wasn't an accident."

"Jeez," said Rickey. He wondered how it felt to know you'd been conceived as bait.

"He didn't, of course, but he took good care of her until she passed away ten years ago. Took care of me too. I made my own fortune, but I started out wildcatting with the proceeds of the trust fund he set up for me. I never have doubted that my daddy loves me."

Rickey sorted through a variety of responses before settling on, "That's good."

"She said she was gonna name me after him, and he told her not to. So you know what she named me? John. Get it? *John?*"

This time Rickey couldn't think of any response.

"John Franklin Firestone—Franklin after her father. I started going by Frank when I got into business—too damn many Johns around. I guess you know what I mean."

"Well, I gave it up in kindergarten, but yeah."

"So you see how I got to be such a scrappy guy," said Firestone, looking as happy as ever. "I knew you'd be a scrappy guy too. Now let's see if you can scrap a little with Cooper and help him figure out how to make food Dallas wants to eat."

They had arrived back at the hotel. As Rickey climbed down from the huge SUV, Firestone called, "Figured you and Cooper wanted to catch up last night, but if you feel like a little company tonight, I can have somebody sent over. I know all the services, a'course."

No way is he saying what I think he's saying, Rickey thought. Looking into Firestone's rather saturnine but amiable face, though, he realized that of course Firestone was saying just that.

"Uh, no thanks, I'm OK," he said.

"I don't care what flavor you like, if that's what worries you. Hell, you want a boy, I can probably get better value for the money."

"No!"

"Suit yourself," said Firestone, apparently unruffled. "Have fun at the restaurant." And the Explorer pulled away, leaving Rickey to stare after it, wondering again what the hell he was doing in this big crazy town.

After changing into his whites, Rickey got the Mustang out of the parking garage and drove to the restaurant. He was already starting to know his way around Dallas; with all the visible landmarks on the horizon, it was easy to stay oriented.

He planned to ease the kitchen into his new menu, doing a few dishes at a time and seeing how customers liked them. He'd discussed his first one with Coop last night: an appetizer presentation of beef Wellington, the classic dish of beef, mushrooms, and foie gras in puff pastry. It was a perfect example of cross-utilization, the economical use of ingredients in more than one dish. Right now there was a thick-cut filet on the menu. The kitchen cut its own meat, and at the end of every whole filet was a piece called the head that usually went to waste. Beef Wellington would use up the heads and any other beef scraps, yet diners would perceive it as fancy. Coop had smiled ruefully at it, and it was the kind of dish G-man would call fossil food, but Rickey suspected his love for old-fashioned cuisine would serve him well in this gig.

"Hey, did you see this?" said Sugar, the sous chef, waving a newspaper in Rickey's face as soon as he walked into the kitchen. Rickey took the paper and saw that it was a quarter-page ad featuring his photograph from *Gourmet*. His glamour shot, G-man called it. The text beneath the picture read CHEF JOHN RICKEY OF LIQUOR, NEW ORLEANS—GUEST CHEF/MENU CONSULTANT AT FIRESTONE'S! Then it listed his various awards and other hype—there was that damn *Bon Appétit* quote about his impeccable grounding in local and global culinary tradition—and gave the dates. Coop's name appeared nowhere in the ad.

"Jeez," Rickey said. Though of course he'd known Firestone planned to advertise his stint, actually seeing his name in another restaurant's ad felt weird and wrong. He'd behaved himself with Coop last night, but now he felt as if he was being unfaithful to Liquor.

"Cute, huh?" said Sugar.

"Yeah." Rickey brushed past her and went looking for Coop, who was back in the walk-in. "You ready to do this?" Rickey asked.

"Ready as I'll ever be." Coop grinned. "Actually, I'm looking forward to it."

There was a nice dark demiglace already prepped, and the beef Wellingtons came out better than Rickey had hoped. Since the ad had mentioned New Orleans, people would be expecting Creole food. Rickey called Coop's seafood supplier to see if he could get a late delivery of Gulf shrimp. If he could, he'd make shrimp remoulade; it was one of the few useful things he'd learned at Reilly's, and he could just about make it in his sleep. The shrimp were available, though the price raised Rickey's hair. He reminded himself that he was hundreds of miles inland from the Gulf now. As he hung up the phone, Sugar said, "Hey, we have lots of frozen shrimp. You could've used those."

"You can't use frozen shrimp for remoulade. They're the star of the dish."

"We used to do it at a Cajun restaurant I worked at."

"Shrimp remoulade isn't Cajun, and I don't care what you used to do. I don't use frozen shrimp for *anything*. They suck."

"Ooo," said Sugar. "A prima donna. Keep trying, maybe you can out-Coop Coop."

Rickey looked around for Coop, but the chef was still in the back. Just as well. "Look," he said, "I don't know what your problem is, but—"

"I don't have a problem. I was just kidding."

The interruption made him see red. He took a deep breath and tried to channel his old CIA instructor, who had always reminded him of a Marine drill sergeant. "*Shut your smart-ass mouth and listen to me!* I don't know what kinda shit Coop's been letting you get away with, but I don't put up with garbage from shoemakers who don't know what the fuck they're doing. I don't care where you used to work, I don't care if you *like* me, I don't care if you *quit* at the end of the night, but as long as you're in this kitchen, you speak to me and Coop with the respect you owe your chef. And if you don't understand why you owe your chef respect, you're in the wrong goddamn business. You understand?"

Sugar turned away without answering. Rickey slammed his knife down on the cutting board, making everybody jump. "*Do you understand?*"

"You're only here for a *week*! You can't talk to us like that."

"Oh, but I can. Do you have *any idea* how much Frank Firestone is paying me to help Coop overhaul this kitchen? I'll give you a hint—it's more than you make in six months." That was probably a slight exaggeration, but it would serve to make Rickey's point. "Look, I'm not trying to be an asshole, but Firestone *wants* me to tell him what's wrong with this restaurant. If I've learned one thing from having my own place, it's how much a chef needs to depend on his sous chef. I don't think Coop can depend on you. Seems like you ought to be trying to change my mind about that—not confirm it."

He went back to what he had been doing without waiting for Sugar's response. A few minutes later Coop came in and said, "Did I just see Sugar crying in the back?"

"Maybe," said Rickey. "She needs to learn some respect for her superiors."

"Well, but Rickey, I can't have my crew subjected to verbal abuse—"

"Coop, can I talk to you in private? Just for a sec." They ducked around the corner into a little alcove near the pass. "I didn't want to say this in front of them," Rickey said, "but I think you've seriously lost control of your crew. I heard Sugar backtalking you as soon as I got here, and a few minutes ago she started backtalking me. I don't put up with that kinda shit at Liquor, and you shouldn't either. Did you let your staff walk all over you at Star K and Capers?"

"Probably a little," Coop admitted. "I'm not much of an authority figure. When I had my own problems, people started coming in late and slacking off, and I never could bring myself to fire them. I know Sugar wants my job. Hell, she'll probably get it when I leave. What'd you say to her?"

"I'm not exactly sure. It sorta came from the gut." Rickey laughed. "I bet it improves her attitude, though. What about the rest of the crew? Can we count on them, or are they gonna send us down the pike?"

"Flaco doesn't speak much English, but he's a solid cook. Diego's a little flaky. He can do the job, but you have to stay on top of him. Hubie—you'll meet him later in the week—well, Hubie's pretty much a waste case."

"Why do you hire people like that?"

"This crew was here when I came to Firestone's."

"So fire 'em and build your own."

"You and your youthful enthusiasm. Wait till you're forty-seven—everything won't seem so cut-and-dried anymore."

Rickey had trouble imagining what could be more cut-and-dried than the need for a dependable crew. He'd worked with bad cooks before, and they didn't just drag down the kitchen, they dragged down the whole restaurant. Waiters got sick of having to fight for their orders; hosts were reluctant to seat too many customers in case the kitchen couldn't handle it; customers didn't understand why they had to wait for food when the place was two-thirds empty, and eventually took their business elsewhere. He wondered if his authority here extended to firing the entire crew, but decided to withhold judgment until after tonight's dinner service.

As they were returning to the line, Frank Firestone entered the kitchen. He gave them a big howdy, then glanced from Rickey's face to Coop's. Some tension must have shown there, because he said, "What's going on?"

"Nothing," said Coop. "Rickey and I were just discussing the chain of command here."

"Chain of command?" Firestone laughed. "Seems to me your link's been cut right out of that chain, Cooper."

It wasn't quite the cruelest remark Rickey had ever heard in a kitchen. Cooks ranked on one another all the time, and managers and owners sometimes got in on the act as well. Coop, though, seemed to deflate like a cut-open parchment roasting bag. He actually put one hand against the wall as if bracing himself. Firestone just watched him, cocking an inquisitive eyebrow: *Yeah, what about it?*

"If y'all want to—" Rickey began.

"Now, Cooper," Firestone went on, "you know we agreed you were to let Rickey take over this kitchen. He knows a little something about running a successful restaurant, which is more than you've been able to claim for a few years now. I don't want to hear about chains of command. There's no chain. Rickey's in charge here, and you agreed to do what he says."

Poppy Z. Brite

"It's not like that," Rickey said. "We weren't—"

Firestone ignored the interruption. "You understand?"

Coop stared at him, dark eyes blazing. Firestone gazed blandly back. There was a terrible raw intimacy to the moment, and Rickey would have given a great deal to be elsewhere. Then Coop's face cleared, as if he had remembered something. "Sure, boss," he said. "Sure I understand."

"Good man." Firestone gave them a sunny smile, as if perhaps they'd all been talking about tonight's dinner specials. "I'll be in the office for an hour or so. If I don't see either of you before I leave, I'll catch you tomorrow."

Rickey couldn't look at Coop. He walked away toward the line, and after a minute he heard Coop following.

Early on, it became obvious that the night was shaping up busy. Rickey wondered if it had anything to do with that newspaper ad; the place had been dead when he ate here last night. He and Coop worked the sauté station while Sugar expedited. Though she didn't say much beyond calling out the orders, she kept up her end of things. He liked working next to Coop, who was fast and rock-steady. Flaco worked the grill as solidly as Coop had promised, occasionally making comments in a mixture of Spanish and English. Rickey learned quite a few words, though he didn't think he would be able to use any of them in polite company. Diego handled salads and cold apps, faltering a little here and there but never fucking up too badly. The shrimp remoulade didn't sell all that well—maybe Rickey had underestimated Dallas's taste for Creole cuisine, or maybe he just hadn't explained it to the waiters in a sufficiently simplistic manner—but the beef Wellingtons fairly flew out of the kitchen.

The cooks gathered in the bar when service was over. Sugar left after drinking a single glass of wine. Rickey felt a little sorry for her—she was obviously no great shakes as a cook, but it really must be difficult for women in the boys'-club environment of a restaurant kitchen. Well, the things he'd said would help her in the long run. She needed to toughen up.

The person he really felt bad for was Coop. Firestone had cut him down right in front of Rickey, had pretty much ordered him to be Rickey's bitch. It had lessened Rickey's respect for both of them, but it had also made him want to help Coop if he could. The struggle between cooks and management was an age-old one, and Rickey would always be on the cooks' side.

When the dining-room manager started making let's-get-out-of-here noises, Flaco and Diego convinced Coop and Rickey to join them at a Mexican bar on Maple Avenue. Rickey would have preferred to go back to the hotel, call G-man, and get some rest, but Coop seemed to want him along. Maybe a few drinks would blunt the impact of that ugly scene. The bar was a tiny, sweaty place decorated with Christmas lights, beer signs, rodeo posters, and icons of the Virgin Mary. Rickey felt like a nodding, grinning idiot until Coop taught him to say "Sorry, I don't speak Spanish." Or maybe Coop had taught him to say "I like buttfucking"; after a few tequilas he didn't much care. Bad things had always happened to Rickey when he drank tequila, but since he was in a Mexican bar, he thought it would be impolite to refuse.

The lights began to run together, gaudy and bloody. It was going to be one of those nights. Abruptly Flaco and Diego were gone, and Rickey and Coop were in a taxi on their way to some uptown bar. They'd left their cars at the restaurant, thank whatever God protected hopeless drunks.

"Fuck you, I'm not going in there," Rickey said when he saw the giant rainbow flag hanging over the door of their destination.

"Come on—it's not a cruisy scene. It's relaxed. You need to get over your homophobia."

"Coop, I don't know how to tell you this, but I'm gay."

"You're gay, but you're one of those gay men who prides himself on not being a fag. Everybody needs to embrace his inner fag once in a while."

"Oh jeez," Rickey moaned, but he was too drunk to resist being dragged into the bar. Coop's idea of "relaxed" turned out to include loud dance music and muscular young men in tank tops, both of which made Rickey feel ancient. He wondered if that was Coop's objective. But the place turned out to have a back room that was much quieter and more comfortable, with old sofas and chaise lounges arranged around a bar that looked like a glammed-up tiki hut. Coop fetched him a shot of Wild Turkey on the rocks. That was how Rickey had begun his night, but the thought of pouring another one on top of all that tequila made him nervous. He sipped it anyway and half-listened to Coop talk about tonight's service.

Gradually Rickey became aware that while Coop was keeping up his end of the conversation, his attention was focused on a spot somewhere over Rickey's shoulder. Rickey turned and saw a shirtless young man whose jeans hung low on his scrawny ass, the waistband surely no more than a half-inch above his pubes. What were kids thinking these days? Rickey felt tireder and older than ever. "Still got an eye for the young stuff, I see," he said.

At least Coop had the decency to look embarrassed. "Sorry. That was rude."

"I don't give a fuck. It's not like I'm your date or anything."

Coop smiled a little at that. "You're not?"

"No. I'm not."

The night had turned into an endless pub crawl, and Rickey slipped into a deeper haze as the hours passed. Without warning they had left the gay bar and were in another taxi; Rickey was unsure of their destination. He was surprised, a few minutes later, to find himself in the elevator of his hotel. Why hadn't he stopped drinking two hours ago, after the Mexican bar? He knew he'd never been able to handle tequila. Was Coop still with him? Yes, there he was, leaning against the mirrored wall. An infinity of Coops and Rickeys was reflected around them, dizzying and slightly nauseating. "What are we doing here?" he said.

"Ah, that's the question we all begin to ask ourselves after a certain age, isn't it?"

"Shut up with your bullshit," Rickey said a little rudely. "I mean, what are we doing in the hotel?"

"You said I could crash here. I'm in no shape to drive."

Rickey didn't remember saying that, but figured he might have. The second half of Coop's claim was indisputably true. Rickey regarded their weaving, goggle-eyed reflections and laughed. They certainly were going to have a beautiful dinner shift tomorrow.

"Wow," said Coop when he saw the room. "Firestone must think you're going to make him a lot of money."

"This is the nicest hotel I ever stayed in," Rickey admitted, neglecting to mention that it was only his fourth one ever. "You want something out the little lowboy here?"

"Lowboy?" Coop laughed. "That's called a minibar. And yeah, I'll take a beer if you've got one."

Lowboy, minibar, what-the-fuck-ever, Rickey thought, scowling at the rows of bottles and cans. He supposed he might as well just have the word PROVINCIAL tattooed on his forehead; famous chef or no famous chef, he wasn't ever going to be able to hide it.

Coop drank a third of his beer in one swallow and sprawled on the bed. "You know you're sleeping on the couch, right?" Rickey said.

"Yeah, yeah, just let me stretch out for a minute. Relax, Rickey. I'm not going to bite."

"Fuck you. I'm not eighteen any more, OK? I'm not scared of you. I'm not even impressed by you." Rickey wasn't sure why he was getting so mad, except that he didn't really want Coop here. He knew nothing was going to happen, but it just didn't feel right. He probably never would have allowed Coop in his room at all if he hadn't felt bad about the scene with Firestone.

"I know you're not," Coop said. "Come on—be nice. I thought we were friends now. Why don't you take off that dirty jacket and sit down?"

Rickey realized he was still wearing his white chef jacket, now spotted with grease and remoulade sauce. He undid the cloth buttons and dropped it on the floor. The T-shirt underneath was a little sweaty, but not too offensive. He was about to take one of the room's several armchairs, then decided *Fuck it—let him see I'm not scared* and sat on the edge of the bed.

"I'm really not looking to interfere with your life," Coop said.

"Who said you were?"

"I don't know . . . I just feel like I put your teeth on edge somehow. I thought we'd gotten over it last night, but now things seem weird again. I don't know if it's because you're still attracted to me or because you can't believe you ever were."

Rickey felt Coop's fingertips brushing the small of his back, but the larger, drunker part of his mind decided to ignore it for now. Later he would realize that was sort of like ignoring a blazing fire on the other side of the room, but at the moment it didn't seem like such a big deal.

"Because I'm still really fucking attracted to you, Rickey, and if you want to do anything about it, I give you my word it'll begin and end in this room. I have no interest in messing with your relationship or trying to be a part of your life. I know you don't want that. But . . ." Coop sighed. "A couple of times since you got here, I thought you were looking at me the same way I was looking at you. I'd kick myself if I let you go back to New Orleans without asking."

"So you're saying we could have sloppy, drunk sex with no strings attached?"

"Pretty much, yeah."

For a moment Rickey saw how easy it would be. He'd never been this wasted without G-man around, so he'd never been tempted to let himself go and blame it on the liquor. They had been involved in their share of sleaze, particularly during their Peychaud Grill days, but nothing sexual. Now Coop's hand was under the hem of his shirt, touching the patch of skin just above his asscrack, and that light, maddening touch made Rickey imagine how the whole night would go. He hadn't felt such a powerful charge of erotic curiosity since he was sixteen and trying to figure out how he could get his best friend in bed.

If he was going to do anything to stop this, Rickey knew he better do it right now and not think too much about it. A picture of his home kitchen flashed through his mind—the red-and-white linoleum, the clean tile countertops, an old blue cake plate they'd had since they got their first apartment—and for some reason that gave him the strength to shake off Coop's hand and stand up. "You gotta get out of here," he said.

"Oh, hell, Rickey . . ."

"Hell nothing. I told you, I'm no kid any more, so save your crappy lines for the underage barflies."

"I knew you didn't like me looking at that boy."

Rickey couldn't believe he'd heard that. "I didn't—" he started to say, then wondered why he was even considering justifying himself to this loser. "Forget it," he said. "Think what you want. But you still gotta go."

"Look, we don't have to do anything if you don't want to. I said I'd sleep on the couch. See, I'm getting up." Coop heaved himself off the bed and listed toward the couch. "But don't make me leave. I don't have anywhere to go."

"Go home."

"I'm too drunk to drive."

"Call a cab."

"I don't have enough money to get to Oak Cliff."

"Here." Rickey fumbled for his wallet, extracted a pair of twenties, and forced them into Coop's hand. He remembered Coop handing him a cocaine-encrusted hundred-dollar bill for train fare all those years ago, and the turnabout gave him enormous (if slightly craven) pleasure.

"Rickey, look, I didn't mean to make you mad."

"I'm not mad. I'm really not. I just don't trust you, and I'm never gonna trust you, and you're obviously determined to fuck with my head, so I'd be crazy to let you sleep here. I'd wake up and find you sucking my dick or something."

"Maybe if you weren't such a goddamn Puritan, you'd have a little more life experience."

"Maybe if you'd ever learned to keep it in your pants, you'd know that spending fourteen years with somebody you love *is* a life experience."

"You're right," said Coop. His head drooped and his body seemed to sag. Rickey almost felt sorry for him, but focused on the image of the blue cake plate and hardened his heart. "But can't I just sleep on—"

"Out. Now. Goodbye." Coop tried to head for the couch, but Rickey grasped him by the back of his jacket and moved him forcibly toward the door. It wasn't locked, and within seconds he had propelled Coop into the hall and slammed the door after him.

A few seconds of silence. Then, in a muffled voice: "Rickey, if you'd just—"

"Jesus, don't you ever give *up*? No! No! The answer is no! Now get the fuck out of here before I call security!"

"But I'm horny."

Rickey stared at the door in disbelief. This was too weird to be happening; probably he'd passed out from the tequila and was dreaming it all. "Go get a blowjob from a crackhead," he said. "You'll still have thirty-five dollars left for cab fare. I'm going to bed, good night, fuck off."

He went into the bathroom, cranked the faucets to full blast, and splashed cold water on his face. When he ventured back to the door a few minutes later, the peephole revealed an empty hall.

Rickey undressed, crawled into bed, and jerked off for the first time in he couldn't remember how long, imagining in lurid detail what it would have been like having sex with Coop. He had never known his imagination was capable of this kind of thing. Coming up with new liquor dishes was more his speed, or so he'd thought, but now he almost believed that he knew the scent, taste, and touch of a strange man. Not just a strange man, but a *different* man: someone who had not grown up with him, was not intertwined through his life like a vein through a heart, did not speak with his accent or know his ways. It wasn't Cooper Stark himself who had gotten Rickey into such a state; it was simply the lure of the exotic. Afterward, he went to sleep feeling like an asshole, but at least this way he wouldn't want to kill himself when he woke up the next morning.

13

"Thanks for everything," said Rickey. "Let me know how things go, huh?"

"You bet," said Frank Firestone. "And thank *you* for everything. I wasn't sure about you at first, but you turned out to be just the scrappy guy I was looking for."

He handed Rickey his personal check for ten thousand dollars. Rickey had expected a check drawn on the restaurant's account, but of course that wouldn't have been as showy. They shook hands, and Rickey walked off toward airport security, the clack of his boot heels absurdly loud on the cement floor. No one around him appeared to notice the sound; he guessed it was a common one in Dallas.

He had never intended to wear the damned cowboy boots. They'd been delivered to his hotel room yesterday, and at first the sight of them had horrified him: black leather with purple-and-gold stitching and a big green shape of Louisiana with the location of New Orleans marked by a little cocktail glass like the one in Liquor's logo. He only tried them on so he could say he had, but they embraced his tired feet like a pair of pneumatic leather cushions. Rickey had never known shoes could feel like this. He was used to his feet feeling as if someone had been pounding on their soles with a hard rubber mallet. Today they barely hurt at all. He no longer cared what the boots looked like, and anyway you couldn't see the shape of Louisiana once he pulled his pants cuffs down.

He thought things had turned out more or less all right. The steak had been the turning point. The morning after his drunken debacle with Coop, Rickey awoke in a mood as black as any he could remember. He left the hotel and drove aimlessly around the city, half-tempted to hightail it to the airport and catch the next flight home. His mind kept repeating the words *ten grand, ten grand, ten grand,* but it wasn't even the money that was really keeping him here; it was his pride. He'd be damned if he was going to slink away, to let Coop think he'd been driven away. Several times he was tempted to call G-man and tell him the whole story. He probably would have if he'd had his cell phone with him, but he still hadn't replaced it. Instead he decided to have lunch, and pulled into the parking lot of a restaurant, some upscale steakhouse he'd vaguely heard of.

I hate Dallas, he thought as he scanned the menu. The city's tastes were aggressively pedestrian; its weather was disgusting; it had no seasonal ingredients. He glared around the restaurant, which was crowded. Steak, steak, steak, that was all they wanted. He knew he wasn't being fair; there was a greater variety of ethnic food here than in New Orleans, and very likely a vibrant fine-dining scene, but it seemed that to make real money you had to have a steakhouse. He didn't even particularly like steak, didn't know why he had stopped here. His curiosity was mildly piqued by a prime bone-in ribeye dry-aged forty-five days, and he ordered it even though it was very expensive. He'd never had meat aged that long, or even seen it for sale.

"Betcha like that cooked medium-rare," said the waitress.

"How'd you know?"

She nodded at his check pants. "I see you're a cook. You know better'n to mess up such a nice steak by ordering it medium or well-done."

"I wouldn't order *any* steak medium or well-done."

"Well, this isn't just any steak. You're gonna think you never tasted beef before. Like some potatoes with it?"

"Sure. You got Lyonnaise?"

"No, but we got Taters'n'Onions."

"That's fine," said Rickey, surrendering.

The steak arrived at the table sizzling, drenched in butter, nearly as big as his head. What had he been thinking? He should have just stopped at one of the little Mexican holes-in-the-wall. Sighing, Rickey cut off a slice of steak and put it in his mouth.

Oh my fucking God.

The complex flavors of aged beef seemed to fill his entire world; he was scarcely aware of the clashing silverware, ringing cell phones, and bragging conversations around him. First was the beef taste he knew, with its elements of iron and carbon, deeper than usual but still familiar. Following that was an almost cheesy flavor—not unpleasant, but rather like a good Parmigiano-Reggiano when it started to get old and grainy. The two layers melded to form an overwhelming sensory experience of meat. How could this be? He'd eaten beef thousands of times, yet this was like the first time he had tasted foie gras or the sharp, briny oysters of the Pacific Northwest, so different from the sweet, fat Gulf oysters he'd grown up eating. He could tell that a taste-memory was encoding itself in his brain, something he would turn over and over and eventually try to repeat.

"This is what they have, dammit," he muttered to himself. "This is what they do best, so they think it's all they want, just like we think all we want is gumbo and fried shrimp and redfish with goddamn lump crabmeat on top."

Though New Orleans was his womb and the place that had shaped him, Rickey knew that in many ways it was a backward food city no matter how much tourists romanticized it and locals defended it. Unfamiliar ethnic cuisines and chefs trying to cook outside the Creole box had trouble finding a foothold. A chef who announced his dislike of crawfish to Chase Haricot was ostracized. Most people were willing to at least try something new, but a sizable and vocal minority of the New Orleans dining public saw the old-line restaurants as their temples, other restaurants as Sodom and Gomorrah. As those people felt about their eternal seafood gumbo, so Dallas felt about steak and the cuisine surrounding it. That was what tasted best to them; that was what they were willing to spend money on. Rickey knew all Dallas diners couldn't be like this, but Frank Firestone wanted to reach the ones who were. God knew why, that was his target audience, and reach them he would with Rickey's help.

He went to Firestone's and worked the dinner shift without incident. He and Coop kept their communication to a bare minimum, all to do with putting out the food. The kitchen was even busier than last night and they didn't have much time to be uncomfortable. Rickey made a few more specials but didn't do anything radical yet. The plan was still taking shape in his head.

After work he went straight back to the hotel and stayed up for hours making notes. He called Frank Firestone several times, running ideas past him. Firestone was enthusiastic about everything. At one point Rickey was tempted to call home and have G-man fax him several pages from a Vietnamese cookbook describing a traditional meal of beef cooked seven ways, but by now it was three A.M. and they didn't have a fax machine at the house. Instead he relied on his memory and his taste.

The next day he called a kitchen meeting. Since business had picked up so much, all the cooks were working tonight. They stood leaning against the stainless steel countertops regarding Rickey with what he couldn't help but see as skepticism: Flaco with his impassive turtle face, Sugar half-scowling, Diego and Hubie goofing off, occasionally erupting in uncomfortable giggles. And Coop. It was strange to be in a kitchen where he had no allies.

"Y'all think Firestone is a big cheeseball," he told them. "Maybe he is, but you're lucky to be working for somebody who doesn't mind spending money to make money. How many places have you worked where management expected you to make great food out of crappy ingredients? You don't have to do that here. Your food costs are through the roof and he doesn't care. He'll buy you all the beautiful ingredients you want as long as you can get customers to eat them."

Rickey glanced at Coop, who was leaning against the reach-in with his arms folded across his chest. He gazed back at Rickey with the barest hint of a smirk, or maybe that was just Rickey's paranoia.

"You been making gorgeous food, but do you ever think of your market? I didn't really understand it until I got here. I had a plan that might've worked in New Orleans, but I threw it out. We need a plan that works for Dallas, and what works here is beef."

"You're turning Firestone's into a steakhouse?" said Coop.

"I looked up steakhouses in the phone book," said Rickey, evading the question for now. "I counted about fifty before I quit looking. Probably the city could support one more, but what would be the point? Steakhouses are institutions. They're like clubs—everybody has his favorite and nobody likes an upstart. Am I wrong?"

"No, but what's your point?" said Coop.

"My point is, you've got access to some of the best beef in the country, maybe the world, and there's hardly any on your menu. Coop, you came up in the seventies and eighties, when America's ideas about food were getting completely overhauled. It's not like that any more. People know a lot more about food and they know what they like. I came up in the nineties in New Orleans, which isn't exactly on the forefront of any culinary revolution, so I'm not interested in iconoclasm." Rickey hoped he had pronounced the word right. He'd actually stopped at a bookstore and looked it up in a dictionary to make sure it meant what he thought it meant, but he had never used it in conversation before.

"You're interested in giving people what they want."

"Well, yeah. And I don't see the point in making it sound like some kinda cop-out. It's food. It's basic. It's emotional. I love giving people something they didn't *know* they wanted and having them realize they like it, but I'm not interested in making them eat a bunch of weird shit. And as good as your food is, I gotta say that's exactly what you've been doing."

Coop laughed, though there wasn't much humor in it. "Making them eat weird shit, huh?"

"Yeah. And I'm not even saying you have to stop. I'm saying that in order to get away with it, you need a unifying theme."

"A gimmick, you mean. Like yours."

"A gimmick if that's what you want to call it, but not like mine." Rickey refused to be offended; he was on a roll. "New Orleans loves liquor. That wouldn't work here—sure, people like to drink, but it's not a unifying theme. You need a Dallas gimmick. But Firestone wants to think he's running a cutting-edge restaurant, so you also need something a little unusual. My idea is to promote the place as a global palace of beef."

Hubie giggled, but Rickey barely glanced at him. "I know that probably sounds stupid at first, but you won't believe how much you can get away with as long as you've got that one comfortable ingredient people can grab on to. An all-beef menu—Firestone might even do an in-your-face ad campaign, like 'If you don't want beef, don't eat here.' You feature really good-quality meat—lots of prime, dry-aged for the recipes that merit it—and make great beef dishes from around the world. I did a real rough menu."

"Do you know how much prime *costs*?" said Sugar, sounding more awed than combative.

"Like I said, Firestone's willing to pay for quality. He also realizes he can use the concept to get some publicity. I've suggested changing the name of the restaurant from Firestone's to Prime, and I think he's gonna go for it.

"Now, I don't know how the Dallas market likes veal. We sell the shit out of it in New Orleans, so I can write you up some recipes if you want, but for now I've just done the beef." Rickey began handing out copies of his menu.

Poppy Z. Brite

PRIME
(*formerly* FIRESTONE'S)

NEW BEEF MENU

Beef Wellington app

Thai spring rolls with beef, lemongrass & peanuts

Ethiopian kitfo (beef tartare) with tomato-jalapeño relish

Wagyu beef sashimi with white radish & scallions

Indonesian beef saté with coconut-chile dipping sauce

Beef short ribs braised in Belgian beer

Fennel seed–cured beef tamales with caramelized fennel marmalade

Bolognese beef ravioli with Parmigiano and candied pumpkin

Côte de Boeuf Rossini with roasted vegetables

*Hazelnut-crusted Wagyu beef filet with
roasted garlic and kirsch glaçage*

Osso buco with mushroom-Gorgonzola risotto

Beef stew à la Bourguignonne (or in winter, pot au feu)

Korean stir-fried beef with kimchee and smoked oysters

Bone-in ribeye with chocolate–pumpkinseed molé

Teriyaki beef with roasted broccolini and almonds

*Vietnamese beef seven ways
(sesame-beef salad with shrimp crackers, beef fondue and
Asian herbs in rice paper, braised beef in coconut sauce,
beef roasted in lotus leaves, beef and shrimp sausages on
sugarcane skewers, shredded beef with black rice and
coral sea salt, beef consommé with rice noodles)*

They all stood scanning it. No one spoke.

"I figure y'all will probably want to add some Mexican and Southwestern dishes," Rickey said. "I don't know a whole lot about that style, so I'll leave it up to you."

The silence stretched out to uncomfortable lengths.

"It'd be real nice if somebody said something."

"I didn't know you were into fusion," said Coop. "I wouldn't have expected that of you."

"It's not fusion! These are traditional dishes. Some of the menu descriptions make them sound more accessible, but I didn't fuck with the cuisines."

"Ah," said Coop. "I must have missed all that coral sea salt they use in traditional Vietnamese cooking."

"Coop, for God's sake, you're gonna be getting fifty-sixty bucks a head for those seven dishes. You can add a few upscale touches without compromising the food."

"Firestone likes this idea, huh?"

"Yeah," said Rickey. "He does."

"Well, then, why are we even bothering to discuss it?"

Coop folded the menu, tucked it into his apron pocket, and walked off. The other cooks stood gazing at Rickey, a semicircle of motionless faces and eyes that were not quite hostile, but were definitely ready to be. Rickey knew whatever he said now would determine how seriously he'd be taken for the rest of the week.

"Do you want to keep working here?" he asked them. "I know Coop thinks this concept is bullshit. Some people in New Orleans think my restaurant is bullshit, but it did six hundred fifty thousand dollars in sales last year. Ten percent profit. If Frank Firestone doesn't start seeing numbers like that, he's gonna close this place and you can kiss your easy-ass jobs goodbye."

"You think this menu can give us numbers?" said Flaco, surprising Rickey with his more-or-less perfect English. Apparently he could speak it when he wanted to.

"I think so," Rickey said honestly. "You can't ever know for sure what'll catch on, but I know how customers like to latch on to a gimmick. And I know how a good gimmick can set you free."

"He's right," said Sugar. "I've been cooking in Dallas restaurants for almost ten years now. I think people will eat this shit up."

At that moment, Rickey decided he liked Sugar more than he'd thought at first. She was no great cook, but her bluntness appealed to him.

So they ordered the ingredients and implemented the menu. Firestone announced the name change to the local food press and ordered a neon sign depicting a glowing red steak superimposed over a globe of the world. A few of the more strenuously ethnic items seemed to puzzle diners, but overall it was a big hit. By the end of Rickey's stay in Dallas the restaurant was booked solid for the next week, and that was without any advertising of the new menu, just word of mouth. When he met with Firestone to tie up loose ends and give his final recommendations, he didn't advise firing anyone. After what had felt like a pretty shaky start, the consulting gig was a success.

"Rickey's a one-trick pony," he'd overheard Coop telling Sugar one day when they thought he was in the walk-in. "He came up with a good gimmick in New Orleans, and I suppose he thinks that's all you have to do anywhere, just take one bullshit ingredient and build a menu around it."

"Aw, you're just a bitter old man," Sugar had replied with her usual tact. "I'm looking forward to having some damn customers for a change."

She didn't know the half of it. Rickey was glad Coop had pushed things too far that drunken night; it had given Rickey the ruthlessness he needed to destroy Coop's vision for the restaurant and build a new one in its place. If they had stayed friendly, the job might not have been nearly as successful.

He'd earned the ten grand, Rickey thought as he took off the hideous, comfortable boots and put them in a gray plastic tray to be shuttled through the X-ray machine. Prime was on its way to being a hot ticket. If he had a niggling feeling that he had taken a world-class restaurant and turned it into a trendy gimcrack, he ignored it. So Coop had made him that one perfect meal. What good was perfect food if nobody showed up to eat it?

Rickey pondered this culinary koan all the way back to New Orleans, but when his plane touched down at Louis Armstrong International, he still didn't know the answer.

Poppy Z. Brite

14

The day Rickey was due home, G-man got a call at the restaurant. "You probably want to talk to Rickey," he said when the caller asked for the chef. "He's out of town right now, but he might be in tonight. Or you can catch him tomorrow for sure."

"Nah, dawg, you the one I want. This is Dirty King. I met you at N-Word's party the other night. You was telling me you felt like bologna sitting on the plate with foie gras."

"Sure," said G-man, remembering what Terrance had told him about the sleek young man on the porch. A couple of years ago, talking to a rap mogul who owned an airplane would have fazed him, but he had grown used to rich fuckers. "Made myself hungry. I had to fix a bologna sandwich when I got home."

"You fry it in a skillet?"

"No, just raw."

"Try it hot sometime. Throw it in a pan and fry it till it humps up. Then fry the bread and slap it together with a little mayonnaise. It's real good like that."

"I bet. So, look, you just called to exchange recipes or what?"

"Nah, actually I got a favor to ax you." Dirty King hesitated. When he spoke again, he sounded almost shy. "It's my parents' thirtieth anniversary tonight, and I dropped the ball. Meant to make a reservation somewhere real nice and forgot all about it. I wondered maybe if I brought 'em in, you could give 'em the special treatment."

"Well, sure. But I gotta tell you, dude, it's the middle of the summer. Slow season. You could probably get in somewhere fancier if you wanted."

"Aw, all those old-line dinosaur places . . . I don't know. My folks ain't Creole or nothing. They just good churchgoing ghetto folks. I rather bring 'em someplace I know they'll get treated right."

"Sure," G-man said again. He made a note of a VIP reservation for seven-thirty and hung up, shaking his head at the intricacy of race identifications and relations in New Orleans. Many light-skinned black people from old families referred to themselves as Creole, and often held high positions in city government and business. There was even supposed to be something called a grocery bag test, in which the person tore off a piece of a brown grocery bag and held it up to his arm. If his arm was lighter than the bag, he could call himself a Creole. G-man had never heard anyone admit to doing this, but in school he had known plenty of kids who bragged about being "light" or "red," and plenty of darker ones who caught shit for their color.

What would Dirty King and his parents most like to eat? King had expressed a fondness for mackerel, so G-man ordered some from his seafood guy. Because he'd been thinking about Creoles, he decided to serve it grilled with a spicy Creole tomato marmalade. Creole tomatoes had nothing to do with Creole people—the moniker described big tomatoes grown in the rich alluvial soil of southeast Louisiana—but the two things formed a sort of pun in his mind. It wasn't something he could have explained to most people, but Rickey would understand it. He wondered when Rickey would get home. His plane was supposed to land around five. G-man had wanted to pick him up at the airport, but Rickey said it was too close to dinner and he'd take a taxi to the restaurant.

G-man had gotten through the week better than he'd expected

Poppy Z. Brite

to. Had no choice, really, but he was proud of himself for not letting his mood sink too low. Being busy with the restaurant had helped. When Rickey called home, G-man was pleased to be able to tell him everything was going smoothly. It wasn't that Rickey hadn't trusted him to run the place, G-man knew. On the surface of it, Rickey trusted him completely. But in his secret heart, Rickey just knew Liquor would crash and burn in his absence, and it would be good for him to see that this was not the case.

Dinner service had already begun and they were having an early rush when one of the waiters told him, "Rickey just got here. He said for you to come back to the office when you get a chance."

"OK, thanks," said G-man, a sense of relief and happiness warming him. Just as Rickey had "known" there would be a disaster in his absence, G-man hadn't truly believed Rickey would get home safely until this very moment. He finished what he was doing, then asked Tanker to take over his station for a few minutes and left the line.

"Hey, sweetheart!" Rickey said as G-man came into the office. G-man kicked the door shut and grabbed him. They kissed once, twice, three times, then just stood hanging on to each other, surprised by the intensity of their reunion. It *had* been more than a decade since they'd spent a night apart, G-man reflected; they were entitled to a little intensity.

"Wow," said G-man. "Damn, I missed you."

"I missed you too. It was like being on another planet."

"Did anything bad happen?"

"No. Sort of. I don't know. I'll tell you all about it later."

They let go of each other, and G-man noticed Rickey's feet for the first time. "Dude!" he said in horror. "What are you *wearing*?"

"Goddamn it! Not you too. People looked at them funny in the airport, and the cabdriver thought I was some kinda oilman."

"Well," said G-man doubtfully, "they're very . . . unusual." He bent and pulled up Rickey's pants cuff a little, exposing the shape of Louisiana and the martini glass marking New Orleans. "Real unusual."

"I know they're hideous," Rickey admitted. "But they're *so fucking comfortable*. You gotta try 'em on later—you'll want your own pair."

"I don't know about that. You're not gonna wear 'em in the kitchen, are you?"

"Jeez, no. You think I want the crew calling me Tex or something worse? Kinda wish I could, though. Anyway, what we got going on tonight?"

"Nothing much," said G-man. He knew that if he told Rickey about Dirty King and his folks coming in, Rickey would insist on staying to help. Rickey looked pretty fried; he needed a night to relax and not think about restaurants. Besides, G-man wanted to look after the party himself. He felt slightly proprietary about Dirty King.

"You want me to stay?"

"No, why don't you go home and get some rest? We got it under control."

They'd more or less disentangled from each other, but now G-man grabbed Rickey and kissed him again. "I'd rather know you're waiting for me," he said. "It really sucked coming home to that empty bed every night."

"You got it," Rickey laughed. He picked up his suitcase and started to leave, his boot heels making a racket on the tile floor.

"Hey!"

"What?"

"You got paid?"

Rickey pulled a check out of his pocket and waved it in G-man's face. "Ten cool G's, G," he said. "And I earned every fucking penny."

Dirty King picked up his fork and cut into his piece of grilled mackerel. The perfectly crisped skin split, releasing a savory little puff of steam. He put a piece in his mouth and followed it with some of the Creole tomato marmalade, which was sweet and sour with a subtle underlying burn.

Poppy Z. Brite

Across the table, his mother was eating her pecan-crusted drum, his father cutting into a thick ribeye steak cooked medium-well. Dirty had tried to convince them to order more adventurously, suggesting the foie gras appetizer and the quail entrée special, but his father just said, "I didn't grow up eating cat food and I'm not gonna start now."

"And look what they want for that foie gras!" his mother said. "Twelve dollars for a little piece of liver, ummm-ummm."

"Momma, it don't matter. I'm rich."

"It *does* matter," she said with an air of finality, tucking her napkin into the lap of her suit. She was wearing one of her church suits, bright purple with matching shoes and earrings. He'd tried to take her shopping numerous times, buy her something a little less Sunday-morning-in-the-hood, but the rigorously color-coordinated suits and pant sets were all she ever wanted. He supposed anything more tasteful would make her seem to be putting on airs in front of her friends.

He didn't really care what they ate or how they dressed, though, as long as they enjoyed themselves. He would never forget his tenth birthday celebration. A budding gourmand even then, he had begged to visit Escargot's at the Hotel Bienvenu, God alone knew why—possibly he had read something about it or heard a teacher mention it. In his addled kid-brain it had become the epitome of fine dining. His folks turned their pockets inside out to take him there. The food was good, or at least it had seemed all right to his uneducated palate, but he and his brother and parents were treated with a casual, annihilating disdain by the front-of-the-house staff. He would never forget the skeptical surprise on the waiter's face when his father asked for the wine list, which had conspicuously not been offered, or the way the check had come immediately after the entrées without anyone asking if they wanted dessert. It hadn't been because they were black, Dirty knew—there were plenty of rich New Orleanians of all colors, and plenty more well-heeled black tourists. Rather, it was because they seemed poor, because they were obviously unused to white tablecloths and leather-covered menus. They had been marked as hicks at the door, declared unworthy.

As young Dirty—then still known as Little Claudius, or sometimes L.C.—tried to find the restroom, he lost his way and found himself in a dank hall that ran behind the kitchen. A middle-aged, light-skinned black man in chef's whites was leaning against the wall smoking a cigarette. The man gazed at him for a moment, then tipped him a long, solemn wink.

"Can you please tell me where the bathroom at?" said Little Claudius, groping for his manners and losing his grammar in the process.

"Back out that door and to the right," said the cook, pointing with his cigarette. "How you liked your food?"

"It was real good."

"Some of our shit ain't too bad. How them penguin-suit motherfuckers treatin you up front?"

The boy thought about it, then decided this man would not appreciate tact. He shook his head.

"What I expected. You know the big asshole showed you to your table? The one looks kinda like Frankenstein if he was constipated for two-three weeks?"

Giggling, Little Claudius nodded.

"He snorts a lotta cocaine. They don't pay him enough to feed his habit, so you know what he does? Sells his motherfuckin shoes to the waiters whenever he needs extra cash. That little fag waiting on y'all done bought five or six pair already, even though he keep complainin that they smell."

"I gotta go," Little Claudius said nervously, overwhelmed by these revelations. But all the way to the restroom, and back at the table, he felt as if he'd glimpsed another, truer world. The snotty host and waiter no longer seemed powerful. He almost laughed when the waiter brought their change to the table, imagining the furtive exchange of crumpled money and used, odiferous shoes.

Poppy Z. Brite

That anonymous cook had changed his life. He still loved upscale restaurants, but no maître d' or server had ever been able to intimidate him again.

He still felt protective of his parents, though. They had tried to give him what he wanted and suffered embarrassment for it. He hadn't dared tell them about the cook or the shoes. Tonight he wanted them to have a perfect experience, and he hadn't trusted any of the restaurants he usually frequented to provide it. Liquor had risen to the occasion better than Dirty dared hope. The host seated them at a prime table decorated with a bouquet of green and silver balloons. The waiter brought them complimentary glasses of champagne and the kitchen sent out an array of *amuses-bouche*. His parents only nibbled most of these, but he knew they were impressed by the gesture.

"This is real good, Claudius," his father said as he cut another piece of overcooked meat. "Believe it might be the best restaurant meal I ever had. You say you know the chef here?"

"I sure do," said Dirty. He looked up from his plate and saw a familiar figure heading for their table. "In fact, here he comes now."

In his monogrammed white jacket, G-man looked taller and more confident than the young man Dirty remembered meeting at the party. His disheveled hair was tucked beneath a tall white paper hat, and his eyes were no longer hidden behind dark glasses (though from his painful-looking squint, Dirty guessed he must need the glasses). He shook hands with the three of them, bowing a little over Dirty's mother's hand as he enveloped it between his two hard, muscly palms. "How y'all liked your meals?"

"Oh, it's all wonderful," said Mrs. King. "I'm still picking at this nice piece of fish."

"Sorry. I tried to time it so I'd get out here after you finished eating, but I'm not used to this. My partner usually makes the rounds. I haven't been out here in so long, I had to get one of the waiters to point me toward the dining room."

"Well, we're happy to see you," said Mr. King in a voice as magnanimous as any Dirty had ever heard him use. "Everything was delicious. I thought it'd be nothing but fancy-schmancy slop. Good to see you got a few things a man wants to eat."

"Dad . . ."

"No, I know what you mean," said G-man, and Dirty, who spent far too much time around posturing fools looking for the next reason to be offended, suddenly liked him even better. "I got nothing against fancy-schmancy slop myself, but when you've seen one salad stacked into a tower, you've pretty much seen 'em all. Sometimes you just want a big old steak."

"Exactly. Young man's got a good head on his shoulders."

"Handsome too," said Mrs. King.

"Calm yourself, woman."

G-man's eyes met Dirty's, and they shared a silent half-humorous moment of perfect understanding: *Parents, what can you do?*

They exchanged a few more pleasantries, and then G-man said, "Well, I'll let you finish up in peace. Thanks so much for coming in. Oh, and happy anniversary. It's great to see people stay together for a change."

"You're not from one of those broken homes, are you?" Mrs. King asked. Divorce was a particular hobbyhorse of hers.

"No ma'am. My folks been married forty-five years this past May."

"My goodness," she said approvingly.

Dirty stopped G-man as he was about to leave the tableside and handed the chef his card. He had written his private cell phone number on the back, something he almost never did. The few people who did have the number, aside from his closest friends and colleagues, were mostly chefs. He loved being in the music business and wouldn't trade his life for anything, but something about these white-garbed, flame-retardant figures had always seemed impossibly cool to him. Their burn-weals and knife-scarred fingernails, their tattoos and heat-roughened skin, the way the hair got seared off their ropy forearms—it was a hard life, and there wasn't even any real money in it unless you were somebody like Lenny

Duveteaux. Dirty admired people who put themselves in the fire for the sheer hell of it. He supposed he had never really gotten over the effect of that lone cook at the Hotel Bienvenu.

He shook G-man's hand again, then bumped knuckles with him. "I owe you one, dawg," he said. "Call me if you ever need to collect."

"I just don't know," said Rickey. "Did I do the right thing, or did I fuck it up?"

They were lying in bed with most of the lights off; only a small green-shaded lamp in the corner illuminated the room. He had told G-man everything, from Coop's amazing tasting menu to the steak that had changed his whole perception of the city, from Firestone's cheerful sleaziness to Coop's drunken fingers brushing the small of his back, from yelling at Sugar to facing the circle of cooks with his new menu. He wasn't sure he should have shared all these details, but he had always told G-man everything. He couldn't imagine any other way of living.

"Well, you fucked up Stark's menu," said G-man. "But, I mean, that's what you were hired to do. Firestone wanted you to turn the place into a hot new restaurant. He wanted you to create buzz. From what you told me, you sure as hell did that."

"I guess. No, I know it. I did create buzz. The place was empty when I got there and packed when I left. But Firestone wanted me to help Coop figure out how to cook for Dallas. He didn't hire me to just implement a whole new menu whether Coop liked it or not, and he sure didn't hire me to change the name of the restaurant."

"Did Firestone like your menu?"

"Oh God. He fucking loved it."

"Then you did your job. If Stark doesn't like it, he can quit."

"He told me he can't. He said he feels trapped there because he's got a free place to live."

"So let him give up the apartment. Maybe he has to live at the Y for a while or something. It won't kill him."

Rickey wondered. Coop's pride had already seemed so damaged, but he'd just begun to salvage it, talking about going to Spain and all. Having to live at the YMCA might finish him off. Or maybe he'd get laid there and calm down a little; Rickey had heard things about the Y. At any rate, though G-man had a generous heart, Rickey supposed it was futile expecting him to feel much sympathy for Cooper Stark.

"It's just," he said, and stopped.

"It's just what?"

"It's just that I think it was a better restaurant when I got there than when I left. That's not a good feeling."

"But nobody ate there."

"No, they didn't," Rickey admitted.

"What good is a great restaurant if nobody eats there?"

This was exactly what Rickey had asked himself on the plane, but he hadn't repeated it to G-man. The fact that G-man mentioned it anyway made him feel a little better. Maybe he had done the right thing after all. He rolled over and pushed his face into G-man's shoulder. "I don't want to talk about it any more right now," he said.

"Fine with me. You sleepy or what?"

"Hell, no."

"Good."

15

Oscar De La Cerda and Woofer Scagliano were having lunch at a popular restaurant on Burgundy Street. They made an odd pair. Woofer was thin and neat, his suit worn at the elbows but well-pressed. De La Cerda was big and sloppy, his hair a little too long, his mustache always in need of trimming, his jacket frequently bearing evidence of a Lucky Dog or a roast beef po-boy with gravy. Nevertheless, they had been friends since their law student days at Tulane, and like most New Orleanians, their favorite social activities were eating and talking about eating (in that order).

The fact that Woofer's boss was now gunning for De La Cerda's most lucrative client and De La Cerda was gunning for Woofer's boss's job in no way affected their friendship. Their ostensible opposition had perhaps brought them even closer, because now there were more favors to be traded. As in the restaurant scene, everybody at the courthouse knew one another and bitter professional rivals were often private friends. New Orleans was a very small town in some ways, and while clients and jobs would come and go, an ally at the courthouse was a blessing forever.

Before he decided to throw his hat in the DA ring, De La Cerda had often tried to convince Woofer to join him in private practice.

Woofer had always refused, citing his belief that he was doing something positive for the city. "It's not possible to do anything positive with Tricker Treat in office," De La Cerda was saying now. "Guy's poison. He's poisoned the DA's office, he'll poison your career."

"Nonsense," said Woofer in his prissy way. "Several of his former ADAs are successful attorneys, magistrates—one's even a federal judge."

"Yeah, and what about the one who's in the nuthouse for setting fire to his law office?"

"Let's not get into that. You know very well that Torchy Stepanovic had emotional problems long before he went to work for Placide."

"Which I'm sure Tricker did his best to exacerbate."

"He hates that nickname, you know."

"I know. That's why I use it." De La Cerda glanced down at the empty table, then looked around for their waiter, whom they hadn't seen in over fifteen minutes. He flagged down a different waiter rushing by with a tray of dirty water glasses. "Excuse me," he said in a tone that made it clear he didn't think he needed an excuse. "Would you ask our waiter if he can get our drinks out pretty soon? It's gotta be half an hour since we ordered them."

"I'm sorry, sir," said the waiter in a tone that made it clear he wasn't. "We have a big party upstairs and we're a little over-whelmed right now."

"Overwhelmed," De La Cerda repeated. "I see. Well, would you ask the chef if he can send out our appetizers? I need to get some-thing on my stomach."

"I'm sure she'll get to your order as soon as she can," said the waiter, and made his escape.

"*She?*" said De La Cerda. "You brought me to a restaurant where the chef is a *she*? You know how I feel about that."

"Actually, Oscar, I don't. But I have no doubt you'll tell me."

"Women can do home cooking just fine," said De La Cerda with the air of a professor beginning a cherished lecture. "They can sling hash, and I guess they can cook Italian food and stuff like that. But they're genetically unsuited for a fine-dining environment."

"That's not only sexist, it's ridiculous."

"No it's not! No-Woofer-it-is-not." De La Cerda poked at the tablecloth with his nail-bitten forefinger. "Men have been cooking haute cuisine for centuries. They're hard-wired for it. They understand that it requires ruthlessness. Women aren't ruthless."

"You should run that theory past your ex-wife sometime. I seem to recall she was pretty ruthless about that beach house in Bay St. Louis."

"That wasn't ruthlessness, that was just pure selfishness. Totally different thing. To be ruthless, you gotta have a streak of cruelty. Women can be mean as hell, but they aren't really cruel."

"Ridiculous," Woofer said again as their waiter appeared and set two plates before them. In the center of each plate's vast white expanse was a sad little heap of food: a few microgreens, a triangle of phyllo, and something shredded. "Drinks!" De La Cerda shouted at the waiter's retreating back, but the waiter gave no sign of having heard.

De La Cerda poked cautiously at his appetizer, then took a bite. "I knew we should've gone to Galatoire's," he said around the meager mouthful.

"Don't be silly. This rabbit confit is a specialty of the house, and I think it's very good."

"I never have liked rabbit. They're too damn cute. What kind of bastard wants to eat the Easter Bunny?"

"Wouldn't cooking it qualify as ruthless, then?"

"No, just mean."

"I give up," said Woofer.

The long-sought drinks arrived at the table. De La Cerda took a sip of his vodka martini and said, "I *knew* they wouldn't make it with Stoli like I told them. I *knew* they'd give me some crappy well brand. I hate this place."

"Do you want to send it back?"

"Hell, no. Took me long enough to get it the first time."

"You shouldn't be drinking at lunch anyway," said Woofer, who had ordered iced tea.

"Drinking? What do you mean? I'm not drinking. This is a single. I'm just having *one drink*. Are you sure you're from New Orleans?"

"Born and raised, as you know. I simply don't think it's necessary to perpetuate the decadence."

"Yeah, yeah, you're like those people who want to clean up the Quarter so much that the tourists won't want to go there any more. They gonna be in Disneyland anyway, they may as well go to the one with Mickey Mouse and roller coasters."

"But no strippers," Woofer pointed out.

"People like you get their way, pretty soon we won't have strippers either."

"I have no interest in putting the ecdysiasts out of work. I confess they don't do for me what they seem to do for your most lucrative client, but they're entitled to make a living."

"Sure they are." De La Cerda had always wondered if Woofer was gay, but didn't like to come right out and ask. "Yeah, Lenny likes his strippers. Course he might not be able to afford them much longer, what with your boss trying to put him out of business and all."

"How was your rabbit?"

"Terrible," said De La Cerda, who had finished it in three bites. "I was hungry, but it gave me no pleasure. Don't try to change the subject. How's Tricker coming along with his case against Lenny?"

"You know I can't tell you anything about that."

"He's listening to all those tapes himself, isn't he? I bet he won't let anybody else touch them. Just nod if I'm right."

"Oh, look, here come our entrées," Woofer said brightly, though he was still finishing his appetizer.

"I hate the service here," said De La Cerda when the waiter had set down the plates and left the table. "They take forever to bring you anything, and then they rush it out all at once. Fucker practically snatched your appetizer plate away so he'd have somewhere to put your entrée. I bet that lady chef is back there crying her pretty little eyes out because she can't handle the rush."

"God, you're offensive."

"I aim to please," De La Cerda said obscurely, taking a bite of his sweetbreads in orange-rosemary sauce. "Hmmmm," he said, chewing. "Hmmmmmmm."

"Well? What's the verdict?"

"Ambitious."

"That's good, right?"

"Not in this case."

Woofer sighed. "So send it back."

"No, no, I can eat it." De La Cerda speared a pale lobe and chomped on it. Watching him, Woofer felt a little sick. He'd never liked sweetbreads. He took a bite of his salmon with jasmine rice and Hindi spice rub. It wasn't bad, though he didn't quite understand what salmon had to do with Hindus.

"You just like to suffer," he said as De La Cerda ate another sweetbread.

De La Cerda appeared to give the matter fair consideration. "Not exactly," he said at last. "I'd rather have a good meal. But if I gotta have a bad one, it's more fun to bitch about it than to suffer in silence."

"Well, I'm sorry. You pick the restaurant next time."

"Ever been to Liquor?"

"No, and I'm not going. I can see it now. The chef comes to the table, you introduce me, he yanks me out of my chair and punches me in the teeth. I've heard about that guy."

"Rickey?" said De La Cerda. "What have you heard about him?"

"Well, he's kind of a hard case, isn't he? Stabbed a man in the throat with a vegetable peeler."

"What was he supposed to do? Sit there and let the guy shoot him?"

"Of course not. It's just a little intimidating."

"You're a real shark, Woofer."

"I can be a shark when I'm cross-examining a witness. I don't especially want to be one when I'm trying to eat lunch."

"That's reasonable," said De La Cerda, mopping up the last of his orange-rosemary sauce with a hunk of bread. Woofer watched him, feeling a little guilty. He knew Placide Treat was bent on taking down Lenny Duveteaux. Treat had become obsessed with Lenny, and had neglected other, more important cases in his zeal to listen to those tapes. There might not be enough for a conviction, but there was probably enough for an indictment, particularly by a grand jury that had received the Treat treatment. That would mean plenty of billable hours for De La Cerda, but it would also be a series of huge headaches and a difficult, possibly unwinnable case. Woofer knew De La Cerda considered Lenny a friend as well as a client, so it would be a double blow if Lenny actually went to prison.

Privately, Woofer hoped Treat would either retire or lose to De La Cerda in the upcoming election. At one time Woofer had loved working in the DA's office; he had come to the job full of idealistic vigor, and neither the long hours nor the abysmal pay had lessened his determination to help send criminals up the river to cut cane and pick cotton. Over the past couple of years, though, he'd found that he no longer liked working for this particular DA. Megalomania, encroaching senility, or something worse had transformed Treat from an eccentric but capable lawyer into a borderline nutcase. Probably Lenny Duveteaux really was a crook—*certainly* he was—but did Treat really believe his misdeeds merited all this time and effort? The streets of New Orleans were a war zone. Vicious killers walked free every week because the DA's office had neglected to build sufficient cases against them. Just recently a crack dealer who'd knifed his girlfriend to death in front of their twin babies had been released on a technicality: the babies were the only witnesses, and they couldn't testify. How did Lenny Duveteaux's corruption stack up against something like that?

So Woofer secretly hoped Treat would be voted out and De La

Cerda voted in. Maybe De La Cerda would keep him on, allow him to do some good. Maybe Woofer would leave the DA's office altogether. Either way, he was overdue for a change; he'd been spinning his wheels under Treat for far too long.

They passed on dessert, but halfway back to the lot where they'd parked, De La Cerda paused at the door of a sandwich shop. "I know you'll think I'm a fucking pig—" he began.

"Oh, go ahead," said Woofer, who had seen him do this before. As De La Cerda bellied up to the counter and ordered a shrimp po-boy (lettuce, mayonnaise, no tomato), Woofer decided to join him in his decadence for once. They really hadn't gotten enough to eat.

Lenny had found himself Uptown while running errands, so he decided to swing by the little house on Marengo Street. Rickey was just getting up and seemed disinclined to let him in, but Lenny stood on the porch talking about this and that until Rickey finally opened the door all the way. Lenny headed for the kitchen and poured himself a mug of coffee. "Where's G-man?" he asked.

"Went to the drugstore. You wanna move that?" This last referred to Lenny's coffee cup, which Lenny had set down on the cover of a cookbook.

"Sorry. So how'd the consulting gig go?"

"OK, I guess. You know more about consulting than I do. The guy was happy with my ideas and I got paid. Does that mean it went well?"

"Sounds like it. What'd you do for them?"

Rickey described his concept for Prime. Lenny listened with mounting concern. He couldn't believe Rickey had been so short-sighted. Despite their substandard educations, he knew Rickey and G-man weren't stupid, but sometimes they could be incredibly naive. "I thought you were just supposed to redo the menu," he said.

Rickey shot him a look. "I *did* redo the menu."

"No, you gave them a whole goddamn concept. A global palace

of beef. You could've based an entire restaurant around that concept, just like you did with Liquor, but instead you let this hick have it for ten lousy grand. What were you thinking, Rickey?"

"I don't *want* to base an entire restaurant on beef. It doesn't interest me that much. It's a good idea for Dallas, not for here."

"You could've opened a restaurant in Dallas! I would have backed it. It's a great idea—I don't know how you come up with them. Instead you just threw it away!"

"I don't want a fucking restaurant in Dallas! I hate the place!"

"You wouldn't even have to run it!" Lenny yelled. "You just hire the crew, put your name on it, and rake in the money! It's a no-brainer!"

"Well, I guess that's why it appeals to you. I don't want to put my name on a bunch of crappy restaurants. I don't want to spread myself too thin and end up letting my main place go to hell."

"Are you saying that's what I've done?"

"Hey, if the shoe fits," said Rickey, smiling in a particularly infuriating way.

"Then you could've sold the idea to me. I would have paid you more than ten grand for it." Lenny wasn't even sure if this was true; he just wanted to goad Rickey. He wasn't used to losing his temper like this, but Rickey could make him angrier than almost anyone he knew. Rickey still had all the smugness and vehemence of youth, and was right often enough to back it up.

"Well, how the fuck was I supposed to know you wanted it? I was desperate, I felt like I wasn't doing what I'd been hired to do, I needed the ten grand—"

"Why do you need ten grand anyway? Liquor's doing great."

"Because I'm sick of being in your pocket. This is all your fault anyway, Lenny. What if you go to prison? We'd have to—"

"I am not going to prison!"

"Yeah, you just keep telling yourself that, but I'm not taking it for granted. You've had your finger in too many pies. I don't want to depend on your ass forever, cause it just might go up in a sling."

"You little bastard!"

"You sleazy crook!"

Lenny took a halfhearted swing at Rickey, who blocked it, grabbed Lenny's arm, and spun him around. Lenny broke away and came back at him. They wrestled for a couple of minutes, not really wanting to fight each other but neither willing to give in first.

"Well, ain't this a nice sight to come home to!" said G-man, entering the kitchen with a plastic shopping bag in each hand. He set the bags on the counter, seized Lenny and Rickey by the scruffs of their necks, and pulled them apart. They stood there breathing heavily, not sure whether to glare at each other or look embarrassedly at G-man.

"Y'all look like a couple of mangy dogs somebody just threw water on," said G-man. "I'm not even gonna ask what's going on. I figured you'd get into it eventually. Couple of goddamn prima donnas."

Rickey and Lenny started talking over each other. "*I'm* not—"
"Well, *he*—"

"I don't want to hear it. You wanna know the truth, I'm embarrassed for both of you. You two can fuck around all day, but I got work to do. See you at the restaurant, Rickey." G-man turned and walked out of the kitchen. A moment later they heard the front door slam.

"He's not really going," said Lenny. "He wasn't dressed for work."

"We got extra whites at the restaurant," Rickey said miserably. "Now see what you did? You're not satisfied to make me feel shitty about my first consulting gig, you gotta mess up my home life too."

"I'm sorry." Lenny was never able to stay mad for very long, and he guessed he *had* given Rickey a pretty hard time. Even though he'd known the boys would want to leave the nest eventually, it still stung a little. "I really did think that was a good idea about the global palace of beef, though. You could've made a fortune."

"Lenny, don't you understand? I don't need a fortune. I don't want to live like you. I got my restaurant and G, and that's all I really want. I like my life. Can't you respect that?"

"I guess I have to. It's hard, though. I want to see good things happen to you guys, Rickey. I really do—I always have. And in my book, more is better."

"I know. But we're not like that, OK?"

"OK."

Rickey stuck out his hand, and Lenny shook it. When their eyes met, they both started laughing. "You fight like a sissy," said Rickey.

"Hey, I can't help it. I didn't grow up in the hood like you."

"No shit."

"I meant what I said, though—I'm *not* going to prison. I'm sorry you've lost faith in me, but you'll see. I'm going to come out of this smelling like a rose, and Placide Treat will be sorry he ever fucked with me."

"You're probably right, Lenny. I hope so. But I gotta protect my restaurant."

"I understand."

"Speaking of which," Rickey sighed, "I guess I better get over there and face the music. Damn, I wish he hadn't walked in on that."

"He'll be OK. He's seen you acting like an asshole before."

"I know," said Rickey. "I just wish he hadn't seen it quite so often."

G-man made it all the way to the corner of Magazine Street before he started laughing. He pulled over to the curb, leaned his forehead against the steering wheel, and let go. He knew he should be mad—Rickey needed to learn to handle his temper, and Lenny had no business provoking him—but how ridiculous they had looked lumbering around the kitchen like a couple of dancing bears!

An old man passing by peered in at him curiously, then hurried on up the street. G-man imagined what he must look like—a scruffy character sitting alone in a car laughing his fool head off—and that got him started again. He gripped the wheel, closed his eyes, took several deep breaths, and finally got himself under control.

Poppy Z. Brite

He'd have to pretend to be mad when Rickey got to work, he thought as he drove on. Rickey had to get his impulses under control. There was still too much of the Lower Ninth Ward in him, the streets where you had to fight anybody who looked at you the wrong way. Back then it had been dangerous, because a lot of those people had guns, and Rickey had mostly acted sensible. Now his ego got stroked all the time and he knew nobody was going to shoot him if he took a poke at them. G-man still believed Rickey would have kicked Humphrey Wildblood's ass right there in Liquor's dining room if given the chance. Now he was fighting with Lenny, without whose backing they wouldn't even have a restaurant. He needed some perspective.

"Glad you could make it," he said in what he hoped was an icy tone when Rickey showed up in the kitchen.

"This is the same time I always come in. I can't help it if you decided to take off like a bat out of hell and got here ninety minutes early."

"I got work to do."

"So do it." Not quite under his breath, Rickey added, "Fucker." He stomped off to place the seafood order. A few minutes later he was back with a case of onions, which he proceeded to chop into a brunoise so small that two or three pieces would have fit on a match head. Even his knife on the cutting board sounded defensive somehow. G-man kept feeling Rickey's eyes on his back. After thirty minutes of silence, Rickey said in a small voice, "Are you really mad?"

G-man turned to look at him, fully intending to say yes. Instead he pictured Lenny's hairy arms wrapped around Rickey's waist and started laughing again. At first Rickey smiled hopefully; then, as G-man kept glancing at him and going off into fresh gales of laughter, he began to scowl. Finally he demanded, "What's so goddamn funny?"

"You!" G-man gasped. "And Lenny! Waltzing around the kitchen—so retarded—sorry—but oh my God, Rickey, it was hilarious!" He caught his breath, took off his glasses, and wiped his eyes. "Clash of the titans," he concluded, and nearly set himself off again.

"Go ahead and laugh. He took the first swing. I was just defending myself."

"I'm sure you were terrified."

"Yeah, right," said Rickey, beginning to see the humor in it. "Fucking Lenny, trying to tell me I should open a fucking restaurant in Dallas."

"What was it all about anyway? I heard the end of it as I came in, but by the time I got to the kitchen, you two were . . ." G-man looked away in case he got started again. "Uh, fighting."

Rickey explained what Lenny had gotten so upset about. "Huh," said G-man. "He really thinks you sold your idea cheap?"

"I don't care what he thinks. It's embarrassing enough to have my name associated with Prime. I'm not about to whore myself out on a permanent basis."

"No, you shouldn't," said G-man, who wasn't anxious for Rickey to do any more traveling. "It's interesting, that's all. You just pull ideas out your ass, and these big wheels think they're great."

"I don't pull them out my *ass*," said Rickey, a little offended. "I spent a lot of time putting together that beef menu. And Liquor is the product of a lifetime's experience."

"Aw, save it for the food rags. This is me you're talking to."

"Well, you know the extent of my genius better than anybody."

"Uh-huh. You want to talk about the dinner specials, genius, or you got some more rich fuckers to beat up first?"

"We can talk about the specials," said Rickey, resigning himself to a day of G-man's ribbing. It wasn't as if it happened that often, and he supposed he had it coming.

Poppy Z. Brite

16

"Rickey!"

"Yeah, who's this?"

"Frank Firestone here. Didn't wake you, did I?"

"Uh . . . it doesn't matter. How's things in Dallas?"

"Great! Just great. Prime's taking off, new gimmick's getting us all kinds of write-ups and publicity. Sign looks great too, with the steak and the world and all."

"How's the Big D coming along?"

"What's that? . . . Oh, the Big D's finished, all lit up fifty stories high on the TransWorld Communication Tower. How come you to ask about that?"

"I don't know. I guess I'm a little sleepy. Glad to hear things are going good."

"Yeah, just great. I was gonna send you some reviews, but Cooper says he's writing you a letter, he'll stick 'em in the envelope before he sends it."

"He's . . . uh, OK, that's fine."

"All righty then. I'll be talking to you, Rickey. Thanks again."

"Sure . . . bye."

"Who was that?"

"Fucking Frank Firestone."

"What time is it?"

"Seven fucking thirty."

NEW ORLEANS ONLINE DINING FORUM

PRAISE A GREAT MEAL, COMPLAIN ABOUT A BAD ONE, OR
JUST FIND OUT WHO MAKES THE BEST SHRIMP PO-BOY!

Address questions and abuse complaints to moderator@nolaonline.com

ANYBODY HEARD ABOUT THIS? by Coonass
I heard a rumor to the effect that John Rickey, head chef at Liquor, recently did some consulting at a restaurant in Dallas. Anybody know if this is true? :O

RE: ANYBODY HEARD ABOUT THIS? by Jazzmatazz
Yes, it is true!! Chef Rickey designed a new menu based entirely on BEEF! Liquor, beef . . . what's next? "Cob," a restaurant that serves only corn products?

RE: ANYBODY HEARD ABOUT THIS? by YatGourmet
LOL, Jazz! All-beef menu sounds about par for Dallas, tho. That Rickey is one smart cookie!

"SMART COOKIE?" (was: ANYBODY HEARD ABOUT THIS?) by WineSnob
John Rickey is no "smart cookie." He's a callow kid who got lucky with one idea and one rich backer, and obviously thinks he can repeat it ad nauseam. Thank God he has perpetrated this abortion on Dallas and not New Orleans.

RE: "SMART COOKIE?" by Coonass
WineSnob: Liquor is one of my favorite restaurants. De gustibus non disputandum. I'll try the beef place if I am ever in Dallas. ;)

RE: "SMART COOKIE?" by WineSnob
It's not as if Chef Rickey has anything further to be ashamed of here. An all-beef menu is certainly no sillier than the Liquor gimmick. He needs to jettison the gimmick, and possibly the do-nothing partner.

Poppy Z. Brite

"DO-NOTHING PARTNER?" (was: RE: "SMART COOKIE?") by DoctorB

WineSnob, you must be a fly on the wall to know so much about the inner doings of Liquor's kitchen. Unless you've worked in a restaurant yourself, you can't possibly understand the duties of a co-chef or sous chef. Gary Stubbs works hard and contributes a lot to Liquor's menu. Why do you snipe at this restaurant? What's in it for you? What secret hatred gnaws at the core of your scurrilous little heart?

YUCK! (was: RE: "SMART COOKIE?") by ismellfish

Mackerel stinks!

RE: YUCK! by DoctorB

Thanks for reminding me why New Orleans, the "great seafood city," has such a pitiful selection of fresh seafood. I forgot we are duty-bound to fear and loathe anything that doesn't bottom-feed in the bayous or swim in the polluted waters of the Gulf.

AGENDA (was: RE: "DO-NOTHING PARTNER?") by WineSnob

Tsk, tsk, more of your paranoia Doctor B. (And enough with the tired Hunter S. Thompson shtick too.) To employ a colloquialism, "I calls 'em as I sees 'em."

RE: AGENDA by DoctorB

Right. And as Rex issues his Proclamation next Mardi Gras, golden monkeys will fly out of his butt. Selah.

RE: AGENDA by ismellfish

WineSnob = Humphrey Wildblood!

RE: AGENDA by Coonass

ismellfish: You think??? : D

RICKEY SUX! (was: RE: "SMART COOKIE?") by SaintsFan

Everyone knows Liquor is only still in business because of that stupid "Dark Kitchen" book! Plus Rickey is a f**

RE: RICKEY SUX!

SaintsFan: Go crawl back in your slanderous cave!!! >: (

RE: RICKEY SUCKS! by SaintsFan

It's "libel," not "slander," you moron . . . but not if it happens to be true!

Placide Treat, in his office long before the rest of the courthouse complex came to life, picked up his phone and dialed a long-distance number. "Me," he said when his party answered. "You got some information for me? . . . What you mean, they didn't? . . . What you *mean,* he didn't? I thought he promised you he would . . . Well, what you gonna do about it? . . . No, no, I'll get what I need some other way . . . these damn tapes, maybe. Yeah. Awright. Bye-bye, Johnny."

Dear Rickey,

I guess you showed me, huh?

From where I'm standing, your life looks like a dream. You're young, good-looking, and talented, with a successful restaurant and a faithful partner you obviously love a lot. Then you get invited to show up the guy who embarrassed you years ago, when you were an innocent kid and he was on top of the world. He's fool enough to make another pass at you, so you throw him out of your room, then do away with his entire menu and replace it with one that's roughly a thousand times more successful. You become a culinary hero in the eyes of Frank Firestone, a clueless but wealthy man. A lot of people must hate you for living this kind of life and having this kind of luck . . . but I'm not one of them. I hope you left Dallas knowing that.

I believe some people are blessed. Not talking about any big religious thing—just mean that the universe smiles on some people. You're obviously one of them. I used to think I was too, but it has become evident that if I am to have any more blessings, I'll have to go and find them myself. Or make them myself—no longer sure of the difference.

Thought you might like to know that I am actually having a lot of fun with Prime. I admit I thought it was bullshit at

first. Maybe it is, but it's cheerful, accessible bullshit that still leaves room for a lot of creative control. This week, along with several of the dishes you left us, I'm doing a Thai shredded beef salad with lemongrass and bird peppers, a grilled flatiron steak with chimichurri sauce, and a Kobe beef burger with a foie gras center. Not the kind of thing I'm used to, but I think that's good for me. I needed a shakeup in my life. Find myself drinking less and enjoying the job more. I've got you to thank for that . . . so thanks.

I expect to stay at Prime for another year or so, until I save enough money to make a new start somewhere. I think I told you about wanting to go to Spain. May do that . . . or may just get on the road and see where it takes me. I don't know yet; just know I feel excited about life for the first time since 1990 or so.

One last matter: Until I am too old to think about such things, I'll probably be a horndog bastard who spends too much time thinking with his dick. Sorry I did that to you again, but whatever happens, I promise it will be the last time. I do admire you and would like one more crack at being your friend. If you find yourself in Dallas any time over the next 12 months, let's get together. Otherwise, I'd love to hear from you by letter, phone, or e-mail, whichever makes you most comfortable. Would enjoy meeting your partner too. Give me one last chance not to be an asshole, huh?

Whatever you do, thanks again for everything. Keep living the dream.

Coop

Coop:

Yes dammit I showed you and that's the last I ever want to hear of you. You haven't changed since the night I met you and I don't think you ever

Dear Coop,

It's good to hear from you. I really did like your first menu and I was not happy to feel like I ruined it, so I'm glad that

Coop,

My life is not a fucking dream, it is a reality I have worked hard for. You act like you're so happy and impressed by my relationship but do you realize you have never once said or wrote my "partner's" name? It is GARY STUBBS and people call him G-MAN and he is a REAL PERSON

Coop,

I've tried to write 3 different letters and I don't know what the hell to say, whether I'm mad at you or not, whether I want to keep in touch with you or not, why you can still fuck with my head so much when I hardly fucking know you

Dear Coop,

Coop,

Coop

FUCK IT

Rickey hit DEL on his keyboard and watched all his attempts at a reply vanish into the ether, sorry that he didn't even have the satisfaction of crumpling a piece of paper and hurling it into the trash.

Poppy Z. Brite

17

"**Goddamn crotch rot,**" Rickey muttered. He was sitting naked on the edge of the bed, doubled over his lap in a most ungraceful position.

"Why don't you let me help you?" said G-man.

"Because two people shouldn't share *everything*, even if they're in love."

Crotch rot was one of the least glamorous aspects of kitchen work in New Orleans. Rickey didn't know if cooks elsewhere got it, and he wasn't particularly interested in finding out. The heat of the kitchen conspired with the natural summer swelter to produce a painful red rash between the butt cheeks, under the balls, and (in severe cases) halfway down the inner thighs. When you had a nice crop of it going, it felt as if somebody had taken a piece of fine-grained sandpaper to your most tender parts. You walked like a cowboy and could pretty much forget about having any kind of sex life until it went away.

"You never get it because you're so skinny," Rickey accused.

"I've had it before. It's got nothing to do with being skinny. I'm telling you, you ought to switch to boxers." G-man stepped into a pair of blue cotton shorts printed with cartoon images of Mr. Peanut. "They make all the difference."

"I don't like 'em," Rickey said miserably. "I just hate to dangle."

G-man laughed.

"You're real sympathetic."

"I'm sorry, sweetheart. I told you, I'll help you put on the butt paste if you want."

"Forget it." Rickey picked up a yellow plastic tube that bore a picture of a grinning baby and the legend BOUDREAUX'S BUTT PASTE. When another cook had recommended this product years ago, Rickey thought the guy was fucking with him, maybe even making some kind of veiled fag joke. It turned out to be a real product, manufactured across the lake and sold at drugstores all over town. Though it was meant for babies' diaper rash, it had achieved a cult status among local cooks as a treatment for summertime crotch rot.

He dabbed on some of the thick, greasy ointment, wincing at the touch of his own fingers. It stung at first, but soon began to ease the fiery pain.

Woofer Scagliano truly didn't want to go to Liquor, so of course that was exactly where Placide Treat ordered him to have dinner.

"I want you to get the lay of the land," the DA said. "See what kinda place it is, who eats there. Find out does this young fella really run it or is he just another tool of Lenny Duveteaux."

"How am I supposed to find out all that by having dinner?"

"I want you to meet him. Don't let on you work for me. Just see what kinda impression you get."

"I'll probably get an impression of his fist on my nose," muttered Woofer, whose entire opinion of Rickey had been formed by the events in the second half of *Dark Kitchen*. He hated these Boris-and-Natasha errands Treat sent him on. In addition to being humiliating, they took valuable time away from his other cases. Though

Woofer knew he was an effective lawyer when he had the time to be, just lately he was as scattered as his boss.

But of course there was no use arguing with Treat. Woofer said a small prayer for the candidacy of Oscar De La Cerda, then made reservations at Liquor for himself and Linda Getty, a policewoman friend he sometimes took to this kind of thing.

Upon their arrival, he was surprised by how traditional the restaurant looked. He had expected a trendy place, but Liquor's design owed more to the old-line steakhouses and the main dining room at Commander's Palace than to the latest hot Magazine Street bistro. Woofer liked that; trendiness made him uncomfortable.

"You could get drunk just reading about this food," Getty commented as they perused the menu. She was a tall light-skinned black woman with a serious demeanor that suited Woofer's temperament. Several years ago she'd been shot during a hostage situation in the Iberville housing project, and she still walked with a slight limp. Even after the shooting, she caught shit in the department for rumors about her sexuality. She resigned, then reapplied a year later. Now she was a district commander who brooked no shit from anybody, but she still wasn't exactly out of the closet. Occasionally she needed a date for some official function or other, and Woofer never minded filling in. Somewhat more frequently, Getty did the same for him.

Woofer thought of himself as rather like a coat hanger or a shoe tree: he fulfilled his function best in the closet and had no compelling reason ever to leave it. His predilection for young working-class Irish and Italian men had broken his heart on several occasions, but since they tended to dislike flamboyance as much as he did, he had always been able to keep his liaisons discreet. (Woofer himself was Italian, but some long-buried gene in his family tree had given him the coloring of an Irishman; his father always said he must be the only redheaded Scagliano who'd ever lived.) Though he supposed some of his colleagues wondered about him, surely they could see that his job kept him far too busy for marriage and such.

"Well, that's supposed to be the gimmick," he told Getty. "They use liquor in every dish. Perfect concept for New Orleans, isn't it?"

"Yeah, just what we need—encouragement to drink. I have to scrape enough people off the streets of the Sixth District, Woofer. I'm not impressed by cutesy-pie shit like this."

A waiter appeared at their table. "Would you folks like to start with a cocktail?"

"Double Maker's Mark and Coke," said Getty. She saw Woofer looking at her. "What? I'm not driving."

"I'll have a glass of the Gewürztraminer," Woofer decided, eyeing the pitiful wine list. In *Dark Kitchen*, Chase Haricot claimed that Rickey hadn't wanted to serve wine at all, but Lenny Duveteaux had pressured him into it. "Is the chef in the house tonight?"

"Yes, sir."

"I'd like to meet him if possible."

"I'm sure you can." The waiter glanced over his shoulder at the crowded dining room. "Might be a little while, though."

"Of course."

"What's your cover?" said Getty when the waiter had left the table.

"What do you mean?"

"Your cover story. Why are you gonna say you want to meet him?"

"Oh, my pretext." Getty rolled her eyes, but Woofer ignored her. "Well, I was just going to say I'd heard a lot about the restaurant. Maybe pretend to be a tourist."

"Woofer Scagliano, I don't know how you ever get through a day in court. You ain't no damn tourist. You got a accent." Getty had grown up in Treme, one of the blackest and poorest neighborhoods in the city, and it crept into her speech patterns when she was irritated. "You might think you've trained yourself out of it, but anybody with half an ear knows you're a New Orleans boy. Hell, just leave it to me. What are you gonna get?"

"Get?"

She waved the menu under his nose. "What are you ordering?"

"Oh. The ribeye, maybe."

"BO-ring. I'm having the duck with kirshwasser-pickled Rainier cherries and weinkraut."

"What's weinkraut?"

"Got no idea." Getty gave him a brilliant smile. "But I'm always ready to learn."

The waiter's name was Charles, and he had always been a little scared of Rickey. Rickey wasn't mean like some chefs, but he was too intense for Charles's liking.

"I'm not making dining-room rounds tonight," he said, pinning Charles with a death stare. "You shouldn't have told him I would."

"Sorry. He looked like a high-class type. I thought you'd want to know."

"Yeah, God forbid I should go talk to anybody from the lower classes—I only come from them."

"I didn't mean—"

"Course not. Nobody ever *means*."

"C'mon, dude," said G-man from his place at the sauté station. "Just run out there and stop by the guy's table for two seconds. It won't kill you."

"I don't feel like it."

"What's the big problem?"

"MY ASS HURTS!" Rickey shouted. Everyone in the kitchen stopped what they were doing and stared at him. It took him a few seconds to realize what they were probably thinking. "Get your fucking minds out the gutter," he said. "I got a bad case of crotch rot, that's all."

"Film at eleven," said Shake.

"What's crotch rot?" asked Marquis.

Rickey glanced over his shoulder at G-man. "See? You skinny bastards never get it. He doesn't even know what it is."

"Yeah, yeah, I already heard your theory on that. Look, we're slowing down—these guys can handle the rest of the tickets. Let's go out to the dining room together. I'll do most of the talking and you can just stand there looking pretty."

"Fuck you!" said Rickey, but he wiped his hands on a side towel and pushed the bandanna up on his forehead, his usual preparations for making front-of-the-house rounds. "And fuck you too," he said when he saw Charles looking at him.

"I'm sorry! I'm just telling you what the customer wants!"

"He knows it," said G-man. "He's just being a dick. Don't worry about it, Sir Charles."

"Why do you always call me that?"

"Just be glad I don't call you the Round Mound of Rebound."

"You basketball nuts are all alike," said Marquis, who knew what G-man was talking about. "Can't give it up once the season's over."

"Aw, hell, Marquis. I saw you wearing an Iverson jersey last week."

"That's different. It matches my car."

"You really don't know what crotch rot is?" said Shake after Rickey and G-man had left the kitchen.

Marquis shrugged. "Never heard of it. Some kinda sex thing, I guess."

"Nah, man, it's not a sex thing. It's a *heat* thing."

Shake proceeded to describe the condition in lurid detail, and understanding dawned in Marquis's face. "Sure, I get that," he said. "Just ain't ever heard it called crotch rot."

"Well, what do you call it?"

"Taint."

"*Taint?*" Shake repeated. "That's disgusting."

"I guess crotch rot sounds so nice."

"You got a point there."

"Ah, the glamorous life of a chef," said Terrance from his grill station. "If only the diners could hear us now, we'd *never* have to worry about getting too busy."

Poppy Z. Brite

Woofer and Getty were just finishing their entrées. Woofer felt a little thrill of satisfaction as he saw not one but two white-coated chefs approaching his table. He looked up and smiled, intending to greet them politely. But all at once his stomach was in free fall, his heart had begun to rocket in his chest, his tongue was a dry leaf in his mouth, and he couldn't say a word.

"*Hi,*" said Getty, turning that megawatt smile upon them. "The duck was delicious. I'm Linda Getty. Louis Earl Getty is my brother, you may know his name, he writes a column in the newspaper? I don't know if you're aware of it but he's doing a book all about the different styles of barbecue in America. He's been to Texas, Memphis, Kansas City . . . all over the place. In fact, I think he's somewhere in North Carolina right now, but when he heard I was coming here he asked if I'd talk to you, see if maybe you were interested in contributing a recipe. Of course it's mostly going to focus on traditional stuff, but he hopes to have sidebars with recipes from famous chefs. You know . . . sidebars?"

She made a sort of gesture with her hands that Woofer supposed was meant to indicate sidebars, though he had never seen such a gesture before.

"Sure," said Chef John Rickey (as the monogram on his jacket identified him). "I haven't done a whole lot of barbecue, but I got a nice recipe for bourbon-basted pork ribs." He looked a little dazed by Getty's torrent of words, but the idea of contributing a recipe seemed to please him. He matched Getty's smile with one just as gorgeous. Woofer barely noticed it. He was looking at the other chef, whose jacket simply said *G-man*.

This G-man wasn't incredibly handsome—Rickey was better-looking by the usual standards—but he had a demeanor that Woofer found irresistible. It had to do with the way he tucked his chin down and looked at the world from underneath his eyebrows, his dark eyes slightly worried like those of a good dog wondering if he'd done something bad. It had to do with the obvious strength of his long-fingered, scarred hands. It was a certain Irish-Italian length of nose and set of chin, perhaps. It could be blamed on any number of things, but mostly, Woofer had convinced himself within moments, it was just his obvious *kindness* showing through. How could anyone look at this young man and not instantly love him?

"I'm William Scagliano," he said, offering his hand. G-man took it, and Woofer felt his cock twitch in his neat flannel trousers when that callused palm touched his. Getty gave him a hard stare, obviously surprised that he'd used his real name, but Woofer didn't care. So what if Rickey hauled him out of the chair and punched him in the mouth? Right now, even a beating would be bliss.

But neither chef appeared to recognize the name. Not surprising; almost every New Orleanian knew who Placide Treat was, but few could name a single assistant DA. "Nice to meet you," said G-man. "How'd you like the food?"

"Oh, it was marvelous. Marvelous. Just . . ." He knew he couldn't say marvelous again. "Just beautiful," he said, and wrenched his gaze away. He pretended to become absorbed in sipping the last two drops of his wine. When he looked back, Rickey was frowning at him.

Woofer tensed, but Rickey only said, "Scagliano? Did your family use to live on Tricou Street in the Lower Ninth Ward?"

"My aunt and uncle do."

"I remember them. They had this little dog that used to get out the yard and crap in my mom's flowers. Drove her nuts."

"That was my dog!" said Woofer, glad of something to distract him from G-man. "He had to stay over at their house because my mother was allergic, but he was mine. Little ginger beagle named Woofer. That's how I got my nickname—everybody said his hair was the same color as mine, so they started calling me Woofer too."

G-man laughed, and Woofer turned large shining eyes upon him. Rickey kept shifting from foot to foot, not-so-discreetly tugging at the seat of his pants. "We better get back to the kitchen," he said. "Thanks for coming in."

"Oh, thank you, thank *you,*" said Woofer, staring at G-man, hoping for another word from that kissable mouth. He knew he was making an ass of himself, but he couldn't help it.

"Uh, sure, no problem," said G-man, and Woofer tried not to swoon in his chair.

"*Well,*" said Getty when the chefs had left the table. "That certainly was an interesting display."

"Oh, God."

"I didn't know I was gonna get a floor show with my meal tonight."

"Was I really that bad?"

"Hon, you were about the worst I've ever seen." Her strong-boned face assumed a moronic cast; her sharp eyes glazed over. "*Mahvelous, mahvelous. Oooo, it was so mahvelous I just want to get down on my knees and suck your big sweaty dick.*"

"Don't," Woofer begged.

"What was the big deal anyway? The other one's way cuter."

"I know."

Getty studied him closely, then shook her head. "You really need to get laid. I know a guy—"

"I'm not interested."

"Woofer, you're not actually gonna try and get with that chef, are you? Couldn't you see they were a couple?"

"I know," Woofer said sadly.

"Poor baby." She reached across the table and patted his hand. "But hey, that was a pretty good cover story, huh? True, even—my brother really is doing a barbecue book."

"Do you think he'll use their recipe?"

"Who knows?" Getty smiled. "All I know is, white boys love it when you act like they can make barbecue. They got an inferiority complex about it."

•

201

"What was *that* all about?" said G-man. They were in the passage that led from the dining room to the kitchen.

Rickey scowled. "I don't know, but I sure didn't like the way he looked at you."

"Aw, c'mon. It wasn't anything like that. His date was a knockout."

"Yeah, and I bet she's as queer as him. Quit fucking around, G. You know that guy was making cow eyes at you."

"It kinda seemed that way," G-man admitted. "But who cares? We'll probably never see him again. And speaking of weird, since when do you bitch at customers about their dogs crapping in your mom's yard twenty years ago?"

"I wasn't bitching. I thought it was funny. Hell, I hardly know what I'm saying. I'm in serious pain, dude."

"Really?" G-man looked more carefully at Rickey, noticed the fatigue in his eyes and a certain slickness to his skin. He really *was* in pain, and G-man felt bad for having teased him about his crotch rot all day. It wasn't a serious ailment, but it could hurt like hell. "I'm sorry. Why don't you go on home and sit in the tub? Run a nice bath, put some baking soda in the water. We're almost done here—Terrance and I can break it down."

"Nah. I'm fine."

"No you're not."

"I will be. I'm not going home early."

"I know what the problem is," said G-man. "You're afraid that guy Woofer is gonna wait for me in the parking lot."

"Way he looked at you, I wouldn't be surprised. I didn't like that one goddamn bit."

"Hazard of the job. Chefs are sexy, you know."

"Yeah," said Rickey, tugging at his pants again. "I'm feeling real sexy tonight. I oughta pose for *Bon Appétit* or something."

"You oughta pose for a Boudreaux's Butt Paste ad."

"Fuck you," said Rickey, but there was no rancor in it. He hurt too much to get really mad about anything.

•

Poppy Z. Brite

A few hours later, Rickey lay in the darkened bedroom drifting toward sleep. He felt much better now. As soon as they got home, G-man had fixed him a tepid bath laced with baking soda. Rickey hadn't thought it would help, but it did. After that, overriding Rickey's protests, G-man made him lie on the bed and slathered another coat of paste on him. He was able to reach the spots Rickey couldn't, and the stuff helped almost immediately. The real reason Rickey hadn't wanted him to do it earlier, though, was because he couldn't help but get horny when G-man touched him in those particular spots, even if it was only to apply greasy medicine. G-man knew how he was, and sucked him off so softly that it didn't hurt a bit.

What would he do without such a sweet soul of a boyfriend? Rickey sometimes tried to imagine what life alone would be like, but his mind always shied away from it before he got very far. Now, because of Cooper Stark and because of the weird customer who had stared so hungrily at G-man tonight, he forced himself to take the fantasy a little further than usual.

For one thing, he would have stayed at the CIA and ultimately graduated with a degree in culinary arts. Whether he'd returned to New Orleans or gone somewhere else, he would have started his career making a decent wage, as opposed to the shit pay he'd gotten at most of his early jobs. That might have been all right. On the other hand, he couldn't deny that there had been something fine about struggling to build a life with G-man in their first crappy apartment. Because they had so little, they'd taken deep pleasure in everything they did have: a comfortable chair they'd found in the garbage, a new saucepan they'd saved up for, a good cookbook, and most of all each other. For the first time in their lives, they'd been able to have all the physical closeness they wanted: not only sex but kissing goodbye and hello, rubbing each other's tired feet, just lying around watching TV. They had cherished that and gorged themselves on it. Rickey knew it wouldn't have seemed so luxurious with someone he'd met after moving out of his mother's house, because they would have no history of denying themselves.

So he would have had more money. And he supposed he would have fucked around a lot; there was plenty of easy sex to be had in the restaurant world. Probably it would have been fun. But what would he have now? He knew plenty of cooks his age, just starting to get broken-down and burnt out, who'd cultivated nothing and had nobody. They'd lost a lot of the bone-burying energy they'd had in their twenties and now spent more time drinking than chasing ass. When they got home, what was waiting for them? An empty bed and their own hung-over faces in the mirror the next morning? Rickey didn't think he could live like that. The Church and government could define marriage any way they liked, but he was the most married man he knew.

He had really dodged a bullet with Coop. A couple of years ago, maybe even a couple of months ago, tonight's incident with the Scagliano guy would have sent Rickey into a jealous sulk at the very least. He'd always hated for anyone else to look at G-man. After what he had almost done, though, he'd have to be the king of all hypocrites to get mad over a moony customer. That night at his hotel in Dallas was easily the closest Rickey had ever come to straying, and it had shaken him to his core. Even now he couldn't deny that he was powerfully attracted to Coop and believed—hell, *knew*—they would have had an intense physical connection. But, again, for what? There couldn't be any hookup worth your whole life. If he had done it, he felt sure he would have confessed. G-man had always known everything about Rickey; to keep something from him would make Rickey feel incomplete, almost unreal. He didn't think G-man would have left him over it. But he couldn't be sure, and even the possibility filled him with an austere, dreamy terror like the fear of death.

It hadn't happened, though. Thank God, it hadn't happened. There was only this life, this pool of shared warmth in the bed, this man he knew inside and out; it was enough for him. *I could stand to do this forever,* he thought, and the idea eased him over into sleep.

Poppy Z. Brite

18

Placide Treat paced from one end of his lawbook-lined office to the other. It wasn't very far, but he was soon out of breath. Woofer Scagliano watched him with some alarm. Treat was a wiry little thing, but he seemed a likelier candidate for a coronary than many of the sleek and greasy three-hundred-pound lawyers Woofer saw around the courthouse each day. Those guys were mostly complacent, which was good for the heart. Treat was driven by an inner fiend that gnawed at his vitals and, Woofer felt sure, would eventually chew right through some indispensable artery or organ.

"You talked to him for a lousy five minutes and didn't find out a goddamn thing!" said Treat. "I bet you don't even know what color his eyes are!"

"They're blue," said Woofer, but he was only remembering that from *Dark Kitchen*, which had included a vivid and melodramatic description of Rickey (broad-shouldered, impossibly handsome, startling turquoise-blue eyes) contrasted with a word-sketch of the former boss who'd tried to kill him (rat-faced and narrow-chested; if Chase Haricot hadn't mentioned the color of the guy's eyes, he had surely implied that they were an infernal red).

"You gotta go back," said Treat. "Try not to pussyfoot around so much this time. Don't have dinner. Hang around the bar. Keep your ears open. Bring me back something."

"What do you expect me to find out? I'm sure you don't think people are hanging around the bar at Liquor discussing the secret criminal dealings of Lenny Duveteaux."

"Course not . . . but people say things that lead to other things. They don't always know what they're saying, either. You're smarter than most people, Woofer. You might know."

"Why not Lenny's own restaurants? Don't you think we might find out more from them?"

"I got Panzeca hanging around Lenny's and Dymond on the scene at Crescent. I think Liquor's more important, though. Lenny's been real careful about covering his ass at his restaurants. He might not have been so careful at Liquor—people don't associate him with it. And look what he's done for those two young kids. Bankrolled their idea, set 'em up in business, taught 'em how to do everything but wipe their asses. I know Rickey's got some kinda information on him. I know it."

Woofer looked carefully at Treat, wondering how much the old man wasn't telling him. He didn't believe for a second that Treat really thought he was going to find out anything useful at Liquor. Sending him there was just Treat's way of trawling for miscellaneous dirt while Treat himself worked on the real case . . . whatever that was.

"Well, I guess I'll just have to go back and look around some more," he said manfully. He was subject to sudden surges of useless optimism, and he experienced one at the thought of seeing G-man again. Of course, the chefs probably didn't spend much time in the bar, but even a glimpse would do his heart good.

"That's my boy," said Treat. "Slow and steady wins the race."

Woofer wasn't sure he liked that, but he supposed it suited him. He left the DA's office full of resolve.

•

Poppy Z. Brite

"Meaningless!" said Rickey. He was sitting at the kitchen table reading the new issue of *Bon Appétit*. "Totally fucking meaningless!"

"What?" said G-man mildly.

"These one-word restaurant names. Seems like all the hot places gotta have 'em these days. Jar! Town! Tru! They don't sound like anybody's name, and they got nothing to do with food, so what the hell do they mean?"

"Couldn't tell you," said G-man. A moment later he realized Jar might have something to do with food, but he agreed that it was a dumb name for a restaurant. He didn't feel like listening to Rickey rant about it, though. Yesterday had been their day off, and if truth be told, he was a little hung over.

"I mean, *our* name is one word, but it describes our *menu*. Plus it denotes a touch of glamour. What's *Jar* supposed to mean? Does everything come out of a jar? I don't think I'd be bragging about that."

"Liquor denotes a touch of *glamour*?" Somehow those words didn't sound like Rickey's. "Who told you that?"

"Well, Coop, actually. He said it was a great name for a restaurant. Makes people think of cocktail lounges, speakeasies, maybe tiki bars . . . a little tacky, but glamorous. He wasn't telling me anything I didn't know, but I thought he had a good way of putting it."

"Huh," said G-man. He wasn't in the mood to hear about Cooper Stark. In fact, he wasn't sure he would *ever* be in the mood to hear about Cooper Stark. Rickey had shown him the letter Stark had written after Rickey's return from Dallas, and G-man had found it a self-pitying and self-serving piece of work. The line about some people being blessed by the universe actually offended his long-buried Catholic sensibilities, not an easy thing to do. In most ways, G-man had left the Church at sixteen, when he figured out what it thought of him and Rickey. He hadn't abandoned all his beliefs, though, and one thing that remained with him was something an otherwise long-forgotten priest had said in a homily: *God loves us all equally, but that doesn't mean He wants us all to be alike. One thing He loves about us is our ability to carve out a niche for our-selves.* G-man had spent half his life watching Rickey carve out a niche for them both, and a good one too. The implication that the universe had somehow gifted Rickey with a big helping of dumb luck was offensive in more ways than he could count. Even the reference to "the universe" itself offended him. Atheists loved to use that term to describe some shadowy force that somehow controlled human destiny, but what the hell did they think the universe *was*? Did they think the stars and nebulae took an interest in their doings, and if they really meant God, why couldn't they just say so?

Rickey hated for him to talk about this sort of stuff, though. The least hint that G-man still harbored any religious faith whatsoever seemed to antagonize him far out of proportion to the weight G-man gave it, so they mostly avoided the subject. He certainly wasn't going to bring it up now, or start an argument about Cooper Stark. Instead he just said, "Didn't Stark once have a restaurant called Capers?"

"Yeah, but at least that's *food*."

And Prime is one word too, G-man thought, but didn't say it.

When they left the house to go to work, the air clung to their faces like hot plastic and sucked all the breath from their lungs. The sky was a clear, pitiless blue like the heart of a flame. Just an ordinary August day in New Orleans. Later in the afternoon, clouds would probably roll in over the lake and there would be a brief but intense thunderstorm. Then the rainwater would steam up off the streets and sidewalks, turning the city into a vast, dirty sauna. Rickey and G-man might hear the thunder, but they wouldn't see the rain; there were no windows in the kitchen.

Rickey had to send back a case of unripe tomatoes, but that wasn't unusual, and nothing else of note marked the afternoon prep work or the dinner service. The weirdness that would define the next few months of their lives didn't begin until after they had broken down the kitchen and were having a drink in the bar. The house line rang, and Karl answered it, then said, "For you, Rickey."

"I hoped I might catch you there," said a woman's voice as soon as Rickey came to the phone. "I got this number from information."

"Who's this?"

"This . . ." The woman paused, and Rickey thought he heard a muffled sob. "Sorry. I'm pretty freaked out right now. This is Sugar from Dallas. You know, Firestone's? I mean, Prime?"

"Yeah, sure. Hey, Sugar." From the corner of his eye, Rickey saw G-man glance across the room at him. "What's going on?"

"I don't know. I mean, I know what happened, but I don't know *why*."

Now a strange emotion began to infuse Rickey's consciousness. It wasn't precisely fear, since he couldn't imagine what he had to fear from Sugar; he supposed it was apprehension. "What happened?" he said.

"Coop didn't show up for work two days ago." She paused to (as far as Rickey could tell from the sound) blow her nose. When she came back, she sounded a little calmer. "We tried to call his apartment, but he didn't answer. I know you thought I was after his job, but I didn't want him to get in trouble, so we just filled in for him and didn't call Mr. Firestone. When he didn't show up again last night, Flaco and I decided to drive over to his place after service. He didn't answer the door, and we couldn't see anything through the window."

Now Rickey felt something more than apprehension. It still wasn't fear, but a sick knot had formed in his stomach and a weird, unpleasant warmth was creeping up his spine.

"I called the police. I hated to do it in case Coop was in some kind of . . . I don't know . . . legal trouble, but I didn't know what else to do."

"Why didn't you call Firestone?" Rickey heard himself say. "He's Coop's landlord. He owns the building."

"I didn't know that. I just knew I had a bad feeling. Anyway, one of the cops broke into the apartment, and Coop . . ."

She began to cry in earnest. The feelings of apprehension and sickness had left Rickey; now he felt very cold and calm. He said nothing, and after a minute Sugar went on.

"I saw him. Just for a few seconds, but oh, God, it was awful. I don't see how he could have done that to himself. Just stuck a gun in his mouth and pulled the trigger like that."

"Are you sure it was him?" Rickey said absurdly. He didn't know why he said it, except that he didn't want to believe Coop was dead.

"Yes, you could still recognize him. But it was horrible. I know you think I didn't like him, and sometimes I didn't, but I never wanted anything like this to happen. If I'd known he was feeling bad, I would've . . . I don't know. I would've done something."

"*Was* he feeling bad?"

"I didn't think so. He seemed pretty happy with the new menu. We were doing a lot of business and he came up with some real good specials. I just didn't think he would ever do anything like this."

Rickey didn't think so either. The letter Coop had sent him a few weeks ago hadn't sounded like the words of a man wrapping up his affairs and preparing to swallow a bullet . . . or had it? He would have to dig it out and read it again. He supposed hindsight could make you read just about anything into such a letter.

"So what happens now?" he asked. "Is Firestone gonna close the restaurant?"

"He says not. I don't know if it can survive the bad publicity, but he's gonna try to ride it out. He even offered me the head chef job." Sugar laughed, but it was a humorless sound. "When Coop was alive, I wanted that job so fucking bad. I just knew I could do it better than him. But now I don't even want to stay in Dallas. This is too weird. I gave a week's notice, and I think I'm gonna take off, maybe try my luck in California. You ask me, I think Flaco will be the next chef."

Well, he's a better cook than you, Rickey thought, but didn't say it. He felt bad for Sugar; it must have been awful going to Coop's apartment, having to deal with the cops, seeing him like that. A gory picture flashed through Rickey's mind, and he tried to push it away. Instead he found himself thinking of the night Coop had kissed him, all those years ago in New York, and that was even worse.

When he hung up, the noise of the bar seemed to take several seconds to come back up to its previous level. The racks of sparkling glasses hanging upside down above the bar, the liquor bottles and drink menus, the faces of his coworkers all had an odd flat look, as if something had sucked most of the oxygen out of the room. He walked back to the booth where he'd been sitting.

"Sweetheart? What's wrong?" said G-man. Rickey knew he must look awful, probably shellshocked; G-man would never call him "sweetheart" in public unless he was really worried. Rickey took a deep breath and began to explain.

What would haunt G-man most was this:

Not the fact of the man's death itself, but the sudden, savage joy he felt at hearing it. No, not so much joy as *triumph*. He thought, *You had your two chances at Rickey, motherfucker, and you didn't get him either time, and now you're all out of chances.*

An instant later he was horrified. That thought hadn't come from any part of himself that he knew or wanted to know. He got up from his side of the booth and crossed over to sit beside Rickey, who was staring at the tabletop as if he saw something awful there. When he put his arm around Rickey's shoulders, he could feel Rickey's heart pounding.

"My God, I'm sorry," said G-man.

Rickey leaned his head against G-man's shoulder. "He just did it," he said breathlessly. "He just fucking did it."

"I'm sorry," G-man said again, still feeling like a liar. He hugged Rickey close to him, ignoring the curious glances of the few people in the bar. In his head he began to say an Our Father. He told himself it was for Cooper Stark's immortal soul, but he suspected it was really for himself, a small and inadequate penance for such ugly thoughts.

Rickey sat in bed reading and rereading his two letters from Coop. G-man had tried to comfort him, but had eventually rolled over and gone to sleep, discouraged by Rickey's lack of communication. Rickey didn't mean to be uncommunicative, but didn't feel he deserved to be comforted either. If Coop really had killed himself, Rickey couldn't help feeling he'd had some hand in it.

Of course, G-man said that was ridiculous. Probably most people would say it was ridiculous, especially if they came from a Catholic background: suicide was a sin, and that was that. But couldn't it be more than that? Couldn't it be a culmination of unbearable things adding up, adding to the weight on a man's soul until life itself seemed unbearable?

Rickey wasn't used to thinking like this. He spent a lot of time worrying over the restaurant, but he was basically an uncomplicated person, never overly troubled by depression or angst. Growing up in the Lower Ninth Ward, he'd lost friends to violence, and a few cooks of his acquaintance had driven drunk once too often, but he'd never known a single person who had killed himself. The act seemed impossible. The fact that Coop had done it anyway made Rickey feel he'd never really known the man.

But of course he *hadn't* really known the man. He had made plenty of assumptions about Coop, and had let Coop piss him off a great deal, but he hadn't taken the trouble to find out what really mattered to the older chef. They had just begun to forge an uneasy friendship when Coop had fucked it up by hitting on him at the hotel that night. Thinking back on it, Rickey wondered whether he could have made a difference by sleeping with Coop, and what G-man would say to that. Then he wondered if Coop's madness had somehow been contagious, because that was a crazy thing to be thinking.

Poppy Z. Brite

He skimmed Coop's first letter again.

This is a good gig. In fact it is my last chance . . . If I can keep this job for another couple of years, I think I can get my shit together and save enough money to go do a few things I really want to do.

Coop had talked about going to Spain, apprenticing himself to some hot-shit young chef there. Rickey believed he had really wanted to do that. And Rickey's menu overhaul—insulting though Coop must have found it—would surely have made it more possible. The place had been unprofitable before; now, according to Firestone and Coop himself, it was a money machine. What had made Coop decide he'd rather stick a gun in his mouth?

Life's an existential comedy, kiddo. I don't know if you believe that, but I do. If I didn't, I think I'd have blown my brains out by now.

Rickey looked at the second letter. Lines that had seemed innocent or mildly irritating now felt like little knives slicing into his heart:

If I am to have any more blessings, I'll have to go and find them myself. Or make them myself—no longer sure of the difference . . .
Thought you might like to know that I am actually having a lot of fun with Prime . . . I needed a shakeup in my life. Find myself drinking less and enjoying the job more . . . I feel excited about life for the first time since 1990 or so.

"What the fuck?" Rickey muttered. "How'd you get from being excited about life to fucking *obliterating* yourself?"

Beside him, G-man made a little sound in his throat, rolled onto his stomach, and buried his head in the pillow. Rickey glanced over at him, then back at the letters. He knew G-man was upset about this for different reasons than he was, but he couldn't worry about that, not right now. There would be time for them to deal with it, if in fact there was anything to deal with. Right now Rickey had to figure it out on his own.

Would Coop be in the Dallas morgue—wherever that was—or would they have sent him to a funeral home by now? Rickey shuddered. He didn't even like medical shows on TV. The things people did in those places were things he never wanted to know about. He supposed bodies had to be made presentable for funerals and such, but cutting up meat was as close as he ever wanted to get to all that.

I don't believe he did it.

The thought came out of nowhere, and Rickey wasn't aware of its significance at first. Of course he didn't really believe it yet; it hadn't had time to sink in. But the words stayed in the back of his mind, gradually getting a little louder, a little louder. He knew Coop was dead; that much he believed. Sugar had seen the body, had been about as freaked out as anybody he'd ever talked to. But did he believe Coop had come home from work one night and put a bullet in his head, thus ending any possibility of going to Spain, cooking good food, getting laid, pissing Rickey off, or doing any goddamn thing at all except lying on a slab until somebody buried or burned him? Rickey found that he did not.

"That's just stupid," he whispered. Surely he wasn't going to try to turn Coop's death into some kind of murder mystery just because he felt guilty about it. Who would want to kill a chef, and a has-been chef at that? Coop was no threat to anybody.

But he didn't really know that, did he? He didn't know anything about Coop's life except what Coop had told him.

Rickey swung his legs over the side of the bed, got up, and went into the bathroom. There was a family-sized bottle of Excedrin PM in the medicine cabinet, and he swallowed four. Back in bed, he stared at the ceiling and waited for them to work. G-man's slow breathing calmed him a little. He wondered what it would be like to go to sleep every night lulled only by the sound of your own breathing, to wake up and see an empty pillow beside you. Maybe Coop had done it after all.

He squeezed his eyes shut and forced himself to begin counting backward from a hundred. He was asleep by thirty-five, but it was not a restful sleep.

19

It hadn't been a good week. Since getting the news about Coop, Rickey was tired, distracted, and generally off his game. He forgot to order things and called out tickets wrong. "I know you're depressed," G-man said rather sharply one night after Rickey asked for an order of redfish when he meant monkfish and the mistake went unnoticed until G-man had all the table's entrées ready. "But can't you try to concentrate? Maybe it would get your mind off things."

"I'm not *depressed*," Rickey said. "Never been depressed in my life. That shit's for artists and little Catholic schoolgirls. I'm just kinda fucked up in the head right now, that's all."

"I know you are. I know it. But we're coasting here, Rickey. We can't afford to keep doing that in the fall when we get busy again. I'm just saying if you won't let me help you, at least try to help yourself."

"I will," Rickey promised. "I'll be OK. I'm sorry."

And he was, for G-man's sake as well as Coop's. It almost seemed that Coop was more of a threat to them now than he had been while alive. He hung like a dark cloud over them, making Rickey feel guilty and—for some reason—scared.

He knew he'd had reason to be scared when he got the call from the Dallas lawyer the following week. It came in on the kitchen line, and he stood there with the A.M. prep work going on around him as the guy blew his mind.

"This is Edwin Crowley from Groden, Kirkwood, Hill in Dallas," said a dry voice with only a faint, refined Texas twang. "I imagine you know what I'm calling about."

"I've never even heard of you."

"Oh, damn. Mr. Stark said he was going to speak to you, but frankly I had the feeling he didn't really want to. In that case, let me explain. You're aware that Cooper Stark passed away recently?"

"Yeah, sure."

"Well, Mr. Stark named you the executor and sole beneficiary of his will."

"HE WHAT?" Rickey yelled. G-man glanced in his direction, but most of the other cooks ignored him, assuming he was talking to a recalcitrant purveyor or somesuch.

"Please, sir. My ear. He named you—"

"I heard you. Sorry. It's just . . . well . . . he can't *do* that, can he?"

The lawyer laughed. "He can and has done it. Of course, you can refuse to be the executor, but the estate is yours whether you like it or not."

"What estate?" Rickey's brain felt as if it had floated right out of his skull and was hovering somewhere near the kitchen ceiling. "Coop was broke and in debt, wasn't he?"

"Not at all. He didn't leave a large estate, but his checking and savings accounts total about twenty-two thousand dollars. Of course there'll be some legal fees, but not large ones, I think."

"I thought he said he was in some kinda credit consolidation program."

"No." Rickey heard papers rustling. "His credit was in good standing. His car isn't worth more than a few hundred—I'd advise donating it to charity and taking a tax write-off if I were you. And of course there's the house."

"What house?"

"The *apartment* house." The attorney didn't sound impatient so much as ostentatiously patient. "Mr. Stark owned the building he lived in."

"No he didn't. Frank Firestone did. Does."

"I can assure you that's not the case. I'm looking at the title right here."

"Mr. . . ." Rickey realized he had already forgotten the lawyer's name. "Listen, can you hang on? I want to take this in my office."

"Certainly."

"What's up?" said G-man as Rickey put the phone down and left the kitchen.

"I don't know," Rickey said over his shoulder. As he entered his office, the name came to him: Crowley, same as a pretty little town in Acadia Parish. He and G-man had driven through it once, on their first real vacation. It seemed very far away now. He picked up the phone and said, "Sorry, Mr. Crowley, but I don't understand any of this. I hardly knew Cooper Stark. Met him once twelve years ago and didn't see him again till I did that consulting gig last month. Even then, it was just a week working together. There was nothing else between us." *Almost true. Technically true.*

"He told me as much. However, he also said you were the only trustworthy person he knew, maybe the only one he'd ever known, and he wanted to make up for what he'd tried to do to you. If you really are that trustworthy, Mr. Rickey, it'll make my job much easier."

"Who are you anyway?" Rickey said—a little rudely, he supposed, but he didn't really care at this point. "I mean, why'd Coop have a lawyer?"

"He came to me a few weeks ago for the purpose of making a will."

Oh, shit, Rickey thought. *Oh crap, oh hell, oh shit and fuck.* He remembered how his thoughts had run on the night he'd learned of Coop's death. *I don't really believe he did it.* Since then he had come a long way toward accepting that Coop must have done it;

Poppy Z. Brite

the other alternatives were even more unlikely. Was that why he had made a will? Had he actually *planned* his suicide weeks in advance, and gone through the preparations one by one, thinking of Rickey the whole time? That was too horrible to contemplate.

"Well, there was nothing between me and Coop," Rickey repeated. "We were just friends. Hardly even that, far as I was concerned."

"So you've said. I'm not entirely sure Mr. Stark felt the same way. He *did* have your name tattooed on his hip."

"Run that by me again," said Rickey, feeling as if he might cry. He remembered his mother reading him *Alice in Wonderland* when he was very young. This was what falling down the rabbit hole must have felt like.

"Your first name—John—was tattooed on his hip. Just above the left, uh, iliac crest, in red and black ink. I have the medical examiner's report here."

"That's not me. Nobody ever calls me John. *That is not my fucking name tattooed on his ass.*"

"I don't believe the iliac crest is quite the *ass*. Anyway, Mr. Rickey, your relationship with Cooper Stark is no business of mine except as it relates to his will. I just need to know how you want to handle these proceedings. Of course, it would be wonderful if you could come back to Dallas—"

"I can't decide anything like that right now. I want you to talk to my lawyer."

"Of course. Put me in touch with him, would you?"

Rickey flipped through his Rolodex and read out Oscar De La Cerda's number. Crowley promised to call him right away, and Rickey hung up feeling as if he'd just escaped a bad dinner party. Of course that was stupid; he hadn't escaped anything, and he hadn't been to many dinner parties either, good or bad. At any rate, Coop had dumped another load of shit on him, and he would have to deal with it sooner or later.

He sat at his desk for a few minutes, staring at nothing in particular, wishing he had never taken Frank Firestone's consulting job.

Ten grand was beginning to look like chicken feed given the gig's repercussions. Why had Coop lied to him about being broke and in debt? Twenty-two thousand dollars wasn't a huge amount of savings, but it was too much to qualify as poor in Rickey's world. (The fact that Coop also owned the apartment house was beyond comprehension at this point, so much so that Rickey had nearly forgotten about it.)

Rickey closed his eyes and didn't open them again until he heard G-man speak. "Dude, what's going on?"

"Fuck if I know," said Rickey.

"I heard you hollering at somebody on the phone, and then you just disappeared."

Rickey tried to explain the conversation he'd just had. G-man's eyes got bigger and bigger behind the lenses of his shades. When Rickey finished speaking, they were both silent for a moment. Then G-man said, "Are you gonna do it?"

"Do what?"

"Whatever you're supposed to do." G-man made a frustrated little gesture with his hands. "Be the executor. Go deal with his shit."

"I don't know. I want to see what De La Cerda has to say."

"I don't think you should have anything to do with it. There's something really fucked up going on here, Rickey."

"You think?" said Rickey, and began to laugh. Nothing was funny; he just felt so confused and worn out by recent events that there wasn't much else he could do.

"Well, it'd be a hell of a lot easier to do all this if you could go back to Dallas for a couple days," De La Cerda told Rickey.

"Yeah, that's what Crowley said. In case you forgot, I got a restaurant to run. I don't really care about making life easier for a bunch of lawyers."

"It'd be easier for you too," said De La Cerda, unperturbed. "You don't have to go right away. Crowley says the apartment house is worth a couple hundred thousand, so that'll have to go through

probate. You don't need to be there for that. Once the probate's finished, though, you'll need to check out the building, decide what
you want to do with it, possibly appear in court to get Stark's
accounts signed over to you. And of course you'll have to go
through his effects."

"His effects?"

"The stuff in his apartment. When somebody leaves you his
entire estate, it's not just the good stuff. All his crap belongs to you
too—his old clothes and used toothpaste tubes and personal
papers. All that kinda shit. You'll want to go through it, decide
what to keep, what to sell, what to throw out."

Rickey could think of nothing he'd want to do less. He tried to
imagine sitting in the apartment where Coop had blown his brains
out, sorting through shirts and cookbooks, and his mind rebelled.
"Can't I just hire somebody to throw everything out?" he said.

"Rickey . . ." He could hear De La Cerda lighting a cigarette.
"Something's weird here. I don't know what went on between you
and this guy—"

"Nothing!"

"So you say," said De La Cerda, echoing the other lawyer. "And
I believe you. You gotta be stupid to lie to your attorney, and I
know you're not stupid. But I don't know why you're mixed up in
this, you say *you* don't know why you're mixed up in this, and it
smells funny to me. If I were you, I'd want a look at whatever's in
his apartment before it goes out on the curb for the world to see."

Rickey couldn't take any more. He got off the phone and went
back out to the kitchen, where dinner service had just begun. "You
expedite tonight," he told G-man. "Let me work the line."

G-man looked at him for a moment, then nodded and moved up
front to the expediting station. Rickey took up his position at the
sauté station, where there was a six-burner stove, a small oven, a
lowboy, and a bain-marie for sauces and hot soup. The sauté cook
was responsible for three of the menu's five appetizers and five of
its eight entrées. It was a demanding station, and Rickey seldom
felt comfortable letting anybody but G-man work it. He hadn't

worked it himself in some time, preferring to be up front directing the flow of the kitchen. Tonight he didn't want to orchestrate; he just wanted to be a cog in the machine, working so hard and fast that he didn't have time to think about anything else.

From his station, G-man called out, "Shake, ordering two green salads, one tomato salad. Rickey, ordering one artichoke, two redfish, two pork."

"One artichoke, two redfish, two pork," Rickey called back, confirming the order. He took three parboiled artichoke hearts and two portions of pork loin out of his lowboy. The artichokes went into a sauté pan with olive oil. While they were sizzling, he dredged the pieces of pork in porcini mushroom flour, then popped them into the oven. When his artichoke hearts were golden-brown around the edges, he slid them onto a plate and topped them with a pepper-vodka-spiked shrimp remoulade. He hadn't been sure of this dish at first, but several customers had praised the combination of hot, meaty artichokes and cool, tangy remoulade. "One artichoke up," he called. A few seconds later, Shake said, "Two green salads, one tomato salad up." A runner came and whisked away the table's starters.

Rickey checked his pork loins, then put a pan on another burner and began to sauté the morels, roasted garlic cloves, and diced artichoke hearts that he would serve over them. After a few minutes he splashed these items with cognac. Not until the pork was nearly done did he slide his pecan-crusted redfish filets into their pan. A couple of minutes on each side and they were ready to go onto plates he'd already sauced with pools of rum beurre blanc. In the meantime, three other orders had come in. The sauté station was exactly what he needed tonight.

"Chef, this is table four," said a waiter, coming in with an armload of appetizer plates from a table that had been served earlier. The phrase was a signal that somebody hadn't finished a dish; if the plates had been clean, the waiter would have just said "Chef, table four." Rickey resisted the urge to leave his station and inspect the leftovers. That was the expediter's job. From the corner of his eye he watched G-man use a tasting spoon to poke through the remains of a green salad. "Looks OK to me," G-man told the waiter. "They say anything?"

"She said she was saving room for her entrée."

"Happens all the time," Shake said. "Chick orders a salad just to be virtuous, then pigs out on the entrée. What's her second course?"

"Ribeye," said the waiter.

"See, what'd I tell you?"

It turned out to be a busy night, and Rickey was glad. By the time the last orders came in at 9:45, they had done a hundred and twenty-six covers. The kitchen hadn't been slammed—it took a lot more than a hundred and twenty-six covers to put this crew in the weeds—but they'd been busy enough that Rickey was able to keep moving and forget about the various conversations with lawyers he'd had earlier. As he started breaking down his station, these conversations came back to him and caused a sick feeling deep in his gut. The night of hard work had been helpful, though. He supposed it had given his subconscious mind time to work on the problem, because now he knew what he was going to do.

"I gotta go back to Dallas," he told G-man as they drove home. "Doesn't look like there's any way around that. But I'm taking De La Cerda with me."

"That'll cost us a fortune."

"Worth it. Anyway, I can pay him out of the estate."

"Why's it worth it?"

"Because he can help me figure out what I'm stepping in. And if it's anything too nasty, he'll be there to help me scrape it off my shoe."

"I guess," said G-man. "I still don't understand why any of this is happening, though."

"Neither do I. I swear to you, G, I really don't. I know how it looks, but if anything had happened between me and Coop, I would've told you."

"Oh, I know that." G-man waved a hand, dismissing Rickey's

reassurances. "I don't think you're hiding anything. I think some-body else is, though."

"G, don't you see? If Coop really did own this building and I can sell it, we'll have enough money to buy out Lenny's share of the restaurant. We'd be free and clear. I figure you'd be in favor of that even if Lenny *doesn't* go to jail."

"Course I'm in favor of buying Lenny out. You know that. I'm just not in favor of putting your life in danger to do it."

"My life's not in danger," Rickey said. He didn't think it was, either. He still wasn't sure he believed the official circumstances of Coop's death, but it wasn't as if he was going to Dallas to poke into things. He just needed to see what was going on and figure out how to collect what was apparently coming to him. If he could find out *why* it had come to him, that would be good too, but he wasn't going to play detective.

20

Sid Schwanz was a professional drinker. Oh, it said *journalist* in the appropriate blank on his tax returns, and he did write human-interest columns and horse racing stories for the *Times-Picayune*. However, that had always seemed like a lark for which he was lucky enough to get paid (or for which somebody was foolish enough to pay him); what he had really dedicated his life to was the art of enjoyable drinking. He was good at it too; he was never falling-down drunk but seldom completely sober.

During the racing season, the majority of Schwanz's drinking was done at the New Orleans Fair Grounds. In the off-season—now, for example—he was fond of Liquor. It wasn't too far from the racetrack (like a moon unable to escape the gravitational pull of its mother planet, Schwanz felt restless if he strayed too far from the track even during the off-season), and the owners liked him. He didn't think the bartender was too crazy about him, but she was easy on the eyes and generous with the pours, so that was all right.

Holding up the long zinc bar toward the end of service one evening, Schwanz noticed a familiar figure on the next barstool, a redheaded, long-faced man who didn't look as if he was having much fun. After studying the man for a few minutes, Schwanz decided he'd seen him on TV, though not in any very important capacity. Just then somebody nearby said, "So they hauled him into Municipal Court," and Schwanz's mind made an association. "Don't you work over at the courthouse?" he asked the man, gesturing vaguely in the direction of Tulane Avenue.

"More or less."

"Assistant DA, ain'tcha?" That was why Schwanz had thought of the man as unimportant: because he'd appeared on the local news with Placide Treat. No one seemed very important next to Treat.

"Yes," said the man reluctantly, as if he were admitting it rather than bragging about it. "Woofer Scagliano."

The newspaperman introduced himself, and they shook hands. "Kinda funny you hanging around here," said Schwanz, "what with your boss beating up on Lenny Duveteaux and all. Say, you ain't spying, are you?"

"No!" said Woofer in a phony-sounding injured tone. "Why would you think that?"

Must be spying, Schwanz decided. He couldn't imagine what the ADA hoped to learn by hanging around the bar at Liquor, but his reaction had been so suspicious that he must be up to something. Schwanz, always loyal to the restaurateurs and bar owners who took care of him, decided to distract Woofer. "Aw, don't pay no attention to me," he said. "I'm always a little goofy when I haven't been to the races in a while. Can't wait till Turkey Day."

"You like the ponies, huh?"

"Like 'em! I'd marry one if it could cook. Or if I could take her out on the town, even. Can you picture me and a high-stepping filly taking a spin around this bar?"

Woofer glanced around the crowded bar. "I can't imagine *anyone* taking a spin in here," he said, "let alone a horse."

Schwanz ignored him; he was off just as surely as his beloved ponies were when the starting gates crashed open. "That reminds me of an old Fair Grounds story. You ever hear about the horse who went to Bourbon Street?"

"Can't say I have."

"It was Grand Wizard, who won the 1960 Thanksgiving Day Handicap. I guess he figured he hadn't done enough celebrating— that night he busted out of the barn and trotted all the way to Bourbon Street. Bourbon wasn't like it is now, neither—they had some real classy strip shows back then. Big old gawgeous girls with tassels and things, not these skinny silicone babes they got today. So Grand Wizard comes up to the street barker at the Sho-Bar and asks to go in—"

"He *asked*?"

"Well, he made it clear he *wanted* in, anyway. And the barker— guy I went to school with, as a matter of fact—says, 'Hell, no, you can't come in here. You're only three years old, and besides, you're a gelding!'"

Sid Schwanz laughed until his gut ached. No matter how many times he told that story, it always tickled him. "Yeah," he said when he finally caught his breath, "the Sho-Bar guy himself told me that story. Legs Cabazon. We was in school together. Course he was a few classes ahead of me."

"Where you went to school?" Woofer asked, not because he had any reason to care but because it was a question New Orleanians asked one another from sheer force of habit, much like commenting on the weather.

"Holy Redeemer. Now my daddy, he was a public school boy. Went to the same place the chefs here at Liquor did—he grew up in the Ninth Ward just like them. Course it's Frederick Douglass now, but it was still Nicholls back when my daddy graduated."

"Really?" Woofer seemed to perk up when Schwanz mentioned the chefs. "You know them?"

"Sure I know 'em. Hell, they let me drink free for a year when they first opened, just so I wouldn't write a particular story about a murder that happened here. Now there's a bestselling book out about it, and I didn't even get to write the damn thing!"

Schwanz launched into this story, and Woofer listened to it with more apparent interest than he had to the tale of Grand Wizard's perambulations.

Woofer thought the newspaperman might talk both his ears off, but that was all right; it gave him an excuse to remain in the bar. He knew there wasn't much chance that he would catch a glimpse of G-man—he'd been here three times since his first visit and had only seen the chef once—but any chance was better than none.

Of course he already knew the story Schwanz was telling; he'd read *Dark Kitchen* when it was published out of simple curiosity at all the hype, and had reread it recently looking for information about G-man. Unfortunately, there wasn't much to be found; Rickey was the star of the book. He'd gleaned all sorts of information about Rickey and fed it to Placide Treat as if he were learning it on his trips to the restaurant. He had no idea if Treat thought he was getting anything useful from this information, but so far it had seemed to keep him happy, if Treat could ever be called happy.

The case against Lenny Duveteaux wasn't going well, as far as Woofer could tell. Treat hadn't discovered anything incriminating on the tapes and still refused to let anyone help him listen to them. Woofer had begun to picture his boss as a mad, one-legged Ahab, though it was more difficult to cast the amiable Lenny as the white whale. Now Woofer himself was in the odd position of hoping the case would stay alive, at least for a while, so he would have an excuse to keep coming to Liquor.

"Call me Ishmael," he muttered, and realized he was becoming quite drunk. That would never do. He couldn't afford to be drunk if G-man turned up; he would disgrace himself for sure.

"What's that, chief?"

"Nothing—just got a frog in my throat," Woofer replied, hoping this wouldn't somehow remind Schwanz of another story.

Rickey didn't like staff to use the public restroom—he had some idea that it gave customers a bad impression, as if they imagined the people cooking and serving their food never needed to go to the bathroom—but somebody was in the employee toilet, and G-man really had to pee. Besides, service was almost over; probably nobody would see him.

As he turned away from the urinal, a tall redheaded man entered the restroom. He looked a little drunk, but that was hardly unusual here. What *was* unusual was the panicked look he gave G-man, as if he were an armadillo on the highway and G-man was an eighteen-wheeler bearing down on him. "Sorry," he said. "I, uh, I didn't know anybody was in here."

That was kind of a strange thing to say, but G-man didn't think much of it; he was too busy trying to figure out where he'd seen the man before. Probably just a regular customer. "No problem," he said. "This restroom's for you, not me."

The man laughed as if this were a witty riposte. Then, abruptly, he lurched over to the sink where G-man was washing his hands. "Listen," he said. "I work for the DA. I can tell you what's going on with the Lenny Duveteaux case. Meet me sometime."

Now G-man remembered where he'd seen this guy before: he'd dined here recently with an attractive black woman, and after Rickey and G-man visited their table, Rickey had claimed the guy was giving G-man the eye. He guessed Rickey had been right. All at once he was seized with a devilish urge to accept the proposition. How surprised and impressed Rickey would be if he turned up some sort of inside information about Lenny's case! G-man had seldom felt a conscious need to impress Rickey, but just lately Rickey was so consumed with the whole Cooper Stark mess; it might be nice to learn something that would make him sit up and take notice.

"Well," G-man said cautiously, "I don't know. That's not exactly ethical, is it?"

"Pshaw," said the guy. G-man had never actually heard anyone say that before. "What my boss is doing isn't ethical either. I'm ashamed of working in the DA's office these days, but I'm trying to fight corruption from the inside. That's why I want to help you . . . and Rickey, of course."

Woofer, that's his name, G-man thought, recalling the story about the dog that had dug up Rickey's mother's flower bed. "OK, Woofer," he said, and watched the guy glow because G-man had remembered his name. It was very odd having this effect on someone, and even odder trying to use the effect to manipulate the man. He didn't much like the feeling, but he liked Rickey's distractedness even less. "I guess I could meet up with you if there's something you want to tell me."

"Really?" said Woofer, as if G-man had promised him an all-expense-paid trip to Tahiti.

"Sure. I mean, don't risk your job or anything, but if you *want* to help us . . ."

Woofer waved a dismissive hand. "Treat's so lost in those tapes, I could have lunch at Commander's Palace with Lenny, Richard Nixon, and Huey Long and he probably wouldn't notice."

G-man wasn't sure he understood the connection between these three personages, but Woofer seemed to feel he had proved his point. He took a business card from his wallet and wrote down the address of a po-boy shop in Marrero. "Meet me here Tuesday noon."

As G-man walked back to the kitchen, he wondered just what he thought he was doing. He'd have to make up an excuse to go to Marrero. This would involve lying to Rickey, something he'd never done. He thought again of the distracted look he'd seen more and more in Rickey's eyes lately, the look that made him know Rickey was thinking about Cooper Stark. It would be worth a small white lie or two to get Rickey to stop looking that way for a few minutes, and to look at G-man with something resembling admiration. Rickey might be planning a trip back to Dallas to find out what had happened to Stark, but Rickey wasn't the only one who could dig up dirt.

Poppy Z. Brite

21

"My God, this is disgusting," said Oscar De La Cerda. He was eating a microwave burrito he'd bought in a convenience store near Longview, Texas. He had agreed to accompany Rickey to Dallas, but flatly refused to fly, explaining that he'd once been on a plane that developed a slow pressure leak and had spent two hours tormented by visions of himself being extruded, ectoplasm-like, through the plane's body. A lapsed Catholic, he had instantly reformed and promised the Virgin Mary that he'd never board another plane if she would only get this one down safely. She did, and he hadn't.

"That's on you," Rickey said. "We could've already been there six hours ago, eating something decent."

"I'd rather eat bad food than die." De La Cerda considered this for a moment. "Yeah, it's a tough choice, but I'm sticking with it."

Rickey didn't actually mind the road trip. De La Cerda had volunteered his own car and wasn't charging Rickey for the driving time, and he was an amusing travel companion, telling stories of crooked judges and crazy clients and epic meals eaten on someone else's dollar. The scenery was deadly dull, but its very emptiness cleared Rickey's head and gave him time to think about what he was going to do once they got to Dallas.

The inside of De La Cerda's car was a landscape of crumpled fast-food bags, empty soda cans, candy wrappers, old legal papers, and (for some reason) dozens of ballpoint pens. "I'm always losing them," the attorney explained when Rickey asked about these. "I'm the Bermuda Triangle of pens. Every time I buy a pack, I throw a few in the car so I'll always have one handy." Rickey grabbed a half-used legal pad and began making a list.

1. Meet with Crowley

2. Go to Coop's apt.

3. Talk to Firestone???

He wasn't sure about that last item. He'd intended to stay in touch with Frank Firestone, to keep tabs on how Prime was doing. Now he thought Firestone might be able to answer some of his questions about the discrepancies between the way Coop had claimed to be living and the way he really had been . . . but what if Firestone blamed Rickey somehow for his chef's suicide? Of course that was ridiculous, but death caused people to think and do some very weird things. Like go running off to Dallas when they had a restaurant to run back home and a partner who hated the whole screwy deal, for instance.

Even so, he needed to talk to Firestone. He'd feel like a pussy if he didn't. He resolved to call Firestone as soon as they got to Dallas.

He gazed out the window at a landscape of sere brown hills relieved only by an occasional cow. "Mind if I nap awhile?" he asked.

"Be my guest," said De La Cerda. "I'm writing a brief in my head anyway. If you hear me mumbling, don't worry—I'm not freaking out or anything."

"I think I might be," Rickey said. He leaned back in his seat, put his forearm over his eyes, and didn't wake up until they were on the outskirts of Dallas.

They checked into a downtown hotel right near the Big D. Rickey remembered that he'd promised himself to call Frank Firestone, and did so, but got shunted off to his voice mail. "Uh, hey, Mr. Firestone," he said, feeling like a horse's ass. "Rickey here. I'm real sorry about what happened to Coop. I'm back in Dallas to . . ." He hesitated, not sure if Firestone knew about the will, not particularly wanting to clue him in if he didn't. "To take care of some other business. I'd like to talk to you if you got a minute. Give me a call." He left the hotel number and hung up.

At Crowley's law office, Rickey had to sign a bunch of papers, after which Crowley gave him the keys to Coop's car and apartment. De La Cerda agreed to drop Rickey off at the apartment, then return to Crowley's office to hash out more details. Rickey would drive Coop's Saturn back to the hotel later.

"You sure you want to do this alone?" De La Cerda asked. They were parked outside the apartment house in Oak Cliff. Rickey could see Coop's decrepit little Saturn at the other end of the lot.

"Hell, no," Rickey said. "I don't want to do it at all. But if I gotta do it, no offense, I don't want somebody sitting there watching me."

"Hey, no problem. I understand it's personal and all."

"Everybody thinks I fucked this guy, don't they?"

De La Cerda blinked. "You don't mince words. No, I don't think you fucked him. You told me you didn't, and it's in your best interests to tell me the truth. Also in my best interests to believe you."

"God, I hate that kinda talk," said Rickey. He knew he was putting off entering the apartment, but suddenly this seemed very important. "Forget the lawyer-speak for a second. In your heart, you think something was going on between us. Anybody would. But I didn't fuck him. I just want one person to know that. I really didn't."

"One person?" said De La Cerda. "Doesn't G-man know it?"

"I sure hope he does." Rickey shook his head. "I don't know. I feel like I don't know a goddamn thing any more."

"Well—" De La Cerda gripped Rickey's shoulder. Rickey had the idea it was meant to be a man-to-man, buck-up gesture, but under the circumstances it felt weirdly intimate. "Just do the best you can. And listen, when you go in there . . ."

"Yeah?"

"The police don't do a lot of cleaning up. The coroner's guys take the body away, and sometimes pick up any . . . well, *chunks*. And that's about it. I just wanted you to be prepared."

"Great." Rickey got out of the car. "I'll see you at the hotel later."

"Be careful!" De Là Cerda called after him.

Rickey climbed the outside staircase to Coop's second-floor apartment and stood at the door for a moment, just holding the keys in his hand. He admitted to himself that he was scared of what he would find in there. He'd never been good with blood and guts, didn't even like cleaning fish if he could help it. He wasn't happy to be going in alone, but having De La Cerda there would have made it even worse. The best thing would be if G-man could have come with him, but that would have been too weird. *Thanks for putting me in the first-ever situation that was too weird to share with my life's partner, motherfucker,* he told Coop silently, and anger gave him the strength to open the door and step into the apartment.

He had expected to encounter some awful mess right away, but the living room looked clean enough, and he realized he didn't know where Coop had died. He moved deeper into the apartment, which seemed as hot as a slow oven. The late afternoon shadows gave the place an empty, spooky feel, or maybe that was just his imagination.

To his right was a tiny kitchen with a door that led to the roof garden where they'd sat and talked on Rickey's first night in Dallas. The kitchen had a refrigerator, an ancient gas stove, and about two square feet of counter space. Rickey opened the refrigerator and looked in. A few condiments. A quart of milk so completely gone over that its plastic sides bulged gassily. A half-carton of eggs and a Saran-wrapped package of bacon turning green. A Styrofoam to-go box from a restaurant. Curious, Rickey opened it and saw a pool of congealed hummus and two desiccated falafel balls. He'd have to throw all this out later, but for now he put it back and closed the fridge. A glance through the cabinets revealed similar contents: an open box of Triscuits, a jar of peanut butter, a bottle of Scotch, an unused bug bomb. It was the lonely kitchen of a lonely bachelor. Rickey no longer felt scared or angry, just sad.

There was still the rest of the apartment to see, though. He left the kitchen and walked down a short hall. Here was the bathroom with its old ceramic tiles and fifties-era fixtures. Empty, but now he became aware of a faint, unpleasant smell, a *meaty* smell, something like the inside of a walk-in cooler that hadn't been cleaned out for a long time. Wherever the mess was, he was near it. He went farther down the hall and looked into a bedroom. The smell was very strong here. The bottom half of the bare mattress was blue-ticked cotton. The top half was a nightmare of blood.

Rickey walked to the edge of the bed, not wanting to but unable to help himself. He couldn't believe so much blood had come from one person. The stain was at least a yard across. There was a black, clotted-looking spot at its center where he supposed Coop's head had lain. The wooden headboard and the wall above the bed were flecked with blood. Most of it was obviously dry, but that black spot looked like it might still be a little tacky. It was so thick that it looked like it might *always* be a little tacky.

Rickey felt his gorge rising and made himself take several deep breaths. Whatever possibilities had once existed between him and Cooper Stark, they ended here. All Coop's possibilities ended here. Rickey had expected to remember Coop kissing him, as he had on the night he'd learned of Coop's death, but instead he found himself thinking of the meal Coop had cooked for him when he first arrived in Dallas. The beautiful tomato consommé, the lemony skate, the falling-apart-tender veal cheek. The dessert that tasted like bananas Foster. That talent had ended right here, had soaked into this mattress without leaving any real residue of itself.

Rickey felt faint. Only the thought of touching that stain kept him from sinking onto the edge of the bed. As he stumbled backward, his elbow hit the edge of the closet door. The door swung open, revealing a few items of clothing on hangers, some sneakers, two pairs of chef's clogs, and a pair of very expensive-looking, very ugly cowboy boots. On the side of one boot Rickey could see the Statue of Liberty done in green leather. Instead of the usual torch and tablet, she was holding a chef's knife and a book upon whose cover was stitched, in tiny red-threaded letters, THE JOY OF COOKING.

Rickey blundered out of the room, back down the hall, and sat heavily on the vinyl sofa. One of the seat cushions was missing. A sharp-edged rip in the other cushion scratched the heel of his hand, and he glared down at it, thinking it represented everything that confused him about this whole deal. Why had Coop claimed to be deeply in debt? Why had he driven a crappy car and furnished his apartment with uncomfortable junk when he had plenty of money in the bank? Hell, when he owned the damn apartment building?

He had said Firestone owned the building, Rickey remembered. Claimed Firestone was keeping him penned up like a little bitch, like his pet chef. And—Rickey hadn't remembered this before, but now he did—Firestone had told Rickey his real first name was John, the name tattooed on Coop's hip. What was *that* all about?

He looked around the room. Other than the sofa, there wasn't much furniture. A cheap bookcase built from a kit, mostly full of cookbooks. An equally cheap stereo. An end table beside the sofa, and on the tabletop, two items: a jelly glass with an inch of liquid in it (the Scotch from the kitchen, by the look of it) and one of Rickey's favorite cookbooks, *Simple French Food* by Richard Olney. A legal pad and pen were stuck in the cookbook as if Coop had

Poppy Z. Brite

been distracted while making notes on a recipe. Rickey picked up the book, and it fell open to a recipe for roasted calf's liver. On the notepad, Coop had written, "Marinate in milk before roasting so not too dry? Try oven hotter or"

That was all; Coop hadn't finished the thought. Had someone knocked on the door, pulling him away from his drink and his notes? And if so, had that happened on the night of his death, or earlier?

Night, hell; Rickey realized he didn't even know for sure what time Coop had died. He'd just been assuming it had happened at night because that seemed like the time when someone would decide to kill himself. For all he knew, it had happened in the middle of the afternoon. No, that couldn't be right, because Coop would have been at work. Morning, then. Maybe Coop had woken up that day and just decided he couldn't stand to cook one more piece of beef. Rickey laughed, not knowing he was going to, not meaning to. The small humorless sound was startling in the apartment's dim stillness.

Back at Crowley's office, the attorney had given him a sheaf of papers: copies of the will, death certificate, title to Coop's car, deed to the building. Rickey realized he was still carrying them. He slid them out of the manila envelope and flipped through them, and sure enough, there was the medical examiner's report. Rickey didn't want to look at it, but once he had it in hand, he couldn't stop himself. Besides, it might tell him the time of death. Why did he want to know the time of death all of a sudden? He wasn't sure.

The ME's report looked like a tax return and was full of heartrending details. Not just the descriptions of Coop's injuries, but the minutiae of his life Rickey had not known, that would never matter to anyone again. Coop's middle name was Marshall. His birthday was September 9, just three days after Rickey's. Here was the notation about the tattoo on his hip that said John. The date of his death was filled in, but the time was left blank.

Rickey skimmed the typed police report, hoping it might say what time Coop's body had been found.

AT APPROXIMATELY 23:20 HRS. DECEDENT'S CO-WORKERS VISITED DECEDENT'S APARTMENT BECAUSE HE HAD NOT SHOWN UP FOR WORK IN 2 DAYS. THEY COULD NOT GET IN AND POLICE WERE CALLED. UNIT 534 RESPONDED, ENTERED THE APARTMENT, AND FOUND DECEDENT IN BED WITH A GUNSHOT WOUND TO THE HEAD. A COLT TROOPER .357 MAGNUM BLUE STEEL REVOLVER WAS FOUND IN LAP OF DECEDENT. THE RIGHT HAND WAS AROUND THE GRIP OF THE WEAPON AND FOREFINGER WAS THROUGH THE TRIGGER GUARD. A MASSIVE HEAD WOUND WAS OBSERVED . . .

Rickey stopped reading and turned back to the ME's report. He scanned the physical description, trying to get that last image out of his head and remind himself what Coop had looked like alive.

HT.: 73 in.
WT.: 180 lbs.
HAIR: Black
EYES: Brown
PUPILS: Contracted
TEETH: Fair to poor—eight fillings, large diagonal chip upper left central incisor

Rickey's eyes stopped moving. He wasn't sure why at first; maybe he'd just had enough of this. *Incisor,* he thought uselessly; the word echoed in his head for some reason. That was your front tooth. Coop's front tooth hadn't been chipped. His teeth may have been "fair to poor" in the ME's estimation, but they had still looked pretty good from the front. Rickey remembered noticing his all-too-rare smile, trying not to see the way it lit up his face and turned his dark eyes devilish.

Oh God, he thought, *how much of this is happening just because I thought the son-of-a-bitch was hot?*

It didn't matter. Coop's tooth hadn't been chipped, unless it had happened in the weeks since Rickey's departure from Dallas. Had he gotten in a bar fight? Had some weird kitchen accident? Drunk too much and slipped in the shower? How many ways could you chip your front tooth? *Plenty,* Rickey told himself, trying to banish the next image that came to him: the barrel of a gun being shoved into an unwilling mouth, opening it by force when it wouldn't open on command.

That hadn't happened.

It could have, though.

Probably he'd chipped it some other way. The shower scenario seemed likeliest. He'd admitted to Rickey that he sometimes drank too much.

Not recently, though. In his letter he'd said he was drinking less, having fun with the new menu.

Oh, hell.

Rickey stepped on his chaotic thoughts and tried to force them out of his mind, the way he did when he was worrying too much about some restaurant matter that he couldn't do anything about. It was time to get out of this apartment. Tomorrow he would come back here with boxes and garbage bags to clean out the place. The gory mattress and other big furniture would have to go eventually, but he could hire somebody to do that after he'd gotten rid of the small stuff. The day after that, he hoped to be on his way home.

Right now he needed a drink.

"Call the coroner's office," said De La Cerda.

"What?" said Rickey. They were in the penthouse bar of their hotel—not the fancy place where Frank Firestone had installed Rickey on his first trip, but a cheaper place downtown. The Big D was clearly visible from here, glowing the deep red of heart's blood against the indigo sky. Now on his second Wild Turkey, Rickey was telling the attorney about Coop's chipped tooth.

"Take another look at the report. Coroner's, ME's, whatever they got here. The doctor who did the autopsy—his name will be on there. Call the office tomorrow morning and ask him about the tooth. Maybe he'll have an opinion on whether it could have happened that night."

Rickey tipped his glass and found it empty. Ice cubes rattled against his teeth. *Incisor,* he thought. "What's the point?"

De La Cerda shrugged. "Make you feel better, maybe. You want my advice, I say don't get mixed up in this any more than you already are. Clean out the apartment, set things in motion to collect your property, and go home. If it all goes smoothly, a couple months from now you'll be a lot richer. And he'll still be dead no matter what you do."

"You got such a nice way of putting things."

"They teach you that in law school."

Rickey wanted another drink, but he knew it wasn't a good idea. That didn't usually stop him, but thinking about the last time he'd gotten drunk in Dallas helped him to push away from the table, pay his tab, and take the elevator up to his room. Frank Firestone hadn't returned his call, and Rickey was no longer sure he wanted him to. What would he say? *Hey, did you give Coop that apartment building, then tell him to lie to me about it? And by the way, was that your name tattooed on his ass?*

It was just ten-thirty. G-man would still be at the restaurant, probably busy closing the kitchen. Rickey wanted to call him anyway, settled for leaving a message at home. Maybe he'd call back later; he didn't think he would be able to sleep any time soon.

He turned on the TV and flipped through the channels, paused to watch a few minutes of sports highlights, finally settled on one of his favorite *Iron Chef* reruns, the foie gras battle. Iron Chef Chinese was making a steamed dome of foie gras and winter melon when Rickey fell asleep.

"You know I didn't have a chipped tooth," Coop told him. "The only question is what you're going to do about it."

"What happened to you?" Rickey asked.

Instead of answering, Coop kissed him. The jagged tooth snagged

Rickey's tongue and he tasted blood. With the skewed logic of dreams, they were lying together on a cracked vinyl sofa cushion in the middle of the dining room at Prime. All around them, people talked and laughed and ate exotic beef dishes, oblivious to the two naked men in their midst. *I'm going to fuck him this time*, Rickey thought. *If I do, maybe he won't die.* A guilty sense of abandon came with the thought. He ran his fingers through Coop's hair, and they sank into the gory mess of Coop's skull.

Rickey awoke gasping, frantically wiping his fingers on the sheet. He had a headache and a hard-on. He turned off the TV, swallowed two Excedrin PMs, found the M.F.K. Fisher book he'd brought, and settled back into bed praying to a God he didn't believe in for dreamless sleep he didn't feel he deserved.

G-man opened his eyes and stared at the empty space on
the other side of the bed. Today was the day he was supposed to
meet with Woofer Scagliano. He'd been worried about that because
it meant he would have to lie to Rickey, but now he didn't have to,
because Rickey wasn't here. Great.

When he got home last night, there had been a message on the
answering machine. "Hey, dude. Just wanted to let you know we
got here awright. Man, what a boring ride. Texas is a fucking waste-
land. Anyway, I'm at the hotel, the number's on the pad by the
phone. Hopefully I'll be able to finish up here and get back home
in a couple days. Miss you, OK? Love you . . . Bye." G-man stood
gazing at the machine, his face not quite expressionless. He hadn't
erased the message when it finished playing, but had gone into the
kitchen, taken a long swig from the bourbon bottle on the counter,
and returned to listen to it again. He didn't like bourbon as much
as Rickey did, but just then he had wanted that taste in his mouth,
thinking maybe Rickey was tasting it too.

Rickey thought G-man didn't mind that he had returned to
Dallas. G-man *didn't* mind, or at least knew he shouldn't; Rickey
really hadn't had much choice in the matter. It was the decent thing

to do, and they would certainly be able to use the money if all this worked out. Still, if he was to be honest with himself, he had to admit that he didn't like Rickey being in Cooper Stark's orbit. Had been surprised to realize how much he disliked it when Stark was alive and didn't like it a damn bit better now that Stark was dead.

G-man rolled onto his back and put his arm over his eyes. It was wrong to think that way about a dead man, and it was wrong what he planned to do today: meet with a guy who seemed interested in him sexually and maybe even lead the guy on in an attempt to get information about Lenny's case, information Woofer shouldn't be giving him.

Why's he doing it anyway? G-man thought. *I'm no beauty*. He was fine with that knowledge, didn't consider himself ugly but had no desire to be a prettyboy. He'd seen people take Rickey less seriously as a chef because he happened to be good-looking, thought it was stupid but probably unavoidable. G-man could think of few things more embarrassing than having food magazines write about his broad shoulders or pretty smile. Rickey made him feel plenty hot when it mattered; the rest of the time it wasn't an issue. Except to Woofer Scagliano it apparently was.

He got out of bed, put on a pot of coffee, called the hotel in Dallas. Though it was early, Rickey wasn't in his room. G-man left a message on the hotel's voice mail, wishing for the hundredth time that Rickey would get around to replacing his damn cell phone. Months had passed since he'd thrown it into Lake Pontchartrain. But they had so little free time, and when they did have a day or two off, there always seemed to be something more important to do. Sleep, for instance. Or go meet some weirdo who wanted to tell you secrets about the District Attorney.

G-man poured milk straight from the plastic jug into his coffee. When Rickey was here, he usually heated the milk first, but it didn't seem worth doing just for himself. He sat at the kitchen table and drank two cups, gradually becoming alarmed at how low he felt. This wasn't like him. Sure, he felt sad from time to time, but it seldom took him long to find the sun behind the clouds. Today he didn't even want to look for the sun. The first time Rickey went to Dallas, G-man missed him badly and had done a certain amount of moping around, but it hadn't felt like this. Now he was acting as if Rickey had died.

A strange urge had been playing around the edges of his consciousness, and this thought turned it into a decision. He finished his coffee, brushed his teeth, got dressed, and left the house. It was still several hours until he was supposed to meet Woofer, but he needed to go ahead and do this before he lost his nerve.

The church he'd attended as a child, Sts. Peter and Paul in the Faubourg Marigny, had closed a couple of years ago. Sts. Peter and Paul was an old church in a poor neighborhood, and attendance had dwindled until the archdiocese claimed they couldn't afford to keep it open. G-man wouldn't have gone there anyway; his mother went to Mass almost every day and he sure didn't want to run into her just now. Instead he drove up Louisiana Avenue to a little church he'd noticed but never entered, Our Lady of Good Counsel. It was slightly decrepit, not at all grand, and he'd always liked the look of it. The morning Mass was about to begin. He genuflected and slipped into a rear pew.

G-man wasn't sure what atavistic urge had brought him here. He hadn't been to church since he was sixteen, when he'd gone to Confession and told the priest he thought he might be in love with his best friend. The priest said that was impossible, but if he really couldn't get such thoughts out of his head, there was always the exciting option of a celibate life. Rickey took the Church's position on their relationship personally and would read G-man the riot act for coming here, if he knew. (*Great, you can hide two things from him in one day,* he thought, then pushed the thought away. He wasn't hiding anything, because Rickey wasn't here to see it.) In his heart, G-man felt that he had left the Church that day. He hadn't stopped believing in God, though, and the Catholic roots went deep enough in him that he wasn't quite sure how to speak to God without coming to a place like this.

Poppy Z. Brite

A small silvery bell rang in the nave and the Mass began. There wasn't a big crowd, just a handful of old ladies. G-man was surprised at how familiar it felt to stand and make the responses to the priest, to be seated and hear the lector read Scripture. *You've been away*, the rituals seemed to say, *but you can never really leave*.

This idea had been repellent to him for the better part of fifteen years, but now it was comforting. Some strange rebellion seemed to be going on in his heart. He looked up at the calm marble face of Christ on the cross, thinking, *No one on earth has the right to tell me I'm living a sinful life, and I haven't heard it from You*. The thought filled him with a deeper peace than he had felt in weeks. Maybe there was something here for him after all.

When the other worshipers began filing up to take Communion, though, G-man remained kneeling in the pew. He wasn't ready for that step, wasn't sure he ever would be again. Besides, he was no longer a Catholic in good standing; you were supposed to receive Communion at least once a year. Instead he watched the people filing up the aisle, opening their mouths or cupping their hands before the priest, then returning to their seats with the body of Christ melting on their tongues and a look of deep concentration on their faces. He remembered how hard it was to let the wafer sit there and dissolve, how sometimes it almost gagged you, especially if you had looked at the priest's hairy wrist as he put the wafer on your tongue. When that happened, his mother said, you were supposed to think of Jesus' agonies and realize you weren't suffering at all in comparison. He'd never been crazy about Communion, to tell the truth.

A tiny old lady with vivid black-and-white-striped hair—"skunk hair," his sister Rosalie called it—was in the pew behind him. He'd felt her eyes on him ever since they exchanged the sign of peace, and as soon as the Mass ended, she leaned over and said in a hoarse downtown contralto, "You Mary Rose Bonano's boy Gary, ain'tcha?"

For a moment he considered denying it—if his mother found out he'd attended even one Mass, he would never hear the end of it—but his manners got the better of him. "Yes ma'am. Mary Rose Stubbs, now."

The lady flapped a dry leaf of a hand upon which several ersatz jewels sparkled. "She always gonna be a Bonano to me. Nothin against your daddy, but I been knowin dat girl too many years to call her Miz Stubbs. I'm Teresa Trepagnier—used to be Teresa Campanella when me and your momma's momma was in school together."

"Pleased to meet you, Mrs. Trepagnier."

"Meet me! I give you a fig cookie one time when you wasn't hardly old enough to chew it. Anyway, I thought Mary Rose told me you done left the Church. Broke her hawt."

"Well . . ."

"Don't worry, I ain't gonna tell her I seen you here. It's *good* you goin to Mass, babe. You tell your momma in your own sweet time. She musta said a rosary for you, though. Dat girl sure says a lotta rosaries."

"My momma can work some beads," G-man admitted. Despite her promise, he couldn't help wondering if this lady planned to run right down to the beauty shop—or wherever she saw his mother these days—and tell Mary Rose she'd run into him here. Well, it couldn't be helped.

"I gotta get goin," said Mrs. Trepagnier. She extricated herself from the pew and lurched toward the aisle, leaning on a four-pronged metal cane. G-man stood up to help her, but she waved him off. "You go on, sugar. Don't let a old lady hold you up."

"No, really, let me walk you out. Can I give you a ride someplace?"

"Aw, you so sweet, but I got my car outside."

G-man escorted the old lady out of the dimness and the smell of candle wax and incense into a bright, hot late-August day. He opened the door of her car—a vast Buick even older and longer than Rickey's Plymouth, though in somewhat better repair—and gingerly helped her in. Though her stripey head barely cleared the top of the steering wheel, she piloted the car smoothly out of the parking lot and went tooling away up Louisiana Avenue, twiddling her beringed hand at him in the rearview mirror.

That was New Orleans. As in any city, you could walk down most streets in relative anonymity, but step into a restaurant, a grocery store, or a Catholic church and you were sure to meet somebody you knew. Maybe she really wouldn't tell his mother she'd seen him at Mass, and what if she did? He could do worse than to make his mother happy once in a while.

G-man felt a hundred times better than he had when he'd woken up, and realized he was ravenous. He drove home and fixed himself a huge breakfast of scrambled eggs, bacon, and toast. After that, he felt completely fortified for whatever the day might bring.

Woofer had spent much of the night in Placide Treat's office, ostensibly organizing files but really searching for some piece of information that would impress G-man. He felt like someone who'd just decided on a method of suicide or embezzled an enormous sum that would certainly be discovered by his employer: a man on the brink of disaster, with all the crazy exhilaration that attended it. What was he doing? He didn't know, but it felt better, *righter* than anything he'd done in months. He had decided he wouldn't be working in the DA's office much longer, whether or not Oscar De La Cerda won the election next year; he needed a fresh start. Even if he had no chance with G-man, maybe he could do one last good thing while he was here.

He knew there were things about the case that Treat hadn't shared with him. That was no sensible way to handle your business, but Treat and common sense, never the best of friends, seemed to have parted ways entirely in the last year or two. Woofer wondered if this would matter to the voters come election time, then laughed silently at himself. De La Cerda was right; sometimes he really didn't think like a local.

He hadn't been able to find anything particularly revealing on

Lenny, though. He pulled out a folder labeled JOHN and flipped through its contents. There were several reviews of a restaurant in Dallas, and a line caught his eye: *Consulting chef John Rickey of New Orleans, brought in to revamp the menu, instead overhauled it to Dallas tastes and turned the restaurant's fortunes around . . .*

Was this a dossier on Rickey? *Dark Kitchen* said he hadn't been called John since he was very young. Woofer kept looking through the file. Here was something that seemed unrelated at first: copies of Dallas police and medical examiner's reports on someone named Cooper Stark, who had apparently shot himself dead a few weeks ago. Woofer scanned the reports, then flipped back to the restaurant reviews. Apparently Cooper Stark had been the chef at the restaurant where Rickey had consulted.

For the first time, it occurred to Woofer that he might have more to lose than his job. If Treat was keeping files on dead associates of Rickey's, could that mean Rickey himself was in some kind of danger? The ME's report in particular sent a chill up his spine. Woofer considered just putting the file back where he'd found it and not showing up for his meeting with G-man. But if he had plenty to lose, it followed that Rickey had even more. However much he might covet the man's boyfriend, Woofer couldn't face the possibility of being responsible for Rickey coming to harm.

Working with quick, nervous movements, Woofer photocopied everything in the JOHN file. When he had finished, he returned the file to its place, locked the drawer, slid his pilfered materials into a manila envelope, and took his leave of Treat's inner sanctum. He knew he might never see this place again, but even so, he was glad to shut the door behind him.

G-man didn't know the West Bank very well and got badly lost on the way to Marrero. His easygoing nature was a bit frayed by the third time he went through the Harvey Tunnel, but at last he found the address Woofer had given him. When he walked in, he thought he'd made another mistake, because the place looked more like a

Mexican restaurant than a po-boy shop. Then he glimpsed the beacon of Woofer's bright red hair in the dimness, and Woofer looked up and waved at him.

"What kinda place is this?" said G-man as he took a seat, glancing around at the maracas, sombreros, and international soccer posters on the walls. He hadn't known anybody in New Orleans cared about soccer.

"It's run by a family from Jalisco. They call it a po-boy place so they'll get the local business, but the Mexican menu is really good. Try the barbacoa tacos. Oh, I'm so glad you came."

"Sure," said G-man a little uncomfortably. "I said I would, didn't I?"

He scanned the menu, then ordered the tacos Woofer recommended and the posole, which appeared to be some kind of soup. He hadn't always been an adventurous eater, but Rickey had drummed into him the importance of subjecting one's palate to all sorts of experiences. At least the waitress hadn't said "You no like," something they often heard when they tried to order items not on the English menu in the local Vietnamese restaurants.

He hoped Woofer would go ahead and tell him why they were here, but instead Woofer started asking all sorts of questions about his life history and how he'd gotten interested in cooking. G-man answered them, making sure to bring Rickey into the conversation as much as possible. It wasn't difficult: he doubted he ever would have started working in restaurants if Rickey hadn't developed such a passion for it. When he said so, Woofer asked him, "What *would* you be doing now?"

"My dad and one of my brothers work at Tante Lou's Confections. I guess I might've gotten on there."

"You don't think you would have gone to school?"

"I *went* to school. Frederick Douglass."

"No, I mean college. University."

G-man laughed. "Do I look like some kinda intellectual to you? My family's poor. They didn't even have the money to send us to Catholic school, let alone college, and I'm sure not smart enough to get a scholarship."

Woofer closed his eyes for a moment, and a small, nearly invisible shudder seemed to pass through his body. "But you've always been good with your hands, right?" he said. "What about trade school?"

"I don't know." G-man was getting tired of this. He'd come here to find out about Lenny's case, not to feed whatever weird working-class fetish this guy had. "I'm not big on thinking about stuff that might've happened. I like the way things are now."

So what did you want to tell me? he was about to add, but just then the waitress brought their food to the table. G-man soon lost himself in the new flavors and nearly forgot about Lenny's case. The posole was a spicy, complex red-brown broth full of tender pork chunks, nutty-flavored hominy corn, chopped cabbage, and diced onion. The barbacoa tacos were filled with the most meltingly delicious beef he'd ever tasted: rich with fat, the shreds seemed to dissolve into nothingness on his tongue. "What part of the cow is this?" he asked.

"I don't know," said Woofer, and waved the waitress back over. When he repeated G-man's question, she gave him a blank look. G-man was impressed when Woofer said, *"Que parte de vaca es barbacoa?"*

"La cabeza."

Now it was Woofer's turn to look blank. Seeing his confusion, the waitress tapped her forehead, then smiled and walked away.

"The head?" said Woofer.

"That makes sense. The head's real fatty—that's why they boil pigs' heads down to make hogshead cheese."

"Ugh."

"Hey, what difference does it make? You liked it before. Are you gonna quit liking it just because it's something you're not used to eating?"

"I suppose that's the best way to look at it."

"I didn't always look at it that way," said G-man. "Rickey taught me it's important to educate your palate."

"He must be quite a guy."

Poppy Z. Brite

"He is."

There was an awkward silence. G-man crumbled a corn tortilla into the bottom of his bowl to absorb the last drops of soup, then scraped up the pieces with his spoon.

"I suppose you know I didn't ask you here just because I wanted to give you information," said Woofer.

G-man shrugged, embarrassed for himself and for Woofer. *I knew I shouldn't have come,* he thought.

"But I *do* want to give you information. I especially want to give it to you—the information, I mean—after what I found last night." Woofer opened his briefcase and took out a manila envelope. "I'm not sure what all this means, but it seems like something you and Rickey should know about."

G-man accepted the envelope. Inside was a slim sheaf of papers. He wasn't expecting much at first, having just about decided that Woofer had arranged this meeting simply to get a good long look at him, but the first mention of Cooper Stark made his heart grow cold. As he examined the rest of the papers, he began to feel dizzy with foreboding. "You got these from Treat's office?" he said.

Woofer nodded. "They were in a file labeled 'John.' He's been keeping tabs on Rickey, I guess."

G-man remembered the tattoo on Stark's hip, the one the Dallas lawyer had told Rickey about the night he learned he'd been named executor and beneficiary of the will. G-man hadn't liked it then and liked it even less now. "It's not Rickey," he said.

"What's that?"

" 'John' isn't Rickey. His mom sometimes calls him Johnnie, but nobody ever calls him John. And look at this." He found the notation about the tattoo on the ME's report and pointed it out to Woofer. "That's not Rickey. Even assuming the worst, even assuming something happened between them in Dallas—which I don't— why would he have a tattoo of Rickey's name?"

"Obsessed, maybe. A *Fatal Attraction* kind of thing."

"But it's the *wrong name.* Stark knew Rickey was called Rickey. No, man, this John is somebody else, and I need to find out who."

"Is there anything I can do to help?"

"Find out who John is," said G-man. "It's gotta be somebody Treat knows. Listen, thanks for inviting me to lunch." He tossed a ten-dollar bill onto the table before Woofer could protest, then scrawled his cell-phone number on a paper napkin. "I gotta go. I got some ideas about who to talk to. Call me if you think of anything, OK?"

"Sure," said Woofer.

"Thanks. Really, I mean it, but I gotta go."

He could feel Woofer's sad eyes on his back as he headed for the door, but he didn't care. He felt very strongly that Rickey was in danger from this John person, and he was going to find out why.

Poppy Z. Brite

23

The alarm woke Rickey early. De La Cerda had advised him
to call the medical examiner's office well before noon, when there
would be a better chance of catching the doctor he wanted to talk
to. He called room service and took the ME's report out of its envelope, wondering when his life had begun to go so wrong that he'd
end up looking at a thing like this before he'd had his first cup of
coffee.

Forcing his eyes away from the gory details, he found the name
of the doctor who had performed Coop's autopsy and called
Information. When he asked for the ME's office, a mechanical voice
recited a number, then informed him that for a charge of thirty
cents it would dial the number for him. Rickey let it, reflecting that
this feature of the automated information system had brought
things full circle to the days when you dialed the operator and
asked her to connect your call. Not that he remembered that, but
his mother had worked as a switchboard operator when she was
very young, and still liked to talk about the lyrical-sounding
old New Orleans telephone exchanges: TUlane, CRescent,
WHitehall 9 . . .

He was distracting himself, and was yanked out of his reverie by a female voice with a slight Hispanic accent saying, "Dallas County Medical Examiner."

"Uh, hi. I'm trying to reach Dr. . . ." He realized he'd forgotten the name already, and glanced at the report again. "Dr. Carter."

"May I tell him who's calling?"

"This is John Rickey. I'm trying to find out about Cooper Stark, a patient of his." *Are you supposed to call dead people patients?* he wondered, too late. *Probably not. She's gonna hang up on me for sure.*

But the woman only said, "Are you the next of kin?"

"I'm the executor of his will."

A pause. Then: "I don' know if Dr. Carter's in yet. I'll transfer you."

"Thanks," Rickey said to a series of clicks. Another phone began to ring; then another voice, this one pure Texas, said, "Holliday Carter."

Holliday? Rickey thought. He identified himself and had begun to frame his question when the doctor said, "I cain't tell you anything over the phone."

"I kinda figured. Well, thanks any—"

"Be happy to talk to you if you can come in."

"Huh?"

"I don't have any posts till later this morning. If you can come in right now, show me you're who you say you are, I'll see what I can tell you."

"To the morgue?"

"That's where you usually find us pathologists, yeah."

"Uh . . ." Rickey remembered his dream. *You know I didn't have a chipped tooth,* Coop had said. *The only question is what you're going to do about it.* So what was he going to do? Wuss out because he was scared of dead bodies? "Sure, I can come in," he said.

The doctor gave him directions from downtown. As they hung up, Rickey's room-service coffee arrived, and he gulped two scalding cups as he got dressed. He'd brought along the fancy cowboy boots Frank Firestone had given him; he was embarrassed to wear them in New Orleans, but people wouldn't stare at them here, and they *were* awfully comfortable. He slid his feet into the buttery-soft leather, then took the elevator down to the hotel's parking garage, retrieved Coop's car, and set off for yet another place he didn't want to go.

The traffic on I-35 was hair-raising, but the interstate swept him along to where he was going in just a few minutes. He exited near the medical center campus, pulled into the complex, and found the building without much trouble. When he punched the glove compartment button to retrieve the envelope of Coop's papers, something else fell out: one of those small laminated grocery-store discount cards. Rickey had two or three of them on his own key-chain. Looking at it made him remember that Coop hadn't been just a source of gore and bad dreams, but a person with the ordinary details of an ordinary life. All at once he felt terribly lonely for the friendship they'd almost had. Maybe their mutual attraction would always have gotten in the way, but if they'd managed to get past that, he thought they really could have *liked* each other. He swallowed a lump in his throat and got out of the car. It was right that he'd come here, no matter how unpleasant the experience might be.

He spoke to the receptionist and was asked to wait in what she called the reception room, a cubicle with a table, a few hard plastic chairs, and a big box of Kleenex. Was this where families waited to find out what had happened to their loved ones? Rickey couldn't imagine sitting here in the sterile light wondering if the body of a person he loved lay somewhere nearby. The room was cold and there was an odd smell, not quite decayed but more as if industrial-strength disinfectants had been used to mask something decayed. He shuddered, and of course the doctor picked that moment to walk in.

"Not exactly the Ritz-Carlton, is it? More like the *Rotz*-Carlton. Don't listen to me—I haven't had enough coffee yet. Howdy." The man extended a hand. "I'm Holliday Carter."

"John Rickey," said Rickey, shaking the coldest hand he'd ever touched. "I haven't had enough coffee either."

"Well, let's see if we cain't do something about that. Conchita!" The doctor went to the door of the cubicle and addressed the receptionist. "You got any of that Texas crude left?"

"You're the only Texas crude thing I see around here," the woman said, but she got up and fixed them two cups of coffee from a pot in the corner.

As he sipped the noisome black brew, Rickey eyed the doctor. He had a long pale head with deep-set eyes and a tufty little fringe of reddish hair that made Rickey think of the orangutans at Audubon Zoo. The backs of his hands were so white that the blue tracery of veins looked like a map of some vast river system beneath the skin. His appearance was pretty off-putting, really, but he seemed friendly enough as he examined Coop's papers and glanced at Rickey's driver's license. "From the Big Easy, huh?"

"Yeah," said Rickey, though he hated that particular nickname for New Orleans.

"What's your connection to Mr. Stark?"

"We worked together."

"And he left you all his earthly possessions?"

Rickey shrugged. "It looks weird to me too. Tell you the truth, Doc, I don't know what to make of any of this. Last time I saw him, Coop seemed anything but suicidal. He seemed happy."

"Sometimes people *are* happy once they make up their mind to do away with themselves. It takes a load off, so to speak."

"I guess. But there was one other thing. In your report, you said he had a chipped front tooth. It wasn't chipped last time I saw him. I just wondered if that could've happened when he . . . you know, did it."

Carter looked up, his cavernous eyes sharp. "You're thinking it wasn't suicide?"

"Well . . ." Rickey took a Kleenex from the box, twisted it around his finger just to have something to do with his hands.

"Mr. Rickey, I know how upsetting it is when somebody close to us decides to take their own life. We wonder why we weren't able to help them. We don't want to believe they could have done such a thing. In this case, though, I feel one hundred percent confident that your friend committed suicide. I'm real sorry, but that's what the forensic evidence told me. There were no signs of a struggle, no drugs in his system other than a little alcohol. His right hand tested positive for gunpowder residue, meaning he did fire the gun himself. It's all in my report."

"I couldn't read the whole thing," said Rickey, feeling stupid.

"Of course not. I'm sorry to have to tell you these things, but I want you to understand my findings. I don't know about the chipped tooth. He could have done it in an accident days or weeks before death. He could have involuntarily bitten down on the gun's barrel when he shot himself. I didn't find the chip in his mouth, but it may have remained at the scene or I may have missed it. I *can* tell you his death was instantaneous. He didn't feel any pain."

"That's good," Rickey said, wondering how somebody willing to stick a gun in his mouth and pull the trigger could be said to have felt no pain. "Look, I'm sorry if I wasted your time."

"Absolutely not. I encourage next of kin—or friends, whatever—to ask me any questions they might have. You cain't really deal with the loss of a person until you understand what happened to him."

I guess I'm not really dealing with it, then, Rickey thought, but he just thanked the doctor and got out of the place as quickly as possible. The not-quite-smell of decay and the bad coffee had conspired to make his guts churn, and the Saturn's interior had become ovenlike during the few minutes he'd spent in the building. Rickey realized he'd never eaten dinner last night. No wonder he felt so crappy; he needed to get something in his stomach.

He stopped at a tiny Mexican diner and had scrambled eggs with chorizo. They were creamy, spicy, and delicious, and as he lingered over them, he began to feel a little better. He'd done what he could. The pathologist seemed sure Coop's death had been a suicide. It was time to leave his uncertainty behind and get on with cleaning out Coop's apartment. The job would take him all day, and he was anxious to get it over with. He'd call De La Cerda from there and let the lawyer know what he was up to.

Rickey picked up some heavy-duty garbage bags at a drugstore, then drove over to Oak Cliff and parked in front of Coop's house. There were no cars in the parking lot and no signs of life around the building; the other tenants must be at work or sleeping in. For the first time, Rickey wondered if any of Coop's neighbors had heard the shot that killed him. Probably there was something about it in one of the reports and he just hadn't seen it. That had been embarrassing, telling the doctor he couldn't read the whole report. He knew the doctor must have thought he and Coop were lovers. Everybody seemed to think so these days.

Lost in his thoughts, Rickey climbed the outside staircase, let himself into the apartment, shut the door behind him. He was halfway across the living room when he registered movement from the corner of his eye, near the sofa: an arm, reaching to click on the lamp that sat on the end table. Rickey froze, his heart pistoning.

"Good to see you again, Chef," said Frank Firestone. "How you liking those boots?"

24

G-man forced himself to stay calm as he drove back across the bridge and headed uptown. He'd tried to call Rickey several more times, but Rickey still wasn't in his room. Damn him for throwing his cell phone in the lake like some silly-ass drama queen. Damn him for not taking the time to replace it. *I should have gone ahead and gotten him one if he wouldn't do it,* G-man thought guiltily. It wasn't his responsibility, but he should have done it anyway. Now if anything happened to Rickey, it would be his fault.

Of course there was no reason to think anything would happen, no reason for the sense of foreboding that curled in his gut like a worm in amberjack. There must be some legitimate reason for Placide Treat to have records on Cooper Stark, or more likely an illegitimate reason, but not a dangerous one. G-man glanced at the envelope lying innocently in the passenger seat, betraying no hint of its gruesome contents. Why the hell would Treat have Stark's autopsy report? What could it mean? These were the circles his mind kept making, and he was very close to panic.

Back home, he tried Rickey again, left another message at the hotel, then had an idea and called Dallas information. There was a listing for Cooper Stark, but when he dialed it, a recording told him the number was out of service. Even if Rickey was cleaning out Stark's apartment, G-man couldn't reach him there.

Placide Treat, he thought frantically. What did he know about Placide Treat? He was investigating Lenny. His son had written a nasty review of Liquor. He liked Tante Lou's Treasure Eggs, or at least thought they were good vote-getters.

Remembering that, G-man paused and forced himself to think more carefully. Who had told him that? His brother Henry, of course. And who had told them something else about Placide Treat? His father.

He picked up the phone again and dialed his father's work number. He would be calm, he promised himself. "Tante Lou's, shipping department," said a gravelly male voice that didn't belong to his father.

"Uh, hello, could I talk to Elmer Stubbs?"

"Lemme see if he's around . . . El*MER!*" There was a clatter and a pause, then, blessedly, Elmer's voice on the line. "Hello?"

Calm, G-man reminded himself. "Daddy, it's me, Gary."

"Gary? What's wrong?"

Either he hadn't sounded as calm as he thought or some parental radar was at work. Without being specific about where he'd gotten the material, G-man explained what had turned up in Treat's files. "It really freaks me out," he concluded, "and I can't get in touch with Rickey. I know you told us some kinda story about Treat last time we had dinner over there, but I was hitting the wine pretty heavy that night and I don't remember what it was."

"I told you about Treat's illegitimate son," said Elmer, sounding as if he were thinking fast. "*Supposed* illegitimate son. I don't even know for sure if he exists, and I got no idea if it'd have anything to do with all this."

"Can you find out?"

"Let me make a couple calls." Elmer hesitated. "You gonna be OK?"

"I think so."

Poppy Z. Brite

"Don't do nothing crazy, awright? Just sit tight until I call you back."

G-man knew he couldn't sit by the phone, so he went into the kitchen and started cleaning out the refrigerator. Into the garbage went a brace of carrots so withered they looked like something out of a voodoo spell, an ancient jar of Patak's mango pickle whose label was translucent with orange grease, a knob of unidentifiable cheese. He was pondering a plastic container with three salt-cured olives in it when he heard the phone ring.

"The son's Christian name is John," said Elmer.

"John," G-man repeated dumbly, thinking of the tattoo Rickey had said they found on Coop's body, the tattoo Coop's lawyer had assumed was meant for Rickey.

"He might be going by another name now. He lives in Dallas. That's all I could get."

"It's enough."

"Gary, you ain't gonna go messing around with these people, are you? I got a friend in the police department—"

"Daddy, I don't think the police can help me with this. I gotta take care of Rickey, if I can. You know that."

"Yeah, I know." Elmer suddenly sounded ten years older than he had at the beginning of the conversation. "Well, call me when you know something. Don't let me sit here and worry."

"I won't," G-man promised. "It might be a while, but I'll call you. I love you, Daddy. Momma too."

"Gary—"

"Sorry. I gotta go." He hung up on his father's voice saying his name again. Rude as hell, but Elmer would sit there all day urging him to be careful.

He tried Rickey's hotel again. Nothing.

Placide Treat had a bastard son named John, and he lived in Dallas.

Shortly before all the shit with Lenny had gone down, Frank Firestone had contacted Rickey out of nowhere offering him a

261

generous sum of money to come to Dallas. He'd worked with Cooper Stark. Now Cooper Stark was dead, and details of his death had been found in the files of Placide Treat.

Treat had gotten one of his sons to write a negative review of Liquor. Was it so far-fetched to think he had gotten the other son to set Rickey up somehow, maybe for something far worse than a bad review?

He remembered what Humphrey Wildblood had told Rickey on the night Wildblood ate at Liquor: *My father can guarantee you never get another bad review in New Orleans if you're prepared to give him information on Lenny Duveteaux.*

Was this all about Lenny, then?

That didn't matter right now. Rickey could be in serious danger, and G-man had to do something about it. Since he couldn't reach Rickey by phone, he would just have to go to Dallas, and he needed to get there faster than any car or commercial flight could take him. He hadn't wanted to involve Lenny, but Lenny was the only person he knew who had the money and power to help him. He picked up the phone again, dialed the first three digits of Lenny's number, then paused. *Was* Lenny the only person with enough money and power to help him?

The night Rickey came home from his first trip to Dallas, G-man had discouraged him from working the dinner shift, not just because Rickey was tired but also because Dirty King was bringing his parents in and G-man wanted to take care of them himself. When he spoke to them at the table, he could see that the meal had meant a lot to the rap mogul, though he wasn't sure why. He remembered King handing him a business card with his personal cell number written on the back and saying, *I owe you one, dawg. Call me if you ever need to collect.*

Maybe this was the time to find out if he had meant it.

His mind tried to throw up all sorts of objections—*you hardly know the guy, this is much bigger than whatever he thinks he owes you, you're probably blowing it way out of proportion anyway*—but he overrode them all. Rickey could be in danger. He felt Rickey *was* in danger. Nothing else was very important to him right now.

They both received a lot of business cards, and most of them ended up jumbled with other crap in a kitchen drawer, but G-man had figured Dirty King's card was important enough to put in his wallet. He found it there now and dialed the number, wondering what the hell he was going to say.

"It ain't even a problem, dawg," said Dirty King. "You took care of my family, I'm a take care of you."

G-man wasn't inclined to argue. They were aboard King's small private jet, which bore the Gold Frontin' Records logo on its sleek sides and all over its black leather interior. In the cockpit was a middle-aged white man King simply called Cap. In the seats behind them were two very large, very armed-looking young brothers King had introduced as his bodyguards, Darnell and C-Ray.

G-man had arranged for Tanker to run the kitchen if he and Rickey weren't back by tomorrow, then rushed off to meet King at the little Lakefront Airport where the millionaires kept their private planes. Thirty minutes out of New Orleans, he had just finished filling in the gaps in the abbreviated version of the story he'd given King over the phone.

"I don't even know for sure if anything needs taking care of," said G-man.

"You got a gut feeling, though."

"Yeah."

"You gotta listen to those. At a Gold Frontin' party one time, I got a feeling about this kid over in the corner. He wasn't doing nothing, wasn't even looking at me, but there was just something I didn't like about him. I had my crew search him when he went to leave. Know what they found? Cassette tape—a rough cut of the new Kryptyk." G-man knew Kryptyk was one of Gold Frontin' Records' biggest acts. "Some fool done left it lying around and this motherfucker just slipped it in his pocket. Coulda sold dupes on the street for mad money if he got out with it."

"Damn." G-man wondered what had happened to the thief, but didn't ask.

"Yeah. So when your gut tells you something, listen to it. But right now, listen to me." King gestured back at the two bodyguards. "These headbusters know what they're doing. We gonna get into Dallas, go straight to this apartment you think your boy's at, check out the scene. If it looks bad, they go in first. You and me stay back. *Way* back. Got it?"

"Sure."

"Yeah, I know that kinda *sure*. It means *I hear you, but when it comes time to bang, I'll do what the fuck I please*. That ain't good enough. If my boys gotta put their lives on the line, your job is to help 'em by staying the fuck out the way. Got it?"

"Got it," said G-man, trying to sound sincere. Of course he and Dirty King both knew—and probably the bodyguards did too—that if he saw any chance to help Rickey, he'd jump at it. But the official chain of command had been issued; he supposed that was part of how these guys psyched themselves up to face danger. He wished he had some similar tricks, but his life had gone in a different direction. In the past couple of years, anyway, he'd faced nothing more dangerous than a long line of order tickets and a stressed-out kitchen crew.

"You wanna watch some videos?" said King, pressing a button that made personal DVD screens slide out of the ceiling.

"Nah, you go ahead. I think I'll try to rest a little."

G-man leaned his forehead against the window and watched Louisiana, or maybe it was already Texas, slipping by below. He knew the airplane must be traveling very fast, but nothing could go fast enough for him. He needed to already be there, to disprove the words—*too late, too late, too late*—that echoed in his head and pounded with his heartbeat, to silence the fear that everything important in his life had suddenly been wiped away when he wasn't looking.

Poppy Z. Brite

25

Firestone had been sitting in the apartment all night, silently psyching himself up for what he needed to do. It was one thing to kill a man in the heat of the moment—in the heat of passion, so to speak. It was quite another to lie in wait for someone, ready to turn him into an example of why no one should ever fuck with you or your family, the family you were finally proving your worthiness to join in full.

He was naked except for his boots, which he might need for kicking. The incident with Cooper had taught him the value of being naked when you had dirty work to do; there was less mess to clean up afterward. Instead of having bloody clothes to dispose of, you could just jump in the shower.

He wanted a cigarette, but would not smoke one in case the smell alerted Rickey. Instead he just sat on Cooper's ragged one-cushioned sofa, the other cushion missing because Firestone had thrown it into the river, and he waited, and he thought about his family.

For the better part of four decades he had been an afterthought in his father's life. He and his mother had been supported by the Geigenheimer fortune, and now that Firestone was a figure of some repute in the Dallas business sphere, Placide Treat occasionally called upon him for a favor. But in the eyes of the world, that pusillanimous pustule Humphrey was his father's son, while John Franklin Firestone was little more than a juicy rumor.

The restaurant had been a legitimate business venture, as well as something he thought might catch Treat's interest; like all New Orleanians, his father loved a good restaurant. But Treat had never come to eat there, hadn't even visited Dallas since the place opened. Not until Firestone learned of Cooper's past with Rickey did the restaurant turn out to be of some use to Treat, and that had been the purest kind of dumb luck.

Firestone and Cooper Stark had met when they were both catting around New York in the early nineties. Firestone had spent most of that decade traveling the world's capitals, but Dallas always drew him back. When Cooper's restaurants folded and he found himself owing money to some people who weren't nearly as patient as your average bank or credit card company, Firestone had paid off his debts for him. He figured having a famous chef in his pocket would come in handy sooner or later, even if the chef was pretty much a has-been.

In return for paying off the debts, Firestone had turned Cooper into his pet chef bitch: made him move to Dallas, installed him in the restaurant, given him a piece-of-shit car, played on-again-off-again sex games with him. Firestone had never been able to resist fucking anything that didn't run away from him: men, women, lawyers, chefs, strippers, it didn't matter. Considering who his mother had been, he guessed that wasn't very surprising. Of course, Cooper had had some power in the relationship too. He had few expenses, so he just kept socking away his paychecks until he had a nice little nest egg. At one point he'd gotten nearly angry enough to leave Dallas, and Firestone had signed over the apartment building to make him stay. The two had fed off each other; Firestone could see that now.

The turning point had come when Cooper was flipping through

an old issue of *Gourmet* one day: "Hey, I know this guy," he'd exclaimed. It had been Rickey, pictured in a write-up of Liquor that mentioned the connection with celebrity chef Lenny Duveteaux. Of course, Firestone hadn't known of Rickey's importance then; but later, when he learned that his father was pursuing a case against Duveteaux, he had put the pieces together.

"Think you could get him in bed?" he'd asked Cooper.

"Well, I couldn't before."

"Think you could try?"

"Do I have a choice?" Cooper asked. But of course it was a rhetorical question; Cooper Stark never had much of a choice where Firestone was concerned.

With Treat's blessing, Firestone arranged for Rickey to come to Dallas for a consulting job. Where Humphrey's offer of good reviews in perpetuity had failed to sway Rickey, Firestone's darker and more effective methods of persuasion would succeed.

But then everything had started to go wrong.

First of all, Rickey remained damnably and steadfastly faithful to his boyfriend. Firestone had found it inconceivable that, given the chance to get off scot-free with someone he was undeniably attracted to, Rickey would refuse to stray. But Rickey had refused.

Firestone had spent the next several weeks in a white-hot rage at Cooper: for failing, for being too sympathetic to Rickey, for acting as if Firestone was crazy for suggesting the plan in the first place. He'd visited Cooper one night, angry about his failure to follow through on the plan. They had ended up in bed as they almost always did. Afterward, they'd argued about what Stark hadn't managed to do with Rickey. Cooper, who'd been drinking, had threatened to call Rickey up and tell him the whole story. Firestone waited until Cooper fell asleep, then got the unregistered gun he always carried in his briefcase, jammed it into Cooper's mouth, and pulled the trigger before Cooper had time to do more than open his eyes. He put the gun in Cooper's slowly stiffening hand and fired it into one of the sofa cushions, because he knew about swabbing for powder residue. He cleaned himself up, talked himself down, took the sofa cushion away and threw it out the car window into the Trinity River.

He had been able to do all that, yes. Probably it hadn't been the wisest thing to do. But he was going to make up for it now. Since he hadn't been able to get information out of Rickey in one way, he was going to get it in quite another. After that, surely he would be his father's favorite son. The implements of his plan were arrayed in the bedroom, waiting.

He heard a key in the door and gripped the can of Mace, ready to do what he had to do.

"What the fuck—" Rickey got out before Firestone Maced him in the face. For an instant there was no pain, and then it seized him all at once, like a spider closing venomous jaws around his head. Once, and only once, he'd cut up a bunch of habanero peppers without wearing rubber gloves. He had washed his hands afterward, but when he thoughtlessly rubbed his eye an hour later, the burning had been huge and instantaneous. This was like that but a hundred times stronger, in both eyes, up his nose, down his throat and snaking into his lungs. His heart was trying to burst right out of his chest. He had forgotten where he was, forgotten Firestone, forgotten everything but the fire in his head and the fight to take a breath.

Somebody grabbed him by the back of his shirt and lifted, dragged, led. *Must be G,* he thought semicoherently, *something blew up in the kitchen and he's got me, but oh, fuck, I'm blind, I'm gonna suffocate . . .* He remembered where he was, began to struggle. Something crashed into the back of his head and he was gone again.

In the blackness, a man waited for him. Rickey saw with little surprise that the man was Cooper Stark.

"Better wake your ass up," said Coop. "Don't let him do you like he did me."

Poppy Z. Brite

"How *did* he do you?" Rickey asked.

But Coop was gone, and a few seconds or hours later, Rickey didn't remember that he had ever been there.

Placide Treat had been pacing for so long that he expected to look down and see a circular track worn through the carpet of his Roosevelt Hotel suite. It was still well before dawn, but he couldn't remember the last time he had slept. Never before in his life had such a good idea gone so damnably wrong.

When Treat found out that the chef at John's restaurant had a history with Rickey, he'd seen a chance to use it against Lenny Duveteaux. Now the plan had gone to hell, one man had died, another was likely to die, and John had ventured so far into the land of lunacy that Treat feared for his son's life too.

Treat believed sincerely that Rickey had information capable of incarcerating Lenny Duveteaux. He'd found no proof of this, but if he was wrong, that meant his instincts were beginning to fail him. He couldn't let himself believe that. And there were rumors of an old man who had been murdered for making a complaint about Liquor's zoning; if he could get Rickey to testify about that alone, it would be plenty.

Humphrey's *Cornet* review had been his first shot across Liquor's bow. It hadn't done a great deal of damage, but it had perhaps put Rickey in a frame of mind where he was looking to prove himself. Consulting gigs were good for that; they made young chefs feel like hotshots. ("Like hired guns riding into town to do what the drunken old marshal cain't," John had put it in his Texan way.)

Treat and John had gambled that Rickey could be tempted to stray in Dallas, especially if he felt sorry for his old flame. This had been their initial mistake. John would never have been born if not for his father's cheating heart, and he had learned some of his satyr's ways from Treat. They hadn't reckoned on a man who would refuse to cheat even when given a golden, risk-free opportunity.

None of that was good, but Treat could have lived with it. Such a plan was never a sure thing. What he couldn't live with was the call he'd gotten late one night. John's voice, usually so self-assured, had sounded like a lost little boy's. "Daddy? . . . Cooper's dead."

Did you kill him? Treat had nearly asked, then cursed himself. You didn't want to say such things on the telephone, even on a secure line like his. And of course John had killed him. He wouldn't have been calling otherwise. John's cold Treat blood had gotten him through it, but now Treat was an accessory to murder, not for the first time ever, but for the first time in service of a cause that was not honorable. The death of Cooper Stark had helped no one.

Now Rickey was back in Dallas. Treat knew this courtesy of Woofer, who ate at Liquor practically every night; the boy wasn't long on brains but at least he was loyal. Treat had been touched by his willingness to return to the restaurant again and again, trying to glean some helpful nugget of information.

Rickey was in Dallas for unknown reasons, and Treat couldn't reach John. He'd tried John's home, the restaurant, his cell phone. John carried his cell phone everywhere, but he wasn't answering it now. Treat felt sure John had learned of Rickey's return and would try to confront him, most likely in Stark's apartment, where Rickey would surely have to go.

This had gone far enough, Treat decided. He had never intended for Cooper Stark to die, but Stark had chosen to involve himself with John. Rickey was a different matter, an innocent party who had no idea what he'd walked into. And if John did try to hurt him, Treat suspected Rickey might put up a better fight than Stark had.

He couldn't risk the death of an innocent man, and he certainly couldn't risk the death of his son. He had hidden John away like a shameful secret long enough. It was time to claim him and try to redeem him. A son who was willing to kill for him—no matter how misguided that act had been—surely deserved as much.

Standing at the window looking out over the sunrise-tinged city, Treat came to a decision. The vista before him had changed dramatically in his lifetime. Where slums stood in his memory, the Superdome now rose white and golden. Where live oaks once formed a canopy over Claiborne Avenue, an interstate highway roared. He could expect to live no more than another twenty years, and he decided to make his elder son a full part of that life. He would go get John—or Frank, or whatever he liked to call himself now—and bring him back to New Orleans. Yvonne had long known of his existence. She didn't like it, but Treat believed she would find it in her heart to accept him. She had wanted another child after Humphrey, but hadn't been able to have one. And Humphrey would get to know his brother at last. John would acquire some of Humphrey's humility, while Humphrey might gain self-respect from seeing that his brother was a flawed, weak-minded man just like everybody else. Treat would embrace his family, his *entire* family, and he would win the DA race again. In another city, admitting the existence of a long-rumored bastard son would be a liability. In New Orleans, he wouldn't be surprised if it gained him voter sympathy. New Orleanians loved a man who had the panache to wear his dirty laundry with pride.

This plan filled Placide Treat's mind and heart so completely that for the first time in months he forgot about Lenny Duveteaux. It could work; certainly it could work, if only he was able to move fast enough. He was going to Dallas, and he was leaving as soon as possible.

When Rickey swam up to consciousness again, he was on a bed and somebody was pulling his arms up over his head. Again he thought it was G-man, that all the Dallas business was finally over and he was home. But the bed was unfamiliar and faintly sticky, and the hands on him were not G-man's. Something cold and metallic encircled one of his wrists. A handcuff.

Rickey caught a breath. It felt like it was ripping his lungs apart, but it brought his mind back from the edge. He remembered where he was, began to struggle. The handcuff, not yet latched, came loose and went flying. He wrenched himself out of Firestone's grasp and up off the bed. A fist smashed into his temple, not hard

271

enough to knock him out but hard enough to make his head swim. He swung back at a spot twelve inches or so above where the fist had been and connected with flesh. Firestone grunted, whether in pain or just surprise Rickey couldn't tell. The sound gave Rickey a better idea of his position, and he kicked out at it. His foot sank into something soft. He felt Firestone stumbling away from him. Rickey turned and groped his way out of the bedroom, down the hall, toward the kitchen.

He still couldn't get his eyes open, but he didn't waste any time looking for the sink to wash his face; his knowledge of kitchen chemistry told him that the compounds in pepper spray wouldn't be affected by water. Instead he raked through drawers and cabinets, hunting for a weapon by touch alone. He found nothing but silverware, a potato masher, a garlic press. Where the hell were Coop's knives?

As he heard Firestone behind him, Rickey finally managed to crack one eyelid. It felt like a hot coal burrowing into his head, but he could see a slice of cabinet shelves. Box of Triscuits. Jar of peanut butter. Bug bomb.

Rickey grabbed the bug bomb and tried to pry off its plastic top as Firestone reeled toward him. It wouldn't come, and he nearly sobbed with frustration before he remembered the one he'd set off in his own house last month. You had to squeeze the sides of the top, then twist, a lame attempt at childproofing. He got it off just as Firestone Maced him again. The pain seemed worse this time because Rickey knew it was only going to keep intensifying. He aimed the bug bomb at the spot where he'd seen Firestone's face a second ago and pressed the trigger. A hissing sound and an awful sweetish chemical smell filled the room. He heard Firestone gasp reflexively, then begin to choke.

Rickey flung the bomb at him and made for the door that opened onto the roof garden. It wouldn't open. Rickey wondered if he should just try to smash one of the glass panes, but then his searching fingers found a deadbolt and slid it back. Behind him he could hear Firestone scrabbling among the things Rickey had raked out of the drawers and cabinets. Any second now a knife would plunge into his back or the bottle of Scotch would come flying at his head.

He flung the door open and lurched onto the flat roof. His knees connected with a planter, and he almost lost his balance. It would be cute if he escaped Firestone only to go toppling blindly off the edge of the roof. He forced himself to stand still and try to open his eyes, and that was when the world exploded and a huge invisible hand seemed to mold itself to Rickey's body and propel him gently into space.

Dirty King's jet touched down at Love Field ninety minutes after it left New Orleans. G-man had already found Cooper Stark's address in the sheaf of papers Woofer had given him. Their ride awaited them right on the tarmac: a late-model Chevy Impala tricked out with spinner rims, tinted windows, an ear-splitting sound system, and four DVD screens. Under any other circumstances, G-man would have been impressed with the car, but now he slid into the backseat without giving it a second look. C-Ray took the wheel, King climbed in behind him, Darnell rode shotgun, and they sped off toward Oak Cliff.

The drive seemed to take hours, though C-Ray knew where he was going and it couldn't have been more than twenty minutes. Finally they pulled into a small vacant lot that had been covered with gravel to form a rudimentary parking area. Beside it was a big old house, slightly decrepit-looking and obviously divided into several apartments. A beat-up Saturn and a fire engine were parked in the lot. As they piled out of the Impala, G-man caught a whiff of wet ashes, and a knot formed in his stomach.

The two bodyguards stood poised for action, their hands straying toward the insides of their jackets. They scanned the area like a couple of predators looking for their next meal, but there was nothing to see except a lone fireman swinging down from the engine's cab. "Y'all live here?" he called.

"A friend of mine does," said G-man. "What's going on?"

"Some idiot in the second-floor apartment set off a bug bomb without extinguishing his pilot light. Bomb rolled under the stove and the fumes ignited. Blew out the back wall of the kitchen. Look, you can just see the edge of the hole from here."

"Was anybody hurt?"

"Yeah, two people, I think. They were the only ones home. One of 'em fell over the edge of the roof garden and the other one was trapped in the kitchen. You missed all the fun, though—ambulance already took 'em to Parkland, and we put the farr out twenty minutes ago. Police been and gone too."

"How bad was it?"

"Don't know. If you wanna see about your friend, you better just go over to Parkland. That's what we told the old man."

"Old man?"

"Yeah, an old man showed up in a taxi while we were still hosing down the hot spots. When we told him the people from the house were at Parkland, he jumped back in the taxi and went peeling off."

"I gotta get to the hospital," G-man told Dirty King, who had come up beside him.

"Just tell C-Ray where you wanna go, dawg."

The two bodyguards climbed back into the car, looking disgusted. "Thought we was gonna get to do somethin," Darnell complained.

"Shut up," Dirty King told him. "Every day you don't gotta do nothing, count your blessings."

Rickey opened his eyes and saw four faces hanging above him. Three belonged to unfamiliar young black men. The fourth was G-man's.

His eyes still burned, the skin all over his body felt lightly crisped, and there was a faraway dull ache in his left ankle. Overlying it all was a lovely floaty feeling that seemed to caress him from deep inside, leaving him detached. "The fuck am I?" he said.

"You're in the emergency room," said G-man, who looked ready to cry but was hiding it well. Probably the other three guys couldn't tell at all. Rickey wondered briefly who they were before the lovely floaty feeling wiped away his curiosity. "You got a concussion and a broken ankle, but you're gonna be fine."

What about Firestone? Rickey started to say, but realized he didn't much care. Besides, talking hurt his throat. He groped for G-man's hand, found it, and let his eyes slip shut again.

G-man wanted to stay, but a nurse shooed them out of the tiny room. "When he wakes up again, you can take him home," she said, and G-man felt a little better.

As they stepped into the hall, an orderly wheeled a gurney past them. The figure on the gurney was completely covered with a sheet except for two feet clad in gaudy hand-tooled cowboy boots sticking out at the end. Placide Treat was hobbling along beside the gurney babbling at the sheeted figure. "John, wake up . . . you gonna be awright, son, Daddy's here . . . Johnny, open your eyes."

He grabbed at the sheet, which slid partly off. Before the orderly could snatch it back, G-man glimpsed the lower half of a naked, scorched male body with the word COOPER tattooed in red and black above its left hipbone.

26

"So Firestone actually *gave* the apartment building to Stark?" said G-man. He was doing most of the talking, since Rickey's throat still hurt from the pepper spray.

Placide Treat nodded. He, Rickey, G-man, and Oscar De La Cerda were sitting in the bar at the top of Reunion Tower. Dirty King and his two bodyguards had flown back to New Orleans earlier this evening. Amazingly, Dirty King had embraced G-man like a brother and told him to call if he ever needed anything else. Rickey knew how much some people appreciated a good meal, but this struck him as extreme.

The gorgeous Dallas skyline sparkled in Rickey's peripheral vision. He tried not to look at it. His head still hurt, and he didn't want to be reminded of his evening here with Coop. It had been Treat's idea to meet here—"a neutral place above it all," he'd said. He seemed remarkably calm for a man whose son had been pronounced dead just a few hours ago.

"He was always giving people stuff," said Treat. "He'd sleep with them and he'd give them stuff. I guess he thought that was how you showed you loved somebody. Guess maybe he learned it from his daddy."

Poppy Z. Brite

Rickey looked down at his feet. One was completely hidden inside a huge knee-high cast that was going to make his life in the kitchen miserable over the next few months. The other was clad in a new, cheap sneaker supplied by the hospital. It wasn't as comfortable as his fancy cowboy boots had been. He didn't know what had happened to the boots. Maybe one of the cops or EMTs had snagged them. Rickey didn't care; he never wanted to see them again.

The doctor at Parkland had said he could get the huge cast replaced with a walking one in a week or two, but until then he was supposed to keep his weight off it. They'd given him a pair of crutches that were already threatening to become objects of his deepest hatred. He wasn't supposed to drink, but he didn't mind that so much because of the pain medication they'd given him. The lovely, floaty feeling he had experienced at the hospital was beginning to wear off, and he looked forward to getting back to the hotel so he could take a pill or two.

"I don't get it," said De La Cerda, who'd come in late. "How'd Stark get mixed up in this in the first place?"

"He and Firestone had a pretty intense relationship in New York," said G-man, repeating what Treat had told them at the hospital. "That was when they got the tattoos, I guess. Is that about right, Mr. Treat?"

Treat nodded morosely, staring into his glass. He'd wanted a Pimm's Cup, but the bartender didn't have any cucumbers, so he had settled for a double martini.

"Right," said De La Cerda. "But I still don't understand why Firestone ended up killing him."

"Coop agreed to help set Rickey up, but then he made a will leaving everything to Rickey. Who knows? Maybe there was a part of him that admired Rickey for not cheating on me. Firestone couldn't stand that."

"It was all about ego," Rickey said. The words felt like tiny knives scraping the inside of his throat, but he could not remain silent on this point. "He could've cut his losses right there—his restaurant was doing great thanks to my silly-ass beef menu, so it wasn't like he got nothing out of the whole deal—but Coop wasn't allowed to defy him. Except Coop did end up defying him. He made that will less than three weeks before he died."

"Christ," said De La Cerda. "What a tale. I'm still not exactly clear on why *you* got dragged into it, though, Rickey."

"Apparently it was all part of the plot against Lenny. They were convinced I had some kinda dirt on him, and they were gonna make me give it up one way or another."

Treat favored De La Cerda with a baleful glare. "I'm aware of your reputation as an attorney and I respect it," he said. "But I don't respect the fact that you represent Lenny Duveteaux. He's a bad, bad man."

"Aw, you just hate him because he wouldn't comp your party at his restaurant that time."

"You go on telling yourself that, sonny. You just go right ahead."

Rickey and G-man glanced at each other. G-man raised his eyebrows inquiringly—*Time to cut out?*—and Rickey nodded.

They took their leave, Rickey struggling awkwardly with his crutches. Placide Treat and Oscar De La Cerda sat staring at each other over the rims of their respective cocktails. Finally De La Cerda said, "You're gonna drop the case against Lenny, right?"

"I can't address that question yet."

"Christ, you stubborn old bat, you just admitted in front of three witnesses that you planned to blackmail Lenny's business partner. In light of that, how the hell do you think—"

Treat began to sob into his drink, and De La Cerda subsided guiltily. After a minute he leaned over and patted the old man's knee. "It's gonna be OK," he said.

Dirty King had entrusted G-man with the temporary custody of the tricked-out rental car. G-man helped Rickey into it, put the crutches in the backseat, and drove to the hotel downtown. They rode in a pall of silence that remained over them as they entered the room.

Rickey collapsed on the edge of the bed and flung the crutches into a corner. His shoulders sagged. Looking at him, G-man thought at first that he was angry. "What's up?" he asked.

"Oh, not much." Rickey laughed bitterly. "I just can't figure out if I'm a whore, a pawn, a dupe, or all of the above. What's up with you?"

G-man realized Rickey was not angry, but deeply embarrassed. Of course he was; his pursuers had pretended to treat him like a serious and talented chef, but had actually treated him like a bimbo. Then a crazy man had gotten the drop on him, would have done God knows what to him if Rickey hadn't managed to get away. Who wouldn't be embarrassed?

He looked at Rickey's hunched shoulders and clenched hands, at his set chin trying not to quiver, at the whole live safe sight of him. He was impossibly beautiful, and G-man loved him so much he could hardly breathe. "Come here," he said. "Come here, sweetheart."

They were on the thirtieth floor, and as they held each other in the darkness, the Big D gleamed above them, advertising nothing except its own location, referring to nothing except itself, sucking up a million dazzling megawatts of wasted power simply because it could.

Back in New Orleans, summer lingered through September, loosened its sweltering grip on the city, and began to turn into fall.

Rickey sat in the bar at Liquor one day, sipping a Coke and reading the paper. He was supposed to be drawing up a menu for a private party who wanted to rent out the restaurant next month, but he couldn't concentrate on it. His concentration hadn't been all that great in general lately. He thought about Coop quite a bit. On the day Firestone had nearly killed him, he had mourned his and Coop's almost-friendship. Now he knew that his almost-friend had been willing to set him up, to ruin his life for the sake of someone else's vendetta. But it hadn't happened, and his almost-friend had died because of him. Was he some kind of psycho magnet? There had been the thing with Mike Mouton when Liquor first opened, and now this. G-man said it was just a coincidence, but Rickey wondered.

He also thought of the things Firestone had planned to do to him there in that blood-smeared room. The police had found duct tape, a box cutter, Coop's missing chef knives, a handgun. Rickey did not let himself think about these things very much.

He'd been back in the kitchen two days after his injury, propped up at the expediting station calling out orders. Once he had his walking cast, he worked the line at least once or twice a week to make sure he didn't lose his chops. The itch of his knitting bones and the clammy, nasty feel of his skin beneath the plaster were a constant bane to him. He'd finished his second refill of pain pills, and the doctor said he should try to avoid getting another since they were addictive. Rickey missed them. They were one of the few things that had ever completely calmed him.

As well as a walking cast and a slight yen for opiates, he also had a fancy new cell phone that could transmit photos, access e-mail, do everything but contact life on other planets. G-man had gone out and bought it for him the day after they returned from Dallas. Rickey had used it to take a picture of his cognac crabmeat au gratin dinner special and send it to G-man's cell phone while G-man was off running an errand. G-man sent back a text message that simply said FOSSIL FOOD.

Rickey became engrossed in a news story about Woofer Scagliano, who had announced that he was resigning his ADA position to seek public office. He was running for Clerk of Criminal District Court. Rickey didn't plan to vote for him.

He looked up as somebody entered the bar. Lenny, looking sharp in his spotless monogrammed chef's whites, the big cheeseball. He'd been amenable to the idea of Rickey and G-man buying out his share of the restaurant, but nothing was final yet; Coop's will was still in probate and no one could guess how quickly the apartment house might sell once Rickey's title to it was clear. He'd have to have the damage from the explosion fixed first, and he hadn't even talked to a contractor yet.

Lenny appeared happier than Rickey had seen him in many months. "Who died and gave you a blowjob?" Rickey asked.

"That's not only rude, it doesn't even make sense." Lenny parked himself on the other side of the booth. "But I'll ignore it, since I'm in such a fine mood."

"How come?"

"Placide Treat's case against me has been settled for good."

They had heard nothing from the DA since their return to New Orleans. Rickey appreciated Treat's attempt to save him, but he would be perfectly happy if he never had to see the old man again. "I figured he was dropping it," he said. "I mean, after what happened and all."

"You'd think so, but we haven't been able to get a yes or no out of him. In fact, no one seems to be hearing quite as much from old Tricker Treat as they used to. I suspect New Orleans might just be getting a new DA when his next term's up, and I think his name might be Oscar." Lenny smiled his demented smile. "But I like to make sure of things, you know. I can't believe I didn't think of this before. Know what I did?"

"What?" said Rickey warily. He didn't think he was up to a tale of intimidation, threats, or pain. He'd had enough of that to last him a long, long time.

"Well, I knew the tapes were the only thing he had that could possibly hang me. I'd thought of getting somebody to steal them, but how obvious would that be? They'd know it was me."

"Yeah, Lenny, I guess they would."

"Well, anyway, getting into the DA's office isn't as easy as getting into . . . some places. I wasn't sure I knew anybody who could do it, until G-man told me about his little go-round with Woofer Scagliano. I was so proud—I think I gave Woofer his very first bribe. He didn't want to take it, but I got him to understand that if he's going to run for office, he needs to learn how to accept favors gracefully."

"So Woofer got you in. What'd you do?"

"Not me. My operative."

"Yeah, yeah. Spare me the Liddy shit. What'd you do?"

"He fixed the plumbing," said Lenny, just about bursting to tell it. "The plumbing in that building's for shit. Has been ever since the place was built—they bid it out and took the cheapest offer. The difference went into somebody's pocket, I'm sure. Anyway, last week the whole fourth floor of the DA's building flooded with sewage. Shit dripping down the walls, water all over the place. Had to shut down the place and set up temporary offices in some Catholic girls' school down the street—Our Lady of Copacabana or something. I heard the contents of Treat's office were a total loss."

"Including the tapes?"

"Including the tapes."

Rickey stared at him, trying to take this in. He had seen a different side of Placide Treat in Dallas, a sorrowful and pathetic old man rather than the dangerous political figure of yore. The one son who remained to him couldn't be much of a comfort. (In September, Humphrey Wildblood had written a rave review of Liquor, making no mention of the scathing one he'd previously published. Not long afterward he had turned up at the restaurant obviously expecting to have his meal comped, but Rickey had told Karl and the waiters to pretend they didn't understand his broad hints. Maybe he would savage them again later. Rickey didn't really care.)

The image of Treat in a room with shit dripping down its walls shouldn't be funny, and it wasn't, not really. But Lenny's undisguised, childlike glee at having slimed his way out of another fix, and the idea of lanky Woofer Scagliano and the "operative" creeping into Treat's office to make the toilets overflow . . . well, that was funny. Rickey looked at Lenny and began to laugh.

"Pretty slick, huh?" said Lenny, laughing too. Pretty soon neither of them could stop, and G-man heard them all the way from the kitchen and came in and stood with his hands on his hips, looking at them and shaking his head. That made them laugh harder, and G-man got started too even though he didn't know what was funny. They laughed and laughed in the dim cool bar with the autumn evening settling over the city, and for the first time in far too long, Rickey thought maybe everything would be OK.

About the Author

Poppy Z. Brite is a native of New Orleans. Her fiction set in the restaurant world includes *Liquor, The Value of X,* and several short stories in *The Devil You Know*. She lives in New Orleans with her husband Chris, a chef, and is at work on another novel about Rickey and G-man.

Poppy Z. Brite's first Rickey and G-man novel is a manic, spicy romp through the kitchens, back alleys, dive bars, and drug deals of New Orleans.

Liquor
1-4000-5007-3. $13.95 paperback

"*Liquor* is world-class satire and perfect New Orleans lit."
—Andrei Codrescu, NPR commentator,
author of *Casanova in Bohemia*

THREE RIVERS PRESS • NEW YORK

WHEREVER BOOKS ARE SOLD

CROWNPUBLISHING.COM